# The Darkening

And when night Darkens the streets,
then wander forth the sons of Belial

*Paradise Lost*
*~ John Milton ~*

# CHAPTER ONE

*- Hindu Kush Mountains ~ Afghanistan -*

Darkness comes early to the Hindu Kush mountains. On this evening, it brought with it a hot, rough wind that buffeted Abasin Niazi, sending the scarf of his turban fluttering behind him as he negotiated the ancient rampart wall, an AK47 resting in the crook of his arm.

An uneven indentation ran along the center of the sand-dusted stone rampart, the worn result of thousands of pairs of similarly sandaled feet that had walked this same path night after night for the last two thousand years or more. Tonight, Abasin could sense the spirits of those men walking beside him more than ever before. A shiver ran down his spine, part pride, part fear, because some of those men, the unlucky ones, were not ghosts. They waited just meters away behind heavy wooden doors with rusty iron hasps and hinges.

He dismissed the thought, forcing his attention away from the cobblestones of the courtyard, and out over the parapet, down past thirty meters of layer upon layer of ancient wind-beaten sandstone bricks, to where the mountain slope dropped steeply into a narrow valley slowly being devoured by the approaching darkness. Beyond the valley, the natural camouflage of the mountain range that

1

surrounded him kept the fortress hidden. A single pathway, the only route through the valley, was known only to the very few entrusted with the secrets Abasin guarded.

After more years of similar nightfalls than he cared to remember, Abasin's eyes had grown accustomed to this strange twilight period; the dying sunlight glinting off the scree covering the bouldered approach created waves of shimmering light that waved and undulated. To Abasin, it looked like a mighty lake, revealed only once a day as the boundary between the day world and the world that accompanied night met, merged and melted into each other. Apart from the occasional whirl of twisting dust caught by a random eddy of wind, all was still beyond the battlements. All was silent, save for the scuff of his sandals against the stone of the walkway.

His job was a lonely one, but one he knew he had been called to. Called to just as his father, his father's father and his ancestors beyond them had been summoned. It was an honor beyond explanation to perform this duty, to keep safe the secrets locked away behind the heavy wooden doors that bordered the edges of the courtyard below, to be a part of the ancient order tasked with protecting them.

There were other men walking the walls and battlements, more still within tending to their duties, ensuring that that which was hidden, remained locked away. All were Abasin's brothers. Some quite literally, others from the same remote village of the Hindu Kush where, as a child, his parents had surrendered him to the cabal where he had remained for the past thirty years. Never stepping farther away from this place than the occasional time he found himself greeting a new arrival or helping the monthly supply delivery to unload their mules and horses.

Carved out of the very mountainside itself, the fortress had been built by Alexander the Great as he swept through what would become Afghanistan on his way to conquering India, and achieving immortal glory. The fortress had had a name once, but that name, along with its location had been lost in the mists of time. Now, its existence was known only to a chosen few, who referred to it simply

2

Scarecrow felt his heart sink. They had all been duped; his team, the CIA, the intelligence assets, every damn one of them. Directed to this place by planted or unwitting local informants. All while Al Abba and his men had patiently lain in wait, ready to spring their trap.

Al Abba shook his head, then leaned in and whispered into Scarecrow's ear. "You are a brave man, even in the face of what you believe to be certain death. But you are mistaken, I am not going to kill you."

Al Abba nodded to the big man holding Scarecrow's right arm, and he felt himself being dragged toward one of the locked cells. Al Abba unlocked the door with a large iron key.

Scarecrow caught a glimpse of a smaller darkened room beyond the doorway. At the back of the room, a second door was hewn into the rock wall, looking like something from a fancy European castle.

"What the hell is this?" Scarecrow yelled, digging his heels into the floor to try to slow his captors. Rough hands forced him into the cell, the only answer to his question the sound of the cell door slamming shut behind him.

Scarecrow pushed himself to his feet.

The scrape of metal locks against ancient rusted hasps was followed by the screech of a small wooden window in the door sliding open. A shaft of light filled the room. Alil Al Abba's eyes appeared at the opening, watched Scarecrow for a moment, then disappeared as the wooden cover slid back into place.

Darkness swallowed Scarecrow. He fumbled for the night vision goggles still hanging around his neck, found them, and slipped them over his eyes as he fought to get his breathing under control. The goggles were still working, thank God. He looked around the room. The prison was as sparse as the other cells he had seen before he was captured. A light layer of sand covered the floor. Ignoring the pain in his muscles from the beating, Scarecrow stumbled to the door at the opposite end of the small cell, his right hand clasped to his side, cradling what he was sure were a couple of fractured ribs.

This second door was an ornate piece of work that looked as

though it had been hand carved. Images of armor-clad warriors had been engraved deep into the ancient wood. Behind them, bodies lay strewn across the ground. Ahead of them, more soldiers in different armor fled in obvious panic, leaving behind weapons and shields, which was strange because the attackers carried no weapons or shields of any kind. Around the edges of the door were what Scarecrow took to be skulls.

It reminded him of a picture he'd seen of the Bayeux Tapestry when he was a kid. The tapestry had been created to commemorate the Battle of Hastings when the Normans had invaded and ultimately conquered Britain in 1066. The carvings on the door in front of him were in that same simplistic, almost childlike style, but the scenes they depicted were anything but childlike. They were vicious and bloodthirsty. Obviously whoever had crafted this wanted to impart the military value of whatever was locked away behind the door.

Despite his dire situation, Scarecrow could not help but be impressed by the exquisite workmanship of the craftsmen who had made this work of art. He ran his fingers slowly over the wood. *There's no lock*, he realized after a few more seconds. *And no handle either.* In fact, there was no visible way for the door to open at all.

He worked his fingers around the edges of the door where it met the wall. He felt the slightest of gaps between the wood and the rock.

Amazing workmanship. The door sat in a slit that had been carved out of the rock face. And somehow the architects of this fortress had slotted the door into that carved space so that the door could only be raised or lowered.

Scarecrow jumped as something banged against the opposite side of the door.

"Boss, is that you?" he whispered, his ear flat against the wood of the doorway.

There was another thump against the door and Scarecrow pulled his head away.

"Boss, it's Scarecrow. Can you hear me? You okay?"

He heard a sound, barely audible through the thick wood of

12

the door; a low keening, almost a mewling, like that of a child.

"Jesus!" Scarecrow hissed. He immediately began looking for a latch or a handhold that he could use as leverage to open the door, but found nothing.

"Shit, shit, *shit!*" Scarecrow stepped back from the door in frustration. He could feel his anger rising, threatening to get the better of him. He needed to get control of himself if he was going to gain any kind of advantage out of this situation.

A metallic rattle, like chains being dragged over a cobblestone floor echoed through the room.

Scarecrow spun around to see the door slowly beginning to lift. A gap of six inches had already appeared between it and the floor. An icy gust of cold air flowed out of the opening, and Scarecrow felt the already chilled temperature of the room begin to drop even lower. He took a step toward the door, reaching down to grab the base of it as it rose higher.

Scarecrow froze halfway there.

A hand, small, almost childlike but unnaturally white to the point that it was virtually alabaster, reached through the growing space beneath the door. Thin spider-like fingers grasped at the empty air. Long nails at the tips of each finger scraped against the rock floor. A second hand appeared, attached to a spindly arm.

Scarecrow took another step back, his hand instinctively reaching for the empty holster on his thigh. His back hit the opposite wall just as a pair of flat, luminous yellow eyes appeared in the blackness of the space beneath the rising door.

The eyes looked around the room and Scarecrow thought he could hear whatever owned them sniffing at the air, like a wolf scenting its prey. Then they fixed squarely on him. A hiss escaped from the creature's mouth, as it pulled itself through the gap, out of the darkness beyond the door.

And in the final moments of his life, as the creature scuttled across the floor toward him, Scarecrow screamed.

•••

The American soldier succumbed, just as the others before him had. History demanded that the American remain nameless other than the call sign Alil Al Abba had overheard; *Scarecrow*. Beyond the wooden door separating Al Abba and his men, the soldier's screams quickly faded to a wet gurgle then finally stopped completely, replaced by a deep slurping sound, like mud forced through a blocked pipe.

Eventually even that sound faded to nothing.

Alil Al Abba observed as this all unfolded through the narrow wooden slit in the door. He watched the pale, skeletal creature sniff the now-still corpse of the dead soldier, the American's mouth agape, a line of bloody drool dripping from between his lips.

The creature, its head bald except for a few tufts of black hair, dipped and lapped at the blood. When it was done, it sidled spider-like around the cell. The creature's eyes locked with Alil Al Abba's, and the living man felt a shudder of revulsion, tinged with a strange attraction that seemed to emanate from the thing's eyes. They shone like pools of shifting molten sand, fascinating, compelling, unrelenting...

Alil Al Abba raised his right hand. Instantly, the cell was flooded with light from a single UV bulb in the ceiling of the room. The creature squealed and hissed, bouncing off the walls, blinded, before vanishing back into the darkness of the room beyond the ornate door.

The gate descended noisily back into place.

"Bring the bodies of the others," Al Abba said, not taking his eyes from the lifeless soldier sprawled on the cold floor in front of him. The change could take as little as a day to take effect, for others two, so there was little time to waste. Every second was precious if his plan was to be successful. "We leave in twenty minutes."

Alil Al Abba continued to stare at the soldier's body. A minute passed, then another. Finally, a grim smile formed on his lips as he whispered "Allah hu akbar," and slid the cover closed.

## ASSOCIATED PRESS—BREAKING NEWS

*The bodies of twelve US military advisors were found this morning near a military base in northern Afghanistan. The military advisors are reported to have been killed by a roadside bomb. According to sources, the advisors were a part of an ongoing effort to train Afghan military units in the war against al-Qaeda insurgents in the area.*

# CHAPTER TWO

Captain Mike Lewis yawned, closed his eyes for a second then blinked them open, then repeated it a couple more times until the instruments on his flight panel finally swam back into focus. This had been a particularly grueling flight—fourteen hours straight in the air—and the lack of sleep was finally catching up with him. But his cargo was considered precious, and this flight, well it was more a mission of conscience for him and his two other crew. He'd brought back bodies from Afghanistan before, but never so many, and never of guys he had worked with on such a regular basis. *It was a crying shame what had happened to them. A goddamn crying shame.*

Captain Lewis yawned again, then spoke into his helmet's microphone, "GM-Heavy-two-niner-one to March tower we are on approach. Over."

The response came almost immediately, "Roger that GM-Heavy-two-niner-one, you are cleared for landing on runway two. Over."

Captain Lewis eased the C-17 Globemaster until the nose of the plane aligned with the lights of their assigned runway twinkling like tiny candles in the darkness ahead of him, about seven miles away. Surrounding that tiny strip of light, the brighter lights of Los Angeles glowed.

Captain Lewis's co-pilot, First Officer Cecilia Fasciano spoke into her microphone, "Loadmaster, we are on approach, please make sure your seats are in the upright position and your ass is in one of 'em."

Lewis smiled at the line, a routine he'd heard played out God knew how many times over the last four years he'd worked with these guys. After all the shit they had been through, they were a tight-knit, well-oiled, team... most of the time, at least. He instinctively paused, waiting for Dave Shafer's usual response of 'Ass down and secured, sir'.

It didn't come. Captain Lewis glanced across at Cece, who caught his gaze and returned it with one that showed her bemusement at the lack of a reply. She followed the look with a shrug of her slim shoulders. Cece leaned in and turned a knob on the instrument panel, switching the microphone to the cargo bay speaker, just in case there was a problem with Dave's headset. It wasn't like he wouldn't know they were on their descent, the landing gear had just come down with a thud that reverberated through the plane as the wheels locked into place. And there was an unmistakable shift in the handling of the aircraft as its aerodynamics changed.

"Dave? We're on approach, you need to let me know everything is okay back there." She paused for several seconds, waiting for a reply. When none came, she repeated the question, but there was still no answer from the loadmaster.

Cece let out an exaggerated sigh of exasperation. She turned in her seat to face Lewis. "Captain, request permission to go and make sure our loadmaster hasn't fallen out the back of the aircraft?" Her voice contained only half the sarcasm the sentence should have carried.

"Make it fast," Captain Lewis said. They were now less than three miles out and their altitude was dropping rapidly. The last thing he felt like doing was making another pass because his loadmaster had fallen asleep in the bathroom.

"Roger that," Cece said. She unbuckled her harness and slipped through the door between the cockpit and the cargo bay of the aircraft.

Thirty seconds went by before Cece's cool professional voice crackled in Lewis's ear, and he could tell by his copilot's tone that she was spooked. "Captain, I'm back here in the hold. There's no sign of Dave. And it looks like a couple of the coffins have—"

Lewis caught a sound that lasted only for the briefest of instants and that could have been the first part of a sharp intake of breath or an exclamation of surprise, but Cece's microphone cut out and left him with just a barely audible static hiss.

"Cece, do you copy?"

Silence.

Captain Lewis felt a cold line of sweat drop from his armpits and run down the sides of his chest. "Cece, get your ass back here, right—"

A loud boom filled the cabin as something hit the cockpit door hard enough to rattle the hinges.

"Jesus Christ," Lewis yelled, glancing back toward the door while keeping one eye on his approach. "Dave, this is no time to be screwing around, get yourself—"

An even louder thump, like someone had just shoulder charged the door, echoed through the cockpit.

The lights of the airport now lay directly ahead of the cockpit window. A rough crosswind of eighteen knots buffeted the C-17. It was all Captain Lewis could do to concentrate on keeping the aircraft's nose pointed where it should be. "Dave, get your ass in your seat," he snapped, unable to keep the anger from his voice. "That's a goddamn order." They were only seconds away from touching down and this kind of idiocy was simply unacceptable. He was going to have to bust Dave's balls later for this out of character BS. *Christ*! If he was drunk again there was going to be hell to pay.

Lewis pulled the cup of the headphones off his right ear and listened.

*Scccriiitch*!

The new sound floated across the space between the door and the pilot's seat. It took a few seconds for Lewis to place it; it sounded like nails being drawn down the metal exterior of the cockpit door.

There was another sound; the unmistakable click of the cabin door's lock unlatching. The sound vanished in the screech of the massive transport plane's tires touching down on the runway.

Lewis began to throttle back. Aiming the nose of the plane toward the lights of a clutch of military vehicles waiting on the skirt at the end of the runway.

"You idiots had better have a really good reason for why you'd pull such a goddamn stupid stunt," Captain Lewis called back over his shoulder.

There was still no reply.

Now he was *really* pissed. Joking around was acceptable, it was a universally understood way to relieve the stress and horror that servicemen and women endured on an almost daily basis. But *this* stunt, this was just plain dumb. The two idiots had put the entire flight in danger, not just their three lives but the lives of those on the ground too, not to mention the fact that they were carrying the remains of twelve of their own in the hold. He was seriously considering filing a reprimand.

*And what the hell was that weird smell?* Lewis's nose wrinkled. "Jeez-us!" Lewis exclaimed as he throttled the aircraft's engines back. He looked back over his shoulder again, expecting to see Cece's and Dave's smirking faces. Instead he saw the pale, ghost-like faces of two dead men. He knew they were dead because of the blood-stained battle fatigues they wore, and by the way their eyes seemed to glow yellow in the dim electronic light of the cockpit's instrument panel.

Captain Lewis had no time to even reach for the pistol he kept tucked in the side of his seat before the two corpses launched themselves into the cabin.

•••

From the runway apron everything looked good with the C-17's approach. The aircraft was lined up perfectly, the pilot expertly shifting the aircraft's attitude as it was buffeted by the California night winds gusting across the base. The wheels touched down and even from where he stood, Major Victor Bobek heard them screech and complain before settling into a low thrum as the pilot throttled back and began to slow the aircraft, easing it toward where he and his repatriation crew of fifteen men and women waited with trucks to transport the bodies of the Special Activities Division teams stowed in the aircraft's belly.

So it was a complete surprise when the plane suddenly veered to the left and began to cut through the grass separating the runway from the ten foot high security fence surrounding the base.

The plane got approximately halfway across the open ground before the wheels shredded and the landing gear dug into the wet soil. The C-17's left wing dipped, dug a deep, ragged furrow into the ground... and stuck. The huge transport aircraft bucked; quite gracefully for such a massive and cumbersome machine, Bobek thought. The tail pitched into the air at a twenty-degree angle as the nose of the aircraft dug into the ground, sending a wave of earth flying into the air. The nose and cockpit crumpled, the left wing detached from the body and went careening out into the darkness, trailing sparks like fireworks behind it. The main fuselage hung upright, and for a second Bobek thought it might just stay that way, but then with a creak of twisting metal, it crashed to the ground, sending a plume of debris and smoke into the air.

A profound silence settled over the airbase, broken a second later by the swell of emergency vehicles' sirens as they began to race toward the crash site. Bobek braced for an explosion, but none came. *The fuel tanks were probably close to empty by the time they landed,* he thought.

"Get me over there," Bobek snapped at his driver. The man nodded and headed around to the other side of the vehicle at a jog while his boss climbed onto the Jeep's foot plate and slammed the door behind him.

*What a complete cluster*, Bobek decided as the Jeep took off across the concrete runway toward the crash site. *A total and utter screw-up*. The emergency vehicles—two ambulances and a couple of fire engines—had already arrived at the broken plane. The wreckage was illuminated by the fire engines' spotlights. A stream of fire retardant foam was already being laid over the smoking engines by one of the fire engines.

By the time Bobek and his convoy of vehicles arrived at the site almost a minute later, rescue personnel were already beginning to move through the wreckage.

Given the violence of the crash, the remains of the aircraft were remarkably intact, Bobek thought as the Jeep pulled to a stop. The main fuselage was more or less still in one piece. A few windows were busted out, and a jagged scar, about twenty feet in length ran from the midway point of the plane before disappearing where the plane's belly lay against the ground. The nose was not so lucky. It was crushed, and the windshield of the cockpit was completely gone. The pilot was visible, still strapped into his seat, his head slumped to his chest. A medic climbed a ladder that had been placed against the side of the plane. He reached the pilot, took a few seconds to check his vitals, then shook his head slowly at Bobek and began to climb down again.

"Goddamn it," Bobek cursed quietly. He'd already lost twelve of his best men in the failed raid in Afghanistan, now he'd lost another. And he didn't hold out much hope for the other two crew members either.

This was turning into the shittiest of weeks.

Bobek opened the door and signaled to his men in the other three vehicles to rally up. One by one the doors opened and his team followed behind as he picked his way through the rutted, debris-littered crash site toward the rear of the aircraft.

The loading ramp was down, as if it had been lowered on purpose, which made no sense. Maybe a fault? Maybe *that* was what caused the crash?

His driver handed Bobek a flashlight as they approached the rear of the wrecked aircraft. Multiple beams of light cut through the darkness, illuminating the cavernous interior of the C-17 like it was a gutted whale. Bobek and his men climbed up the ramp and made their way inside.

Flashlights played left and right through the darkened interior. Close to the front section of the plane, a woman's body lay crumpled and broken. Bobek could see she was undoubtedly dead; the right side of her face crushed to the point of being unrecognizable. A surprisingly small amount of blood surrounded the remains of her head like a crown, clotting in her long hair. Despite the terrible injuries, Bobek still recognized her as the copilot, Cece.

"Cover her up," Bobek ordered one of the rescue teams while he continued to make his way carefully through the wreckage.

Most of the coffins of the twelve-man strike team were still laid out in two neat rows. The couplings that secured them to the cargo bay floor had done their job, for the most part. Three of the coffins had been dislodged from their fixtures and lay askew. Another had come away completely and lay almost upright against the right side of the C-17's bulkhead, but the crash must have dislodged the locking mechanisms of all of the caskets because every one of the lids was wide open.

Bobek walked slowly between the two lines of coffins, shining his flashlight into each of them one after the other.

"Holy. Shit," someone enunciated slowly from behind Bobek.

*Holy shit indeed*, the Major thought as he stared into the final coffin. Each and every one of the caskets was empty of its occupant.

Presumably, somewhere in the plane's wreckage was the body of the Loadmaster, but apart from Cece's corpse, there wasn't a sign of any of his strike team's bodies.

"Check with whoever is in charge of the emergency services and see if he or his people have found any of our men outside," Bobek ordered a corporal sifting through the debris. "And if he *hasn't* found anything, take four of our guys and start working your way back to the runway. See if you can find them."

This just did not sit right with the major. A crash he could understand. That could be put down to bad luck or bad piloting, but this was all just too damn weird. Where the hell were the bodies of his

22

men? They couldn't have just gotten up and walked away. And why had the copilot been back here when the plane was landing?

Bobek had spent his life relying on his instincts. It was why he was still above ground rather than buried in some unmarked grave in some shit-hole country most Americans had never even heard of, let alone could find on a map. He was alive because his instincts were good, reliable. He trusted them. And right now, his instincts were screaming that something was wrong, something was terribly wrong.

•••

In the shadows surrounding the runway, twelve shapes made their way through the darkness from the broken remains of the C-17. One after the other they clambered over the security fence like spiders navigating a web, the razor wire slicing through skin almost to the bone but leaving no blood, causing no pain, eliciting no reaction. Dropping to the ground on the opposite side of the fence, the figures paused and stared at the sleeping city that lay before them. Despite the chilly air, not a single breath escaped their mouths, their chests remained still, their skin as pale as the cloud-blanketed moon.

A single thing bound the twelve; a desire to feed.

One by one the dead men began to move toward the houses, apartment buildings, and businesses of Los Angeles, and an unsuspecting humanity that slept silently in their beds, unaware of the storm that was approaching.

*- LOS ANGELES -*

*Nine days later*

# FRIDAY

The night is darkening round me,
The wild winds coldly blow;
But a tyrant spell has bound me,
And I cannot, cannot go.

*"The Night is Darkening Round Me"*
*~ Emily Brontë ~*

# CHAPTER THREE
CHAPTER THREE

Tyreese felt like a man hanging on a cliff's edge by his fingertips, slowly slipping toward oblivion.

In the movies it was easy to move on; writers just gave the lead character a couple of months and they were blissfully emptying out their dead wife's or husband's closet, falling in love, finding someone new. Leaving the past behind.

In reality, it wasn't anything like that. Emma's clothes all still hung in the closet. Her hairbrush, makeup, even a half-empty bottle of her pain meds were still exactly where she had left them on the dresser.

Sometimes, when the pain of her loss just got so bad he felt like he could not take it any longer, Tyreese would open her side of the closet and bury his face in her blouses, skirts, and t-shirts, moving slowly from one to another, trying to find a remnant of her scent. Trying to find *something* that would ease the pain that squeezed his heart, something that would resurrect her in his mind, triggered by the fading molecules of a perfume she had worn, or the faint musk of her body odor. As the years after her passing moved by him, those moments of relief became harder and harder to find. Strangely, the weight of Emma's loss became lighter and lighter. Memories faded, so her presence became less real, and bits of her began to be chipped away, leaving a space within him that was a perfect vacuum in the shape of his life with Emma. But the pain of his wife's absence grew heavier and heavier. It was a weird, contradictory experience; a circular feeding frenzy of despair and loss and emptiness.

Two nights ago, he'd woken from a dream just after midnight unable to remember Emma's face. He had thrown back the covers, his consciousness straddling the thin, hazy line between dream and wakefulness, and in his panic he'd forgotten that he had lost his legs and tried to make it to the kitchen for a glass of water. He had, of course, fallen to the floor, his face thumping against the musty carpet. He didn't know how long he'd lain at the side of his bed, his confused mind trying to make sense of where he was, what had happened.

When his mind had finally staggered back to this world, Tyreese found himself huddled in the corner of the closet, an old t-shirt of Emma's balled up around his fist like a boxing glove, soaked through with his tears.

First his legs. Then his wife. Gone.

Now his mind.

He was losing it, he realized, sliding down into a black pit of despair and loss that there was no getting back out of. Where only death awaited.

And that was okay.

That, he welcomed.

# LOS ANGELES TIMES

The Los Angeles Unified School District announced today that it is taking precautionary measures for its 649,000 students by immediately closing all school campuses throughout Los Angeles County. Due to the forecast of heavy rainfall leading to anticipated widespread flooding across Southern California, all 900-plus public schools and 187 charter schools within the district will remain closed for the next seven days.

# CHAPTER FOUR

Birdy ran. Each sneaker-clad foot momentarily touching the gym floor, kissing it, then lifting again as she accelerated herself toward the waiting vault box. Her heart thrummed in her chest, a finely tuned, supercharged V6 engine, her lungs pumping fuel to it with rhythmic ease. Muscles expanded and contracted with the fluidity of a natural-born athlete. Sweat popped on the young girl's forehead, dripping toward her eyes, she caught it with the quick stroke of the back of her hand and flicked it away.

*You are alive*, her body sang. *Alive.*

Birdy launched herself into the air, pushing forward off her left foot, her arms outstretched ahead of her, as though she were diving into water. Her torso was almost parallel with the gym floor, her hands reaching for the top of the vault box. Both hands landed with a slap as Birdy pulled her knees almost to her chest and allowed her momentum to carry her forward and over the box before landing perfectly on the foam crash mats on the opposite side.

"Awesome!" Bryanna, Birdy's trainer, yelled, spontaneously applauding as the girl landed and immediately dropped into a forward roll, only to bounce up again and jog back to where the rest of the class waited.

Birdy was in complete awe of Bryanna. She had participated

in the TV show *American Ninja Warrior* three times. The last time, she had been one of the small but growing group of women to make it to the final stage; Mount Midoriyama in Las Vegas. Bryanna had *been* to Las Vegas *and* she had appeared on TV. Birdy had downloaded all her videos and watched them on her phone. Bryanna was her hero. Birdy tried, but could not conceal the smile she felt ease onto her lips at her trainer's effusive praise.

"And that, kids," Bryanna said, turning to the class of children, most of whom were not much older than nine or ten, "is exactly how you perform a Kong vault. So, who wants to give it a try?"

Hands went up immediately amid calls of "Me! Me!" The ten kids, all of them younger by a third than Birdy's fifteen years, excitedly vied to be the next to learn to fly. And flying was *exactly* how Birdy would describe what she experienced when she was here.

Parkour—free-running, whatever you wanted to call the sport—was what Birdy loved, and she was damn good at it too, even if she did say so herself. She taught kids with Bryanna three nights a week, and weekends when she could. In fact, *any* time Birdy could spend here at the YMCA was better than being at home. Because around this neighborhood, the Y was the closest to after school activities as you could get without either running with or from one of the local gangs. Or spending time sitting mindlessly in front of the TV or a computer screen. The freedom parkour gave her, the way it had altered her perception of the world, transformed buildings and apartment blocks into her personal training ground, and allowed Birdy to turn the towers and multi-level apartments into ladders to escape their confines, rather than the prison walls almost everyone else she knew regarded them as. Instead of concrete obstacles, now she was surrounded by adventure.

Birdy was young, just two months past her fifteenth birthday, but the second she turned eighteen, she would be gone from here, and parkour was going to be her golden ticket out. She just needed to practice, practice, practice.

"Okay, I'm going to form you up into two groups. This half," Bryanna split the group of kids down the middle with a chopping, sweeping motion of her hand, "you're with me. The rest of you guys go with Birdy."

Obediently, each group of kids followed their assigned trainer.

An hour later, as the last child left with his mom, Bryanna and Birdy were alone in the YMCA gym.

Bryanna grabbed her training bag, stuffed a sweat-dampened towel into it and zipped it closed. "Nice work today," she said to Birdy. "You need a lift home?"

Birdy shook her head. "Nah! I think I'll stay and practice a bit, if that's okay?"

"'Course. Just put the equipment away when you're done."

Birdy nodded.

"See you," Bryanna said, as she slipped through the exit with a final smile at Birdy.

Finally alone, Birdy turned, inhaled and exhaled a deep breath, and surveyed the gym. She loved Bryanna. Adored the kids she tutored. But it was only when she got this place to herself that she really felt *present*. This was *her* time. She looked at the clock on the far wall: 3:30 pm. That gave her just about an hour to herself before she had to get home. She had been trying to master a few moves over the past week and she felt confident she was on top of them, but a half hour with each wasn't going to hurt.

•••

The next time Birdy checked the clock, her hour was almost up. She dutifully put all the equipment away, then jogged over to where she had left her duffel bag, pulled a towel from it and wiped the sweat from her body. *I'll shower when I get home*, she promised herself. She tossed the towel back in the bag, pulled a light sweater from within, threw it on, and headed for the exit.

Outside, the sky was a sullen gray, the threat of rain distant for now, but the usual warm California air was instead chilled and Birdy congratulated herself for anticipating she would need a sweater. Home was a twenty-minute walk from the YMCA, past block after block of four, five, and six story apartment buildings, the only difference between them the color each was painted. To Birdy's fifteen-year-old mind, the stark utilitarianism of the apartment buildings was the norm. This was her neighborhood and, even with the gangs and the shootings and the drug dealers hanging around the street corners, she loved it. Had no intention of spending the rest of her life here, mind you, but it was still home. For now, at least.

Birdy tapped in the code to her apartment building's security gate and let herself into the forecourt. The locked gates were a pointless feature, she'd always thought, because *everyone* knew the code to her building, just as she knew the one to every other building on her street. Still it probably made the old people feel a little more secure.

She thought about using her usual route around the back of the building, but Mom would be home by now and she didn't want to spook her by suddenly appearing from her bedroom, so instead she climbed the stairs to the third floor.

•••

"Hey, baby. Is that you?" Elizabeth Finch's voice floated down the hallway to Birdy from the living room. Her mom was watching a TV show; the actors' tinny voices chattering in the background.

"Yeah," Birdy called back. She locked the front door behind her.

"How was your training?"

"Good," Birdy called back. She walked into her bedroom, tossed the gym bag into the closet, pulled her sweater over her head and balled it up; her mom always kept the apartment warmer than Birdy liked. She tossed the sweater onto a pile of other clothes collecting in the corner of her room.

"Don't leave those clothes on the floor," her mom called out. "That's what we have a washing machine for."

Birdy sighed. She still wasn't convinced her mom wasn't psychic, or maybe she had put hidden cameras in her room. Birdy began picking up the clothes.

"What're you doing for the rest of the day?"

Birdy turned and saw her mom's head peeking around the door frame.

"Nothing much," Birdy said, grabbing a stray sock she had dropped. "I was thinking of going to the mall before it rains."

Elizabeth Finch smiled at her daughter. "Just make sure you get your chores done by the time I get home from work, okay?"

Birdy nodded.

"Good girl," said Elizabeth, moving aside to let her daughter squeeze past. "Wash them on cold," she called after her kid as she disappeared toward the kitchen.

•••

By the time Birdy got out of the shower, her mom had already left for work.

Birdy toweled herself dry, slipped on fresh underwear, then pulled a pair of running pants from the closet. She finished her ensemble with a gray hoody over her t-shirt, and her ratty pair of sneakers.

If her mom had still been at home, Birdy would have had to take the stairs. Instead she decided she would go the back way. It would save her a five-minute walk to the bus stop.

Birdy grabbed her MP3 player and plugged the headphones into her ears. She walked over to her bedroom window, eased it open and looked down toward the flat roof of the adjacent apartment block, a couple of stories below. She climbed nimbly up onto the windowsill, switched on her music player, and swung herself out into thin air. She grabbed ahold of the thick drain pipe that ran from the roof gutter two stories above her along the face of the apartment down to a drain grate at ground level. The pipe was cold and bits of paint flaked off as Birdy grasped it with both hands, then placed her feet against the apartment building's wall on either side of the pipe. She quickly lowered herself down until she was parallel to the flat roof of the building butting up against her apartment block, and stepped off onto the roof.

•••

Tyreese sat at the bedroom window and looked out over the neighborhood.

The screech of a window sliding open drew his eyes down, just in time to see the girl who lived in the apartment below his deftly swing herself out onto the ledge of her window. She grabbed the drainpipe running up the side of the apartment building and lowered herself into the gully separating his building from the upper level of the adjacent apartment's roof. The only reason he knew she was a girl—she dressed her skinny frame in a drab charcoal hoodie, army surplus pants and a similarly colored baseball cap on her head that effectively made its owner androgynous—was because he had heard her mother call her Annabelle.

Tyreese smiled as he tracked the girl's movement across the roof; the kid was something to behold. It would have been easy to be jealous of the girl, watching her move so sublimely, while he was stuck in this damn wheelchair, but he felt only awe at her speed and agility. This kid was *fast*. He looked down to where his own legs should have been, felt a brief ghostly memory of the pain from when he had lost them, and dismissed it. On the other side of the room, leaning against the wall near the door were his legs; two prosthetic limbs that were as repellent to him as his own missing, decomposed legs would be. A wooden walking cane leaned against the wall next to the boot-shod prosthetics. Tyreese looked away, his eyes instinctively moving back to the girl.

The first time he had seen her, Annabelle, do this little trick, he had about had a heart attack, sure she was going to fall the thirty feet to the broken concrete path below. But he had quickly learned that this girl was as gifted an acrobat as one of those performers he'd seen on *America's Got Talent*.

This was the part he always loved to watch. It never ceased to amaze him how a girl her size could be so strong and so damn nimble too. She was fast as a jackrabbit and about as agile as Spiderman. Still, he held his breath as he watched Annabelle lower herself hand over hand down the pipe until she was almost parallel with the flat roof of the adjacent building. In one fluid movement, she let go of the drainpipe and launched herself backward, pushing away from the apartment wall with both legs, rotating through the air before landing sideways on the concrete roof ten feet away. She rolled once across the ground before disappearing between two large aluminum air conditioning vents.

When Annabelle reappeared, she was on her feet and jogging across the roof to the opposite side of the building.

•••

Halfway across the roof, Birdy stopped. She had the distinct impression that someone was watching her. She turned and looked back at her apartment block and found the window to her bedroom. Her eyes drifted up one floor to the window above hers... and there he was. The Window Guy, she called him. She didn't know his name, she just knew that he always seemed to be sitting there at his window. So he became the Window Guy.

He probably thought she didn't see him, hadn't noticed him all those times she'd watched him from the corner of her eye while he watched her. But she *had* noticed, she just hadn't bothered to let him know. She didn't think he was a creeper, he just seemed, well... lonely. What was that word she'd learned today? *Melancholy*. She had come across the word in a book she was reading. The author's name was Emily Brontë. She absolutely *loved* that name. Why couldn't her mom have given her a name like that? Instead she was labeled Annabelle Finch. But it wasn't the writer's name that had attracted her to the book, it was its title: *Wuthering Heights*. What was *that* about?

She'd begun reading and had immediately been drawn into the world of Heathcliff and Catherine and their doomed love story. That was where she'd come across the word... melancholy. She'd looked it up on her phone and found the definition meant perpetually sad. That seemed to fit the Window Guy; perpetually sad. He looked crumpled, like he was folded in on himself.

She didn't know why she chose to make it so obvious, maybe she just wanted to make a connection with someone, it wasn't like she had a lot of friends, none at all really other than at school. Her eyes took a second to adjust to the glare of the diffuse light trying to force its way through the cloud-packed sky; there he was, the Window Guy. He was looking right at her; she could see the sudden tip of his head as he realized that she could see him looking at her.

Then it was Birdy's turn to be surprised when the Window Guy raised a hand and waved. Beneath the cowl of her hoodie, Birdy felt her face flush red and a smile crease the edges of her mouth. She waved back. Then, embarrassed and a little confused, she spun around and sprinted toward the edge of the roof, looking for *the* spot, the one safe spot. She aimed for it as she had a hundred times before. She used her right leg to propel herself off the edge of the roof, forcing her body to relax as she flew through the air, until her feet hit the iron landing of the fire escape fixed to the side of the opposite building with a metallic clang that rattled the entire structure. She rolled once and then was up. Two paces to her left and she dropped through the space where the ladder to the ground should have been (that lay ten feet below, rusted and broken and useless) and caught the metal lip with her fingertips, allowing her momentum to carry her forward then backward. On the second swing she let go.

This was where Birdy felt she finally lived up to her name; when she was airborne. And in the eternal second between her fingers releasing the cold metal and her feet hitting the concrete of the alleyway, she was truly flying.

# CHAPTER FIVE

His real name was Gerald, but no one had called him that in over fifty years. Everyone just called him Rat. He hadn't gotten the nickname because he looked like a rodent, he'd gotten it because he'd lived on the streets of LA longer than anyone else most street people knew. And, just like his namesake, Rat knew where all the best places to hide, sleep, and find food were.

At 68, Rat was also the oldest homeless person any of them knew, and he knew just about everyone who lived out here. So if you needed information, Rat was the one you asked. But tonight, he was having problems answering the one question the five other people standing with him all wanted to know: Where had all their friends gone?

"I ain't seen Jimbo or Wonky Alan or Delilah in three days," said ChoCho, a fragile looking Asian woman with a permanent look of fear in her eyes. "Now you know those fools as well as I do, and they ain't gonna miss a meal at the Kitchen."

"Yeah," said Jay, "and when was the last time you didn't have to wait in line at the Kitchen? I can't even remember."

He was right, Rat thought, he was definitely right. The others huddled around the flaming oil drum nodded in unison.

The Kitchen was the nickname for the church over on Burbank Boulevard where a meal was served every night like clockwork. Normally the lines could stretch fifty people deep at the door and some days you'd have to wait a good hour or more to even see the inside of the building. But for their last three visits, Rat and his friends had barely had to wait at all. And every night it seemed like the wait was getting shorter and shorter.

"The cops rounding us up?" Piper asked. She was only seventeen, but she was smart.

Rat shook his head. "The cops don't do that no more. Besides, it would've been in the papers. Ain't seen nothing."

"Well they sure as shit ain't moving to Miami," Eugene joked.

Everyone laughed, but it was half-hearted, nervous. They had all been on edge since the first street people had turned up missing about eight days ago. Sure, people came and went all the time, that was the nature of living on the streets. But the majority of homeless were out here for years, and you'd see their faces on a daily basis. So when old timers started to vanish, that was when people really started to notice.

And that was also when Rat had taken action. He hadn't lived this long by being a sucker. He'd pulled the people he trusted the most; the ones that weren't sick, or whose drug habit was at least under control.

"Safety in numbers," he'd told them. "We all stick together and we'll be safe."

So it was thanks to Rat that the six of them now sat under this concrete overpass, huddled around an oil drum fire, while cars and trucks rumbled across the Ventura Freeway above them. It wasn't like it was cold out here, not compared to some nights. The rain was bad, sure, but everyone just gravitated to the fire because it felt *safe*. The night was closing in quickly. And darkness was when people disappeared.

"We just gotta stick together," Rosy said. "We stick together, we'll be okay." She took a swig from a can of Old Milwaukee and passed it to ChoCho who also took a pull then passed it along.

41

Rat had his people organized; during the day he'd sent some off to grab water and food, while he and two others had scrounged up enough wood and cardboard to keep the fire burning for the next three nights. *Have to be prepared. Have to be ready for anything*, Rat had told them. Which was why they also had an array of makeshift weapons from knives to spears. The spears were improvised from the firewood they had collected. If whoever was targeting the homeless came looking for Rat and his people, they were gonna be in for one hell of a surprise, yes sir.

"Thing is," Rat said, "Whoever's doing this, they gonna slip up some time. Gonna make a mistake. And when they do, the cops are gonna—"

"Hey! Hey! Who's that out there?" Marcellus called out, as he tapped Rat rapidly on the arm with one hand and pointed into the darkness beyond the light of the fire with his other.

Rat strained to look where Marcellus was pointing, but his eyes had gone to shit years ago and all he could see was a blur of shadows and shapes and darkness. "I don't see—" he started to say but was interrupted by ChoCho.

"It's Jimbo," ChoCho said. "Jimbo's back."

Rat could hear the excitement in ChoCho's voice. She and Jimbo had been an item at some point in the past, and everyone knew she still had a thing for the poor guy. ChoCho scrambled to her feet and started to walk toward where Marcellus was pointing.

"Hey, ChoCho; wait up," Rat said.

"It's Jimbo," ChoCho repeated matter-of-factly, and continued on her way.

Despite his crummy eyesight, Rat could still see ChoCho's shape as she walked off into the darkness. He also saw her stop abruptly and heard a collective gasp of surprise from the others still standing around the fire.

"What... What's wrong with his *eyes*?" Jay whispered. "Why they shinin' like that?"

PAUL ANTONY JONES

Before Rat could ask what Jay was talking about, a terrible scream filled the night, drowning out even the constant thrum of vehicles on the overpass above their heads.

"Oh Jesus, what's he doing to her? Oh my God! Run!"

Rat saw his group break and run in all directions and he ran too, although he didn't know why. More screams erupted from all around him and he willed his old legs to move faster while trying to avoid the scattered junk and potholes that littered the waste ground around him.

Ahead of him, he saw Marcellus' broad back. He was heading toward a pile of rubble that half-hid an entrance to one of the storm drains interlacing the city.

"Marcellus! Wait for me!" Rat called out.

The big Mexican stopped and turned to look back at Rat. "Come on," he said, beckoning for Rat to hurry. "You got to *run*." Rat could hear real fear in Marcellus' voice, which was frightening in and of itself because the bear of a man had been an Army Ranger back in the eighties, until drugs, PTSD and Reagan had gotten the better of him. And up until today, the former Ranger had never given any indication that he was afraid of a single goddamn thing.

Marcellus turned and began to scramble up the mound of rubble, but as he did, something inhumanly fast burst from the shadows and covered the thirty feet between it and Marcellus in four loping bounds.

"Look out!" Rat shouted, just in time for Marcellus to half-turn and see the shadow leaping at him. Marcellus screamed and tried to duck but the shadow hit him hard, bowling the big man over like a cat would a bird. Marcellus began to scream and thrash at the silhouette fastened to his throat like some giant tick.

Rat could see no other way but to run past whatever it was that had managed to take down Marcellus. He tried not to look—didn't really want to know, as he limped his way as fast as his gimpy legs could toward the storm drain opening—but Rat couldn't help himself. He glanced down at the two bodies tangled on the ground.

Marcellus was pinned on his back, his eyes wide, face contorted in pain and terror as the... the *girl*—Rat could see it was just a girl now that he was close enough. It was just a little goddamn girl, but somehow she was stronger than Marcellus.

The girl hadn't noticed Rat; she was interested only in Marcellus. Her face was buried in the man's neck and there was a strange sound, an obscene sucking noise. It reminded Rat of when he was a kid and he'd suck a Slurpee through a straw. Marcellus reached a hand toward Rat, his eyes beseeching him for help, his mouth moving but no words coming out.

*It's just a girl*, Rat told himself, took a step toward his friend. "Hey!" he yelled, "Get off him."

The girl's head spun in his direction and instantly dissolved all of Rat's remaining bravado. Her mouth was smeared with blood, Marcellus' blood, Rat could see the two puncture marks on the side of the man's neck, blood seeping from them both.

Blood dripped from the girl's mouth, oozing over her chin in thick globules. *And oh, dear God in Heaven, her* mouth. Rat saw teeth, gleaming in the meager light from the fire. Awful, dreadful teeth. But it was her eyes that terrified him the most; they glowed a golden yellow.

They were the eyes of a predator, of a killer with death on her mind.

The girl opened her mouth wider than should've been possible and hissed at Rat as though she were a rattlesnake and he had disturbed her.

Rat screeched an expletive and began to half-run half-stumble his way up the pile of rubble that hid the entrance to the storm drain system. He was aware he was mumbling to himself incoherently. He felt fingernails break and splinter as he pulled himself hand over hand up the rubble and debris. Something sliced his right leg and he felt warm blood trickling down his calf, but there was no pain. Not yet. As he neared the top of the rubble pile, Rat glanced back in the direction of the camp and saw the indistinct outlines of several bodies

44

lying on the ground near the fire can. Shadows knelt beside or on top of them, golden eyes burning in the night.

To Rat's right he saw someone being dragged into the deeper shadows. It was a woman, he thought, by the sound of the screaming, but he couldn't tell who it was. He turned back and pushed himself up and over the top of the debris pile. Exhausted, he allowed himself to roll down the opposite side. At the bottom, Rat pulled himself to his feet and staggered toward the storm drain entrance, squeezing himself between the metal security bars he and Marcellus had forced open just two nights earlier. He turned and looked back through the bars; there was nothing there. Whatever those... *things* were, they had not followed him.

Rat exhaled a sigh of relief and started to get his breathing under control. It was only when he turned to head deeper into the sewer and saw the four pairs of golden yellow eyes waiting in the darkness ahead of him that he realized he was doomed.

Rat tried to scream, but the first pair of fangs ripped the sound from his throat.

**SATURDAY**

# CHAPTER SIX
CHAPTER SIX

A man's voice crackled from the speaker of the phone resting in Tyreese's lap.

"Hello. How can I help you?" The store clerk on the other end of the phone sounded frazzled, tired.

"Hi, yes, this is Mr. Douglass," Tyreese said, quickly pulling the cell phone to his ear. "I was expecting a delivery today. It's usually here by now, but no one has shown up."

The delivery guy was *always* here by now; Tyreese was beginning to suspect that maybe there had been a screw-up. The sky was thick with gray and black clouds, pregnant with the threat of the storm to come. It sucked the color from the landscape, painting everything in desaturated, muted monochrome. It felt more like a winter evening than a Saturday morning.

"I'm sorry Mr. Douglass—" The man's voice became fainter as his attention was drawn away by someone out of range of the microphone. Tyreese heard him apologizing to someone, then he was back again. "—half my staff haven't shown up for work today and that includes my delivery driver. It's this damn storm warning or the flu or something. I'm sorry but you're going to have to come in to the store in person."

"If I wanted to pick up my food myself, I wouldn't have scheduled a delivery, would I? Jesus! There's no one there who can drive a truck?" Tyreese could feel a knot of tension beginning to tighten in his gut. *Breathe*, he told himself, *just breathe and keep calm*. In the background, Tyreese could now make out the unmistakable sound of angry voices, all vying for the clerk's attention.

"I'm sorry, I don't have enough staff to pull orders, let alone deliver them. There's really nothing I can do," the man said, already distracted by what sounded like a developing commotion in the background.

The line went dead.

Tyreese disconnected the phone at his end too. His eyes wandered around the room as though the delivery guy might be hiding in there with him somewhere. He took a deep breath, held it for several seconds and then exhaled slowly. The anxiety had already spread throughout his stomach and was now climbing toward his throat.

"Breathe," he said to the empty room. "Just breathe." Anxiety was a wall of static in his head. It blocked his memories, confused his thoughts, distracted him. And it hid *something* from him. Something that he wanted to look at but which this fog, like some malevolent trickster, chose to hide. It made every day the same; colorless, muted, frightening. The continual feeling of agitation almost never left him; it was like a second skin of electricity fitted over his own, firing off random nerves that made Tyreese twitchy and restless, and set his stomach in a constant twisting and turning soup of emotion. He took in a few more deep gasps of air and felt the knot of panic loosen its grip on his intestines just a little.

A few more minutes of deep breathing and the stress had subsided enough that Tyreese did not think he was going to have to pop a Lorazepam. That was a win. He hated taking those damn pills, they fuzzed his brain.

Tyreese wheeled himself across the room to where his legs waited. He stared at them for a moment, his heart thumping at the idea of what he was going to have to do. Steeling his resolve, he pulled up his phone's web browser and tapped in what he was looking for, then quickly scanned the search results. He tapped the top choice and listened as the phone rang.

"Hello," he said when a gravelly female voice answered after a couple of rings. "I need a taxi as soon as possible."

•••

Tyreese sat in the foyer of the apartment building, waiting for the taxi he'd ordered to show up. When he and Emma had first moved to their home at *Riverview Apartments* there had been a sofa right here, second-hand, but nice. Now the place smelled like piss, and the sofa had been replaced at some point in the last three or four years by one of those park-bench style seats you can pick up from Walmart for thirty bucks; all wooden and damn uncomfortable... and chained to an exposed water pipe that ran along the baseboard.

Had it really been that long since he had been down here? Tyreese pushed the thought out of his mind along with the fluttering of unease at the idea of just how much time had passed. This place had been clean and new back in '04, the paint fresh, the rest of the residents smiling, he'd known them all by name. That had been back when Emma was still with him. Now the paint on the walls was peeling. There were spots of mold in the corner opposite him, near a brown water stain on the ceiling tiles. What the hell was this place coming to? And he knew no one, well, not unless you counted Annabelle, the girl who lived in the apartment below his.

The sound of a car horn honking alerted Tyreese to his taxi's arrival. He pushed himself unsteadily to his fake feet, using his wooden walking cane to help him keep his balance. Through the grubby glass double doors of the entranceway he saw his taxi waiting at the curb.

*Outside. I'm going to have to go outside.*

Tyreese's heart thumped against his ribs at the thought of having to leave through those doors, and for the second time since he had stepped out of the elevator, he wished that he had taken that damn anxiety pill.

Tyreese took a deep breath and stepped toward the exit, the anger he felt at himself helping to force his anxiety down deep inside. He got by on his anger a lot these days. He pushed the door hard and it flew open, bouncing back on its hinges as he shouldered himself through and headed to the cab waiting at the curb.

The taxi driver was a sour-faced Mediterranean man who glared at Tyreese as if he had just stolen his life's savings. No offer of help from him.

"Where to?" the man grunted as Tyreese maneuvered himself awkwardly into the back seat of the cab, pulling his legs up after him before tugging the cab door shut. He rattled off the market's address, then tried to relax as the cab pulled away from the curb.

It was only a three-mile drive to the store but within the first half-mile, Tyreese had begun to *really* regret skipping the anti-anxiety meds.

Maybe it was the grime-smeared taxi window, but the streets seemed even dirtier than they did from his apartment window, the few people he saw on the eerily deserted sidewalks looked more like shadows than people. They seemed to slink past each other, merging with the equally gray facades of block upon block of apartment buildings. Even the trees looked wilted and colorless in this dour gray-filtered daylight. It was as if the air had suddenly become poison.

Tyreese leaned his head against the glass of the cab's window and stared up at the leaden sky, even thicker with clouds now. It was the first vanguard of the El Niño-driven storm that was inbound to the West Coast. This storm was predicted to be hellacious. The one back in '97 had been bad enough. Streets had flooded, power had been intermittent at best, and then there was the looting. The experts said *this* one was going to last twice as long. The authorities had recommended that anyone who was able to leave town should do so. They should head inland or at least away from LA, which the weather service had all but promised was going to get hit the hardest.

*Good luck with that around here*, Tyreese thought. The majority of folks in these apartments could barely afford the rent. He was confident none of them had a vacation home in Aspen or a place in Tahoe or Las Vegas where they could wait out the storm. Christ, most of them couldn't even afford a car and had to rely on public transport to get anywhere. And the second the storm hit, the roads would flood and the bus service would shut down and then what? If the authorities didn't do something fast then they'd turn on themselves, that's what. And when had anyone ever given a damn about anyone around here? Not in a long time.

The taxi pulled up to the curb outside the store.

"Thirty bucks," the driver said, turning to stare at Tyreese through the security Plexiglas separating them.

"*How* much?" Tyreese asked, unable to keep the surprise out of his voice.

"Thirty. Dollars," the driver repeated the words slowly as though he were dealing with an imbecile.

Tyreese scowled at the obvious scalping he was getting but he pulled out his wallet, counted out the exact fare and slapped it into the man's hand. "Wait here," Tyreese ordered. "I'll be ten minutes."

The driver said nothing, turning his eyes to the front as Tyreese opened the door and maneuvered himself out onto the sidewalk. No sooner had Tyreese slammed the door shut than the driver slipped the car into gear and pulled away.

"Hey!" Tyreese yelled, waving his cane in the air after the rapidly disappearing cab. "Goddammit!" You simply couldn't rely on anyone these days.

It took only a few moments for Tyreese to realize just how much space there was around him. How open the area was. How exposed *he* was. Only another moment for the anxiety to begin to flood his system. His muscles began to tighten, the time between each of his breaths coming shorter than the one before as panic began to take control of his respiratory system. The saliva in his mouth disappeared as though his teeth had suddenly become sponges. His knuckles cracked as his hand tightened around the grip of his cane, fingers turning into a fist. He was a statue, caught by the vibrations of fear that told every atom of his body to flee, yet greedily resisted its neighbor's desperation, pinning him to the spot.

Then Emma was there and talking to him. *Close your eyes, baby. It's okay. Just close your eyes.* He heard Emma's dead voice as if she was standing right there on the street next to him. Although he knew it was just the memory of his wife, he obeyed, because even the ghost of her was an irresistible force. Even so many years after she had gone, Tyreese still carried her willingly around within his head and heart. What else was he supposed to do with the love of his life, when the only thing that remained of her was her spirit? That was better than the alternative.

Distilled light filtered through the lids of his eyes. He squeezed them shut as tightly as he could until there was only blackness. He allowed his mind to listen to his wife's voice speaking to him, easing him down as she had always been able to. He felt his heart begin to quieten, his shoulder muscles relax, as he focused on his breathing just like Emma had taught him.

*Slow baby. That's it, just relax,* Emma's echo whispered. Her beautiful face—the way she used to be, young and smiling, not the withered, pain-riddled one she wore at the end—filled his mind and he smiled back at her. He felt his shoulders relax, his heart rate slow more, and—

"Hey! Hey, mister!"

Tyreese started, his eyes flickering open at the sound of a woman's voice, not his wife's; this one was dry and raspy. He turned around, saw a woman standing just a foot or so away to his left. Her skin was burnt a deep coffee brown from constant exposure to the California sun, wrinkled, with deeper brown age spots—or maybe dirt? It was hard to tell—along the length of her arm. Her hair was a tangled blonde mess. She was wearing a stained summer dress that fell limply from her emaciated frame. The dress might have been older than Tyreese. A shopping cart waited for the woman like an obedient dog a few feet away, its insides bursting with plastic containers and spent cans of soda and beer. *How the hell had she gotten to him without him hearing her?*

Tyreese blinked twice in quick succession, not sure if he was imagining the woman, but judging by the smell of dirt and urine that wafted from her she was all too real.

The woman smiled a gap-toothed smile at him. "It's coming," she said, her words slurring. "Can you feel it? It's coming."

"What?" he asked, even though the answer should have been abundantly clear. "What's coming?"

The woman's grin grew even wider as she threw her head back and laughed a gurgling maniacal laugh. "Something you never expected." Her head bobbed back and forth as she howled wildly at the sky. "It's coming for you. It's coming for me. And there ain't no escaping it."

•••

Tyreese walked as quickly as he could toward the entrance of the market. 'Market' might have been too strong a word for the building he was approaching, if he was honest, it barely made it past corner-store level but it was where he got his supplies every week, delivered a couple of hours after his order was placed... usually. He walked up to the entrance, pushed the door open and stepped inside.

He felt better instantly, the remaining anxiety slipping away at the sight of the store's comforting box-like design.

An Indian man in his mid-thirties with tired eyes sat behind one of three checkouts. His nametag read 'Mike' in large white letters, and 'MANAGER' below that. This was probably the guy he had spoken to on the phone earlier.

Tyreese commandeered a metal shopping cart that had been left near the entrance, nodded at Mike then headed toward the canned goods aisle. There were two other customers in the store, a far cry from how chaotic the place had sounded when Tyreese had called earlier. It quickly became apparent why. The shelves were all but empty, and it wasn't hard to imagine the swarm of panicked humans who had descended on the store like locusts, picking it clean.

"Well isn't that just special," Tyreese muttered to himself, limping down the nearest aisle. The right-front wheel of his shopping cart seemed to have a will all of its own, wobbling and squeaking, intent on forcing its three brethren to follow it in the opposite direction Tyreese wanted to go.

The shelves had been laid bare. It wasn't hard to imagine the throngs of locals who had descended here like a proverbial plague of locusts, stripping the aisles clean of almost everything. He found a couple of boxes of Hamburger Helper and tossed those into the cart. On the second aisle he found a row of six cans of green beans and a single can of carrots. The bottled water section was completely empty, but the freezer still contained plenty of bags of ice, so he grabbed six and added them to the cart. The ice would hopefully stay frozen long enough for him to get them home and allow them to defrost into containers that he could use if the water supply dried up. There was no telling what would get blown into the reservoirs when this storm hit. Clean drinking water could be in short supply.

By the time Tyreese forced his rebellious cart to the checkout he had added a clutch of Ramen noodles, some dried chicken bouillon, and a handful of candy bars.

Mike the Manager gave a perfunctory smile and began ringing up Tyreese's haul. The man looked weary as he pecked away at the cash register's keyboard. He announced the total and packed the items into plastic bags while Tyreese pulled the money from his wallet.

"Have a nice day," Mike said as he handed Tyreese his change.

"Sure thing," Tyreese muttered. He lifted the bags into the cart and pushed it toward the exit.

"Hey!" Mike the Manager shouted, suddenly animated, pointing at Tyreese's cart full of groceries. "You can't take that outside."

"Just gonna load my car," Tyreese lied, and pushed the cart through the doors before Mike had a chance to object.

# CHAPTER SEVEN

Birdy hopped a DASH bus at Figueroa, flopped down onto an empty seat and watched the streets roll by. She allowed her mind to drift away.

The first time she had seen parkour on TV she had fallen instantly in love with it. It made her feel like she could be a superhero. She watched tutorials on YouTube, and downloaded old episodes of *American Ninja Warrior* off the Internet to study during breaks at school.

And she practiced.

It was a *lot* harder than she thought it would be, but Birdy soon found she had a natural athletic ability, an ability that quickly developed into a skill, thanks to her passion for the sport. Finding Bryanna at the YMCA had been the best day of her life. She set herself a goal of being the youngest girl to ever compete on *American Ninja Warrior*, the show that first got her interested in parkour.

At 7th Street, Birdy jumped off the bus and headed in the direction of the mall, a couple of blocks away.

The Figueroa Mall had three floors, and *lots* of stores; everything from jewelry to kitchenware to perfumes. There was even a *real* bookstore Birdy liked to visit when she could. But today she was only interested in one particular store, which was located on the third floor. She pushed through the double doors, and headed past kiosks and stores. She ignored the elevator and took the stairs, loping up them two steps at a time, her excitement supplementing her already abundant energy. At the top she hung a left, weaving her way through the throngs of people chilling, browsing, and shopping, until she stood outside the store she was looking for. *Footsie,* the red neon sign over the door read.

Inside she headed toward the shelves on the right wall where the sneakers and sports shoes were displayed. She was halfway across the store when she heard someone call her name. Not 'Birdy' but...

"Annabelle, hey! How you doing?"

Birdy looked toward the voice. It was Trenton, his six-three basketball-player frame disguising the fact that he was almost a full year younger than Birdy. "What you doing here, girl?" he asked, smiling casually. Another guy, one she didn't recognize, stood to his right. He looked nervous, his eyes constantly moving around the store.

"Just looking," Birdy said, not really sure what else to say. Trenton had never even said a word to her before today, just eyed her up when he passed her in the hallway or during lunch breaks at school. Flattering, but not something she was interested in.

"That's cool. Me and my bro are just browsing, right man?" Trenton turned and gave the nervous looking kid next to him a hard punch on the meaty part of his shoulder. The other kid barely even registered it, he just glanced in Trenton's direction then glared at Birdy as if she'd been the one who hit him.

"Anyway," said Birdy, forcing a smile, "I gotta be going. See you in school."

"Yeah, yeah, girl. See you around." He flashed her a smile that showed off his perfect white teeth. And with that, Trenton and his friend headed to the opposite side of the store and began browsing through a rack of football shirts.

Birdy found the sneaker she was looking for, tracked down an associate and handed it to her. "Size eight. In black, please," she said.

A minute later the woman was back with a box. She handed it to Birdy before disappearing to help an older woman who was trying to find something for her daughter.

Birdy sat on a bench with a slanted mirror at its base. She stripped off her scuffed and scraped sneakers, laying them on the floor next to the bench. The shoebox sat next to her on the padded seat. She lifted the lid reverently, as if the box contained the Holy Grail itself, moved the packing paper aside, and reveled in both the sight and smell of the brand-new pair of sneakers within, each one toe-to-heel with the other, like twins in a mother's womb.

They were beautiful.

Birdy lifted the left sneaker out of the box, pulled out the cardboard support then loosened the laces. She slipped the shoe on and felt the soft material cling to the shape of her foot as though it were a second skin. She did the same with the right sneaker, then stood up.

They felt *amazing*, like she wasn't wearing them at all, but with all the support and protection she needed. Birdy skipped a few paces, hopped to the left and right, then jumped up and down in place a couple of times. She couldn't help but smile; these were going to make her training *so* much easier. She reached into her jacket for her wallet.

"That's her!" a stern voice announced from behind Birdy.

Birdy turned to look and saw a man with a manager name-tag pointing at her. Next to him was a guy who looked to be seven feet tall and almost as broad, wearing a mall security uniform. About ten feet behind that guy were two more security guards; one held Trenton in an arm lock, the other had his friend.

"She was the other one with those two. She's an accomplice," the manager declared.

"What?" Birdy asked, utterly confused.

The guard stepped toward her. "Don't give me any trouble, kid. Just come with me and we'll sort this out." He reached a meaty paw toward her.

Birdy sidestepped it. "I didn't do anything," she cried. The panic in her voice was nothing compared to what she felt.

"Hey! Don't be stupid. Just come with me." This time the security guard lunged at her. His hand almost closed around her wrist, but she dodged away, spun sharply, and before she even knew she was doing it, Birdy ran.

"Grab her!" The security guard yelled as she sprinted for the exit.

The two rent-a-cops in front of Birdy looked torn; they would have to release their grips on the two boys to apprehend her. Birdy used their indecision to slip between them.

Trenton hooted in delight. "Yeah! Run Annabelle. Let go of me, pig!"

*Not real helpful*, Birdy thought as she zagged toward the exit.

"Stop her!" The manager yelled, and Birdy saw heads turning in her direction. Birdy slid under a rack of clothes to get by a young sales associate who had positioned herself in a half-hearted attempt to block Birdy's escape, then sprinted through the exit.

Birdy headed back along the walkway at a jog, weaving through the throng, trying to keep a low profile but knowing a dozen security cameras were probably following her progress. A couple of shoppers looked in her direction, decided she wasn't their problem and kept on walking.

"You! Yes, you. Stop!"

Birdy flashed a look behind her. A security guard was pushing his way through a gaggle of teenage girls who had just exited a Nike store, about six bodies back. Another rent-a-cop angled in her direction from the food court on her left, while a third jogged up the opposite walkway, his lower body obscured by the safety barriers that blocked the open space of the central atrium that split the mall. The guards were trying to block her from getting to the elevators and stairs, figuring if they could cut off her escape route they would have her. They were right, too, Birdy thought. There was no chance she could get to either the elevator *or* the stairs before the two security guards. And as if to confirm she had no chance of escape, a fifth security guard appeared at the top of the escalator from the floor below, cutting off any possibility of escape in that direction.

Birdy's heart had been thudding with the adrenalin of the chase, but now it slowed as she urged her muscles to relax. It wasn't really a conscious effort on her part, it just happened, and Birdy thought it was just one of those genetic quirks of her fight or flight response. Some people froze or ran away when confronted by danger, she just seemed to relax. It wasn't like her senses sharpened, it was just that everything else—the noise of the crowd, the thumping of her heart, the heat of fear—they all faded away and things became... clear. Birdy took a final look over her shoulder at the guard who was now just six feet away and closing in on her fast, a confident smile of victory already on his lips. He knew she was done. He thought there was nowhere for her to go.

He was wrong.

Birdy dodged right, pushing her way in front of a line of shoppers then headed to the glass safety barrier surrounding the atrium. Metal balustrades held thick panes of reinforced opaque glass. The top had a brushed aluminum banister you could lean on and look down over the two floors to ground level, far below. Birdy took hold of the banister with both hands and climbed over the barrier, swinging her body around to face back toward the walkway, her toes slipping into the two-inch gap between the floor and the lower edge of the glass panel.

She heard people yell. Saw a woman browsing in the Victoria's Secret store directly across from her staring open mouthed in a silent gasp of astonishment, had time to register the confused look of the security guard as he hesitated... then Birdy let go of the banister and stepped out into space.

# CHAPTER EIGHT

The air had grown colder during the time Tyreese had spent searching the store. A gusty breeze pulled leaves from the line of trees along the curb and sent them skittering and flying down the street. He zipped his jacket closed and pulled the collar up tightly around his neck. He hadn't exactly expected to have to walk the three miles back to his apartment block so he was dressed only for the cab trip with a light windbreaker. It would have to suffice. He cursed the cab driver under his breath then scanned the streets on the off-chance that the guy might have had a crisis of conscience and decided to come back, or maybe another passing cab might miraculously appear, but the street was deserted.

Tyreese consoled himself with the knowledge that the crazy woman who had accosted him on his way into the store had moved on. He half expected her to be lying in ambush for him, but she had vanished as quickly as she had appeared. At least she had given him the idea for the shopping cart. He'd figure out how to get it back to the store when he could.

The stumps of his legs itched badly against the prosthetics. This was the first step up the ladder that would quickly move to pain and muscle cramps. He cursed himself for not wearing the damn things more often.

He pushed the cart to the edge of the curb, looked up and down the street for any sign of a taxi, sighed when he saw nothing, and began to walk back to his apartment block.

•••

Tyreese was just over two miles into his journey home, his thighs throbbing in pain with each step he took, when he knew for certain someone was following him. He looked back over his shoulder and saw two smirking kids, probably seventeen, tops, jogging quickly toward him. They split either side of Tyreese and ran a few paces ahead, stopped and turned, blocking his way.

"Hey old man, whatcha got there?" said the taller of the two, laying a hand on the front of the shopping cart, forcing Tyreese to a standstill. The kid grinned at Tyreese, looking him up and down, assessing him like a snake checking out its next meal.

Tyreese had seen kids like these all around the area. Hell, he had been just like them himself when he was their age; cocky, sure of their invulnerability, and dumb as rocks.

Tweedledumb and Tweedledumber, he decided, were apt names for these two.

Tweedledumb wore a baggy t-shirt that Tyreese knew probably hid a wiry muscular frame from days spent playing street ball. His friend, Tweedledumber, was a little shorter but a lot wider, his face a caricature of what passed for tough these days. He stood just off to the left, eying the contents of Tyreese's shopping cart. This one was fidgety, constantly shifting from foot to foot, maybe from nerves, maybe something else; kids could pick up any drug they wanted easier than candy around here, these days.

Tyreese had placed his walking cane in the wire basket of the cart next to the plastic bags containing his supplies. Tweedledumber reached for it. Tyreese grabbed the cane, swung it in a tight arc, and brought it down with a sharp crack across the kid's knuckles, hard enough to make the kid yelp in pain but not enough to do any real damage.

"Boy, didn't your momma ever teach you to keep your hands off of other people's property?" Tyreese kept his voice level, cool.

The kid rubbed his knuckles, his face flushed bright red, his eyes little thunderstorms of anger. He looked up at Tyreese and cursed, took a step closer. "I'm going to—"

Tyreese brought the cane up again and smacked it hard against the meat of Tweedledumber's shoulder with a resounding thwack that sent the kid skittering backward, grabbing at his arm. A combination of pain and anger and confusion stitched the kid's mouth shut. He was really living up to his new nickname, Tyreese decided.

"I said keep your hands off my—" This time it was Tyreese's turn to be surprised. The taller kid placed both hands on the front of the shopping cart and shoved hard against it.

The cart's handle caught Tyreese in the stomach, the back two wheels smacking against his shins, hard enough that if they had been actual legs it would have hurt like hell. Instead he felt his prosthetic legs buckle as he lost his balance, and he began to drop toward the pavement.

Before he even hit the ground, the two boys had made a grab for the plastic bags in the cart, but Tyreese managed to twist as he fell toward the uneven paving slabs of the sidewalk, torqueing the cart to the right. Tweedledumber missed, but the taller one managed to grab two of the bags, hooking them out of the cart.

Tyreese hit the ground hard, forcing a deep "Oomph!" from his mouth as his muscular frame slapped the concrete. He managed to get his left hand between the sidewalk and his head, the skin on his knuckles splitting but saving him from a concussion or fractured skull. The shopping cart clattered to the ground in front of his face.

Tweedledumber had managed to recover his composure. He stepped in close, brought a sneaker-clad foot back and aimed a kick at Tyreese's head like he was aiming to put a football down field. Tyreese turned instinctively to protect himself and felt the kid's foot connect with the muscles of his back. The force reverberated around his chest cavity and a burst of pain shot down his spine.

Tweedledumber let out a yelp of anger and pain, the thin material of his sneaker doing nothing to protect his foot from Tyreese's tightly muscled back.

Through the wire meshing of the overturned shopping cart, Tyreese saw Tweedledumb already ten feet away and yelling at his friend to *move his ass*. Tweedledumber had apparently not learned his lesson, because as Tyreese rolled onto his back he saw the kid raise his foot again, readying himself to stomp on Tyreese's head.

Tyreese lashed out with his right arm, punching the kid in the leg just below the left knee. The boy screamed in pain and collapsed to the ground, all thoughts of continuing the assault replaced by the agony of a badly bruised, maybe even torn, calf muscle.

Tyreese moved his attention back to Tweedledumb. The kid's face had a look of utter surprise and confusion. His mouth was open so wide it looked like he had a large O in the middle of his face, shocked that this easy mark had the audacity to fight back. The kid glanced around the street, walked a couple of feet away as though he intended to leave his friend then apparently had a change of heart. He began moving back toward Tyreese, the two bags of supplies he'd managed to steal still clutched in his hands.

The shopping cart lay on its side next to Tyreese. He reached out a hand, placed it on the side of the cart and tried to push himself into a standing position, but when he looked down at his feet he saw his right prosthetic leg was twisted at a ninety-degree angle. *Shit*! He was going to need to reset it unless he wanted to hop all the damn way home. He'd dropped the wooden walking cane when he fell, it lay beneath the cart. He was a sitting duck for this punk.

Tweedledumb was still moving toward Tyreese, just a few feet separated them now, and Tyreese pushed himself upright until he was in a seated position. At least he could defend himself from the little bastard.

But instead of coming at Tyreese, the kid remained at a respectable distance, circling around the overturned cart and the man beside it until he reached his friend. Tweedledumber was still cursing, tears of pain and rage streaming across his cheeks, both hands holding his knee, which Tyreese thought was probably already swelling beneath the baggy jeans. His buddy reached him, never taking his eyes off Tyreese as though he thought the man would leap after him at any moment.

"Get up, dumb-ass," Tweedledumb said, lightly kicking the other boy's back with the toes of his sneaker while keeping a watchful eye on Tyreese, like a snake watching a mongoose.

"He broke my knee," the boy on the ground cried out, his voice a mixture, of pain, anger, and disbelief.

Tyreese didn't think he had hit him hard enough to break anything, but you never could tell. He hoped he had.

The taller kid dropped his gaze to his prostrate friend, then back to their intended victim, and Tyreese could tell he was again trying to calculate whether to help his compatriot or beat feet out of there and save his own ass.

Surprisingly, apparently there was loyalty among thieves, because the kid dropped one of Tyreese's bags, bent over and grabbed Tweedledumber's outstretched hand, and pulled the still cursing kid unsteadily to his feet. He bent to pick up the dropped bag, but abandoned that idea as his buddy teetered unsteadily on his one good leg, and instead threw his arm under the injured boy's shoulder. He shot Tyreese a hate-filled glare, accused him of doing unnatural things with his mother, and then the two of them began to stagger north like two old drunks.

Tyreese watched until the kids disappeared down a side street. When he was sure they would not be coming back, he allowed himself to lay back on the cold concrete of the sidewalk, his eyes staring upward at the bruised California sky.

*Could this day get any worse,* he wondered?

As if to answer him, a shadow crept across his face as the first fat drops of rain began to hit the ground, splattering like tiny bombs against his body.

# CHAPTER NINE

Shoppers screamed as Birdy stepped away from the security banister into nothing. She dropped fast through the air until her fingers grabbed the lip of the floor. She hung there, her legs swinging in the space between the upper and lower floors.

The drop between the two floors was only ten feet, Birdy estimated just as the head and shoulders of the security guard appeared at the safety barrier above her. His face was pale with shock, then relief, then horror when he realized she was only holding on by her fingertips.

Birdy knew he had expected to see nothing but her mangled body splattered across the tile of the ground floor. *This probably wasn't in his training manual*, she thought. She was tempted to raise a hand and give him the finger, but she wasn't an idiot. She'd figured out long ago that there was a point where calculated risk gave way to stupidity, and while she had no problem walking that line, she had no intention of stepping over it if she could help it. Instead, she swung her legs, once, twice... and let go.

Birdy landed on the floor of the second level just in front of a crowd of startled onlookers. She performed a perfect forward roll to dissipate some of the energy her fall had collected, leapt to her feet, looked around to check that none of the security guards had managed to make it to this level, then began to sprint toward the stairs.

Birdy took the steps down two at a time, dodging past couples who were too entranced by their consumer high to even notice her as she zigged and zagged between them.

The second her feet touched the ground floor she slowed to a brisk walk, trying her best to mingle with the rest of the shoppers as she headed for the exit. But as soon as she pushed through the exit doors, Birdy took off, racing as fast as she could across the parking lot toward the bus stop. If she had to, she would keep on running in the direction of home, but a bus had already pulled up to the curb. She sprinted the last hundred feet, catching up to the bus just as it was about to pull away. She banged on the pneumatic doors and gave the driver her best 'please don't leave me' look.

The driver must have been in a good mood because the doors opened with a hiss of air. She stepped on board, handed over her money and moved to the back of the bus, falling onto the seat. Exhausted, but exhilarated.

It was only when Birdy was halfway home that she realized she was still wearing the sneakers from the store.

•••

By the time Birdy made it back to her apartment, the meager sunlight had already begun to drain from the sky, replaced by a ferocious bank of snarling black clouds that was well on its way to devouring the western half of the sky.

Her mom was still at her day job, so Birdy headed for the kitchen. She was ravenous. She had meant to grab something to eat at the mall, but those plans had gone up in smoke. She opened the fridge, peeled the last couple pieces of ham from their plastic container, stuck them between two slices of bread then glued it all together with a thick layer of mayonnaise. She added a glass of milk and made her way to the living room sofa where she quickly devoured the sandwich. She chased it down with half the milk, forced herself back to her feet, and headed back to the kitchen where she washed the plate and knife she had used for her food.

On the way to her room, Birdy let out a loud belch. She giggled to herself as she flopped down on her bed. Her smile was replaced by a pang of guilt when she looked at her feet and remembered the sneakers she'd stolen from the store. *Bright and shiny and new.* She hadn't *really* stolen them, she told herself, not *technically.* She *had* been ready to pay, and besides, she had left her own sneakers behind. *And* they'd tried to arrest her for something she hadn't done. What was she supposed to have done?

Birdy stood up and walked over to the window. Thick shadows had begun to suck detail from the world beyond her bedroom, devouring the color and resolution from the buildings, roads, and trees. Even the few people she saw on the street seemed less real, insubstantial somehow; like the difference between a black and white photograph and a modern color one.

A storm was coming; it was all over the news. That meant no practice, no chance to try her new sneakers. *Life just isn't fair*, she decided. She walked back over to her bed, put her earbuds in, pressed play on her phone's music app and lay down.

After a few moments of staring at the ceiling, she felt her eyes close. She allowed herself to relax, the music soothing her mind, the bed soothing her body. *I'll just lie here for a little while*, she told herself.

Two minutes later Birdy was fast asleep.

•••

By the time Tyreese finally got back to his apartment, the rain was hammering down. Drops as big as marbles zinged onto the pavement so hard it sounded like bacon sizzling in a hundred frying pans. He was already soaked through to the skin, the thin windbreaker he wore no match for the driving rain. And *damn*, if the rain didn't *hurt*. Each impact stung like a mother as it pummeled his shoulders and buzz-cut skull.

At the steps to the apartment, he grabbed the remaining bags of supplies then abandoned the shopping cart, allowing it to roll and clatter to the gutter. All but one of the bags held ice, only slightly melted. The last bag, the one the punk had dropped in his rush to get his friend's ass out of trouble, had half of the food he'd bought. Tyreese hurried inside as fast as his battered body would let him.

The foyer was deliciously warm. He wiped the rain from his face and eyes, then headed to the elevator. He hit the call button with a clenched fist and leaned his forehead against the wall as he waited for the elevator car to arrive. He rode the elevator to his floor, stepped out and made his way to his apartment, leaning against the wall the whole way, the pain in his leg stumps agonizing now, his exhaustion almost total. He fumbled his key into the lock, opened the door and stepped inside.

Tyreese dumped the grocery-filled bag on the counter near the refrigerator, stuffed the remaining bags of ice into the freezer, then stumbled to his wheelchair and collapsed into it. He undid the ties of his prosthetic legs, rolled the sleeve down and pulled them from the sodden material of his jeans, before dropping them unceremoniously on the floor.

He wheeled himself into the bedroom, straight to the closet, pulled out a dry set of clothes and quickly discarded the wet ones into a pile on the carpet.

His back ached from the kick he'd received from that one punk. It twinged as he maneuvered himself into the fresh shirt and jeans. His knuckles were swollen, the skin grazed and bruised, and the stumps of his legs felt as though they were being rubbed with coarse sandpaper. He massaged them one after the other with both hands, wincing at the pain of the pins-and-needles he felt shooting up his thighs.

*Coffee*, Tyreese thought. *I need coffee.* The desire to drop a shot or three of whiskey into the mug from the bottle he kept in the kitchen cabinet was tempting, but it was only mid-afternoon. He needed his wits about him. Although, looking out through the kitchen window at the darkening street, he could be forgiven for mistaking it for late evening. The granite-gray clouds blanketing the sky were thick and full, like he was looking at a mountain range rather than a storm front.

Tyreese waited next to the pot while the coffee brewed, his mind running back over the events of the last few hours. How long had it been since he had actually set foot, so to speak, outside? It had been just after Emma's funeral. Jesus! That meant it had been almost two years. Tyreese sucked in a stuttering breath of the apartment's stale air, his chest fluttering as he fought back the pain of the memory of his wife's death. It felt so fresh, her loss. How could that be? Wasn't the pain supposed to fade? It was a question he asked himself often. He'd never received a satisfactory answer. Sometimes he would wake in the middle of the night sure that she was lying next to him. In those few moments between sleep and wakefulness the illusion seemed so real he could smell her musk, feel the warmth of her body, hear her breathing. And then the moment would pass and he would be alone again, the cold emptiness of her absence filling his every fiber.

Tyreese dismissed the thought and took a mug from the draining board. The coffeemaker's carafe was only half full of coffee but he pulled a mugful from it anyway, then added cream and sipped at the coffee before he wheeled himself back to the living room.

The rain thrummed against the windowpanes, driven by a gusting wind that had already swept most of the leaves from the trees that lined the street. The fallen leaves danced and spun like crazed fairies along the street. The gutters of the road below his window were awash with spill water, it ran like a brook on either side of the street, pouring down the black holes of the street's storm drains. The clouds had all but swallowed the sun, but the light that did manage to make it through painted the street and apartment buildings in a shadowy twilight gray.

Tyreese sipped his coffee, felt the liquid warming his throat and belly.

A car rolled down the center of the road, the first Tyreese had seen in a while, its wipers manically shuttling back and forth, the face of the driver pressed almost to the windshield in an attempt to see through the curtain of rain.

The heating kicked on with a barely perceptible thrum. Tyreese felt warm air begin to wash over his exhausted body. He leaned back in the wheelchair, allowing his muscles to relax, his mind lulled by the hypnotic beat of the rain and the gradually rising temperature of the room. He placed his coffee cup on the windowsill. His eyes were feeling heavy now and, try as he might, he knew he would be no match for the fatigue creeping over him.

Tyreese's head nodded once, twice, toward his shoulder. The third time he did not move, slipping into a deep, dog-tired sleep.

# CHAPTER TEN

"Bitsy, stay away from the God damn water," Frank Schwartz yelled, as his dog headed toward the edge of the pond with the obvious intent of diving right in... again. He had no idea why the damn dog had such a fascination with the water. He never could quite figure out the little mutt's psychology; weren't Dachshunds supposed to be afraid of getting wet? Frank shrugged his heavy shoulders and reached down to pet the dog as it circled back to him, running around his legs, yapping with excitement. At sixty-eight, bending down *and* getting back up again was a pretty big achievement in and of itself, especially for a man of his size, but he was in pretty good condition for his age, he thought. Yeah, he could still turn a head or two down at the old folks' home. He laughed to himself, a deep rumbling bear of a laugh for an equally large bear of a man.

He was alone and happy, thank you very much. Since Laura—God rest her soul—had passed on almost five years ago, there had never been another woman in his life, at least not one he would ever want to spend any more than a few hours with. Nope, he was quite happy by himself. And Bitsy of course, she was the only female company he needed in his life.

The dachshund gave a high-pitched, excited bark, running ahead of her master along the path leading out of the park. Frank had to smile. The dog had been his wife's; sometimes he had teased Laura that she'd loved the mutt almost as much as she did him. To which his wife had replied with a wry grin that she loved the dog way more. God, she had been beautiful.

Frank missed his wife terribly.

Still, life must go on. And he counted himself as one of the happy few, with a heavy emphasis on *few*. After almost forty years with the LAPD—thirty-two of them spent as a beat cop, the remainder behind a desk—Frank had retired, happily. He'd known enough old-timers over the years who had not lasted much more than a year before they had eaten their pistol or drunk themselves into the grave. Frank had decided early on in his career that he was not going to be one of them. He had prepared, both financially, and more importantly, psychologically for the sudden withdrawal of authority, prepared himself for that loss of relevance. Because in the end there was always someone who would simply step into his shoes and do his job. It was *just* a job, after all. And after so many years of dealing with nothing but the inhumanity and the vulgarity of some of the most hateful crimes inflicted on one human by another, Frank Schwartz was happy. At peace even. He *had* made a difference, as much as any one man could, and he had paid the price for making that difference. Now he was reaping the rewards.

The crash over at the air base earlier last week had dampened his spirits for a while. He'd been in the back yard watering Laura's roses (she had loved those roses in life and Frank had promised his wife he would take care of them after she was gone) when he'd heard the crash. The base was over six miles away but he had heard the plane hit and the deathly silence that had followed. The news said it had been one of those big C-17 Globemaster troop transporters, crewed by a recovery team bringing back bodies from Afghanistan. All the crew died, God rest their souls, but he'd also heard other rumors, just scuttlebutt really, about how the bodies they had been transporting back had not been found after the crash. It was all bullshit, of course; the product of overactive imaginations. But damn if it hadn't sent a shiver down his spine when he'd heard about it.

Frank and Bitsy exited through the park gate and turned left in the direction of home. "Come here, Bitsy," he called out. The dog instantly hurried to him, this routine a familiar one they played out every day during their evening strolls around the neighborhood. Frank bent down and attached the leash to the dog, who proceeded to trot along obediently at his ankles, sniffing at the pavement and an occasional streetlamp.

And what was up with the streetlamps, anyway? Almost every one he'd passed on his evening constitutional had been vandalized. Shattered pieces of their light covers and bulbs lay strewn across the sidewalk and road, as though someone had methodically gone from one to the next, smashing them as they went. *Has to be kids*, he supposed.

"This way, Bitsy," Frank said, guiding his dog around the broken shards of plastic and glass.

He just didn't get why someone would want to do that. It seemed like an awful lot of trouble to go to just for kicks. Kids today though, with their tablets and phones and whatnot. Not like when he was a youngster. Even with so much to keep them occupied, there was always going to be the occasional malicious little bastard who thought it would be fun to do this kind of crap.

It was going to get dark early, tonight, Frank thought, his eyes drifting back to the blackening sky. The dense clouds created a premature twilight that cast long, ominous shadows over the sidewalk as he and Bitsie walked the quarter mile back toward the small yellow bungalow they called home.

Their street was quieter than usual, he mused as they rounded the corner to their road. Normally, Frank would pass at least a couple of kids playing out on the sidewalk, or a young couple walking hand-in-hand, even the odd stranger out for an evening stroll, and he would always greet them with a smile or a wave. It was just *that* kind of a neighborhood; picturesque, quaint even, he supposed, but he loved it. In fact, now that he thought about it, he had not seen much activity for the past couple of days. Both the streets and the park he and Bitsy visited daily seemed almost deserted.

Maybe it was because of the promised storm. Maybe it was something else. But now that he thought about it, Frank felt an old familiar tingle of his cop's sixth sense, honed by all those years on the force, that told him it was the latter. Something was just not right around here, he was sure of it. Frank suppressed a shudder of apprehension. He would keep his eyes open. Not just for himself, but for the people of the neighborhood he called home.

People like Jenny and her little boy, a beautiful kid, just turned a year, named Caleb. Hell, at twenty-two, Jenny was barely older than a child herself. But unlike so many single mothers of a similar age, Frank thought, Jenny had her head screwed on nice and tight. She was working her way through college (she was studying to become a Human Resource Manager) and still managed to spend the rest of her time with little Caleb.

Frank and Bitsy had kind of unofficially adopted the mother and boy ever since they moved into the Section-Eight rental next door to his, about nine-months earlier; he becoming Jenny's surrogate father, Bitsy Caleb's playmate. Frank had no kids of his own, had never been blessed with them, but he considered Jenny to be like the daughter he never had. And as old-fashioned as that might sound to anybody else's ears, he did not give a God damn crap. She was sweet and kind, attributes that were hard to find together these days. Frank had seen the worst that life could mete out to someone as lovely as Jenny, if she had the misfortune to catch the eye of some of the assholes who hunted people like her in this town. No way was he going to let that happen if he could help it.

The two companions stopped at the rusted iron gate and cracked concrete path leading up to Jen's front door. There were no lights visible in the windows, and the curtains were pulled tightly together. Frank pushed the gate open and took two steps up the path then stopped as the dog leash in his right hand suddenly went taut. He turned and looked down at his dog.

Bitsy had planted her butt firmly on the sidewalk outside the gate and refused to move.

"What the hell is wrong with you?" Frank asked the dog, a little exasperated. He tugged on the dog leash to try and encourage her to move.

Bitsy hunched down to her belly on the pavement, her ears drooping as she stared up at her master, a pathetic whimper whistling from between her tightly clenched jaws.

*Odd*, Frank thought, scowling. Normally Bitsy would be ecstatic at the idea of paying Jenny a visit; it usually meant a treat and a bucketload of energetic, if occasionally rough, love from the little one. Maybe Bitsy wasn't feeling good. Or, more likely, she was hungry.

Frank gave a last look at the darkened windows of Jen's house, then, with a sigh of resignation, turned and headed back through the gate, walking the few additional yards to his own home, next door.

"You're a pain in the ass, mutt," Frank said, slipping his key into the front door's lock.

By the time the old man and his dog made it to the living room, Bitsy was her normal ebullient dog-self again.

•••

Frank stood at the window of his front room, staring out into the street, a glass of whisky resting loosely in the fingers of his right hand. Only three other homes showed any sign anyone was home on his street, the dim glow of light leaking from behind drawn blinds and curtains. Jenny's house was one of those still dark. He'd called her a couple of times, but she hadn't answered, so he had left a message on her cell. Actually, he'd left several messages; but who was counting.

As far as Frank knew, there was no current significant other in Jenny's life. And it wasn't his place to ask. She had told him that her boy's father was somewhere in Upstate New York; the split had been amicable, according to Jenny. But Frank got the distinct impression, 'amicable' was probably a euphemism for the boyfriend not giving a shit about his child. Of course that could have changed. He hadn't seen any strangers in the area over the past few days (fact was, now he thought about it, he'd seen far fewer people than he would have expected out and about during his walks with Bitsy), but that didn't mean Jenny's ex couldn't have shown up and caused her grief. After so many years of making other people's problems his own, Frank was reticent to step in between two feuding former lovers, especially when there was a child involved.

He took another sip of his nightcap and tried to crush the feeling of disquiet he felt swelling within his gut. He had learned to trust that basic instinct over the years as a cop, but he did not want to hear from it now, not here.

Beyond the window, night's claim on the city was now complete. Besides the light shed by the lamp on Frank's bedside cabinet and the few other homes where he could see the faint glow of a bulb, there was nothing but darkness and shadow outside. Frank hadn't known fear in a long time, but tonight, standing here with only a thin pane of glass separating his reality, the darkness seemed extra oppressive; insidious even. He pulled the curtains closed and drained the rest of the whisky from his glass.

"Tomorrow," Frank said to Bitsy. "Tomorrow morning we'll both go check on her." And, cursing his cowardly heart, he and his dog headed to bed.

•••

Frank woke with a start.

For a confused moment, he lay in his bed, heart pounding, his hand frozen halfway to the bedside table drawer where he kept his .45. He had no idea what had woken him but after a few seconds of silence, he heard Bitsy's fearless growl buzz like an electric saw in the darkness. He forced his pounding heart to slow, drawing in a few calming, deep breaths, his hand suspended in the air near the cabinet, his fingers almost able to touch the brass handle of the drawer. Bitsy, her form a darker shadow on the bed next to Frank, growled again as the unmistakable sound of the doggy-door in the kitchen squeaking open was followed by the sound of it swinging closed again.

"God damn that cat," Frank sighed, then relaxed. He pulled his arm back from the cabinet drawer, pulled the comforter aside and swung his legs out of bed. He glanced at the red glow of his alarm clock: 3:22 in the morning. "*Goddamn* cat," he repeated, this time with a little more venom in his voice.

One of his neighbors—he did not know which, but he suspected it was the cantankerous old lady who lived a couple of doors down on the opposite side of the street—owned a big ginger tomcat that occasionally liked to sneak into the house through the doggy door and scarf any of the food Bitsy had left uneaten. He'd tried taking the dog food up at night, but then the little ginger bastard had started snagging his furniture in retribution. The damn thing had even pissed in the potted fern he kept in the living room.

Frank turned on the bedside lamp.

Bitsy had moved to the end of the bed, an ear cocked to one side, listening. She growled, barked once, then leapt from the bed and disappeared through the open bedroom door, her nails scratching against the hardwood floor.

"Hold on, Bitsy," Frank sighed as he climbed to his feet, steadied himself for a moment as his eyes grew accustomed to the light, then began stumbling his way after his dog. He shambled carefully down the corridor toward the kitchen, naked feet squeaking on the cold floor, his slippers forgotten in his enthusiasm to catch the feline intruder. He was going to show it what-for if he got his hands on it.

Bitsy was already in the kitchen and her barking grew more insistent. Louder, with a sense of urgency Frank had never heard before.

"You got the little bastard cornered, Bits?" Frank called out. "Just give me a second to—" Frank stopped mid-sentence as Bitsy's barking suddenly turned to a panicked yelp then into a scream of pain that instantly shattered Frank's nerve. For a second he thought the scream was the cry of a human child, it was so high pitched, so terrified. It was only the interspersed sound of Bitsy's bark and the obvious sound of a violent struggle that confirmed otherwise; it was his dog, and something nastier than that old tomcat had her.

"Jesus Christ! Bitsy! I'm coming," he yelled, forgetting his aches and pains. Frank jogged as quickly as his old joints would allow toward the kitchen and the screaming dog.

*It has to be a raccoon, or maybe a coyote. Shit! What if it's rabid? Why didn't I bring my pistol?* These thoughts all raced through Frank's mind as he stumbled his way closer, but in the back of his mind, his gut instinct screamed at him to be careful, to be real goddamn careful.

Bitsy screamed again; a pain-filled screech of terror that sent a shudder of fear and anger down Frank's spine. He resolved there and then that whatever had his dog, he was going to end its miserable life, with his bare hands if he had to.

Frank rounded the corner into the kitchen, his hand instinctively reaching for the switch to turn the light on just in time to see Bitsy's rear legs disappearing through the doggy door that led out into the backyard. Fat drops of blood left a morbid trail for him to follow from the center of the kitchen floor to the door.

Frank ran to the back door and drew back the security bolt. He started to reach for the door handle, but stopped midway and ran back to the cutlery drawer. He pulled open the drawer, grabbed the large Chef's knife he kept in there, then turned and ran to the back door, his bare feet almost sliding out from under him as he slipped on the trail of Bitsy's blood.

Frank simultaneously flipped the switch to the back porch light and opened the door. Stepping out onto the porch, he followed the trail of blood over the wooden deck and down the steps onto the lawn, his eyes trying to adjust to the sudden light/no-light transition. He came to an abrupt halt, freezing in his tracks just a few steps out onto the grass, as his eyes finally adjusted to the night.

Nestled in a burr of dead grass, caught in a vague shaft of light from the porch light, sat a small, pale form. It was a kid; Frank could tell that much. A naked child, facing away from him. The child's head was dipped, exposing each knuckle of its spine against the oh-so-pale skin of the child's back. It cradled something in its arms, clutching the limp form to itself as though it was the most precious toy imaginable.

"Caleb?" Frank recognized the boy's shock of ginger hair. It was Jenny's boy. Naked and alone out here in the darkness. *How the hell did he end up out here?* Frank wondered as he took another step toward the child, lowering the kitchen knife to his side as all his earlier fears about Jen and her boy suddenly became very, very real.

"Caleb? It's Uncle Frank," he said as gently as he could, given the pounding in his chest. "What are you—?"

The boy's head whipped around and Frank gave a startled cry of horror. Yellow, feral eyes stared out from deep pits of black, and a steady stream of blood trickled from Caleb's lips over his chest and legs.

"Fuck... Me...," Frank whispered, as he took another step forward. If the kid was in this kind of a state, then what about his mother? Frank felt his heart sink even further.

Caleb turned completely toward the old man, flipping suddenly like some pale bloodless reptile, both hands and feet thudding firmly onto the ground, the thing in his hands falling with a wet thump.

"Bitsy?" Frank said, recognizing the limp body of his dachshund, blood still pouring from two puncture marks in her throat, her tongue lolling from the side of her jaws.

"What? What?" Frank repeated as his eyes moved back and forth from the body of his dog to the child. "What?" The two images just did not make a coherent picture: Caleb, naked and blood soaked, sitting on his lawn in the middle of the night had *killed* his dog. Had crept into his home through the fucking doggy door. His mind simply could not process it; it kept jumping back to the moment he had stepped outside, and repeated the twenty seconds that followed over and over like the stuck needle of a record player.

With a blood-freezing hiss, Caleb began to scramble toward Frank. The child's arms and legs—legs that until this moment had barely been able to even support the kid—propelling him with inhuman swiftness across the damp grass.

Frank staggered backward, stumbled, one foot slipping off the edge of the steps, arms windmilling through the air. This slip, this simple twist of fate, was assuredly what saved him. As Frank fell backward, he saw the boy launch himself through the air like some kind of hybrid human-frog. Caleb passed through the space where the old man had momentarily stood, and Frank saw the boy's mouth open, exposing four needle-like teeth; two curving from the upper gums, two from below. The child's jaws snapped closed with an audible *crack*, barely missing Frank as he stumbled backward.

Frank hit the ground with a jolt, mud slurping around his butt. He pressed his hands into the wet ground, they sank an inch or so as he tried to push himself to his feet, but the ground was slick with rain, and Frank's bare feet slipped from under him as he tried to pull himself up.

Caleb came at him again, scuttling across the space between them.

Frank instinctively kicked out with his right leg. His muddy foot connected with the boy and sent him spinning away. Frank managed to push himself to his feet. He staggered as quickly as he could back toward the house, mud clinging like concrete shoes to his bare feet.

He rushed through the open door, slamming it behind him. He fixed the bolt into place and leaned back against the door, panting hard. *This could not be possible. Caleb was some kind of... of... monster.* Frank's mind, delirious with fear, tried to make some kind of sense of what he had just seen. Caleb was just a little boy; how could he possibly have—

Something slammed hard against the door with an audible thump that shook the door in its frame.

Frank yelped. He was not a particularly religious man, but he found himself praying silently to any god that might be listening, that this would just turn out to be a nightmare.

The doggy door creaked between Frank's ankles and began to open.

Frank bleated in fear, a strained, high-pitched noise that he barely recognized as coming from himself. He dropped to his knees and forced the doggy door closed. On the other side of it he heard Caleb growling and snarling like a crazed dog. He fumbled in the darkness for the doggy door's plastic lock, and pushed it into place.

A thought, small but nagging even over his sense of disbelief and panic occurred to him: *Didn't I leave the kitchen light on?* Frank, his face covered in sweat, glanced around the kitchen, the darkness was almost complete, his eyes barely able to make out the shape of the countertop where he kept the phone. He needed help. 911. The cops. He climbed to his feet and began to move carefully across the kitchen toward the phone, his hands extended out in front of him like a Romero zombie.

Frank stopped dead in his tracks, a shocked noise somewhere between a sigh and a yelp escaped from between his lips.

Two luminous yellow orbs had appeared in the darkness in front of him.

"What the..." he started to say but was interrupted by another voice.

"Hello, Frank." The voice was low, husky, female, with a slight sibilance that bordered on a lisp. It took Frank a second to realize that the voice came from where the two yellow lights floated in the darkness. Another second to realize that the 'lights' were eyes. By the third second he recognized the voice as Jenny's, Caleb's mom.

"Oh no," he whispered, then turned and ran blindly toward the doorway leading back to his bedroom. If he could just get to the bedroom, he could barricade the door, and there was another landline there. He just needed to—

It was the damn kitchen table that did him in, Frank decided a second after he collided with it and went skidding across the tiled floor. His head cracked against something hard as he slipped. *One of the chairs*, his mind told him as he lay dazed, face down against the floor. He tasted blood in his mouth, and something warm was trickling down the back of his head.

Frank tried to push himself to his feet, but he couldn't move. He felt weight against the small of his back, pinning him to the cold floor. Hands, impossibly strong, grabbed his shoulders. He was flipped roughly onto his back as if he weighed absolutely nothing.

Frank let out a shriek of horror. Kneeling over him, her face just inches from his, was Jenny. Her terrible inhuman eyes glowed coldly in the darkness, a thick stream of dark saliva dripped from the corner of her mouth, splattering against his cheek. She smelled faintly of decay.

"Oh, Frank, you didn't think I'd leave you behind, did you?" Jenny cooed. Her voice sounded almost the same, but there was something different he could not quite identify. It sounded... off. Like something good that had been left to spoil.

"Jenny, please," he whispered.

Jenny did not answer him. Instead she lowered her head to Frank's neck and bit deeply into the flesh of his throat.

Frank tried to scream but the sudden shock of Jenny's fangs slicing into his jugular vein paralyzed his tongue. He tried to roll her off him but this ridiculous waif of a girl somehow had him pinned firmly to the ground. He felt his blood leaving his body, drained from him by the creature that suckled at his throat. His heart thumped and thumped, faster and faster as he gasped in pain.

Then a greater pain exploded in his chest, like lightning, racing through his body. Frank's back arched and his teeth clenched tightly together as his heart finally gave out.

Mercifully, the heart attack swept Frank Schwartz away on a tidal wave of pain to be with his Laura, but the creature that had once been Jenny continued to drink from him until she could drink no more.

# CHAPTER ELEVEN

A scream snatched Tyreese from sleep. He sat bolt upright in bed, the comforter scrunched up just below his chest, instantly alert. The scream had not been his, he realized after a few seconds. Wasn't a dream either. Not tonight, at least.

Tyreese looked at the alarm clock on his bedside cabinet. It was just after two am. He replayed the last few seconds through his mind: It had sounded like a child's panicked scream, or maybe a woman. It hadn't come from anywhere within his apartment building, he was pretty sure of that. The voice had been distant, muffled, so it most likely had come from one of the other apartment buildings that surrounded his. When you lived this close to so many families, you heard just about everything a human could do to themselves and others, over time. But this scream had been different, it had carried a note of terror to it that he had not heard in a long, long time.

A dog barked somewhere; three short *gruffs* then became silent.

Tyreese lay back in his bed and closed his eyes in the hope that sleep would be ready to reclaim him, but after a couple of minutes of staring at the inside of his eyelids he knew there was no chance of that happening. His grazed knuckles hurt and the muscles of his bruised back complained as he turned on his side trying to find a more comfortable position.

Finally, he pushed the covers aside, and with a sigh maneuvered himself to the edge of the bed, then into his wheelchair.

He rolled across to the fridge, pulled out the half-empty milk container and filled a mug. He nuked it in the microwave until the milk was just the right side of hot and took up his position by the window, sipping his drink slowly.

A blanket of ugly clouds enveloped the sky, blocking all light from the moon and stars. The curve of sky above was nothing now but impenetrable black. The streets seemed somehow darker too. It was only after a few minutes of sitting, allowing his eyes to acclimate to the darkness that Tyreese noticed entire buildings along this block were completely dark, not a single light was on. He'd spent plenty of sleepless nights at this window, woken suddenly by the nightmare that was his regular nocturnal visitor, and the one constant of all those nights was that no matter what time it was, there was *always* someone else awake on the street, always a couple of lights on in every apartment block.

*Always*!

Now as he looked down from his window at the row of buildings stretching away into the darkness on either side of him, he counted at least four buildings that were completely dark, not even the dim glow of a lobby light on the ground floor. This block had its fair share of brown outs, but that wasn't what was happening here, he could see the orange glow of lights in the buildings on either side of the dark ones.

The apartment was cool, but Tyreese felt a single bead of cold sweat drip from the nape of his neck and trickle down his spine. *Something's just not right.* He couldn't put his finger on what it was exactly, but there was *something* that just felt out of place. Wrong.

He took another sip from his milk... and froze mid-swallow, the hairs on his naked arms standing up like they'd been ordered to attention.

Directly across the street, in the shadows between one of the darkened apartment buildings and its lit neighbor, he saw movement.

A shadow had detached itself from the darkness and was moving quickly across the parking lot of the blacked-out building, flitting between the few cars parked there. The shadow was indistinct, but fast—really fast. It moved with a speed and confidence that could not be expected from a human moving while surrounded by virtual darkness. The shadow stopped momentarily next to an old Lincoln that Tyreese could not remember ever seeing moved from its parking spot, merging with the gloom surrounding the derelict car. Tyreese leaned in closer, the worn armrests of his wheelchair creaking.

Two yellow points of light appeared in the darkness beside the car. It took Tyreese several moments to realize what they were: eyes. Maybe they were reflecting some of the light from his apartment building back at him? The eyes disappeared for a second then reappeared again, as though whomever or whatever they belonged to had shifted its position, or was looking around, before reappearing again, looking back at his apartment.

Tyreese got the distinct and disturbing impression that those luminous disk-like orbs were fixed on *him*. That even though he knew he was completely hidden within the darkness of his own apartment, the eyes saw him. That whatever it was down there was aware of him, was watching him closely.

He'd seen the occasional coyote prowling the street late at night, picking through garbage cans looking for scraps. Hell, he'd even seen a raccoon once, but Tyreese didn't get the feeling this was either of those nocturnal prowlers. This was something else, something new.

As if it had heard his thoughts, the eyes blinked again, and then disappeared as the shadow detached itself from the car and moved quickly toward the apartment building directly across from where Tyreese sat, mesmerized.

The shadow moved toward one of the few buildings whose lights still shone, heading toward an apartment where a window still glowed in the darkness. Tyreese followed the shadow as best he could as it moved silently toward the front of the building. The window was on the third floor, and Tyreese watched as the shadow positioned itself beneath it, pausing as if considering its next move.

"Jesus!" Tyreese exclaimed, the mug momentarily slipping from his fingers, spilling warm milk into his lap as the shadow suddenly leaped six feet into the air... and attached itself to the apartment building's exterior wall.

Tyreese leaned closer to the window, his heart thumping so loudly he could hear it above his suddenly panting breath. The shadow began climbing up the apartment building, a darker splotch within the lighter shadow. It climbed the way Tyreese imagined a bat or a lizard would, hand-over-hand diagonally toward the lighted window on the third floor.

"You have *got* to be kidding me," he said. He rubbed his eyes, sure that what he was seeing had to be some kind of an optical illusion, that he was still half-asleep. There was no way something so large could climb the stucco exterior of the apartment building unless it had suckers... or claws.

In Afghanistan, he'd seen a few camel spiders. Those bastards were big, eight or nine inches, and they could climb the side of your tent and even a building, but whatever he was watching move up the building's front, well, this was human sized. In fact, as it grew closer to the umbra of the light spilling from the third story window, it looked more and more like a human to Tyreese. He was just too far away to be able to see clearly. He cursed silently to himself, and wished he still had his night vision goggles.

The shape stopped just below the sill of the apartment window. Tyreese had to squint to even be sure that it was still there. After a few seconds had passed with no movement, he began to doubt his own mind.

Then the shadow moved again.

A thinner shape — an arm, maybe? — reached up toward the lighted glass of the window.

"Oh shit," Tyreese exhaled when he realized his neighbor's apartment window was open. As he watched helplessly, a hand worked its way into the gap between the window and the jamb.

The window swung open.

*Phone, get the phone. Call the damn cops, right now,* his mind said, quite calmly considering the panic he felt. He had to call the police and let them know that someone... some *thing* was breaking into his neighbor's apartment. His hands reached for the rim of his chair's wheels. He was in the process of turning, his eyes never leaving the window across the street, when the shadow exploded like an arrow from a bow into the room. He saw the drapes flutter like a ripple on a lake and then be still.

Tyreese froze mid-turn, his breath held tightly within his chest as his vision focused exclusively on that small square of orange light less than three hundred feet from where he sat. For what seemed like an eternity he waited, a silent watcher in the darkness.

Maybe later he would admit that the reason he did not move was because he was afraid, afraid that whatever that shape was, it might really see him, might decide to come pay *him* a visit next. But at that moment, he would admit to feeling only a morbid fascination to see this strange event play out to its conclusion.

The rain continued its downpour, but above its static hiss he thought he heard something, faint, and distant. A man's desperate yell of surprise, he thought. It lasted for only a second or so, indistinct above the noise of the storm. But there was no mistaking the screech of fear that followed seconds later only to abruptly and absolutely cease.

Tyreese leaned forward in his wheelchair, his hands clutching the tips of each armrest until his still-scabbing knuckles turned white.

There was no sign of any movement beyond his neighbor's apartment drapes. A minute passed, then another. Tyreese began to turn for the phone again then stopped. "Oh, sweet—" The words caught in Tyreese's mouth.

Across the street, the light within his neighbor's apartment had gone out.

# SUNDAY

# CHAPTER TWELVE

Lizzie Finch was already up and preparing breakfast in the kitchen by the time her daughter rolled out of bed.

"Morning," Birdy said, between yawns. She leaned in and gave her mother a kiss on the cheek.

"Have to expect it's going to take me an extra half-hour to get to work in this weather," Lizzie said, as she spread butter on two slices of toast then handed them to her daughter.

Birdy could hear the resignation in her mother's voice. She worked so hard already, and this rain wasn't going to help by slowing everything down. Birdy knew from previous experience in this kind of weather that there was the possibility that the bus that took her mom the eight miles to where she worked the morning shift at McDonald's might not even show up.

"Thanks," Birdy said. She flashed her mom a sympathetic smile as she flopped down into a chair at the cheap wooden breakfast table near the window. The rain hadn't eased off at all overnight and a sheen of rain drops coated the glass of the kitchen window, blurring the image of the street. A constant *drip-drip-drip* of water fell from the top of the window frame down onto the sill with a syncopated rhythm.

Lizzie finished preparing her own toast, refilled her coffee mug then sat down in the chair across from her daughter.

"What are you planning on doing today?" Lizzie asked after

she swallowed the first couple of bites from her breakfast. She sipped from her coffee mug while she waited for her daughter to answer.

"I'll probably just go to the YMCA," she said. Birdy's gaze drifted out through the window again, trying to judge how bad the rain really was.

Lizzie grimaced. "It's raining so bad out there. You think anyone is going to show up in this?"

Birdy looked outside again. "It's not *that* bad."

Lizzie made a *tsk tsk* sound with her tongue. "Take your coat and make sure you stay dry. I don't need you getting pneumonia."

Birdy understood the implied concern. There was no chance her mom could take time off work to look after her if she got sick. And forget about a visit to the doctor. There was no way they could afford that.

"Of course," she said as if the very idea had been ludicrous.

Lizzie stood up and began to gather the dishes.

"It's okay," Birdy said, placing a hand on top of her mother's, "I'll get these."

Lizzie smiled, pushed her chair back and walked out to the hallway. She took her raincoat from the hook, picked up the old umbrella that rested in the corner near the door.

"See you later, baby," she said and blew her kid a kiss.

"Bye, Momma," said Birdy as her mom closed the door.

Birdy headed back into the kitchen, quickly washed up the breakfast dishes, setting them to dry on a draining rack next to the sink. She headed into her room, grabbed her duffel bag with her workout clothes from under the bed. She'd already decided she would shower at the YMCA after training, as she swung the bag onto her shoulder. She took her own lightweight rain jacket from the hook in the corridor and put it on. It had a hood that unzipped from the collar but it didn't look very cool so she left it down.

Birdy opened the front door, stepped outside, closed it behind her and gave the handle a gentle twist and push to make sure it was locked.

She stopped for a second.

Something felt out of place, something she couldn't quite put her finger on. It took her several moments before she realized what it was: the building was usually filled with noise. The corridor echoing with the muffled sound of people talking, babies crying, music playing *way* too loudly. But today it was quiet, except for the sound of a TV from a couple of doors down and the distant indistinguishable notes of some rap song she couldn't place.

*Probably just the rain freaking people out,* she decided, and headed toward the elevator.

•••

As soon as Birdy stepped out into the rain she changed her mind about not wearing the hood.

Water cascaded from an awning over the apartment entrance as though someone had trained a hose on it. The air hissed with the sound of falling rain hitting concrete. It drilled the blacktop, thrummed as it hit the roofs of the few cars parked in the lot. Birdy waited beneath the awning while she weighed the possibility of being spotted by someone she knew wearing something so blazingly uncool as the hooded rain jacket against getting thoroughly soaked.

She decided the chances of seeing anyone at all were slim to none. The streets were completely empty. She unzipped the collar of her jacket and pulled out the hood, flipping it over her head.

Birdy looked at her phone, it was almost 9am but the other apartment buildings on the street were just ghostly shapes hidden behind the pall of rain. It was *so* dark out here. Clouds filled the sky above her head. Not the usual fluffy white Californian clouds she was used to, either; these were angry, dark, roiling swaths of gray and almost-black that blocked almost all of the sun, casting a twilight illumination across Birdy's world.

Ducking to avoid the waterfall running off the awning, Birdy stepped out onto the concrete path leading to the gate in the security fence around the apartment building. Instantly her ears were filled with the thud of rain hitting her neoprene jacket. It sounded like fingers manically tapping away at one of those old keyboards. She walked to the security gate, opened it and stepped out onto the street. The gate squeaked shut behind her.

Up and down the street, Birdy saw... nothing. Not a single person. A couple of lights still shone from windows in adjacent apartments, but the majority of buildings still had their yellowed blinds closed or their faded drapes pulled together.

*Weird*, she thought. *It's like everyone's gone into hibernation.*

The shushing sound of tires rolling through what was essentially a stream drew Birdy's attention to her right. A silver Suburban, its paint rusty and flaking, moved slowly up the center of the road, its driver straddling both lanes to avoid the deeper pools of water collecting near the curbs of the road, the drains already choking on the constant flood of water rushing into them. Birdy watched the car pass, the driver invisible behind the heavily tinted windows. The car's trunk was open, filled with the car owner's belongings. A poorly fastened blue tarpaulin had been tied over the furniture, but one corner of the tarp had come free, it flapped and waved as the car drove past. Rain and dirty water kicked up by the tires had already soaked the legs of a wooden chair that peeked out from beneath the tarp.

Someone was making a run for it, trying to outrun the coming storm. Birdy felt a faint desire to sprint alongside the car and jump in. Instead, she began to walk in the direction of the YMCA.

•••

The doors to the YMCA were unlocked but the lady who usually sat behind the reception desk in the foyer wasn't in her seat. Birdy waited, thinking the receptionist might be in the bathroom, but after five minutes she had not returned. Birdy signed in on the clipboard sitting on the countertop and headed to the changing rooms.

Instead of the usual sounds of hairdryers, and showers, and people chatting, the changing room was silent. Birdy's footfalls echoed off the tiled walls as she walked across the dry floor, pulled her gear out of her bag and quickly changed. She stowed her clothes in the locker, took her cell phone with her, and secured the locker with her padlock.

She had to walk past the swimming pool on her way to the gymnasium. She exhaled a sigh of relief when she saw a couple of teenagers—boyfriend and girlfriend Birdy presumed by the way they touched each other—frolicking in the water. But the lifeguard's seat was empty and it looked as though the normal throng of early-morning wrinklies doing slow laps around the pool hadn't made it in today. A lone player thumped a ball back and forth in one of the squash courts, his sneakers squeaking loudly as he darted left and right, oblivious to Birdy as she walked past. The weight room was empty.

And that was it. There wasn't a sign of anyone else.

Birdy pushed open the big wooden doors to the gymnasium and stepped into an equally empty space. Not even Bryanna had shown up today. Probably the weather, Birdy supposed, but it hadn't stopped Bryanna before. And where was everyone else? The kids not showing up she could understand, but she had never seen the rest of the YMCA this deserted.

Birdy pulled her cell phone out, sat down on one of the wooden benches lining the wall of the gym, and hit the speed-dial for Bryanna's number. It rang once, twice. On the third ring Bryanna's bubbly voice filled Birdy's ear: "Can't get to the phone right now, so leave a message."

Birdy waited for the beep then spoke. "Bree, it's Birdy. I'm at the Y, but no one else is here. Call me back." She hung up. She'd wait a little while longer and see if anyone decided to put in an appearance.

Ten minutes passed and there was still no sign of any of the others and no call back from Bryanna, either. That meant something was going on, but Birdy had no idea what exactly.

"No sense in wasting a perfectly good gymnasium," she said aloud, then instantly regretted speaking. The sound of her voice in the hollow room only drove home just how creepy the place was when no one else was about.

Birdy moved to the rock climbing wall. Normally Bryanna would insist on Birdy getting strapped into the safety harness and belay rope, but with no one else here to hold the rope if she fell, it was pointless. She'd free climb instead.

There were multiple routes up the wall, each progressively harder, the urethane-resin handholds color-coded by difficulty. Today was a blue day, she decided; the most difficult route up the forty feet of fake-rock face.

Birdy took three large steps backward, wiped her hands against her t-shirt as she eyed her chosen route up the wall... and ran. When she was a few feet from the base of the climbing wall she jumped, her hands reaching for two widely spaced blue handholds, about seven feet up the face. The fingers of her left hand closed on the first, gripping it tightly as she used her momentum to swing her body counter-clockwise a few feet and reach her right hand up to the next highest blue handhold. She got a firm grip and pulled herself up, her feet moving automatically to the holds she knew were below her.

Birdy pulled her tummy in close to the rock wall, arched her back and head slightly so she could see clearly up the uneven fake-rock face and began to climb hand over hand, pulling herself toward the summit.

The difficult part came halfway up. A simulated four-foot overhang stuck out above her. There were no holds on the outward slanting face of it, they were on the upper lip of the overhang, invisible from where she hung so precariously. Birdy wasn't tall enough to reach them, instead she would have to launch herself off the face, outward and upward.

A youthful inability to consider her own vulnerability mixed with a justified confidence in her skill meant failure was the furthest thing from Birdy's mind. She positioned her feet on the tiny toe-holds for maximum leverage, fixed her eyes on the prize, bent her knees, and exploded outward. The fingers of both her hands found their targets, a minimal handhold that strained the muscles and joints of her fingers.

Birdy's entire body now hung thirty feet in the air, supported only by the tips of her fingers. Her grip was strong and true. Birdy waited for her body to stop swinging, then calmly pulled herself up and over the lip of the outcropping and began to climb the final ten feet of the obstacle.

Her forearms burning, Birdy reached for the final handhold, preparing to pull herself up and onto the flat surface of the wall's summit.

"Hey! What are you doing in here?" The sharp crack of a man's voice came from nowhere, amplified by the empty gymnasium.

Birdy instinctively reacted by turning her head toward the voice, her fingers scraped the handhold she was reaching for... and missed. She gasped as she felt her body drop unexpectedly, all her weight shifted onto her weaker left arm. Birdy's eyes flicked back and upward as one finger, damp with sweat from the exertion of the climb, slipped away.

"Crap, crap, crap," Birdy hissed, her feet scrambling for a toehold and finding nothing. She stretched toward the summit with her right hand but it was just out of reach. Birdy scanned the face of the rock to her left for any kind of leverage—panic beginning to flood her system with adrenaline—again finding nothing within reach. She turned her head to the right, her face smooshing against the cold fiberglass of the cliff-face.

There! A handhold just out of reach but if she... could... just... she used the little grip her toes found on the smooth surface of the wall to begin a gradual pendulum-like swing. Her fingers hurt now, the entire weight of her body suspended by just three digits. Her forearm was almost numb. She swung once, twice, and felt the fingers of her right hand graze the handhold. One more time and she managed to hook her pinky onto it, then another finger. Birdy gripped it hard and allowed her right arm to take the majority of her bodyweight as she swung herself a little farther to the right until she found another foothold.

The relief was immediate. She took a second to breathe in deeply then used her right arm to pull herself up onto the flat surface of the climbing wall. She rolled onto her back, her heart sounding a rapid succession of sonic booms in her chest. She took three deep breaths and waited for her thudding heart to slow.

Birdy flipped over onto her stomach to see who it was who had almost gotten her hurt. In the doorway to the gym a man dressed in a white shirt and black tie stood, both hands planted firmly on his hips as he looked up at her. Birdy thought she had seen him occasionally behind the desk of the YMCA's administrator's office when the door was left open.

"You're not supposed to be on that wall without a supervising adult and a safety partner," the man said, his voice carrying the same tone she had heard from teachers when they had caught her practicing her moves in the schoolyard.

"Sorry," Birdy offered, meekly.

The man stood there for a few moments as if considering climbing up to fetch her. Finally, he said, "Get your ass down here. The complex is closing early today."

Birdy stood up and stepped closer to the edge.

The man flinched and took a step toward her then stopped.

Unperturbed by the thirty-foot fall mere inches away, Birdy spoke, "Why are you closing so early?"

The man sighed. "Not enough staff. Now get yourself down here before I call the cops to come and get you."

•••

The YMCA manager waited outside the changing room door while Birdy switched into her street clothes then quickly ushered her out of the building. The boy and girl she had seen in the pool were already walking away, huddled together under the canopy of a big black umbrella.

Birdy turned and looked back toward the YMCA entrance in time to see the manager locking the doors, before giving them a sharp rattle to make sure they were secure. He walked up to where Birdy stood under the portico and stopped next to her, his face turned toward the sky.

"You'd best get home," he told her, his eyes never leaving the angry clouds spilling rain onto the city. "This storm's going to get a

97

lot worse before it's over." He pulled a copy of the LA Times from under his jacket, then held it over his head and jogged out into the parking lot before climbing into an old Toyota Corolla. Seconds later the car had disappeared around a corner, leaving a trail of exhaust fumes behind it.

Birdy adjusted the position of her duffel bag on her shoulder; head down to avoid the driving rain, she pulled up her hood and began her walk home.

•••

Birdy's mom arrived home around four-thirty that afternoon, her raincoat still dripping water as she stepped into the apartment. She took the coat off and hung it on a hook near the door to dry.

"Hi Mom," Birdy chirped, poking her head around the door of her bedroom. "Jesus!" she exclaimed when she saw her mother's soaked hair sticking to her head and face. "Did you fall in the river?" she chortled.

"Annabelle! What have I told you about taking the Lord's name in vain?" Lizzie said, moving into the small bathroom at the end of the corridor, leaving a trail of water behind her.

Birdy followed her mom to the door, her eyes drawn to her mother's reflection in the mirror above the sink as she toweled her face and hair dry. She used a brush to wrangle her hair back into a close approximation of its normal style.

*She looks tired*, Birdy thought, the deep rings under her mother's eyes more pronounced tonight against the brown skin of her face. The wrinkles and worry lines around her mouth and eyes were deeper. Birdy knew that a lot of those worry lines were there because of her; her mom worked two jobs, six days a week, to make sure there was enough food on the table and to put a little something away for Birdy's college fund.

"How was your day?" Lizzie asked, as she continued to towel herself dry.

"Wet. Boring," Birdy called back as she moved to the kitchen.

Birdy filled a mug three-quarters full with water then nuked it in the microwave for two minutes. She added a dash of milk and a bag of English Breakfast tea—her mom's favorite—from the stash she kept in the back of the drawer next to the sink.

"Here you go, Momma," Birdy said, presenting the steaming cup of tea as her mom applied the finishing touches to a new layer of makeup.

Lizzie turned to her and smiled, the makeup doing an almost perfect job of hiding the flaws in her mother's face. "You're an angel, Annabelle," her mom said, taking the mug of tea from Birdy's outstretched hand and sipping it. "Mmmm! Perfect." She placed the mug on the sink counter and turned back to the mirror to finish her preparation.

"You're working tonight?" Birdy asked. This was supposed to be her mom's night off from the Gas 'N Go.

Lizzie paused, her upper lip painted with the lipstick she now held in her hand, her lower lip still bare. "Roberto didn't show up for his shift so they called me and asked me to come in."

Birdy's mom worked a second job four nights a week from six to midnight at a gas station on Figueroa, but tonight was supposed to be her night off. They were supposed to watch TV together on the couch. Birdy hated that her mom had to work two jobs, but this one especially worried her because she would be alone in the little convenience store adjacent to the gas station pumps for most of the night.

"Isn't there someone else who can cover the shift? Do you *have* to go back out there?" Birdy asked, leaning against the door frame. "It's so wet and the weather report says it's just going to get worse. Why do you have to go in?" Birdy hated the way her questions sounded like she was whining, but the truth was she didn't want her mom out there tonight. The weather was getting worse by the hour and it was dark so early.

Lizzie smiled at the barrage of questions. "I don't want to, baby girl, but there's no one else to cover Roberto's shift. I can't let the boss down; besides we can always use the extra money."

Birdy searched for the right words to convey the fear she felt lurking just below the surface of her senses. "But you'll be alone," she said finally.

Lizzie turned and smiled sweetly at Birdy, as if sensing her concern. She reached out a hand and cupped her child's cheek.

Birdy, closed her eyes and pressed against the soft skin of her mother's palm.

"I'll be behind the security screen all night," Lizzie said. "There's nothing for you to worry about." The gas station store had an area behind the counter screened off by glass that was supposed to be shatterproof and even bulletproof, but Birdy wasn't convinced of either of these claims. The night sales clerks were supposed to lock themselves away behind it.

"You promise?" Birdy said.

"I promise," Lizzie replied. She looked at her watch and frowned. "Now let me finish making myself look respectable. It's going to take forever to get anywhere in this weather." She took another couple of sips from the tea and Birdy felt a little tingle of happiness at the obvious pleasure her mom took from this simple act of love on her behalf.

Lizzie smiled back then checked her watch. "I don't have time to change," she said. "I'm going to be late if I don't leave now." She walked back to where her raincoat still dripped water into a small puddle on the linoleum, took it from its peg, shook it, and slipped into it. "You going to be okay here on your own for a while?" she asked.

"'Course," said Birdy. Being on her own was what she did best, apparently.

"You're a good girl, Annabelle." Lizzie downed the last of the tea and handed the empty mug to Birdy. She took her daughter's face in her hands again, and smiled, "I'll see you for breakfast, Chiquita." She bent down and took the small retractable umbrella from where it leaned in the corner crease of the wall. With a final kiss blown to her child she was gone through the door.

Birdy was once again alone.

# CHAPTER THIRTEEN

Elizabeth Finch watched the rain gather in ever larger pools on the concrete forecourt of the Gas 'N Go. For the first hour or so, as the remnants of the evening sun struggled weakly through the clouds choking the sky, she had allowed herself to imagine she was sitting on the shore of a lake, not behind a Plexiglas security screen in some hovel of a gas station on a forgotten plot of Los Angeles.

Lake Tahoe. Yeah, that's where she was. Sitting in the trees watching the water ebb and flow against the shoreline. It was somewhere she had never been, but had always wanted to take Annabelle. *One day,* she told herself, *before the kid grows up and gets on with her own life, we'll sit together on that shoreline and talk about how we made it out of here. Together.*

Lizzie smiled at the thought. Her daughter was so damn smart, and if Annabelle continued to apply herself there was no telling what she could achieve, where she might end up. It was why Lizzie worked so hard; to put away enough money so her child, her only flesh and blood, would get the kind of education she had never had the chance at, an education that would help her escape the crippling poverty that came with growing up in one of the poorest areas in Los Angeles county. Who knew, maybe she might make—

Lizzie's reverie was broken by a sharp tapping on the Plexiglas screen.

"Hey! You awake in there?" A man, a biker judging by the look of his sodden black leather jacket, long greasy-looking hair that still held droplets of rain, and an unruly salt-and-pepper beard lined with a nicotine-yellow demarcation zone stood in front of her. "Gimme a soft-pack of Marlboros," he growled, with what sounded like an accent from somewhere east of Colorado. He nodded toward the shelves of cigarettes at Lizzie's back.

Lizzie swiveled in her chair and reached behind her for the cigarettes, her eyes automatically falling to check that the security bolt of the booth she sat in had not somehow mysteriously unlocked itself while she was not looking. It hadn't. She deposited the pack of cigarettes into the two-way drawer. "That'll be six twenty-five."

The man held her gaze for two or three seconds, a slimy smile on his face as he eyed her up and down. He reached slowly into the inside pocket of his jacket as if he was reaching for a weapon... and pulled out a bunch of singles, with a smirk.

He was going out of his way to try to mess with her, scare her even, Lizzie realized. She did her best to look like she hadn't noticed and didn't care.

The biker placed the damp bills on his side of the security slot. "You alone here, Mama?" he asked nonchalantly, following Lizzie's hands with his eyes as she pulled the tray with his money to her side of the security booth.

Lizzie said nothing. She deposited the money into the cash register, counted the biker's change out next to the pack of cigarettes, then slid both to the man.

"Thank you. Have a nice night," Lizzie said.

The biker pocketed both the cigarettes and the money into his leather jacket but did not move. He leaned in, folded his arms, and rested them on the ledge running along the front of the booth. He moved his face closer to the Plexiglas until his forehead touched it. Lizzie could see the grease stain it left. "You didn't answer my question, *mamacita*!"

He spat the last word with such venom that it made Lizzie

flinch.

"I'll give you ten seconds to get your sorry ass out of here, Mister," Lizzie replied, trying to keep the buzz of nervousness from her voice. She was used to these kinds of losers; you could usually count on at least one every week who thought she was as loose or as stupid as the women they usually hung around with. These guys were pretty harmless, *mostly*, and usually went back to whatever scummy thing it was they did after a few minutes of her ignoring them or threatening them with the cops. But this guy wasn't budging. He fixed her with an intimidating stare, his bloodshot eyes flicking from her face to the swell of her breasts beneath her work blouse and back again.

"How 'bout I just stay here till you get off work? You can show me what you got hiding under that pretty little uniform. Sound good to you?" He leered at her.

Lizzie reached for the phone, but as she did so she heard the ding-dong chime of the door opening. She leaned her head around the biker to get a better view and found herself smiling. Two cops, both regulars, had just walked in. She exhaled a silent sigh of relief.

The biker glanced nonchalantly over his shoulder, spotted the cops who were now eying him suspiciously, and when he turned back to Lizzie he was pouting—actually pouting for God's sake. Like the cops had ruined his playtime or something.

"Everything okay here, Lizzie?" the younger of the two police officers asked, but his stare was fixed on the scumbag.

"All good," said the biker, raising both hands in mock surrender. "I was just leaving. It's *allll* good."

The cop's eyes flicked from the biker to Lizzie. She smiled, and nodded that she was okay. *Nothing I'm not used to*, her eye roll said.

The biker was almost at the exit when the door alarm chimed again.

Roberto, three hours late for the shift Lizzie was now covering, stood in the doorway, blocking the biker's exit. Lizzie felt a spike of anger; Roberto could at least have called. Now here he was, showing

103

up out of the blue half-way through his shift. Well he sure as hell had better not think she was going to just walk out of here. She needed the money and she would be more than happy to let him know.

Roberto took a single step over the store's threshold toward the biker. Lizzie squinted. She didn't have her distance glasses on, so she couldn't be sure, but she could swear Roberto was dressed in only pajama bottoms. And he was soaked through, his black hair plastered to his head. Streams of rainwater dripped over his bare chest and down his legs, forming a small puddle at his feet. And he was *oh so* pale. In fact, he looked really sick.

"Roberto, are you—" The sentence lodged in Lizzie's throat like broken glass as Roberto reached out a hand toward the smirking biker. The biker batted it away.

Roberto was a portly guy in his late fifties. The biker on the other hand, had a good four inches in height over Roberto. The biker looked like he was solid muscle, judging by the tightness of the leather jacket against his back.

The biker called Roberto a derogatory name. "What you think you're—"

It was so fast, Lizzie barely had time to register what happened. One second the biker and Roberto—pudgy, soft-spoken, never-hurt-a-fly Roberto—stood almost face to face. The next, Roberto launched himself forward and lifted the surprised biker off his feet with a single hand beneath his throat. The two men staggered into the store and fell behind a rack of snacks, with a muted thud. Lizzie saw the biker's booted feet sticking out from behind the rack. They shook and jostled as though the man was having an epileptic fit... then they disappeared completely behind the shelving.

The cops hadn't seen anything. They stood three rows over, by the coffee dispenser talking loudly to each other, their radios squawking while they argued over which brew tasted better.

Lizzie banged on the Plexiglas window with the flat of her fist until the cops' heads twisted her way. She pointed, jabbing her finger toward the exit. She could hear nothing other than the radio playing through the store speakers and her own rapid breathing.

Both cops drew their weapons and began to move down the center aisle toward the door.

Lizzie continued to gesticulate toward the last aisle. There was no sign of the biker or Roberto now.

The younger cop signaled for his partner to move up the aisle running parallel to the one Roberto and the biker had fallen behind. His pistol held in both hands, the young cop covered the end of the aisle near the doorway until his partner reached the opposite end. With a nod to his partner, the young cop side-stepped into the farthest aisle... and staggered back, shock staining his face, his eyes wide, mouth agape in disbelief at whatever it was he saw behind the shelves of soda cans and candies. He brought his weapon up and yelled something that sounded like "Hands in the air!" or maybe "Hands where I can see them!"

His partner stepped into the same aisle at the opposite end, and Lizzie saw shock register on his face too. And something else, she thought. Horror? Or fear? She could not decide which. He began to bring his weapon up then screamed as he was suddenly yanked from his feet. His hands flew upward, sending his pistol cartwheeling into the back wall where it scattered boxes of cereal across the floor.

The younger cop yelled something that seemed to just melt together into an incomprehensible sentence. The cop was moving back and forth from one foot to the other, his weapon extended out at arm's length. He looked to be trying to position himself for a shot, but couldn't seem to get an angle. He stepped forward then back again, then repeated the steps over twice more, like some weird dance move. Lizzie almost laughed at the ridiculousness of it; he looked like a character from one of the children's shows Annabelle used to watch when she was young; like he needed to pee *real* bad. His voice was high-pitched, way past the normal authoritative voice she had heard cops use to move vagrants off the forecourt of the gas station or scare some punk who thought he could shoplift.

Then the young cop turned, and, almost in slow motion, began to run back toward the security booth, just as Roberto appeared from the bottom of the aisle. Roberto was on all fours, his muscles working like a big cat's; head up, hands pulling him forward, eyes blazing...

They glowed, Lizzie saw; Roberto's eyes burned with a yellow phosphorescence that fully encircled the pupil.

...as his feet slipped momentarily, skidding out from under him, leaving a smear of—what *was* that? Blood! It was blood. Roberto's naked feet were covered in it, hampering his traction momentarily as his toes smeared tracks across the floor. For a split second, Lizzie's eyes locked with Roberto's. She saw darkness there. And something else... desire; savage, naked desire.

Roberto sprang, lunging forward off all fours, launching himself through the air with amazing agility; agility Lizzie knew Roberto did not possess. Mid-flight, he twisted his body sideways and used both hands and feet to propel his body off an end cap of automotive oil cans to ricochet through the air. He struck the terrified cop high on the shoulder when he was less than three feet from Lizzie's booth.

Lizzie screamed as both men disappeared below the counter and out of her line of sight. She tried to lean over the counter and look, but it was just too hard an angle for her to see past, and, if she was honest, she did not *want* to see what she thought might be happening down there. Even so, she forced herself to lean as far as she could, then screamed wildly, as a hand, blood pouring from what looked like two deep puncture marks in its wrist, slapped wetly against the front of her bulletproof cocoon.

Lizzie staggered back, fumbling for the cell phone she kept in her handbag. Her hands were shaking so badly she dropped the phone twice then finally cupped it with both hands and held it tight while she dialed nine-one-one with her right thumb.

The bloody hand had disappeared again, but it had left behind a wet red smear across the Plexiglas.

"Help me...," Lizzie half-screamed half-sobbed as soon as the emergency operator picked up. "Help me. Please, dear God."

"Ma'am. You need to keep calm and tell me what service you require," a man's voice said calmly in Lizzie's ear.

"Police," Lizzie cried, almost choking on the bile that now rose to the back of her throat. "I need the police here right now. Oh my God... he killed them."

The emergency operator recited the address for the Gas 'N Go. "Is that correct, Ma'am?"

"Yes, for God's sake hurry."

"The police are on their way. Right now I need you to stay on the line with me and—"

Lizzie did not register anything else the operator said because his voice was replaced by a deep base thumping in her ears—*my heart*, a voice somewhere deep inside her skull whispered. *That's my heart*— as the face of the young cop rose in front of her.

Lizzie felt bile rise to her throat. She gagged then vomited over her feet.

The cop's head had been torn from his body; Lizzie could see the ragged edges of the skin around his neck where it had been torn away from the shoulder. The dead cop's eyes were wide open; one stared directly at her, the other toward the ceiling. His mouth hung open, the tongue was missing. Whether it had been torn or bitten off, Lizzie did not know. The cop's trachea hung like a flaccid worm below the flap of neck skin, twisting and jiggling as the head was lifted higher, and higher. Blood still poured from it as the cranial cavity drained out.

Roberto appeared at the window, holding the dead cop's head by its short blond hair, raising it above his own head like a lantern... *Or a trophy*, Lizzie thought. Roberto's face was just inches from hers, separated by only the reinforced Plexiglas security screen.

Roberto had changed... physically. His face was gray as a corpse, his brown eyes now glowed with a preternatural yellow ring of fire, and his face seemed squeezed somehow, like it had been pressed between something heavy.

And then there were his teeth.

Lizzie felt her mind stutter when she saw them protruding between the thin, pale lips of his mouth, black snake-fangs curling from his upper and lower jaws.

And the blood, dear God he was soaked in it.

In the distance, Lizzie heard the wail of approaching sirens. *Just a minute or two now*, she told herself. *They're almost here.* She stepped back until the cigarette rack pressed painfully into her back.

Roberto fixed Lizzie with a stare. His tongue slipped from between his lips and kept coming. It was twice as long as it should be, Lizzie's inner voice observed, coldly. *How can that be?* Roberto proceeded to lick the blood from his face, his eyes never leaving her.

Something thudded against the floor right around where Roberto's feet should have been. *He dropped the cop's head*, Lizzie realized a second later, as both Roberto's hands appeared palm down against the clear plastic of the security screen.

The first hammer-like punch shook the security screen as though it was nothing.

Lizzie screamed a high-pitched squeal of terror.

The second punch sent a latticework of cracks through the glass. The third punch fired a shower of shattered Plexiglas cascading over Lizzie's upturned arms as she instinctively tried to protect her face.

Roberto leaped over the countertop, landing directly on Lizzie, knocking her to the floor. His claw-like hands ripped at the collar of her uniform, tearing the blouse down one side.

Lizzie screamed in terror. She beat her hands against Roberto but it was like hitting a wall.

Roberto forced Lizzie's head back, exposing the soft skin of her neck... and bit deep into her flesh.

Two seconds later, Lizzie's scream of fear had turned to one of pain, then faded to a wet gurgle before finally being replaced by the obscene sound of the creature that had once been Roberto, sucking the life from Lizzie's already limp body.

# CHAPTER FOURTEEN

"Next," the desk sergeant yelled from behind the station's front desk. He didn't even look up as Genie Prescod stood up and walked over to him.

"How can I help you?" the cop asked, his eyes not leaving the pile of papers he was looking at.

"My daughter's missing."

The desk sergeant was in his late fifties, overweight by a good thirty or forty pounds. His body odor wafted to Genie's nose; he smelled like he hadn't taken a shower in a week, which might be true, judging by how undermanned the police station seemed to be. When Genie had arrived, almost six hours ago, she had been told to take a seat in the waiting area alongside twenty or so other members of the public until she could be helped. She had overheard two tired-looking detectives talking as they hung around a brewing pot of coffee about how seriously understaffed they were, something about cops not reporting in.

Genie didn't care about how undermanned they were, her baby girl was gone and she needed their help to find her.

"And how long has your daughter been missing?" The cop finally raised his eyes from the desk, watching Genie through a pair of smudged bifocal spectacles perched halfway down the bridge of his nose.

"Since last night," Genie said. "She didn't come home after work. She always lets me know if she's gonna be late, but she never showed, never called neither. And that just ain't like her. So I want to file a missing person's report."

The sergeant took a form from a drawer.

"Name?" he said.

"My name's Geannette Prescod. But everyone calls me Genie."

The cop gave another long sigh. "The name of the missing person," he said slowly, as if talking to an idiot.

Genie smiled with embarrassment. "Ophelia. Ophelia Prescod. She's only twenty-two."

The cop wrote the details on a sheet of paper, regurgitated a slew of questions about height, weight, distinguishing marks before he asked, "Got a recent photo?"

Genie reached inside her coat and pulled out a photo of her daughter that she'd removed from the frame she kept on the sideboard.

"We live together, my daughter and me," Genie said, offering the photo to the police officer.

The cop took the four-by-six photo and looked at it appreciatively. "Pretty girl," he said, thawing slightly.

Genie smiled. "My pride and joy. A *good* girl." Genie had taken the photo just last Christmas. It showed Ophelia sitting on the sofa, smiling into the lens of the camera as she opened the present Genie had bought her. She was a beautiful girl, slim, a dazzling smile with damn good teeth, her shoulder-length hair sleek and shiny. She was lovely. She was Genie's baby.

Truth was, she was the spitting image of her mom when she'd been that age. Not now of course, with almost thirty years between them, and about an extra seventy pounds, give or take. *Still, that's all part of getting old*, Genie thought, and while she knew she no longer turned the heads of many men, she held herself well. And she was happy. At least, until today.

The cop disappeared into a small room off the waiting area. He came back a minute later with a color photocopy of Ophelia's photograph and handed the original back to Genie. He fastened the photocopy to the missing person's form with a stapler, signed the bottom and added it to a three-inch tall pile of similar reports sitting on the right side of his desk.

"We'll be in touch," the cop said, his eyes already back to the report he was filling out. "Next."

•••

Genie left the police station and headed back in the direction of her apartment. It was a thirty-minute walk. Even though it was drizzling rain and heading toward dusk, Genie did not mind because she was going to put the walk to good use. From beneath the folds of her coat she took a roll of flyers she had had printed at the local FedEx Office that afternoon. She walked toward the light of a 7-Eleven just a little farther down the street, the roll of flyers clutched tightly in her hand.

The store's night clerk was the exact opposite of the surly desk sergeant Genie had just dealt with, in both age and demeanor, although both shared the same tired look in their eyes as though they had been worked close to their limits.

She held out one of the flyers. "Can I post this in your window?" she asked, then added, "She's my girl."

The kid stared at the flyer. There was honest sadness in his eyes when he looked back up at Genie. "Sure, go ahead. But it's not like anyone's going to see it for the next couple of days, what with the storm, and all. You're only the second person I've seen since three this afternoon, and I don't expect many more." The kid had a southern twang to his voice; Alabama, maybe, Genie guessed. "Leave a few on the counter here, too, while you're at it," he said, pointing at the roll of posters Genie still clutched in her hand.

By the time Genie left the store she felt a little better, touched by the kid's honest concern and kindness. But that lasted only as long as it took her to walk out of the glow of the 7-Eleven's lights. The streets beyond were dark and deserted. Genie had never seen them this way before. It was like everybody had just up and left and not bothered to tell her. Well, to hell with them if they had, because she wasn't going *nowhere* until she found her baby girl.

Genie walked a little farther then stopped at a streetlight. The light at the top of the post was not working. Genie had noticed that a lot over the past couple of days. It seemed like every night there were fewer and fewer streetlights. She took a small LED flashlight from her handbag, flicked it on, then pulled a poster from the roll hidden beneath her coat, carefully shading it from the rain with her body to eke out a few extra dry seconds. She wiped the cold metal post with the arm of her raincoat then used a roll of sticky-tape to paste the poster to it. Genie stepped back and inspected her work: MISSING, the title read in bold black letters. Below that was a black and white copy of the photo Genie had handed the cop at the front desk, then Genie's cell phone number. She looked at the image of her daughter for a moment, smiling back at Genie like she almost always did. *You can see the smart in that girl*, Genie thought, wiping a tear away from her cheek before the rain could do it for her. If she could have, Genie would have had the posters laminated to protect them, but that was just too expensive. Still, it would last through the night, maybe, if the rain eased up a little, but Genie knew that by this time tomorrow evening it would be nothing but a blurry mess. But that was okay, though, because by tomorrow night, Jesus willing, she would have found her Ophelia. And if she hadn't, well then she would be out here again until she *did* find her. Her kid was a *good* girl, and Genie had worked hard, given up *oh so much* to make sure she had the best start in life a mother could give her child, or at least a better one than Genie had gotten.

And Ophie, God bless her, Ophie had grabbed at that chance. She was working at a store three days a week, then community college to study computer programming for the other two days, and a couple of evenings thrown in for good luck, as well.

So something like *this* was not *supposed* to happen to good girls like Ophelia, no sir. Not supposed to happen at all.

For the umpteenth time that day, Genie's mind drifted back to the previous morning, trying to drag a little more understanding of what had happened. Ophie had set out for work as usual over at the boutique on Topanga where she worked. Six-thirty that evening, the time Ophie would normally have arrived home, came and went, but Genie wasn't concerned. Ophie could be late sometimes; all it took was a missed bus or backed up traffic because of an accident and she could expect to get home an hour or so later. Just to be on the safe side though, Genie had put both their dinners in the oven to keep warm.

By nine o'clock that night, Genie was beginning to feel the first queasy hints of panic in the pit of her stomach. Ophie had a cell phone but hadn't used it to call her momma, so Genie called her.

The phone rang several times then went to message. And it was then, right at that moment, Genie knew with heartbreaking certainty that something dreadful had happened to her daughter. She felt it as surely as if someone had dropped a black cloth over her heart and condemned it to never see the light of her sweet girl's face again.

Genie called twice more over the next hour with the same result. Then she called all of Ophie's friends that she knew. They hadn't seen her, but they would be sure to let Genie know if they did, they had all promised. There was no boyfriend, not that Genie knew of anyway, and she was certain that her daughter would have told her if there was.

At ten o'clock on the dot that first night, Genie had called the cops.

"Is your child a minor?" the cop on the other end had asked.

"No, she's twenty-two."

"Do you think maybe she's gone to a friend's house? Or her boyfriend's?" the cop asked.

"I called all her friends, and there's no boyfriend. And Ophie wouldn't go nowhere without calling her momma."

The cop sighed. "Well I can take her details over the phone, but my advice to you is to wait until the morning, just to be sure she's not out with some new friends. Come down to the precinct with a recent picture of her and file a report in person. Assuming she doesn't turn up in the meantime."

Genie had not slept a wink that night. She sat the whole night in the chair facing the front door of their apartment, waiting for it to open, waiting for her child to walk back into her life.

It never happened.

In the morning Genie took a taxi to the store where Ophelia worked. She sheltered from the rain in the doorway until the manager showed up. Genie explained who she was to the middle-aged white woman named Sandra. Sandra, who looked like she hadn't slept very well herself, told Genie the last time she had seen Ophelia was when she left the store around six the previous evening.

"Have you been to the cops?" Sandra asked.

Genie shook her head. "That's my next stop."

Sandra seemed genuinely concerned. "Let me know when you find her," she had said after Genie thanked her for her help.

Genie had gone straight home, rushed to the bathroom and thrown up in the toilet. No one who knew Genie would ever describe her as an overly emotional woman, she was tough but fair, never one to overreact. But laying there next to the commode, Genie felt a wave of despair the likes of which she never imagined she could ever have experienced. She sobbed into her vomit-speckled hands, caught by a wave of nausea-inducing fear and sadness.

"No!" she spat, "Not going to happen." She forced back the tears as she pushed herself to her feet, embarrassed at her momentary weakness. The only person who was going to help her daughter was staring back at her from the bathroom mirror. She quickly washed the vomit from her lips and hands then headed into the living room.

From the top of the bureau Genie had taken the Christmas photograph of her daughter from its frame, then headed to the kitchenette where she pulled out all of the emergency cash she kept stashed in a fake can of Heinz beans on the top shelf of the pantry.

Genie walked to the nearest FedEx Office store where the man behind the desk had spent the next hour helping her put the missing person flyer together, and then given her a discount on five hundred copies. Genie would have preferred to have had the flyers printed in color but it would have cost so much more. She had decided to go with quantity rather than quality.

From the FedEx store Genie took a bus the short trip across town to the police station. The bus, usually standing room only, seemed almost as deserted as the streets. *Maybe there's something going around*, Genie thought as she settled in for the twenty-minute journey. As the bus rattled its way through the wet LA streets, Genie could not help but connect the missing passengers with her missing daughter. And as she had stood up for her stop a block away from the police station, Genie had wondered if there was some kind of a link.

•••

Thirty minutes after filing the missing person report with the cop, Genie had begun to regret not giving in to her urge to call a taxi to take her home. The rain was coming down even harder and a cold wind had kicked up, digging through the layers of her clothing and laying siege to her bones.

She had stopped at almost every streetlight and stuck one of the missing posters to them, but now the rain was coming in almost horizontally, driven by the biting wind, which howled and raged, buffeting Genie left and right, threatening to tear the roll of posters from her hand. It was almost as though the storm was working against her, as though it did not want—

Genie's phone buzzed against her thigh. It was probably ringing too, but the pounding rain and howling wind drowned out all other noise. She dug the phone out of her pants pocket, looked at the screen... and gasped. Genie's hand flew to her mouth to smother the sob that had sprung to her throat.

HOME CALLING the phone's display flashed. It was all Genie could do not to drop the phone, her hands were suddenly shaking so much.

"Thank you, Jesus. Thank you, Jesus," she whispered, her head turned skyward. There was only one other person that would call from her apartment... Ophie.

"Ophelia? Baby. You're home," Genie all but shouted, pressing the phone tight against her.

There was silence on the line for a moment, then Ophelia's voice was in Genie's ear: "Momma, where are you? I came home for you, Momma, but you're not here?"

Genie let out a little cry of joy and clutched the phone hard to her breast, her eyes cast skyward as she again thanked Jesus for returning her child to her.

Genie placed the phone to her ear and spoke: "I'm coming home, baby. I'm coming home." Already Genie's feet were moving with a newfound purpose as she headed through the ever-growing darkness, the beam of her flashlight swaying from side to side. The driving rain and wind seemed suddenly less powerful as Genie half-ran half-quick-marched in the direction of home. Her mind was filled with *so* many questions. But only one was truly important, "Ophelia, are you okay, baby?"

"Are you coming home now?" Ophelia asked, avoiding the question. "I'm waiting for you, Momma."

Genie wasn't sure, but she thought she detected a subtle change in her child's voice that she could not quite put her finger on; a flatness to it, maybe, something forced that she had never heard before. Genie knew that there was no way Ophelia would have knowingly put her through the fear and emotional pain Genie had gone through since Ophelia had vanished. She also knew that whatever had happened to her child, it had been forced on her, against her will. *And God knew what had happened to her.* But none of that mattered, not now. Scars could heal, Genie knew this from her own past. There was nothing that love could not make better, given enough time. And what *did* matter was that Ophelia was *alive*, and she was home, and anything else, anything at all, they could fix together.

"Yes, baby," Genie said, "I'm coming home."

Abruptly, the call disconnected.

Genie huffed and puffed, her body sweating from the exertion of running like she hadn't done in twenty years or more. But she barely noticed, because in her head angels were singing.

"I'm coming home," she repeated into the night, and cut across the road toward the entrance of her apartment building.

•••

Despite the driving rain and the biting cold of the wind, Genie was a hot sweaty mess by the time she arrived at the door of the ground-level apartment she shared with Ophelia. Perspiration ran down her back, soaking the thin blouse she was wearing beneath her raincoat. The shirt's material stuck to her skin like cold, clammy hands. The rain had done a number on her hair, too. It adhered to her forehead, loose strands occasionally breaking free and falling into her eyes.

Genie noticed none of this, she was concerned only with reaching her child. She fumbled for the key she kept in the inside pocket of her jacket where she kept the roll of missing posters. Her cold fingers found the keychain and pulled it free, dislodging the roll of posters at the same time, sending them flying from her pocket. They spewed into the air and fluttered to the corridor floor like giant confetti. *That's okay,* Genie thought as she looked at a hundred copies of Ophelia's face staring up at her from the concrete, because she did not need them anymore, her baby was home. She would pick them up later; she and Ophelia. Together.

Genie went to push the key into the lock... and stopped. The door was ajar. She eased the door open with the flat of her hand. Inside, the apartment was dark except for a narrow beam of illumination that extended halfway up the hallway from the overhead light in the ceiling of the corridor she stood in.

"Hello?" Genie called out, her voice quieter than she expected because of the unexpected lump that had lodged halfway up her throat.

"Ophelia? It's Momma. Where you at, darlin'?" She sniffed the air. Something smelled... off. Like someone had thrown up then cleaned it up, the smell lingering in the air.

"Ophelia?" Genie called out again. She stepped over the threshold, reached for the light switch; the switch moved beneath her

117

fingers but the apartment remained dark. "What's going on?" she asked, then took another step inside. Something crunched beneath her feet. Illuminated by the dim light filtering in from behind her, Genie saw the shattered lamp fixture and the remains of its bulb on the floor. Genie's heart began to thud loudly in her chest and she gasped a deep breath, her nose wrinkling at the faint but very real fetidness.

Something was terribly out of place but it was all too confusing for her to process. There was no doubt in Genie's mind that the voice on the phone had been that of her child, no doubt whatsoever, but this was not like Ophelia. Ophelia was a *good* girl; she would never get mixed up with drugs or gangs or anything like that. If something had happened it was because of someone else's interference, Genie was certain. And that meant that someone might be here in the apartment, holding her daughter against her will. Waiting for Genie. But if that was true the next question would be *why*? Why would someone kidnap her daughter, hold her captive, then bring her home and try and lure Genie here? They weren't rich, they had next to nothing. So that only left one other thing that Genie could think of, and she had met enough sick bastards over her life to know that the possibility that some monster had diabolical plans for the both of them was not as farfetched an idea as it might sound.

"Ophelia?" she called out again. This time Genie's voice was barely above a whisper. She reached into her pocket and found the small flashlight. Pulled it out and switched it on.

Genie's heart leapt into her mouth.

Her daughter waited at the end of the hall, illuminated by the white glow of Genie's flashlight. Genie took a step toward her then stopped, something inside, some ancient, primeval instinct that still remembered what it felt like to be prey warned her to not move. She needed to stay perfectly still. Her child was... wrong. Genie took a second and looked, *really* looked at Ophelia.

Ophelia's hair was a disheveled mess, clumps of dirt and even a couple of leaves were caught up in its tangles. Her mouth was covered with what Genie first thought was dirt but after another second she wasn't so sure; it was black and smeared and flaky. *Dried blood*, Genie realized, *it's dried blood*, but she instantly rejected that thought. Ophelia's jeans were soaked and smeared with grime, her blouse ripped in two places, covered in blotches and more stains. Her exposed arms and face were so pale, so cold looking. Two raised bumps on the side of Ophelia's throat caught Genie's attention. Were those puncture marks? It was so hard to tell in the meager light, and Genie's eyes just weren't what they used to be.

But it was her *daughter's* eyes that caused Genie's heart to stop dead in her chest. Her child's eyes were glowing in the beam of her flashlight, shining a deep yellow, like the cat's-eye lane markers on a freeway.

"Oh, my Lord," Genie whispered. She grabbed for the crucifix that hung at her throat. Genie's voice found some of its normal strength, bolstered by the surge of anger and grief she felt swelling within her. "Oh, my baby girl. My beautiful baby girl. What have they done to you?" Genie had no idea who 'they' might be, but she knew that something terrible had been inflicted on her child. Her daughter would never have willingly allowed this to happen to her.

Ophelia spoke. "*Motherrrr.*"

The word was drawn out until it sounded like a purr, or maybe a growl, Genie thought. Her daughter's voice had lost its soft edge, replaced with a sharpness that reminded Genie of the rasping of a saw against wood, as though her daughter's throat was choked or blocked.

"Have you missed me, Mother?" Again, the final consonant was drawn out to a sibilant growl.

Genie stood transfixed in the hallway, silent, her tongue frozen, unable to reply as fear gripped her.

Ophelia swayed gently back and forth, rocked by a breeze only she could feel. Then she spoke again, "So good to see you, and home just in time for dinner." Ophelia giggled as though she had just shared a funny joke with her terrified mother. As she laughed, something thick and black oozed from between her lips, splashing onto her dirty sneakers. "I've missed you, Mother," Ophelia said, matter-of-factly, then suddenly strode straight toward Genie, her head swaying from side to side like a cobra.

Genie gasped and took a step backward, her flashlight illuminating her child's pallid face and glowing eyes as the girl moved purposefully toward her mother. Something was wrong with her daughter's mouth, it was weirdly unhinged, opening wider than any human mouth should be able to, and revealing—

"Oh dear God, no. No. NO!" The last word was yelled, as though the mere utterance might prove strong enough to negate what she was seeing: Teeth. Rows of black teeth, punctuated by upper and lower sets of fangs that curved up and down from Ophelia's jaws.

Genie staggered back out into the corridor. Her child did not seem in a rush as she continued onward, but her movements were insect-like, her limbs snapping from one step to the next rather than flowing. It gave her a menacing, purposeful gait. Completely alien.

The heel of Genie's right sneaker clipped the raised wooden threshold of the doorway. Genie fell backward, her hands windmilling... and found the door frame. She grabbed on hard and steadied herself. A powerful anger had begun to rise in her breast; decades of oppression and humiliation, year upon year of trying to keep her head above water just to survive, to provide for her child, to make sure Ophelia had something better than her life had been. And now all of that hard work, that suffering, and sacrifice had been reduced to... what? Nothing.

"Lost," Genie said, tears beginning to flood down her cheeks. "It's all lost." She staggered out into the exterior passageway, the cold wind and biting rain instantly hammering her but she felt neither. All she felt now was a cold, growing hatred deep within her core, the bastard child of her despair.

Genie looked up and down the corridor, there was no one else around. She thought about knocking on one of the doors, calling for help, but that had never been her thing. She had always handled everything herself, her own way. "Only way to be sure anything ever gets done," she said aloud as she spotted the box fixed to the wall about twenty feet away.

Ophelia stalked toward Genie, her lower jaw dropped almost to the swell of her young breast.

Her child was a *beast*. A *demon*. A *monster*. Genie staggered toward the box, praying it would not be empty.

"Mother, where are you going?" Ophelia demanded.

She ignored Ophelia's mocking question, concentrating instead on flipping the two clasps that kept the glass front panel of the box locked. Her fingers fumbled them open, she and reached inside, grabbing what she found there with both hands.

She swung around and found herself face-to-face with her child. It was only now, so close to each other, that Genie realized Ophelia was not breathing, that her eyes had not blinked once since she had first illuminated them with her flashlight.

A black tongue slipped from between Ophelia's bloodless lips and slithered through the air separating mother from daughter, the tip of it brushed against Genie's right cheek.

Genie let out a faint whimper and stepped away until she felt the cold of the wall at her back.

Ophelia stepped closer, her mouth opening wider, wider, as her head tilted to the side, her eyes fixed on her mother's throat, black liquid drooling from her lips.

"I'm sorry, baby," Genie cried out and swung the fire-ax with all her might.

# CHAPTER FIFTEEN
CHAPTER FIFTEEN

It was almost dawn by the time Detective Phillip Collins pulled up in front of the Gas 'N Go.

*Dawn? Not so you'd have noticed,* he thought, the clouds were so thick there wasn't even a hint of daylight on the eastern horizon. The exterior of the gas station was teeming with cops. The discovery of the abandoned police cruiser at the station meant every officer within a six-mile radius was either here already or on the way. Collins put his car in park, pulled the collar of his rain coat up around his neck and stepped out into the rain.

Overhead, a police helicopter moved back and forth, its searchlight playing across the ground and nearby buildings, its engines roaring.

"Hey, Garcia. What are we looking at?" Collins asked. He ducked under the yellow crime-scene tape and walked over to where Sergeant Rafael Garcia waited beneath the cover of the gas station's front awning, inhaling the remains of a cigarette between thumb and forefinger.

"See for yourself," Garcia said grimly. He tossed the butt into the rain and nodded toward the gas station's entrance.

Collins looked silently at the glass front of the gas station as he pulled on a pair of latex gloves. He stepped up to the door, pushed it open and was instantly hit by the unmistakable coppery smell of spilled blood. *Lots* of spilled blood judging by how overwhelming the smell was in his nostrils. He slowly scanned the interior of the store, taking in everything before he moved any farther.

There were two distinct pools of blood along the aisle closest to the exit, one at either end. Bloody footprints (actual footprints, he noted, like someone hadn't been wearing any shoes) led through the pools of blood toward the security booth at the opposite end of the store. They stopped halfway across, before, disturbingly, starting again about ten feet from the booth, as though whomever the prints belonged to had vaulted the twenty feet or so of clean floor.

A display of plastic oil containers lay scattered across the tiles. Just in front of the security booth was another large pool of congealed blood. The glass of the security booth had been shattered, large pieces of it lay on the counter and scattered over the floor. A patrol officer's cap lay flat-side down near a rack of magazines a few feet away.

Collins had been working homicide for going on fifteen years now. He had seen some things in that time, but this, this was a first.

"It's like a goddamn slaughterhouse," Garcia whispered at Collins shoulder.

Collins took another step inside, sniffed the air like a dog. The place was rank with the stench of spilled blood, but that was about it. There was no residual scent of gunfire, there were no blast marks that he could see, either, so he could probably rule out a shotgun having been used. Which meant to spill this amount of blood, the weapon had to have been a blade of some sort. He walked toward the security booth, carefully avoiding treading in any of the blood splatter, his eyes scanning the other aisles as he passed them.

"Who the hell gave permission for the M.E. to remove the bodies?" Collins said angrily when he reached the opposite side of the store and found not a single victim.

Garcia laughed. "There *weren't* any bodies, Phil," he said. "No sign of them at all. It's like they just up and walked off." He clenched his right hand into a fist and exploded the fingers outward. "Poof! Gone."

"Security camera?" asked Collins, almost absentmindedly.

"We checked. Nothing. Doesn't look like it's worked in a long time."

Collins leaned his head through the shattered security glass, careful not to touch anything. The booth was empty. There were smears of blood on the inside counter, what looked like a bloody palm print on what was left of the front pane, but beyond that, no sign of a struggle. He noticed a woman's purse on a cupboard below the rack of cigarettes. It was open and lay on its side, a tube of lipstick and some tissues had spilled out. The cigarette display cabinet on the back wall was still filled with packs of cigarettes, though some had spilled onto the countertop. The register's money tray was closed. He'd have to check later to be certain it hadn't been gone through, but right now it didn't look like the motivation was robbery.

He thought for a few moments as he slowly scanned the area.

*Maybe* it was a robbery that had just gone bad. *Maybe* whoever had done this had been surprised by the two beat cops walking in just as he was kicking off. But how the hell would someone manage to take down two armed officers? That was unlikely for a lone perp. Especially if all the attacker had was a knife or machete. It didn't make any sense. And no bodies. Why in God's name would someone remove the bodies? It just did *not* make sense at all.

"There was no assistance call from the two officers?" Collins asked.

"Nada. Not a peep," said Garcia, standing in a growing puddle of rainwater dripping from his slicker. "They went code-seven and that was the last we heard from them. It was only when dispatch got the call from the service station attendant and the mobile unit showed up on scene that we even knew any of our people were involved."

Collins nodded. "When the forensics guys get here, tell them I want the inside of that security booth swept like it was their own mother they were looking for, got it? And have someone run a background on the attendant too. Make sure she's not in the system already." The idea that the service station attendant—what was her name again, Finch? — could be behind this seemed implausible, but this was LA. The impossible and the improbable happened on an almost daily basis here, and he was long past being surprised at what new bullshit the city's residents could cook up to screw up his day.

Collins pulled his head out of the security booth, then changed his mind and leaned in again as his eyes caught something he'd missed. "Well that makes even less sense," he said, not meaning for anyone else to hear.

"What?" asked Garcia, straining to look over the detective's shoulder.

"The door to the booth. It's bolted."

"So?"

"From the *inside*. It's bolted from the inside."

# MONDAY

# CHAPTER SIXTEEN

Birdy had never needed an alarm to wake her. So even though Monday's school had been cancelled because of the rain, the natural rhythm of her body's internal clock roused her just before six a.m., as it did on almost every other normal school day. That internal alarm had rarely failed her, which was why she felt a momentary confusion as, bleary eyed, she glanced around her room and saw that it was still dark. A meager light flowed sluggishly through her bedroom window, bleeding a wan glow throughout her room. Turning to her bedside cabinet, Birdy touched the screen of her cell phone. It was 6:04 am.

She swept her legs out of bed and shuffled to the window, wiping sleep out of her eyes. Outside, gray clouds the same color as the skin of some of the ancient women who lived in the apartments around her, had stolen the sky. The vast bank of cloud blocked all but the tiniest amount of light from the invisible sun, hidden deep within the clouds' suffocating folds. A steady wall of rain still fell, adding to the growing lakes of water that had collected overnight on the sidewalks and small patches of grass dotting the street. The gutters and storm drains gushed. Trees dripped. The smell of wetness, dank and cold, hung heavily in the air.

This would not be a day to be outside, Birdy decided quickly.

There was no sign of anyone on the street. Usually, even at this early hour, Birdy was used to seeing a steady flow of people walking to their cars or to the bus stop. Today nothing moved. She pushed her feet into a pair of slippers and shuffled out of her room, yawning. Her mom's bedroom door was closed, which wasn't unusual after she had worked a night shift at the gas station. Birdy stretched. She must have slept extra deeply last night because she hadn't heard her mom come home.

In the kitchen she pulled the last four slices of bread from their bag and slotted them into the toaster—two for her, two for mom. She filled the coffee maker with water and coffee and turned it on, then leaned back against the counter while she waited for both machines to do their jobs.

When the toast popped, she buttered each slice and spread a thin layer of raspberry preserves on her mom's, strawberry on her own, took down two mugs, filled them with coffee and a smidgen of milk, loaded everything on a tray, and headed down the hall to her mom's bedroom. The mugs rattled against the plates of toast as she walked.

"Knock, knock," she said outside the bedroom door, her hands too occupied with holding the tray to perform the actual action.

There was no response.

"Mom. Wakey, wakey. I'm coming in so you'd better be decent." Birdy used her knee to push down on the door handle, bumped the door open with her butt and eased in backward, her focus on keeping the tray from spilling its contents. "It's six-fifteen," she said, turning around. "You're going to be late if—"

Mom's bed was empty, the sheets still tucked hotel-tight, the way she made it every day before leaving for work.

"Mom?" Birdy set the rattling tray down on the highboy. "Mom?" Still nothing other than the sound of the rain beating against the side of the apartment. Maybe she'd missed her somehow and she was in the bathroom? Birdy checked but the bathroom was empty. "Mom?" she called out again as she headed to the living room to see if she'd fallen asleep on the sofa, a note of unease creeping into Birdy's voice. Mom wasn't there either. That left... nowhere.

*Maybe she's left for work already*, Birdy reasoned. But that wasn't like her mom. No way would she have gone off to work without saying goodbye to her little girl. *No way*. That left only one possibility: Mom had to still be at the gas station. That had to be it. The weather must have been so bad last night she had spent the night at the Gas 'N Go.

Birdy walked back to her bedroom and checked her phone. There were no messages. She scrolled through the contacts list on her cell phone until she found her mom's number, pressed the dial button and waited.

After seven rings the call went to voicemail.

"Hello, you've reached Elizabeth Finch. I can't get to the phone right now, please leave a message and I'll get right back to you."

Birdy spoke at the beep. "Mom, it's me. Where are you? Call me as soon as you get this message. I'm going to call the gas station." She tried but failed to keep the displeasure she felt at her mom's lack of consideration out of her voice. Birdy hung up and again scrolled through the phone's contact list, this time looking for the number for the gas station where her mom worked.

The phone picked up after just one ring and a man with a voice Birdy didn't recognize said, "Hello?"

"Hi, is Mrs. Finch there? I need to talk to her."

"Who is this?" the voice on the other end asked.

"This is Bir— This is Annabelle, her daughter. Who are you?"

"Annabelle, my name is Detective Collins, and I need you to stay on the line with me."

The man's voice was calm and soothing but that didn't stop a burst of panic from pummeling Birdy. She felt her throat go dry and her heart begin to pound. How had the police tracked her down so quickly? Maybe from the mall's surveillance video, or maybe Trenton had told them who she was. But why had they gone to where her mom worked? Were they arresting her? *Oh my God, Mom is going to kill me*, Birdy thought.

"It was an accident, I didn't mean to do it," she blurted into the phone.

"What?" The word was spoken sharply and with surprise, as if she had just slapped the man on the other end of the phone. "What did you say?"

"It was an accident," Birdy repeated. "It wasn't my mom's fault. I'm the one who took the sneakers, but it was an *accident*. I was trying them on and then the security guys tried to blame me, and—" The words fell from her lips as quickly as the rain.

"Annabelle, hold on. Hold on," the detective said. "This isn't about... sneakers."

Birdy breathed a sigh of relief, berating herself for giving her secret away.

The detective continued, "I need you to verify something for me, Annabelle, okay?"

"Uh huh," said Birdy, unsure whether she should actually agree to do anything for this random guy who had answered the store's phone.

"Tell me your mom's name."

"Elizabeth. Elizabeth Finch."

"And she works here at the Gas 'N Go station, right?"

"Yes," said Birdy. "She works nights. She was supposed to be off last night, but Roberto didn't show up for his shift so she went in to cover him. Where's my mom?"

The detective ignored her question. "And she was definitely working last night?" he continued, his voice so devoid of emotion that it instantly got Birdy's attention.

"Yes. Where's my mom? I want to speak to her *right now*," Birdy demanded.

There was a pause, "She can't come to the phone, Annabelle. Listen, how about I come and pick you up, so we can talk in person? Tell me where you live."

Birdy felt a flutter in her chest, like a bird suddenly realizing it was trapped there, beating its wings against her ribs, trying to get out. She felt a tear roll down her cheek but she didn't know why. Her mind was suddenly enveloped in a cloud of white; she felt disconnected from her body. "Please let me speak to my mom," she heard a high-pitched voice say, but it did not register as her own.

"Just tell me where you live, Annabelle. Can you do that?"

Birdy told the man on the phone where she lived. Two minutes later she realized she was still holding the phone but the detective had already hung up.

•••

Birdy jumped. The heavy knocking on the apartment's front door had startled her from her seat on the living room sofa. At some point between the detective's phone call and now she must have turned on the TV because two black-and-white cowboys were facing off against each other on some dusty movie studio back-lot. She turned off the TV, headed to the front door, and opened it.

"Hello," said a man who looked old enough to be her granddad. He was dressed in a knee-length gray raincoat, its collar pulled up around his neck. He must be at least fifty Birdy decided. "I'm Detective Collins. We spoke on the phone." His voice had a rough sound to it, like gravel. The man's gray receding hairline was plastered to his skull by rain. He looked tired, with dark bags under his eyes and a complexion so pale it looked like he hadn't seen the sun in a long time. But he had nice eyes. Kind eyes. "You must be Annabelle." He smiled.

"Birdy. Everyone calls me Birdy."

The detective nodded and smiled some more. He had a nice smile too, Birdy decided. Behind him, a policewoman, a few wisps of blonde hair visible beneath her cap, dripped water into a puddle on the corridor's linoleum just behind the detective.

"This is Officer Mulroney," the detective said, gesturing a thumb toward his partner. "Can we come in?"

Birdy stepped aside. "I suppose," she said.

"Thank you." The two police officers stepped inside. "Are you alone?"

Birdy nodded.

"Okay," said Collins, smiling again. He placed a hand against

Birdy's shoulder. "Let's sit down, okay?"

Birdy nodded and began to lead the way to the living room. She caught the subtle nod in the direction of her bedroom that the detective gave Officer Mulroney. The female officer slipped inside the room and gave it a quick look, then moved across the hall to the kitchen as Birdy led Collins toward the sofa.

It was still so dark outside that Birdy flicked the overhead light on as she passed the switch. She saw Officer Mulroney move past the door and down toward her mom's room, only to reappear a few seconds later.

"Just the kid," Mulroney said as she stepped in to join them.

"Where's my mom?" Birdy asked, trying to sound forceful.

"Sit down for a second," the detective said, taking the chair and gesturing Birdy toward the loveseat.

Birdy complied, leaning forward with her hands pressed between her knees.

The detective took a few seconds to compose his thoughts. "Annabelle... Birdy, last night there was an... incident at the gas station where your mom works. Some people were hurt, including some police officers—"

Birdy felt the tears begin to roll down her cheeks and a sob that sounded more like a croak bubble from her mouth. "Is my mom okay?" she managed to blurt out.

Detective Collins smiled again, but this time it seemed awkward. "The truth is, we don't know. We can't find her and we were hoping you might be able to tell us where she might have gone." He paused for a moment then added quietly, "Or if there was anyone who you think might have wanted to hurt her?"

"No!" Birdy cried out, leaping to her feet. "No," she said again, as though if she repeated the word enough times it would somehow negate the reality looming in front of her. "There's no one who would hurt her. No." The final *no* came out sounding more like a plea. She flopped back down onto the sofa.

"Okay, kiddo. It's okay." Collins nodded at Mulroney. She moved across the room and sat next to Birdy on the sofa, placing a still-wet arm around the girl's shoulders.

Birdy shook the cop's arm off.

Mulroney fished a soggy bag of Kleenex from her breast pocket and offered Birdy one.

Birdy shook her head.

"Listen, Birdy," said Detective Collins, "is there anyone you can stay with or someone who can stay here with you? Until we find your mom?"

Birdy shook her head again, not lifting her gaze from her feet.

"No one at all?" the detective asked again.

"No."

Collins let out a long weary sigh and got to his feet. "Mulroney, get Child Protective Services over here."

The policewoman stepped into the hallway and began to speak into her radio. The detective turned back to face Birdy. "Annabelle, I need you to pack a bag of clothes."

"What? Why?" cried Birdy, getting to her feet. She took a big step away from the cop.

"We can't leave you here alone, so, until we sort this all out, we're going to put you in the care of the state. Just for a little while." He sounded genuinely sorry.

"No. No way," said Birdy.

"Birdy, it's okay. It'll just be until we find out what's happening with your mother. Then you can come home."

Birdy knew he was lying; well, maybe not lying, but she could hear the lack of belief in his own words now. This man did not think her mother was coming home. Not ever.

Birdy began to cry. Deep wracking sobs of fear that washed over her like storm waves battering a shoreline.

The detective stepped in close, he put a meaty hand gently on the girl's shoulder. "It's okay. I promise you I'll keep looking for your mom."

Birdy had covered her mouth with one hand to try to keep the tears and fear inside. She looked up at the detective, sure that she would see a lie behind his eyes, but all she saw was sadness, a man who was weary of having to go through this same routine on an almost daily basis. She was about to tell him that she knew it was all an act when the front door bell chimed twice.

•••

Birdy looked up, wiping the tears from her cheeks with the backs of both her hands.

"Are you expecting—" Detective Collins said, but didn't finish the sentence.

"Mom!" Birdy yelled and rushed toward the front door.

"Hey!" Mulroney said as Birdy ducked the woman's outstretched arm and ran to the door.

Birdy flung the door open and let out a quiet gasp.

In the doorway was a black man sitting in a wheelchair. It took a second before Birdy recognized him, because she had only ever seen him from a distance, and then only his head and shoulders framed by his apartment window.

It was the *Window Guy*.

They stared at each other silently for a few seconds. Startled, Birdy gave a little jump when she felt a strong hand land on her right shoulder.

"And who might this be?" asked Detective Collins from behind her.

"Umm... Umm..." Birdy stuttered, her eyes still locked on the Window Guy. She had no idea why, maybe because of the threat of being hauled off by Child Services, but her next words were out of her mouth before she even had time to register what she was going to say: "This is my uncle, David."

She saw the Window Guy give three quick successive blinks.

"He lives upstairs," she continued, "and comes down to help me and Mom sometimes."

Window Guy's eyes grew wider but he didn't say anything to counter Birdy's lie. His eyes moved from her to the detective standing behind her.

"Oh, really?" said the detective, his voice unable to hide his cynicism. "And on whose side of the family?"

"My dad's," said Birdy. "He's my dad's brother."

Window Guy hadn't uttered a word. Birdy gulped down a deep breath then turned to face the cop. "So this means you don't need to call Child Protective Services, right? I can stay here 'cause my uncle can look after me, right?" She turned back around to look at Window Guy, her eyes silently beseeching him not to give her away.

The detective ignored Birdy and stepped closer to the door. "Detective Phillip Collins," he said, flashing his shield.

There was another moment of silence that Birdy felt would last forever.

"You mean like Phil Collins, the singer?" Window Guy said finally, a smile cracking his face.

The detective sighed loudly and rolled his eyes. "Yes," he said, his voice taking on a bored like-I-haven't-heard-this-a-hundred-times-already tone. "Just like the singer."

"Who's Phil Collins?" Birdy asked, her face screwed up in confusion.

Both men exchanged a look of *you've got to be kidding me*!

"And you are?" Collins said.

Window Guy reached up a hand toward the detective. "David. David Douglass," he said. "I'm Annabelle's uncle."

•••

Tyreese had only the vaguest idea what was going on, but by the look on Annabelle's face, it was serious. And hadn't she said something about Child Protective Services? He had no choice but to roll with it, but he wasn't sure the detective was buying what he was selling.

"I'm Annabelle's uncle," Tyreese said. He offered the detective his hand. The cop's grip was firm. Tyreese quickly assessed the man: He was a broad-shouldered fire-plug of a guy. Probably been a cop all his adult life, maybe military before that, Tyreese thought by the quiet confidence he saw in the man's eyes. He guessed the cop was somewhere in his late forties, but his face looked much older. Tyreese knew the look; too long on the front lines. He empathized, he'd seen the same look in his own eyes for years after he got back stateside. Still saw it some mornings when he woke up, yelling and thrashing, terrified by his own mind and the nightmares contained within it.

Collins looked at Annabelle then focused back on Tyreese. "So, why's your name different from Annabelle's here?"

Annabelle gave a little gasp of astonishment; sure she had been found out, but with barely a pause Tyreese smiled, nodded knowingly, then said, "We're stepbrothers. Different mothers."

Collins raised a questioning eyebrow, but said nothing.

"Where's my sister-in-law?" Tyreese asked nonchalantly as he wheeled himself down the hallway toward the living room, following the two cops and Annabelle back inside, as though he knew where he was going.

"Well, Mr. Douglass, that's the thing," the detective said, turning to face Tyreese just as they reached the living room. "Say, can I talk to you in the kitchen?" He glanced at Annabelle and smiled reassuringly, but when his eyes returned to Tyreese, the smile was gone, replaced by a grimness that Tyreese had also seen before. More times than he had cared to when the notification of the latest KIA for his unit came down.

Tyreese nodded and followed Collins into the kitchen.

"Listen," said Collins, swinging the kitchen door closed behind them, "last night there was an incident at the gas station."

Tyreese tried to keep the look of confusion from his face but failed.

Collins sighed. "You know, the place where Ms. Finch, *your sister-in-law*, works." The cop changed the tone of his words just enough to put virtual air-quotes around sister-in-law.

Tyreese silently cursed himself. He got the point. This cop read people like he was browsing the trashy mags they put at the supermarket checkouts. "I know," Tyreese said, and thought he saw a slight raising of the corners of the cop's mouth.

"Last night Birdy's mom was supposed to be covering the night shift at the Gas 'N Go. We got a call of a disturbance and by the time we got there, she and several other patrons, two of them cops, had vanished. But there was blood, lots of blood." He let that sink in for a moment. "Now, bearing in mind the area, we have reason to believe that this might be gang related. So if you know anything," he leaned in close, putting both hands on the armrests of the wheelchair, "anything at all that might help me with my investigation, I want to know about it, right now."

*Well, shee-it!* Tyreese thought. What the hell had he gotten himself into? He thought back to the previous night and the shadow he had seen climbing the outside of the apartment block across the street. How it had entered the open window, the scream moments before the light had been turned off. He thought about telling the detective, but tell him what exactly and why? Hell, he wasn't even sure if he'd actually even been awake.

"You're sure it was gangs?" Tyreese said finally.

The detective pushed himself away from the wheelchair and looked down at Tyreese. "What the hell do you mean by that?"

Tyreese shrugged. "Things don't seem, I don't know, strange out there to you?" He nodded toward the window where the rain still drummed against the glass like fingers.

"I don't follow you," said Collins. Something about the cop's tone gave Tyreese the impression he was stonewalling, that he knew exactly what Tyreese was referring to but wanted to hear it directly from him.

"Man, you're supposed to be the detective. The people! Where are all the people?" he hissed.

Collins sucked in a deep breath through his nose and held it for a few seconds, all the while looking stone-faced at Tyreese. When he eventually exhaled, his voice was lower, softer. "It's the weather," he said, "People are staying indoors because of the weather."

"Uh huh," said Tyreese skeptically. "And where's everyone around here gone? You think they can just jump in their private jet and head to the Bahamas until this all blows over?" Tyreese's voice got low, almost a conspiratorial whisper. "You *know* something's going on, man. Something's not right around here."

From beyond the kitchen, the sound of Mulroney's radio, staticky and unclear, crackled. It was quickly followed by the muffled voice of the policewoman's reply. A second later there was a knock on the kitchen door and Mulroney's head appeared around the jamb.

"Sorry, detective. Dispatch just relayed a message. We've got a lead in the missing persons case."

"Yeah, well it can wait," said Collins.

"I don't think so, Detective. They've found our guys—at least, what's left of them."

"Christ!" whispered Collins. Tyreese thought the man aged about twenty years in the few seconds after he heard the news.

The detective reached into his jacket's inner pocket and pulled out a small metal case. He flipped it open, slid a business card from it, handed it to Tyreese. "If you or Annabelle think of anything, or you just want to talk some more, call me. Understood?"

Tyreese nodded that he did.

"Let's go," said the detective to Mulroney. He turned and walked out of the kitchen, followed by his partner. A moment later the sound of the door slamming shut signaled that Tyreese and Annabelle were the only people left in the apartment.

# CHAPTER SEVENTEEN

"You want to tell me what's going on?" Tyreese said once the cops had left. "Your uncle? Really?"

Birdy stared at her feet and mumbled, "It was the first thing I could think of. And I don't know your name. Sorry."

Tyreese watched the kid for a couple of seconds, then let out a deep sigh. "Tyreese," he said eventually, "My name is Tyreese. And you're Annabelle, right?"

"Birdy," she corrected. "Only my mom calls me Annabelle." She cocked her head to the left. "How'd you know my name?"

"I've heard your mom yell it a couple of times," he said, adding a slight smile.

At the mention of her mother, Birdy's head dropped again. Tears began to roll down her cheeks, then she was sobbing, quietly, her shoulders rising and falling in quick succession.

Tyreese did a double-take. "What? Did I say something?"

Birdy shook her head and tried to speak, but couldn't do anything more than gasp like a little fish on the shore.

Tyreese wheeled himself closer. He laid a hesitant hand against the girl's shoulder. He didn't know how much the cops had told her about what had happened to her mom, so he kept the question as vague as possible. "I heard the cops say something about Child

Protective Services... did something happen?"

Birdy looked up, her face flushed bright red, her cheeks stained with tears. "My mom," she said, then hesitated as though unsure whether she should say any more.

"It's okay, you can tell me."

The girl gulped air. "She's gone a lot, because she works two jobs, so I get left alone. Someone must have reported her. The cops came to check on me, but my mom's at work now."

Tyreese knew the kid was lying about her mom, given what the detective had told him in the kitchen about her being missing, but he kind of understood why she needed to keep that information to herself right now. He didn't need to ask where her father was, it was the same story he'd lived; an absent father, and a mother who'd tried her best to look after him and his older brother. He understood how hard it was for Birdy's mom, how hard it was for the kid, too. Left alone as much as she was, the temptation to find some kind of stability could lead down an easy path, the wrong path. His brother had chosen that path and had paid the price for it, gunned down in the street outside their home over twenty years ago now. His mom had never been the same; she had become a sad shell of her former self. Tyreese had joined the army to get away from that life. His mom had died six months later. He would always feel responsible for that, even though he knew he really wasn't.

"Is there anyone who can come and stay with you?" Tyreese asked.

"I'm fifteen; I can look after myself," Birdy mumbled, staring at her feet.

"Of course you can, but I'm not sure the cops are going to see it that way."

"My mom will be home soon. I'll be okay."

Tyreese watched the girl wipe the tears from her cheek with the back of her sleeve. She wasn't being honest with him, that was obvious, but the kid wasn't his responsibility. The cops would be back, and in the meantime, he could keep an eye on her as best he could.

"Listen, you know where I am," he pointed a finger toward the ceiling. "If you need me, come find me, okay?" He spun his wheelchair around and rolled toward the front door.

•••

Birdy didn't feel good about lying to Window Guy... Tyreese. *Had no choice*, she told herself. *If I told him the truth, he would have called the cops back and they would have taken me away*. She needed time. Time to think. Time for her mom to come home. What the cops had told her, it made no sense; there was *no way* her mom would leave her alone. Her mom would be okay. She *had* to be.

Birdy stood in the doorway of her mother's bedroom for a few seconds, then walked to the bed and pulled the comforter from it. She buried her face deep into the material, drawing in her mother's musk, then threw the comforter over her shoulders and pulled it around her, wearing it like a poncho.

Birdy made her way back into the living room, turned on the TV, then lay on the sofa, resting her head on the armrest. She pulled her mom's comforter tight around her until she was cocooned within its soft, fluffy embrace. Birdy closed her eyes, hoping that when she opened them again, this would all turn out to be nothing more than a horrible nightmare.

# CHAPTER EIGHTEEN

Detective Collins eased the Crown Victoria into a spot behind a coroner's van, about a block away from the Gas 'N Go station where the two cops had disappeared. Single story houses on tiny lots of land lined the street on either side. Some were quite nicely kept, the remains of lawns neatly manicured, the paint only a few years old. Others could have been abandoned decades ago; their lawns dead or overgrown, oil stains on the driveway, rusting cars up on blocks. But they all shared two similarities, he noted: they all had security bars on the outside of the windows, and the curtains and blinds in every single window were closed. There wasn't a soul to be seen cop-watching through any of those windows either, Collins noted. Never in all his years on the force had he ever been to a crime scene and not seen *someone* watching, either in a gaggle of gawkers behind the yellow perimeter tape, standing on their front lawn, or watching from their porch, cigarette dangling from their mouth. But this morning, despite the flashing lights of the cop cars, ambulance, coroner, and fire department, not a single soul had bothered to come out and see what was going on.

Collins checked his Timex. It was just after eleven in the morning, but he'd have forgiven anyone for thinking otherwise; the rain and clouds were a wet shroud over this, and every other street he and Mulroney had driven past to get here. A permanent twilight pall had descended over the city.

The few street lamps that lined the road were all dark. Collins glanced up at the nearest lamppost; the cover that was supposed to protect the bulb was shattered. The remains of the bulb lay in pieces around the base of the post.

Collins stepped out of the car and stood for a second near the curb, looking up and down the street, his hand raised above his eyes to shelter them from the insistent rain. It was like he was standing in a scene from some fifties noir movie. Everything was a shade of gray, depressing, drab... and deserted. The words of the guy he had met back at the apartment building came back to him: *The people. Where are all the people?* he had asked. It had hit a note with the detective when he'd heard it. He'd noticed a distinct lack of humans on the street over the past week or so, a gradual but unmissable reduction in the number of busts, the streets were quieter, even before the rain had moved in. But over the last few days it had become even more noticeable as fewer and fewer calls came in to the station. And it wasn't just the civilian population, either. His precinct had had a few no-shows amongst the admin staff, even a couple of cops that had simply not reported for duty; three during his shift last night. But he'd heard scuttlebutt of precincts losing half their staff. If it hadn't been for the corresponding drop in crime, the city would have been well and truly up the proverbial creek without a paddle.

What was most disturbing, what really got the little hairs all along the length of his spine standing at attention, was how *quiet* the city had become. If it wasn't for the constant background hiss of the rain, he would have begun to wonder if he'd lost his hearing.

"Fuck!" Mulroney's slowly exhaled expletive pulled the detective's attention back to the present. "It's like the end of the world or something." She whispered the last sentence as though she were standing in a library, not the middle of some hell-hole of a neighborhood being pissed on from on high.

Collins gave a half-hearted nervous laugh. "Worried about zombies, Mulroney?"

The female officer turned and looked him dead in the eyes, her face emotionless. "I've been fighting zombies from the day I started this job," she said. *"This..."* she nodded first up and then down the deserted street, *"this* is something new. This is some Stephen King kind of bullshit, right here."

"Canvas a couple of the neighbors," the detective said. "See if they saw or heard anything, 'kay?"

His partner nodded, but she didn't look happy. He saw Mulroney's hand drop to her service weapon as if she was checking that it was still there, then she headed toward the next house over.

The detective walked quickly toward the house, ducked under the yellow perimeter tape and pushed open the creaky iron gate to the path leading up to the front door. The front door was open; a bored-looking cop Collins didn't recognize stood on the porch sheltering as best he could from the rain. Collins flashed his badge to the cop, who nodded.

"Do we know who owns the house?" Collins asked as he brushed rain from his head.

"Belongs to some guy named Roberto Hernandez. He works at the Gas 'N Go station where our guys were last heard from. I spoke to the owner of the gas station and he said the guy hadn't shown up for work two nights in a row."

Collins nodded. Roberto. That had been the name Birdy had given him when he asked about her mother. He had been scheduled to work, but hadn't shown up last night so Birdy's mom was covering his shift. "Do we know where Mr. Hernandez is?" Collins asked.

The cop gave a grim smile. "Oh, he's in there too, Detective."

Collins let out a long sigh. "Any relatives?"

"Nope. Not married. No kids. Lives alone."

How much of a coincidence, Collins wondered, would it have to be for the bodies of two cops to somehow mysteriously disappear from the very same place this Hernandez guy worked and then end up at his home? Was he maybe some kind of a serial killer? Or maybe Hernandez had just had a bad day, flipped out, and managed to kill the cops in some sneak attack; these crazies could take months to formulate a plan. Wouldn't be the first time it had happened. Couple of years back, some guy had walked into a pancake joint and wasted four cops while they sat around eating lunch. Or maybe Hernandez had gotten caught up with some of the gangs operating around here? Maybe he was an inside man for a heist that had gone wrong? There were so many reasons for why this shit went down, he'd lose track if he tried counting them all. Whatever the reason, he wasn't going to find out standing here with his thumb up his butt.

Detective Collins stepped into the house and a surprisingly neat living room.

"Did you turn the TV on?" Collins called back to the cop at the door.

"No. It was on when I got here. Figured I should leave it that way."

A small coffee table sat between the TV and a sofa. A TV dinner tray lay on the table, the food untouched. It looked like it could have come right out of the microwave.

Collins walked through the room and into the kitchen. A few dishes waited in the sink in dirty gray water. It all looked so normal; lived in. Nothing really out of place. No sign of any kind of a disturbance.

A short corridor led off from between the kitchen and dining room. Collins saw the first splatter of blood on the wall about halfway down the hall; just a trickle, like someone had cut their finger badly. A forensic tech knelt next to the stain with a camera in his hands. The flash exploded, blinding Collins momentarily. Just beyond the CSI tech were two more rooms. The door to the first room was ajar; Collins could see the tiled floor of a bathroom. The second door, which was closed, he guessed led to the home's solitary bedroom. Collins pushed the bathroom door ajar with the end of a ballpoint pen he kept in the breast pocket of his jacket.

"Shit!" he said quietly. The bathroom was about five feet by ten. A commode on the left, a sink unit with a mirror and a shelf cluttered with a selection of cheap aftershaves directly opposite the door, and to the right was a bathtub that doubled as a shower.

A body lay in the tub. It was a male, recently dead Collins guessed, by the lack of lividity and the rosiness of the corpse's skin. The hair was cut military short to match the dirt and bloodstained uniform the corpse wore. It wasn't one of his guys, the uniform looked more like military. The body was curled up in an almost fetal position, the knees tucked up tightly to the chest, the arms crossed over them as though the guy had been trying to hug himself when he died. Or more likely he had been positioned like that by whatever sick bastard had brought him here. There was no sign of how the man had died, but the wounds could be easily concealed behind the dirt and blood covering his body.

"Notice anything?" a voice asked from just behind Collins.

"Jesus Christ on a bike!" Collins hissed, his heart jumped at the sound of the CSI tech's voice so close to his ear. Collins turned and gave the guy his hardest stare. The tech was oblivious. He just kept on talking, his jaw working a piece of gum between words.

"Notice anything out of place, detective?" he prompted, an ear-to-ear grin splitting his face.

Collins looked around the room one more time. "Nothing that springs immediately to mind," he said, allowing disdain to color his words.

The tech leaned in close and dramatically sniffed twice. "No stink," he said. "In fact, there's almost no smell at all."

Collins spun back around and, after checking that he wasn't going to walk on any evidence left on the floor, stepped into the bathroom and leaned over the body. He took a hesitant sniff, then a deeper inhalation. The tech was right, there was no smell of decay, just an odd staleness, like stagnant water, and below that the faint aroma of dried blood and grass from the dead guy's tunic.

"Hell of a thing, eh?" said the tech.

"Yeah," said Collins, his eyebrows furrowing. "Hell of a thing."

"It's like he's been embalmed already. Fucking wacky shit, if you ask me."

*Well thankfully nobody's asking you*, Collins thought, but said,

"The others in there?" He nodded toward the closed bedroom door.

The tech drew himself up to full height, his grin widening, the flash of pink gum visible between his teeth. "Oh yeah." He raised both his eyebrows like he was privy to some kind of sordid secret. "I'm done in there. You knock yourself out."

Collins pushed the bedroom door open and stepped inside. The window blinds were closed and the room was dark. He fished out his mini-flashlight and switched it on, playing the beam around the room.

He almost gagged at the sight of the uniformed but headless corpse splayed across the bed. This had to be one of the two cops who'd been unfortunate enough to get caught up in whatever shit had gone down at the gas station. Collins tried not to look too closely at the ragged flap of torn neck skin where the head should have been, his eyes lingering only long enough to note that there was no blood on the bed linen.

"Jesus!" he whispered. He turned his head back to the crime scene tech in the corridor. "Where are the others?"

"Check the closet."

"Great," Collins muttered to himself. He walked over to the closet on the opposite side of the bed. Bloody handprints marked the wall near the door. Flakes of dried blood coated the handle.

Collins pulled a latex glove from his jacket and snapped it on his hand. He reached out and opened the closet door, allowing it to swing all the way open. There were two bodies in the cupboard, one in each corner, both in the same fetal position as the body in the bath tub. The closet was so small their knees almost touched. It looked like they too had been posed very specifically by whoever had killed them.

Collins took a knee. He played his flashlight slowly over the bodies one by one. The first was the other missing cop. There was some blood on his neck, but that was it. Collins shifted his position, his knees complaining. The second body looked to be of a male Hispanic. Hernandez, maybe?

Just like the corpse in the bath, neither body showed any sign of lividity that the detective could see, both seemed to simply be asleep. He leaned in and sniffed both bodies one after the other. There it was again, that faint stagnant water smell.

A throbbing pain had started to pulse just over his right eye about an hour earlier, now it was turning into a full-blown migraine. He massaged his forehead with his fingers but that only made it worse. He needed to get something to eat and some rest, he'd been up a straight nineteen hours, and he hadn't eaten a thing for the last six or seven of those. And all this weirdness, it wasn't exactly helping.

"Detective?" Mulroney stood in the doorway of the bedroom, doing her best not to stare at the decapitated body on the bed, but her wide eyes betrayed her shock and disgust.

Collins used the wall to help himself get to his feet, his knees unhappy with the abuse. "What you got for me?" he asked, taking Mulroney's elbow and guiding her into the corridor. He closed the bedroom door behind them.

"Nothing," she said. "I hit every house on the street. Didn't get an answer from any of them. It's like everyone just up and left."

Never greet a stranger in the night,
For he may be a demon.

*~ The Talmud ~*

# CHAPTER NINETEEN

Officer Steven Sova eased his police cruiser through the storm and darkness at a steady five miles an hour. He'd switched the car's headlights to high beam, and they reflected off the rain as it fell in sheets across the road ahead of him, turning each droplet into a tiny falling diamond. He glanced at his watch: It was 20:18. The street ahead of him was dark; not the LA eight-thirty-at-night kind of dark that meant lit streetlights and a glow in the windows of every apartment building along the road. It also wasn't the street-light kind of dark that meant you could easily spot those inevitable die-hard civilians who refused to stay off the sidewalk just because of the rain, or chose to sit on their balcony, smoking a joint or barbecuing. And it wasn't the kind of dark you could guarantee *someone* would be hanging out in an apartment lobby, shooting the breeze or waiting on a pickup. As far as Officer Sova could tell, every lobby on the street was deserted, but it was hard to be certain because not one light, not even an emergency light, lit any of them.

No, tonight was none of *those* kinds of dark.

*This* was an impenetrable black-as-the-hobs-of-hell kind of dark. The kind of dark that Officer Sova thought might just consume the entire world if he switched off his patrol car's headlights.

There was not a single hint of illumination visible anywhere ahead or behind him along the street. The residents around here were used to going without power every now and again; maybe a blown transformer meant the power company would have to come out (not something they were in too much of a rush to do most days), or maybe they just couldn't afford the bill that month. Whatever the reason, the residents were always prepared and there would be the inevitable glow of candles flickering through windows or flashlights cutting through the darkness. And there would *always* be music playing somewhere. He rolled down his window for the second time in as many blocks and listened.

The only sound was the hiss of his tires on the wet blacktop and the *swish-swash* of his windshield wipers.

It made Sova nervous. *Really* nervous. In his twelve years on the force, he could not recall ever feeling this... freaked out. He thought about calling for backup but decided against it. Didn't want to seem like an idiot and he sure as hell did not want to have to deal with the grief he knew he would suffer from the rest of the guys once he got back to the station. Besides, the shift was stretched so thin right now, he'd hate to take a cop away from a situation where he was really needed, just because he felt nervous.

Sova switched on his cruiser's spotlight, then maneuvered the beam until it illuminated the front of the apartment block on his right. He moved the spotlight slowly across the building from window to window. Something was out of place. It nagged at him like a mother, but he just couldn't put his finger on what it was. He played the light over each floor, then switched it to the apartments on the opposite side of the street to confirm his suspicion.

Sova's foot involuntarily hit the brake, stopping the cruiser in the center of the street. He finally realized what it was that was bugging him; the drapes, he realized, it was the damn drapes. He moved the light back to the apartment on his right just to be sure. No doubt about it, in every single window, either the drapes were drawn, or the blinds tightly shut.

A shudder, like someone had drawn an icy finger down his

spine, rattled his muscles.

Moving the spotlight to ground level, Sova quickly found the entrance to the lobby of the apartment complex to his right. He gunned the engine and pulled in to the curb, then turned on his cruiser's light bar. Instantly the area around his car for a good hundred feet or more was soaked with red, blue, and white light. He waited, watching the windows of the apartments.

Minutes passed and not one drape twitched, not a single blind was raised.

Sova pulled the radio microphone from its hook on the dash. "William-Mary-four-two."

A second passed then a crackly reply. "William-Mary-four-two, go ahead."

"William-Mary-four-two, show me code three at," he glanced at the fading sign above the entrance to the apartment building, "Benson Apartments."

"William-Mary-four-two. Do you need back up?"

Officer Sova thought about it for a second. "Negative," he replied.

He engaged the cruiser's run-lock, pulled the keys from the ignition and stepped out into the rain.

•••

The light from his cruiser provided more than enough illumination for Officer Sova to find his way to the apartment building's entrance, but a hedgerow that acted as a privacy fence between the building and the sidewalk blocked the light from reaching any farther than the steps to the lobby.

Sova stood at the double glass doors. It was full dark within. He pulled a flashlight from a loop on his belt, switched it on and played the powerful beam over the interior of the lobby. The windows were coated with a reflective material to keep the sun out, so the majority of the flashlight's beam simply bounced back at him.

He cursed under his breath. He had hoped he wouldn't have to go inside. It was an irrational fear, he knew, but still. He reached down and pulled his Glock from its holster, then raised the pistol in line with the flashlight, pushed the door open with his foot, and stepped through the gap into the foyer.

The first thing that hit him was how cold the building was, as though the heat had been turned off for hours. For a second he relaxed. That played into his theory that the street had suffered a localized brown-out, lost all power. That theory lasted for approximately two more seconds before his nose picked up on a scent, so strong he thought he might gag; it was the unmistakable coppery smell of blood. Lots of blood.

He played the flashlight across the lobby from wall to wall.

With the entrance at his back, the lobby had two more exits at three and nine o'clock leading to ground-level apartments. A stairwell gave access to the upper floors. The steps led from the ground floor to a small landing then a second set of stairs 180-degrees opposite it. Next to the stairs were the cold aluminum doors of the elevator. The floor was made of some kind of tile or linoleum; it was impossible to tell which because it was covered in pools of congealed blood.

Sova's breathing doubled, his heart began to thump hard in his chest. He swept the flashlight and pistol left and right; a trail of blood led up the stairs, another through each of the ground floor doors. There were footprints in the blood, so many Sova could not tell how many people had been here when whatever had gone down had happened. And he could see what looked like drag marks, as though a body had been pulled through the still-fresh blood then down the corridor to the right. He played his light over the walls and then the ceiling, revealing the unmistakable marks of arterial blood splatter. *No bullet holes. No spent casings, either. Not a one.*

Vomit pushed its way up the officer's throat. He gagged, covered his mouth with the back of his hand, and barely managed to keep the gorge down. It was a charnel house. He swallowed hard, clearing the residue from his throat, and backed up until he felt the door at his back. Only then did he holster his pistol so he could key his radio's microphone.

"William-Mary-four-two. Officer requires urgent assistance at my location. I repeat, officer needs urgent assistance. Multiple homicide, assailants may still be on scene. Send SWAT." He was surprised at how level his voice sounded, a calm that belied the gut-wrenching fear he actually felt in the pit of his stomach.

His radio crackled an acknowledgment, followed a second later by the dispatcher transmitting his request for assistance at his location.

Sova played the light over the interior one last time and pushed his back against the door until it began to open.

*Thump! Thump! Thump!*

Sova froze, the flashlight's beam instantly flicking to the source of the sound.

It was a ball, a child's bright yellow toy ball. It rolled across the first landing of the stairwell, dropped off the lip and bumped its way down the remaining steps, rolling across the floor until it stopped in a pool of blood six feet from where Sova stood.

Sova flicked the beam of his flashlight back up to the stairwell.

"Hello?" he called out, painfully aware of the note of nervousness his voice carried. "Los Angeles Police Department, come out with your hands above your head."

Someone giggled. It was a child's laughter. A boy, Sova guessed, maybe six or seven years of age.

Sova kept his weapon trained on the stairwell and took a step closer, then another, and another until he was just a couple of feet from the first step. "It's okay," he said, "I won't hurt you. Can you come down to me?"

There was another giggle, this time longer. Something dropped from the darkness, too fast for him to follow, and landed with a wet splat at his feet.

Sova looked down and saw eyes staring back at him; it was the head of a man, maybe mid-forties, his eyes wide open, mouth agape in a final scream of fear. A jagged ridge of skin hung around the neck of the head. The flap of skin was ragged, as though it had been torn from the torso it belonged to. The man's windpipe still hung limply from the remains of his throat.

Sova staggered backward. His boots slipped on a thick pool of half-congealed blood and he fell hard on his ass, jarring the flashlight from his hand and sending it rolling off to his right, the beam pointing back toward the street.

"Jesus! Oh, Jesus!" Sova's voice belonged to someone else now. The panic he felt coursing through his body felt distant, his awareness regressing deep into the center of his brain as fear took over his body. He flipped over and began to move on all fours, instinctively heading for the light of his flashlight.

Someone was moving down the stairs, he could hear the sound of them hopping down each step, giggling to themselves.

There were just a few feet between him and the flashlight. He ordered his arms and legs to move faster, but his limbs found little traction in the slick of blood he was crawling through.

"Tee-hee-hee!" This time the childish giggle was directly behind him.

"Oh God. No! No!" Sova reached a hand toward the flashlight.

Something heavy landed between his shoulders, knocking the air from him, pinning him to the floor.

Sova threw out his right hand, scrabbling for a grip on the flashlight that lay just beyond his fingertip's reach.

Whatever had him in its grip now began tearing at his uniform, pulling his tunic away from around his neck, shredding the cloth and skin beneath it. He felt something terribly sharp pierce the skin of his throat. Felt warmth begin to flow out of him.

Officer Sova screamed but there were no humans left in the building to hear him.

•••

The street was still, with only the constant thunder of rain to disturb the otherwise silent world that existed within the two block radius of Officer Sova's cruiser, its lights still painting the road red, blue, and white. A minute later, the first strains of approaching emergency vehicles began to echo off the buildings.

The SWAT team arrived first, their APC roaring to a halt next to Sova's cruiser. The twin doors at the rear of the armored personnel carrier flew open and twelve black-clad figures exited, weapons drawn. They immediately began to fan out into a defensive configuration, taking up firing positions around the apartment entrance where Sova had radioed his position from, their weapons sweeping across the front of the building.

Four more cop cars arrived, pulling up around the APC to form a cordon, the uniforms jumping from them, their weapons at the ready, using their vehicles for cover.

Lynda Turner pulled her ambulance up to the perimeter, making sure the vehicle was out of the line of any potential fire but close enough she could move in at a moment's notice if the need arose. Her partner, Jeb, sat in the back, his arm resting against the headrest of her chair as he leaned in and watched the circus unfold in front of them.

A stillness settled over the street as the police waited for their go signal.

When the signal came it was from one of the SWAT members, his arm chopping the air toward the apartment entrance. As one, the SWAT team flicked down their night vision goggles, leveled their weapons and advanced at a quick jog to the entrance of the apartment. The lead cop pulled the door open, waited as his team flowed inside, and when the last man was in, tagged onto the end.

The door slowly swung closed behind the last man.

Minutes passed with only occasional radio chatter as the SWAT team updated their position as they moved through the apartment building, level by level.

"Holy shit!" Lynda jumped as gunfire suddenly erupted from inside the apartments. She could see muzzle flashes behind the windows on the second floor, hear glass shattering as bullets, fired wildly at God knew who, exploded out of the walls of the building.

The screams began seconds later; horrible, terrifying yells that the cops on the street heard over their radios and through the walls separating the SWAT team from safety. It created an eerie Doppler effect as the delay of the transmission played back the sound of the men's screams a quarter-second after the wind carried the actual screams to their ears. Twenty seconds after the first shot had been fired, silence descended over the street yet again.

Then all hell broke loose. The cops out on the street were either yelling into their radios or sprinting toward the apartment building, weapons in hand.

"We're gonna need more units here," said Jeb from the back of the ambulance. Lynda could hear him busying himself prepping equipment. There was little doubt in either of their minds that this was going to be a mass casualty situation.

"I'll close th—" Jeb's sentence was cut short.

Lynda glanced in the rearview mirror but couldn't see him. The back door of the ambulance was wide open. She turned to face the rear compartment, but it was empty.

"Jeb?" she called, confused. There was no answer.

A scream sliced through the night, cutting Lynda's nerves as sharply as a scalpel. It was coming from above her, the paramedic realized, from the roof of the ambulance. She looked up in time to see a hand appear at the top of her windshield. The hand moved down the glass as Jeb, his face contorted with terror, pulled himself over the windshield toward the hood of the ambulance.

Lynda was barely aware of the other screams that had erupted around her. Her mind registered the barrage of gunshots filling the night with thunder only in passing, her mind stuttering as it tried to deal with the horror of Jeb's face as he thumped weakly on the windshield with a bloodied fist.

*Let me in*, he mouthed silently, blood trickling from the corner of his mouth. *Help me, please.*

And then he was gone. Something had snatched him back up onto the roof of the ambulance, leaving a slick red mark across the windshield that almost instantly began to dissolve as the pouring rain washed it away.

Jeb's screams of horror weakened to a bleat and then nothing.

"Oh, God! Oh, God!" Lynda repeated as she stared through the blood-smeared glass of the ambulance out into a scene of utter confusion and horror beyond.

Through the haze of falling rain, Lynda saw shapes moving among the shadows. She didn't remember there being so many people here a moment ago, where had they all come from? Gunfire exploded from her right. She saw a shadow get hit, fall to the ground, and a moment later spring back up and charge the cop who had fired at it. In a second, the cop had disappeared beneath a wave of darkness.

*Get out of here. Got to get out of here now.* Lynda's brain had finally found a low enough gear to begin functioning again. She reached a hand toward the gear stick, throwing the ambulance into reverse.

Machine gun fire crackled through the night. Lynda yelped in fear and turned just in time to see a lone cop standing on the roof of his cruiser blasting away at a ring of human-shaped shadows surrounding the car.

Lynda released the brake and began to reverse the ambulance away from the nightmare.

The cop was still firing even as he was pulled from his feet. Lynda saw him drop hard to the roof of his cruiser. She had just enough time to register the muzzle flash of his weapon before the first stray bullet shattered the windshield and struck her in the shoulder. Mercifully the second bullet struck her a second later just below her right eye, and all pain ceased.

# CHAPTER TWENTY

A breath caught in Tyreese's throat and he startled awake. The unmistakable sound of small-arms fire rattled nearby, and for a moment his sleep-confused mind told him he was back *there*, in Afghanistan. It took him a couple more seconds before he realized he was actually lying in his bed and it was probably just a—

A scream, bleeding pain and terror, pierced the night, louder even than the constant thrum of the rain against the building.

Tyreese sat bolt upright in his bed, throwing back the covers. The scream—it belonged to a man, he was sure—echoed through the bedroom, followed by another short burst of gunfire, this time from a pistol. Something major was happening, and close by, too. Tyreese swung his lower torso off the side of the bed, used his powerful arms to move from the bed to the wheelchair and pushed himself to the window, staying as low as he could.

Blue, red, and white light leaked through the space between the apartment buildings across the street; the telltale imprint of LAPD's presence. Whatever was going down was either happening in the street directly behind the adjacent apartments or the one beyond that, it was hard to tell where exactly because the rain-covered windows diffused the light from the emergency vehicles into wispy splotches and streaks. Tyreese released the window's security latch and forced the complaining window up, blinking away the rain as it splashed against his face, the cold air bringing goosebumps to his naked arms and chest. He squinted and listened.

Gusts of wind cut through the street, rattling the branches of trees, whistling between gaps, making it hard to pick out other sounds that might explain what was happening. Tyreese thought he heard raised voices, *panicked* voices, but couldn't be sure. There was another burst of gunfire, multiple weapons firing simultaneously, some of them full-auto, followed by more screams for help. He could see the flashes of the weapons as they discharged, followed by the *rat-tat-tat-tat-tat* of gunfire.

Then there was nothing.

Tyreese craned his neck to try to get a better angle, ignoring the rain. Tyreese felt a chill, colder than the one blowing over him, run up his spine and down his arm to the tips of his fingers. Over the entire length of the street that was visible from his window, some nine or ten apartment buildings, only three lights had turned on. Every other window was dark. Hell, he had known nights when the entire street would light up just so the locals could listen (and offer their own commentary and opinions) on a couple's squabble that got out of hand. Tonight, with this kind of excitement, the response was as good as nothing.

For the first time in years, Tyreese felt a hot knot of fear begin to tie itself in the pit of his stomach. Something was terribly wrong here, and he had no idea what it could be.

•••

Birdy's eyes flickered open, her mind foundered for a moment unsure of what the noise that had startled her awake was, or where it was even coming from. It took a few moments for her sleep-misted brain to realize she was in her mom's room; she had fallen asleep on her bed. Her mother's scent still lingered on the pillow, and she breathed it in deeply.

Then she yelped loudly as the unmistakable crack of gunfire

reverberated around the room. It sounded close, very close. She held her breath and waited, counting the beats of her heart thumping against her chest: one, two, three, four, five...

This time the gunfire was continuous, a sustained barrage of shots that sounded like it was coming from some war movie being filmed nearby. She crept to the window on all fours, afraid of stray bullets, raised her head just far enough above the bottom of the window to be able to look out at the street and see the red, blue, and white lights of cop cars leaking through the gully between the apartments across the street. The intermittent flash of what was obviously gunfire lit up the buildings, making millisecond-long shadows jump across the walls of the apartments. More flashes followed by the *rat-tat-tat* sound of a machine gun on full auto reached her ears a half-second later.

Before she really knew what she was doing, she had pulled on her clothes, laced up her sneakers and headed back to the window. She pulled it up, turned her head from the sudden pinprick spray of rain that splashed across her face, grabbed hold of the slick drainpipe, swung herself out, and quickly climbed down.

•••

A scraping noise drew Tyreese's attention down to the floor below him just in time to see Birdy's hoody-covered body maneuver out onto the drainpipe and begin to climb down to the ground.

Where the hell was she going? She couldn't be so stupid as to actually be heading *toward* whatever was playing out over there, could she?

*Never underestimate the amount of stupid a kid is capable of*, his old man had once told him not long before he left, back when he was probably as young as she was now. He hadn't understood what his Pop had meant back then, but as he aged he had come to a grudging belief that his father was a lot smarter than he had given him credit for, God rest the old bastard's soul.

Tyreese watched as Birdy dropped to the ground and, at a low crouch, crossed the road heading toward the gully running between the two apartment buildings opposite his.

"Stop!" Tyreese yelled, just as a sustained burst of automatic fire erupted again, drowning out his voice.

He saw Birdy duck behind a car. She knelt next to the rear wheel for a moment, then she was up again. If the kid had heard him she showed no indication. Tyreese felt his muscles tense as he watched her disappear at a jog into the shadowed mouth of the gully.

•••

The second Birdy's feet hit the ground, she ran to the safety of a nearby tree, listening to the darkness. Other than the constant hiss of rain and the creaking of wind gusting against the apartments, the block had become deathly silent.

Birdy took a deep breath, then sprinted into the road. Halfway across, a short burst of machine gun fire hammered the night and she dove for safety behind the rear wheel of a car parked on the street, sure that someone was shooting at her. A man's voice, barely audible, began begging some unknown assailant for his life before abruptly shifting to a terrified, pain-filled scream, which then just as abruptly ended.

Birdy's hands shook. And she thought she might have peed herself a little. She heard her mother's voice chastising her; *What are you doing, Annabelle? Get home, right now. Do you hear me?*

No! Something had changed over the last few days, since the storm had shown up. It had brought *something* with it, something that had insinuated itself gradually into Birdy's community and then directly into her life. First the storm, then the people who had just vanished, then her mom's disappearance, and now this... a firefight just a few hundred feet away. It was all linked, all connected, Birdy just *knew* it was.

Her legs felt soft and unresponsive, as though they were rebelling against her. She ordered them to move and used her hands to push herself up the side of the car until she was able to peek over the trunk toward a gully.

A concrete path about a hundred feet or so long ran between the eight-foot high security fences of two apartment buildings. Tufts of grass grew along the edges of the paving stones, starting to turn green again after so much rain. A single streetlight stood midway along the length of the gully, but it was out, the cover shattered, the bulb busted too. There was still light though, it came in swirling blues and reds and whites that played over the opposite end of the gully. Water pooled on the uneven paving stones, reflecting the light of the cop cars into what would have been, on any other night, a pretty kaleidoscope across the walls and windows of the apartment buildings. Tonight however, to Birdy, it looked like searchlights scouring the area for her.

Birdy took a deep breath and sprinted the remainder of the distance toward the deepest shadow within the gully, her feet splashing through the half-inch of water collected on its surface. She silently chastised herself for acting like the idiot she knew she was as she squeezed closely against the chain-link fence and set it rattling. She dropped a knee to the ground, her nerves so jangled she didn't feel the cold water seeping into her already-soaked jeans. A second later, once the cop-car lights had swept past, she began to pick her way along the path, using the shadows as best she could. The light from the cop cars—she could see now that there were at least three of them—turned the gully intermittently dark then filled parts of it with swirling colored light, causing her to squint uncomfortably as her night vision tried to accommodate the rapid switch between dark and bright.

Halfway along the gully, Birdy saw there were more vehicles parked in the street; an ambulance, and what looked like some kind of a tank but without the big gun, the word SWAT emblazoned along its side and on its open rear doors. There was no sign of anybody, but she was crouched so close to the ground she couldn't see over the three-foot-high red brick wall that ran parallel to the road, partially blocking her view of the street.

In the next patch of darkness, Birdy scooted herself across to the opposite side of the gully, this time lacing her fingers into the wire of the fence to make sure it did not give away her presence. She could hear the low rhythmic thrum of the vehicles' engines still running. She edged closer still.

A sudden squawk from a police radio, the voice coming from it panicked and incomprehensible, scared her so badly she almost ran. Then the voice was gone, abruptly cut off. Now only the sound of the constant rain, a continuous white-noise hiss, was left. That and her ragged breathing. Birdy forced her lungs to perform the way *she* needed them to; slowly, rhythmically, pushing back against her body's fight-or-flight instinct with deep, controlled breaths of the wet air.

Staying low, Birdy edged along the final fifty feet or so of the gully until she reached the point where the security fence met the low red brick wall. An LAPD black and white was parked on the road directly across the gap of the gully's exit to the street. It blocked her view of the area beyond it, but also gave her cover from anyone who might be on the other side. The cop car's driver's door was wide open, rain thumping against the leather seat. The dim glow of the car's electronics and dome light illuminated a wet patch of the path running alongside the curb.

Birdy peeked around the corner post of the fence. A second black and white was positioned thirty feet ahead. Both its doors were open too. On the opposite side of the road, in the space between the two police cruisers, was a SWAT van. She looked to her right and saw an ambulance, and a third black and white in the middle of the road. The ambulance's windshield was riddled with bullet holes, and it looked like it had reversed into a streetlight. A thin wisp of steam rose from beneath its hood.

There was no sign of anyone alive on the street. No bodies either.

The gunfire had been so loud, so ferocious, that there was no way *someone* had not been hurt. And where were the cops? They should be all over this area. There should be helicopters, maybe even the National Guard, Birdy thought. If people had been hit, there should be bodies, or talking, or *something*. Anything but this deserted, silent scene laid out around her. The rain could have washed away any blood she supposed, but where were the people?

Birdy stood up. She waited, using the meager cover the metal fence pole gave her, standing as still as a statue, barely breathing. She allowed her eyes to slowly scan her surroundings, looking for any clues to where the cops might be. In the middle of the road, just beyond the open passenger door of the second police cruiser, a large flashlight lay in a puddle of water, its beam pointing across the street and under the SWAT vehicle. A police officer's cap lay a few feet beyond that, upside-down, slowly collecting water. Now that she was standing, Birdy could see that the roof of the police cruiser parked at the curb in front of her looked like it was dented, and there were bullet holes in it too.

Birdy made a quick dash to the driver's side door, huddling into the V where the open door met the car's front quarter-panel. The inside of the vehicle smelled of sweat, stale coffee and... something Birdy could not quite identify. She peered through the door's window, up the path running alongside the brick wall in front of the apartments on the left side of the street. The car's radio hissed and crackled with occasional static, like steam escaping from a vent.

Beyond the reach of the car's headlights and flashing light bars was only darkness. Here and there along the pathway, trees stood guard over the street, their upper branches mostly hidden within shadow. Birdy placed a hand on the driver's seat and eased herself up toward the windshield to get a better look, but stopped halfway when her fingers touched something wet and sticky. She almost gagged when she saw she had placed her hand in a pool of half-congealed blood. Birdy screeched with disgust and frantically rubbed the blood into her pants until only a light stain remained on her fingers. She plunged her hand into the steady stream of water running beneath the car, rinsing the remaining blood off.

"Oh my God! Oh my God!" she hissed, unable to stop the words from tumbling from her lips. It was as if she had lost control of her tongue; the words repeating over and over. She threw her hand up to her mouth, forcing her jaws together to stop the tumble of words from escaping, her lips tasting the faint tang of blood that still remained on her fingers.

*I have to get out of here, right now.*

Whatever had done this to the police was still here, somewhere. She knew it. And even though she could not explain how she knew it, her intuition told her that everyone within the darkened apartment blocks had also succumbed to whatever had chosen this place as its home. She had to alert *somebody*. Somebody had to come and help her, help whoever there was left.

When she was finally sure her lips would not betray her, Birdy removed her hand from her face, aware of how badly that hand now shook. She leaned into the cop car's cabin, carefully avoiding the pool of blood, and unhooked the radio's microphone from the dash. Pulling it to her lips, she keyed the microphone.

"Hello," she whispered. "Can anybody hear me? Please!" When she released the key there was a short, sharp burst of static, followed by silence. She waited for an answer, but none came. She keyed the mic again. "*Please*, this is an emergency, I need help. Something... something has happened to your policemen. Can anyone hear me?" She checked the front of the radio, but the knobs and readouts made little sense to her. Her fear began to turn into frustration. In all the movies and TV shows she had ever seen, the cop's radios were always bursting with noise and voices. It was like there was no one out there listening...

The thought forced a cold shaft of fear into Birdy's spine. What if there was no one left to answer? *That* would explain why her call had gone unanswered, and why no backup had arrived to help the cops that had been in these cars.

She had to get out of here. Back to her room. Back to where she was safe. She would call the cops from her phone. As she turned to head back toward the gully, something on the blacktop just ahead of the front left tire of the cop car caught her eye. It had been obscured by the car door until now, and she stopped and looked at it for a moment.

The pistol lay about five feet in front of the car, tiny droplets of rain collecting on its gray metal surface. Birdy stared at it for several seconds, her mind assessing the possible actions available to her. She had never even held a gun, let alone fired one. But how hard could it be? All you had to do was point it where you wanted the bullet to go and pull the trigger, right?

She continued to stare at the pistol, her breathing gradually increasing as she psyched herself up for what she was about to do. Then with one last look toward the gun, Birdy pushed herself off with her right foot, hoping the tread of her new sneakers would not betray her, and sprinted out into the road, ignoring the voice in her head telling her she was crazy. She slowed long enough to reach down and grab the pistol by its barrel—it was a lot heavier than she had imagined it would be—and then she ran. She ran like she had never run before, ducking back into the gully, her eyes fixed on her apartment. She thought about going back up the drainpipe, but the rain was so heavy now she wasn't sure her grip would hold.

As she sprinted out of the opposite end of the gully, she angled her feet toward the security gate. Entered the security code as fast as her cold fingers would allow, shouldered her way through the gate, and slammed it behind her, then slipped and slid her way across the grass verge that was now nothing but mud. Finally, breathless more from fear than the exertion, she pulled open the door to the lobby and slipped inside. She paused for a second to catch her breath, then jogged toward the stairs.

Outside, in the branches of a sycamore tree just across the street, a shadow with yellow luminescent eyes watched Birdy as she stood panting in the entryway. The shadow dropped silently to the wet pavement, pulled itself erect, and began to follow her.

•••

Tyreese decided to give chase to Birdy as soon as she disappeared into the darkness of the gully. He'd yelled for her to come back, but the cacophony of gunfire and the storm smothered his voice. The kid was smart, no doubt, and she was fast, but she was still just a kid, with a child's inability to understand when they were stepping into some serious shit. There'd been no sign of anyone else out on the street, despite the amazing commotion of bullets and screams, and there was no way in hell he was going to leave Birdy to the mercy of... whatever *it* was out there. He still had no idea *exactly* what was going on, but his instincts were screaming at him that it was not good. Not good at all.

So he had strapped on his legs, grabbed his wooden walking cane and headed to the elevator.

He pressed the call button and waited... and waited. Five minutes and some aggressive finger prodding of the call button, and the elevator indicator still showed the cab to be on the ground floor.

"Jesus," he said, exasperated. He walked as quickly as he could to the stairwell and pushed open the door. This was exactly what he'd hoped to avoid; he wasn't comfortable with steps, especially not this many.

All the light fixtures in the stairwell were out, so Tyreese grabbed the lone fire extinguisher from the wall near the entrance and propped the landing door open with it. The light from his floor illuminated about halfway down to the next landing. Better than nothing, he supposed.

He breathed in and took a tentative step down. He just needed to pay attention and keep his cool and he would be all right, he told himself. Two more steps down and Tyreese misjudged the next step, the heel of his boot caught its lip, and he stumbled forward. If it hadn't been for the walking cane he held he would have surely fallen hard, breaking God knew how many bones. Instead he pushed the end of the wooden cane onto the step below him, which gave him enough time for his right hand to grab for the aluminum handrail that ran along the side of the stairs. The handrail was supposed to run all the way to the bottom floor, but it was missing most of the way down, the result of some hard-up junkie who had stripped it and sold it for his next dose. He wobbled for a second or two, the cane's handle biting into the soft skin between his thumb and first finger as it took most of his weight, then he pushed himself back upright until he found his balance.

"You have *got* to be out of your mind," he said aloud, taking in a deep breath to help ease his thundering heart. He allowed himself a second to catch his breath before starting down again.

*One. At. A. Time*, he told himself.

Tyreese froze as the sound of a door opening then creaking shut on squeaky hinges echoed up from the shadows of the stairwell below. Footsteps, rapid and light, followed.

"Who's down there?" he called out, mustering as much menace into his voice as he could find. His grip on the cane grew tighter.

The footsteps stopped abruptly. Tyreese edged closer to the guardrail, leaned over, and looked down into the darkness. A blank pale face looked up at him, then suddenly broke into a smile.

"Tyreese!" Birdy yelled, the relief in her voice taking him completely by surprise.

In what could only have been a few seconds, the girl had bounded up the remaining stairs to Tyreese, rounded his flight of stairs and all but flung herself at him. Her arms tried but just failed to reach all the way around his waist, her head buried deep into his solar plexus.

Tyreese wobbled with her impact, his free hand moving to her back to hold her to him, mostly to stop the two of them from falling. He felt a swell of relief that she was okay (and also that he would not have to follow her out into the night), that quickly began to turn to anger that she had forced him into this position. He pried Birdy from him and placed a hand tightly around her upper arm. His meaty hand swallowed her arm entirely.

"What the hell were you thinking?" he said, loudly. He held Birdy at arm's length until she was almost leaning backward. Her face, covered by a sheen of rainwater, her skin pale in the meager light looked up at him, her joy now turning to fear as she teetered on the edge of a step. If he let go, she would have no chance, he realized through the haze of anger that had overtaken him. She would fall.

"Tyreese," Birdy bleated, her voice fearful. "You're hurting me." Tears streamed down both her cheeks now.

Jesus! What was he doing? He felt a sudden burst of shame that he had let his own fear overtake him. He pulled her toward him, releasing her arm then sat down hard on the step two above where her feet were planted.

"I'm sorry. I'm... I... I just...," he stuttered, unable to put into words his shame. He watched her rub the part of her arm where he had grabbed her. "I saw the firefight. Saw you out there heading to—" His eyes fell to the waistband of her pants. Now it was his turn to sound shocked. "Is that a pistol?" he hissed, his eyes trying to focus through the gloom on what he was sure was the butt of a Glock sticking out of the waistband of Birdy's pants.

Birdy dropped down one more step and pulled out the pistol, her hand around the grip, her finger caressing the trigger guard as she held it in front of Tyreese. "I found it on the street," she said, turning it sideways as she continued to examine it. "It was just laying next to one of the cop cars, like it'd been dropped." Her finger moved over the trigger. "Hey!" she yelled as Tyreese snatched the weapon from her. "That's mine."

Tyreese pulled back the slide—there was a round in the chamber—and dropped the magazine. It was half-full. He slid the pistol into his own waistband. "You could have been killed," he said quietly.

"I'm not stupid. I know not to pull the trigger."

"I'm not talking about the gun! I'm talking about out there." He pointed his chin outside. "Something's going down. I don't know what it is, but you ain't stupid. You know there's no way what happened tonight wouldn't have brought a massive goddamn response from the cops. Jesus! There's not even a news crew out there. And you decide to go crawling around in the dark?" He waited a few seconds for his words to sink in. "You could have been killed," he repeated quietly.

Birdy's eyes dropped to the steps. "I... I know. It's just— Ummmph!" Her words became an unintelligible muffle as Tyreese's paw of a hand suddenly covered her mouth.

"Shhhhh!" he whispered.

From below, the sound of the ground floor door creaking

slowly open again reached them in the semi-darkness.

Birdy's eyes grew wide.

"Did you see anyone else out there?" Tyreese whispered, his hand still clasped over her mouth.

Birdy's eyes got even wider. She shook her head no. If she hadn't seen anyone out there, then whoever had just entered the stairwell hadn't wanted to be seen.

They both heard the sound of bare feet slapping against concrete steps. Tyreese strained to see through the darkness, but the light from the top landing only went a short way into the shadows.

"Who's down there?" Tyreese's voice boomed. He released Birdy's mouth and struggled to his feet.

A few seconds passed without another sound, then without warning, from the edge of the darkness one landing down, a woman's voice, soft yet somehow disturbing to Tyreese, echoed up the staircase, "Baby, it's Momma Are you there?"

Birdy gasped and pulled herself free of Tyreese's grip. "Momma?"

The disembodied voice took on a tone of relief. "Annabelle, baby. I've been looking for you *everywhere*. I can't see you. Come down here to your momma"

Birdy took two steps into the darkness before Tyreese's heavy hand grabbed her by the shoulder and pulled her back, his fingers digging into her flesh.

"Stop!" he hissed.

"Let go of me. Let go," Birdy yelled, struggling to free herself from his grip. "Mom, help!"

"Baby, what's wrong? Who's that with you?"

Now Tyreese's voice sounded like thunder as it echoed around the stairwell, "Why don't you come up here, where we can see you in the light."

A drawn-out hiss rose from the darkness below. Tyreese imagined it sounded exactly how a rattlesnake would if he'd kicked it out from under a rock. When the woman's voice returned, it had taken on a keening, almost simpering tone. "Baby, I'm hurt. Come here to me, please. I need you."

Birdy struggled harder, but Tyreese's grip was vice-like. She turned to face the man who held her. "Let me go!" she screamed, spittle flying as tears of both frustration and relief rolled down her cheeks. "That's my *mom*."

Instead of releasing her, Tyreese took an unsteady step back up the stair, pulling the still-struggling Birdy with him.

"Let go of me! Let me go!" she screamed.

There was a sound of rapid movement, feet scuttling over concrete. To Tyreese it sounded like many limbs working at once, not like a human, but more like a spider, huge and black scrambling up the concrete walls.

"Birr-dyy!" the voice sang; it was much closer now, just a few feet away in the darkness. The voice was not much louder than a whisper, cajoling, "Birdy, I'm right here, baby. Come to me." Then, demanding, "Now!"

Tyreese felt Birdy flinch at the sharpness of the last command.

"Mom?" Birdy allowed the word to fall from her lips, all hope suddenly evaporating from her voice.

Tyreese felt the girl stop struggling and he eased his grip on her shoulders a little.

"Back up, now... slowly," Tyreese whispered into Birdy's ear, his hands now resting gently on each of her shoulders, the left awkwardly gripping the cane beside her. He eased himself up another step, the heel of his right prosthetic scuffing against the lip of the step above. The small hairs on the back of Tyreese's neck tingled, the cold air of the stairwell chilling the sweat that he felt covering his skin. Squinting, he tried to look deeper into the darkness just a few feet below, but there was nothing to see other than shades of black.

They had almost made it back to the top landing when a shadow detached itself from the darkness and moved into the orange glow leaking from the open door behind Tyreese and Birdy. The shape eased into the long shadow the man and girl cast down the stairs, as though their darkness was preferable to even the meager amount of light illuminating the steps.

Tyreese felt his mind grind to a halt right at that moment, his sense of reality suddenly as fragile as a thin sheet of ice across a pond. Birdy sagged beneath his hands as though she were a deflated balloon, her breath hissing from her with shock. Tyreese's own breath was held deep within his chest, and he wondered if his heart would ever start again.

"Holy fuck!" Tyreese finally gasped.

Birdy whimpered at the apparition just a few steps below them. She spun around and, unable to push by Tyreese, buried her head into his side. It *was* Lizzie Finch, Birdy's mom. Tyreese recognized her, albeit barely, from a photograph he'd seen in the girl's apartment.

Lizzie Finch was shoeless, the uniform she wore soaked with rain, clinging to her body, the fabric torn in many places and missing a huge strip down the front that exposed the left cup of her bra and a long swath of pallid skin down to the waistband of her pants. Her wet hair clung to her face, her arms and legs were as pale as the skin of her exposed belly, save for the blotches of dirt and streaks of caked blood the rain had not washed away.

But it was the woman's face that scared Tyreese. He had seen similar expressions during his time in Afghanistan on the faces of insurgents and suicide bombers, usually just kids or young men; cold, deliberate, hungry for death. And her *eyes*; what was wrong with her eyes? They seemed to glow with an otherworldly yellow light, like when you shine a flashlight in the eyes of a dog or a cat at night. *Or a wolf*, he thought. A hungry, rabid wolf.

Lizzie Finch's face was as colorless as the rest of her body. But her lips, in contrast, were a bright ruby red, as though she had painted them with the gaudiest red lipstick she could find. She swayed constantly back and forth, like a reed in a light summer breeze. But *those* golden eyes; there was a greed behind them, Tyreese thought, a hunger. And they remained fixed squarely on her daughter. And, Tyreese thought, he was sure the woman hadn't blinked, not once in the entire time she stood there.

When Lizzie Finch spoke, it was with a demanding, disdainful voice. "Daughter, why won't you look at me?"

Tyreese felt his bladder almost give way because even in this minimal light he could see her teeth were black, completely black, like obsidian. And jutting from her top jaw were two fangs—like a snake's—that curved down to a serrated lower set of teeth.

Birdy twisted her head to face her mother. "You're not my mother!" she spat, still holding tight to Tyreese, but refusing to turn her head away from the ghastly creature.

Lizzie Finch climbed up onto the next step.

"Get behind me," Tyreese ordered Birdy. With his free hand he pried the girl from around his waist, moving the walking cane aside long enough for the girl to duck under his arm. She had to stand two steps up to be able to see over the big man's shoulders.

Lizzie Finch, or what had once been her, advanced up the stairs one deliberate step at a time. Her thin arms were outstretched, one hand pressing against the wall, the other running over the top of the guardrail, her shoulders hunched, head low, her golden eyes never leaving Birdy.

*She's making sure we can't get past her, blocking our way*, Tyreese thought. She wasn't scared of them; she was *stalking* them.

Lizzie's nails scraped against the flaking paint of the wall with a dry scratching sound. She stopped abruptly. "Child, come to your mother." The creature was just four steps down from them now. Its eyes flicked from Tyreese to Birdy then back to Tyreese. "Give her to me," the woman demanded.

"Not going to happen, lady," Tyreese said, aware of the tremor in his own voice. "Now back the hell away from us."

Lizzie Finch waited, her head tilting first left then right as though she was trying to crack a knotted neck muscle. For a moment Tyreese thought *maybe* he had actually managed to scare her off. But then she threw her head back and laughed, a mirthless cackle that trailed off to a gurgling as her lower jaw suddenly distended, dropping down three inches. Tyreese could see the skin stretching like elastic, the black teeth glinting in the paltry light from the landing.

"You have *got* to be shitting me!" Tyreese pulled the pistol from his waist and aimed it at the monster standing in front of him before he even realized he was going to do it. There was a tremendous bang as Tyreese pulled the trigger on the Glock.

Birdy screamed as the gunshot exploded deafeningly in the confined space of the stairwell.

Tyreese saw the bullet clip the top of the exposed cup of Lizzie Finch's bra. It was a perfect shot, right through her heart. He saw the material of her bra fray as the bullet tore into her, saw the skin pucker as the .45 caliber round hit, knocking her backwards, and then disappear as the wound almost instantly began to close up again. The bullet hit the wall behind Lizzie Finch with a twang and ricocheted away into the darkness.

Tyreese pulled the trigger three more times in rapid succession, aiming for center of mass, with the same result; the bullets seemed to just pass right through the woman. And what should have been fatal wounds vanished seconds later, like she was made of some kind of jelly rather than flesh. He put a fifth round through the woman's right cheek. It knocked her down a step, but then she was up again and scrambling up the stairs toward them.

"Run, Birdy!" Tyreese screamed, his mind still trying to deal with what was happening. This was impossible. *Impossible!*

Tyreese started to turn, using his body to block the creature so it could not slip past him and make a grab for Birdy. She was standing on the landing a few steps above him, her eyes wide with horror, her hands clasping the railing as though it was her last fragile grip on reality.

"Get to my apartment. Run! *NOW!*" Tyreese raised his left foot to take the next step but his leg refused to move. He looked down in time to see Lizzie Finch's dirty, blood-stained hands clasped around his prosthetic leg just as she ripped it away, tearing the fake limb from his pants.

And then Tyreese was falling. Tumbling backward into the darkness, his arms flailing as he tried to find something to grab hold of, the cane he held in his left hand whirling like a bad Charlie Chaplin impersonation. Tyreese's body twisted as he fell, pivoting on his one prosthetic leg, his hands coming up instinctively to protect his head from the impact he knew was coming.

Time slowed. Tyreese saw Birdy's mother clawing her way up the stairs toward her terrified child who stood rooted on the top landing. Saliva dripped from the monster's distended jaw. He heard the screeching wail that emanated from its mouth. Saw the teeth flashing in the dim light. And he felt a terrible certainty that he had failed the girl, failed himself, again. They were both *doomed.*

Tyreese's body juddered for a second as the cane he held in his left hand slipped between two upright posts of the guardrail and jammed. He teetered against the handle for a moment, the wood bending, slowing him enough that he thought he had a chance to recover. But then Tyreese heard the wooden shaft snap with a retort almost as loud as the pistol's. One piece of the cane dropped into the narrow center shaft between the floors, the other part tumbled from his fingers to the steps. His momentum altered, Tyreese now fell sideways instead, hitting the steps hard, the edges digging into his already bruised forearms. He rolled to his right and hit the wall, saw the creature just inches away from him still focused on reaching the girl above.

Tyreese threw a hand toward the creature, managed to snag its leg just above the ankle, his fingers grabbing hold of the wet material of the pants leg. His two-hundred-and-twenty pounds of muscle and momentum did the rest. He rolled down the steps toward the next landing, pulling the creature down with him.

Tyreese hit the concrete hard, knocking the air from his lungs. A snarling, screeching Elizabeth Finch landed next to him, her legs trapped beneath his torso.

Through the semi-darkness, he saw a mouth full of fangs heading for his throat. He rolled away just as the jaws snapped shut, but in doing so he lost his grip on Elizabeth Finch.

The creature exploded into the air and landed on the thin metal guardrail, perching there for a second like some monstrous bird. Her eyes blazed down at him, her head tilted to the left in such a way that, if it hadn't been for the terrible sight she presented, it would have completed the avian image.

Then Birdy was standing just one step up behind her mother, easily within reach of the creature.

Tyreese recognized the same bloodlust in Birdy's eyes as he had seen in the creature just moments earlier. Tyreese tried to call out to Birdy, yell at her to run before the thing grabbed her, but he was still gasping for air and the pain in his ribs was so intense all that came out was a weak huff.

"Mom!" Birdy cried.

The creature snapped around to face her child. "Birdy," it hissed, drool trickling from the corner of her lips.

"My name is *Annabelle*!" the girl said calmly as she raised a piece of the broken cane above her head and plunged the pointed end deep into her mother's heart.

The thing that had been Elizabeth Finch did not explode like a burst balloon full of blood, she did not catch fire. What happened was nothing like in the movies. She simply gasped. Her left hand grabbed the shaft of the wooden pole embedded in her chest and tried to pull it free.

Birdy gritted her teeth, shifted her hands to get a better grip on the makeshift stake, and leaned all her weight against it. There was a tearing sound as the pointed end suddenly appeared out the back of the woman, pieces of her skin hanging from it.

Elizabeth Finch began to scream then—a terrible, high-pitched animal wail made all the more terrifying by the confines of the stairwell.

Birdy, all hatred gone from her eyes, gasped, her hands flying away from the shaft of the stake as though it was on fire. She staggered back two steps as her mother collapsed onto the landing next to Tyreese. The woman writhed and thrashed in agony, her hands beating the ground as a black fluid, too thin for blood and too viscous for water, flowed from the puncture marks on either side of her chest. Her hands were clasped around the shaft of the wooden pole embedded in her chest, but her strength seemed to be draining away as quickly as the black liquid leaking from her.

"Mom!" Birdy cried out and took a step forward, her hands reaching toward the handle of the walking stick.

"No!" Tyreese yelled, kicking at the child with his one good leg to keep her away from the thrashing creature. "Let her die, Birdy. For Christ's sake, let her die."

Elizabeth Finch's writhing grew slower, and slower until finally an exhalation, like wind through a tunnel, escaped from the woman's mouth. Then she moved no more.

•••

The rhythmic beat of rain against exterior walls was broken only by an occasional gust of wind that roughly shook the apartment block, squeezing creaks and groans from the building's joists and beams.

Birdy sat silently on the steps just above where her mother's body lay. The girl's face was a blank mask, and though her cheeks were still wet with the tears she had already shed, no more came.

Tyreese eyed the body of Elizabeth Finch sprawled next to him, a hand still wrapped around the broken cane jutting from her chest. The woman's face was turned toward him, her eyes sightless, their ethereal glow gone, her distended jaw agape, teeth like a bear trap just waiting for him to get close enough to snap closed. He hadn't noticed it before, between the way Lizzie Finch had avoided the light and the smears of dirt and blood that covered her skin, but this close the two puncture marks on her throat were unmissable.

*This cannot be real*, Tyreese thought. A pool of the black liquid that had bled from her body when Birdy impaled her mother still trickled from beneath her torso. It oozed slowly toward Tyreese as though it were alive.

"Shit! Shit! Shit!" Tyreese sat up and pushed himself away from the expanding pool of black blood, not sure if whatever had turned Birdy's mom into this... this... *nightmare*, might be infectious. He'd watched *The Thing* when he was a kid, and he sure as hell wasn't going to take a chance on ending up like the late Mrs. Finch, thank you very much. He looked around for his other prosthetic leg, saw it on the step just below where Birdy sat.

"Birdy, throw me my leg," he said, aware of how utterly ridiculous that sentence sounded given the circumstances.

The girl did not move. She sat, knees together, leaning forward, her elbows resting on her lap, her eyes fixed on her mother's body.

"Birdy?" he said again. He snapped his fingers at her in the gloom. Nothing. The kid was completely out of it. Tyreese scooted his butt over to the corner of the landing, pushed his back into where the two walls met, then used the flats of his hands against the wall to lever himself up to a point where he could use his one good leg to get him the rest of the way up.

*Oh, Christ, did he hurt.* His elbows felt like they'd been hit by a baseball bat, and he thought he might have thrown something out in either his shoulder or his neck. He took a second to wait for the pain to pass, then, leaning heavily against the wall, he hopped along it until he was at the base of the steps, his eyes continually moving back and forth between Birdy and the dead woman lying not five feet from where he stood.

"Birdy? Hey, can you hear me?" he asked, catching his breath as he leaned against the wall at the base of the stairs. "My leg? Can you kick it to me?"

The girl continued to stare blankly ahead.

Tyreese let out a long sigh. He turned around until his back was to the stairs then lowered himself down as gently as he could until his butt was on the third step. He used his hands to push himself up a step at a time until he was sitting on the step just below Birdy.

"Hey!" he whispered, "are you in there?" he reached out a hand and gently laid it against her forearm. No reaction. From here he could see how wide her eyes were, the pupils completely dilated, hear her ragged breathing. The kid was in shock. He'd seen this before in soldiers not that much older than the girl sitting on the step above him, witnesses to Hell on Earth. He leaned across and grabbed his prosthetic leg, repositioned it and tied it off, then stood unsteadily and faced Birdy.

"Birdy, we're going to get up now, okay?" He stepped up next to her, reached his hands under her shoulders and pulled her to her feet. She didn't resist him, but she also didn't move when he tried to ease her up the remaining steps.

Whatever had happened to Elizabeth Finch, the probability that she was the only victim of whatever had turned her into that murderous creature was almost impossible, Tyreese reasoned. The entire street and maybe even farther had gone dark over the last couple of days, and he was willing to bet his last dollar that one of the reasons was lying dead on the landing just a few steps beneath him. There had to be more, maybe hundreds of others like Birdy's mom in the apartments all around them, he was convinced of that now. If another one of them showed up, he didn't know if he had the strength to deal with *it*, and if there was more than one... He allowed the thought to trail away.

*It*! He found he could only refer to the creature in that indefinite way, but a part of Tyreese's mind knew what Elizabeth Finch was, knew *exactly* the name for what she had become, but his rational mind could not say the word. It was just beyond reason.

Tyreese slipped one arm around the kid's waist, the other under her knees and lifted her up. She didn't resist him but her body was rigid, every muscle tensed. Birdy weighed about as much as her namesake, he thought, as he began to carry her up the remaining stairs. By the time he reached his apartment door, Birdy had at least relaxed a little, her body limp, her head lying lightly against his chest.

"I've got to set you down," Tyreese said, gently. Still no reply from the girl, but when he lowered her to the ground outside his apartment door, she stood on her own, her head bowed.

Tyreese fished his door keys from his pocket and opened the apartment. "Go on in," he said.

Birdy stepped across the apartment's threshold and stopped.

Only when he had locked the door and thrown the deadbolt into place did Tyreese allow himself to start breathing again.

"Come on, sit down. Over here." Tyreese led Birdy into his

living room and ushered her over to the sofa. After she silently complied, he hurried to the kitchen counter and quickly found the business card Detective Collins had given him. He dialed the detective's cell number, his mind racing over what had just happened in the stairwell as he waited for the cop to pick up.

*Vampire*! That *thing* out there had, until just a day earlier, been a woman, a mother. She was a goddamn vampire. His mind continued to resist allowing him to say the name aloud, as though the word was electrically charged and would shock him if he spoke it. But that was what she was, he had little doubt; the way she had avoided the light when she could, the teeth—Dear God, those *teeth*—the puncture wounds on her neck, the makeshift stake through the heart that ended her life. He realized suddenly that unless it had been a lucky shot, then Birdy had already figured out what her mother had become too, that's why she had aimed for the heart.

"Jesus!" he whispered into the phone.

"*Hello, this is detective Phillip Collins. Please leave your name, number and the case you are calling about and I'll get back to you as soon as I can.*"

Tyreese waited for the beep. "Detective, this is Tyreese Douglass. Ummm... Annabelle Finch's uncle. You said to call you if there were any new developments. Well there's been some developments, Birdy's mom came home. Only it's not her. *Shit*! You need to get over here right now." He hung up.

# CHAPTER TWENTY-ONE

In the few seconds it had taken Detective Phil Collins to run from the store entrance back to his idling car, the rain had soaked almost all the way through his overcoat. If it hadn't been for the suit jacket he wore beneath it, he knew he would be feeling mighty uncomfortable right about now.

"Bit wet out there?" Mulroney asked from behind the wheel, smirking at his discomfort.

"What the hell is going on in this town?" Collins asked as he closed the passenger side door behind him, a note of exasperation creeping into his voice.

The entire strip mall, while lit up like any other night, might just as well have been abandoned for weeks. He'd stopped to pick up a sandwich and some coffee but when he tried the 7-Eleven's doors, he'd found them locked. A couple of cars were parked out front, so someone was probably inside. He'd hammered on the glass front of the store a couple of times but no one had answered. Quite literally, the lights were on but there was nobody home.

And this was the third location they'd stopped at. The last two—one an all-night liquor store, the other a gas station—had been equally deserted.

"Maybe they listened and got out of town before the storm

hit?" Mulroney offered.

Collins could tell by the lack of conviction in her voice that she did not believe for one second that that was what had happened.

Mulroney continued, "You got a call while you were out fishing," nodding at Collins's phone sitting on the dash.

Collins dialed his mailbox and listened to the message from some guy named Tyreese. It was only when he heard him explain about Birdy that he understood who the message was from. When he had showed up at Birdy's place earlier, the African American guy in the wheelchair had said his name was David, Birdy's uncle, which, as he had suspected, had turned out to be a fabrication.

"Turn us around," said Collins, jerking his thumb over his shoulder.

"Where we going?" Mulroney asked. She shifted the car into reverse, pulled a U-turn on the deserted street and headed east.

Collins filled her in on what the message had said.

"Christ, could he be any more fucking cryptic?" Mulroney said, when Collins was done.

The detective's headache from the previous night's shift had never really left, and now he felt it starting to creep back. He needed caffeine. He'd had a cup when he got up this evening, but that was it. Without it his mood was as miserable and dark as the weather. If he had his way, he'd just go home, get under the covers and wait for this whole goddamn storm to blow over. But there was something in this Tyreese guy's voice, something that had tickled his detective's instincts.

Mulroney drove out of the parking lot and headed back in the direction of Birdy's apartment. "Look on the bright side," she said, still smirking, "maybe they'll have coffee."

•••

Mulroney pulled the car to a stop directly out front of the entrance to Birdy's apartment block, turned the engine off then pocketed the keys.

"Sometimes I wonder if I should have chosen another line of work, something simple like playboy jetsetter," Collins joked quietly, as he squinted through the constant back and forth of the windshield wipers at the front of the apartment building. Only two windows were illuminated out of what must be at least a hundred apartments. It was pretty much the same for every other building the two cops had passed on their way here. "I don't like this one bit," he said quietly, looking into the darkened foyer.

"Jesus, boss, you're starting to worry me," said Mulroney, "Want me to call for backup?"

Collins considered it, but the station was so understaffed right now they could be waiting here for hours before anyone got to them. Besides, the radio was on the fritz, Mulroney had called dispatch on the way over here and all they'd gotten back was silence. One of the hazards of this fucking weather, he supposed. *When it rains, it pours*, he thought, grimacing at the irony. "No need, we can handle this. Come on." Collins opened his door and stepped out, he jogged to the relative dryness of the apartment's portico, avoiding the sheets of water gushing from it like Niagara Falls.

Mulroney splashed her way over to join him, cursing as icy water found its way between her jacket's collar and her spine. Something crunched under her boot. "What the?" It was the remains of a light bulb. Mulroney looked up at the broken portico light fixture. "They need to hire a better maintenance guy," she said flatly.

They simultaneously pulled their flashlights out and directed the beams through the glass double-doors of the entrance. Inside, everything seemed normal, if you ignored the fact that there were no lights and no people. Collins unbuttoned his coat and adjusted the shoulder holster, unclipping the safety strap that kept his pistol in place. Mulroney raised her eyebrows, but did the same with the pistol on her hip.

Collins opened the door and stepped inside, holding it open with a foot for Mulroney while he ran his flashlight over the room.

"Someone wanted to make sure there was no light," said Mulroney, moving her flashlight from broken light fixture to broken light fixture along the walls and ceiling. The cops walked briskly over to the elevator and pressed the call button. The elevator indicator above the door glowed a dim orange showing the cab was on the ground floor, but it still did not open. Collins jabbed at the button a couple more times with his index finger and stepped back to stare at the floor indicator.

"Screw this," he said, turning around and heading to the stairs. "Let's go."

"Right behind you," said Mulroney, following him through the door.

The stairwell was even darker than the lobby. They were one flight up when the beam of a third flashlight cut through the darkness from above them, partly blinding the two cops. Instinctively they ducked for what little cover there was.

"You better get that goddamn light out of my eyes and identify yourself if you want to see the morning," Collins yelled. He didn't like the way his voice echoed up the shaft of the stairwell.

"Detective, it's me, Tyreese. I was just making sure you weren't... something else."

Mulroney gave Collins a quizzical look. *What the hell did he mean 'something else'?*

"Turn off the flashlight and step out where we can see you," Collins ordered. "Put your hands in the air."

The light went out and the sound of shoes shuffling over the bare concrete floor filtered down.

"Cover me," Collins told Mulroney, then moved cautiously up the stairwell.

On the second floor, hands raised above his head, squinting hard as the detective's flashlight illuminated him, stood the African American male he had met earlier, the man who had identified himself as Birdy's uncle. He'd been in a wheelchair then but was standing perfectly well now.

"Interlock your fingers above your head."

Tyreese complied. "I don't have—"

"Shut up," said Collins. He moved in close, put the flashlight down on the steps and began frisking the man.

"Got any weapons on you?"

"No," Tyreese answered flatly.

When the detective knelt down to pat Tyreese's pants he felt the two prosthetic legs below his knees. *Well that explains that*, he thought. Collins stood and looked the guy square in the eyes, relaxing a little.

"Mulroney, come on up," Collins called out.

Mulroney joined them, her pistol leveled at Tyreese. Collins shook his head and Mulroney lowered her weapon.

"Where's the girl and her mother?" Collins asked, more a question than a demand this time.

Tyreese hesitated. *Never a good sign*, Collins thought.

"I'll show you." Tyreese nodded in the direction of the next flight of stairs.

"Lead the way."

Tyreese began climbing the steps one at a time. Collins had seen plenty of amputees before, a couple of the guys in the precinct had lost a leg overseas. They all seemed almost as adept with their prosthetics as they had been with their real limbs. This guy, he looked awkward, uncomfortable, as though he was still getting used to them.

"Lose them recently?" the detective asked.

"No."

"Born like it?" Mulroney blurted out. Collins shot her a look that said *could you be any less subtle*?

Tyreese sighed. "No. I lost them in the war. Afghanistan."

"What branch?" said Collins, but before Tyreese could answer, the detective saw the outline of a body lying on the landing just a couple of steps up. He could tell by its shape that it was the body of a woman, but her head was facing away from him so he couldn't see who it was. But there was no mistaking the wooden spike driven through her chest, he could see the pointed end of it protruding eight inches out of her back, a dead hand clasped around the shaft. What looked like unusually dark blood had congealed into a pool around the exit wound. Ribbons of it hung over the lip of the landing like disgusting stalactites.

"Get your hands in the air," Collins screamed, pulling his weapon and pressing it into the back of Tyreese's head. "Get on your goddamn knees. Now."

Tyreese fell forward, the weight of the pistol pushing him off balance, dropping to his knees next to the body of Elizabeth Finch.

"Where's the girl?" Collins demanded. He held Tyreese's hands together above his head with his left hand while his right beckoned back to Mulroney for her cuffs. She slapped them into his hands. Collins jerked Tyreese's arms behind his back and fastened first one of his wrists then the other with the cuffs.

"Just look at her," Tyreese said calmly.

"I said, where's the fucking girl?"

"She's in my apartment. She's..."

*Again with the pause, still not a good sign*, Collins thought.

Tyreese continued, "Birdy's okay, I think. I don't know."

"What the fuck do you mean you 'think'?" Collins demanded.

"She's alive. Just... she's not talking. Please, just take a look at the body."

"What apartment is she in?" Collins demanded.

"Thirty-three."

"Go check on the girl," Collins said. Mulroney nodded and jogged up the stairs past the body.

"Please," Tyreese's voice was almost a whisper now which somehow made his plea seem more insistent. "Look at her face. Just look at her face."

"Get up." Collins didn't wait for him to comply, he grabbed the cuffs and heaved. Jesus the guy was heavy. He helped Tyreese steady himself. "Okay, walk."

Tyreese stepped up onto the landing and skirted the body. He stopped at the bottom of the next flight of stairs up.

"Come on, move."

Tyreese refused to budge.

"If I have to ask you again, it'll be with the butt of my pistol. Move."

Tyreese held his ground, squared his shoulders.

"For Christ's sake." Collins moved the flashlight from his right hand to his left so he could reach his holstered pistol, sweeping the light across the landing... and the corpse.

"Mary mother of God!" he hissed when he saw the frozen features of the dead woman. Could he even call what he saw human? The dead woman's eyes were wide open and staring sightlessly. Even in death they reflected back the light from his flashlight with a yellowish tone. Her face was bloody and dirty and distorted. Collins registered the two puckered puncture wounds on the side of her slender white throat. But it was her jaw, distended, wide open, with two sets of vicious midnight-black fangs and serrated teeth that would give him nightmares for the rest of his life, he was sure of it. A large pool of black ooze had seeped from between the dead woman's lips. Collins moved up a step so he could face Tyreese.

"Is that Elizabeth Finch?" he asked.

"Yes."

"Did you do this?"

"No."

"You know who did?"

"Yes..."

*There's another one of those damn pauses.*

"Who?"

Before Tyreese could answer, Mulroney's voice interrupted them from somewhere beyond the door leading to the third floor corridor.

"Boss, you better get up here. We got a problem."

"No shit," he said. He forced his eyes to leave the horror on the ground. "Move it," he told Tyreese, urging the handcuffed man upward.

•••

Mulroney sat next to Birdy on a loveseat that had seen better days. The girl's hands were clasped tightly together and wedged between her knees. Mulroney's hand was resting on the girl's back. She was speaking softly to the child but Birdy showed no sign of even knowing there was anyone else in the room with her; she just stared straight ahead.

Collins maneuvered Tyreese over to the window. "Don't move," he ordered, placing the flat of his hand against the man's chest, then turned his attention back to Birdy. He walked to the sofa and knelt down directly in front of her, his knees creaking and complaining. "Hi Annabelle," he said gently. "Do you remember me?"

Birdy blinked, but that was her only response.

"Can you tell me what happened?" the detective coaxed, a little more insistently.

Birdy gave a low moan and the detective saw her knees press even tighter together. Her hands were beginning to grow pale from lack of blood flow.

"It's okay," Collins continued, "take your time." He placed a hand gently against her knee.

Birdy's head tilted up enough that her eyes met his. She whispered something so low he couldn't make the words out.

"What did you say, sweetheart?" He leaned in closer. Tears glistened at the edges of the kid's eyes, and Collins felt his heart, hardened by almost twenty-two years on the job, buckle just a little.

"I didn't kill my mom," she said. "I didn't."

"We know you didn't, sweetheart."

"I didn't kill her. I killed a monster."

Collins felt the words like they'd been carved into a two-by-four and he'd been hit in the face with it. He glanced across at Mulroney. He could see the shock in her eyes.

"What? What did you just say?" he asked.

When Birdy met his gaze this time, there were tears on her cheeks, but her eyes were filled with steely certainty. "She *wasn't* my mom. She was a monster. She wanted to kill us. I had to... had to kill her."

"*Jee*-zus!" Mulroney hissed, pulling her arm away from the kid.

Understandable, thought Collins, after all, she hadn't seen the face of the body on the stairs. He looked over to where Tyreese still stood patiently waiting where he'd been ordered to wait. The man met his gaze unfalteringly. Collins stood and walked over to join him.

"Tell me what happened," he said.

Tyreese paused for a moment as though he were considering whether he should, but Collins realized he was probably just taking a moment to get his thoughts together before he spoke.

By the time Tyreese finished telling his story, Collins found himself sitting on the edge of a nearby table, his legs weak, his mind unsure of how to process what he had just been told.

"Jesus," he whispered. On any other day of any other week, he would have nodded politely and called for the boys in the white coats to come and take this guy to psych, because what he said was so obviously crazy. But... Between the disappearing bodies, the silent apartments, and the empty streets, Collins knew this was no ordinary day. And then there was Elizabeth Finch, or what had once been Elizabeth Finch. His mind was still trying to process what he had seen, but he was as sure as he could be that whatever had caused her to change so horribly, it had not been her daughter, Birdy, or the man standing before him in handcuffs who had caused it to happen.

"Toss me your cuff keys," Collins said to Mulroney.

Mulroney just about jumped to her feet. "Oh come on. You don't actually believe this BS, do you?" she said. "I mean, come on."

"Toss me your goddamn keys," the detective ordered.

Mulroney grudgingly complied.

"If he so much as blinks at me the wrong way I'm going to light his ass up," Mulroney said, her fingers touching the butt of her service pistol.

"Sure," said Collins, "but in the meantime, we've still got a suspicious death to process, so why don't you get us some backup?"

Mulroney grumbled something beneath her breath, walked to the kitchen and began talking into her radio. She reappeared thirty seconds later, a look of frustration on her face. "No dice, radio's still down. This weather's screwing with everything," she said. "I'll try the radio in the car."

Mulroney was halfway to the front door when Collins called out, "Hey, Mulroney, hold up."

"Boss?"

Collins prided himself on being a good detective, one of the best if he was truly honest with himself. He closed more cases than were left open, and he did that by being methodical, particular. But he also knew when to listen to his instincts, and right now his gut was telling him they needed to stick together.

"I got a better idea, let's all go."

Mulroney looked at him like he'd just suggested they all take a long hot shower together.

"Humor me," he said then turned his attention to Birdy. He knelt back down in front of her. "Hey sweetheart, you want to take a ride with us?"

She looked up. "Is Tyreese coming?" she whispered.

"Wouldn't have it any other way," the detective replied, glancing in Tyreese's direction.

"Okay," the kid said. She stood up.

"You go with Officer Mulroney then." He turned his attention back to Tyreese, "And you, you're with me."

•••

"Annabelle, why don't you stay on this side of me, okay?" Detective Collins stood between the girl and the body of the creature that had once been her mother, positioning the beam of his flashlight to ensure the body remained hidden within the shadows.

"That's not my mom," Birdy insisted almost nonchalantly, her chin thrust up as the group walked past Elizabeth Finch's body. But despite her bravado, the girl refused to look at the remains of her mother.

"I know sweetheart."

"Birdy, my name is Birdy," the girl insisted.

"Sure thing, Anna... Birdy."

Mulroney's flashlight momentarily illuminated the face of the dead woman, long enough for the cop to finally see what Collins had seen. Mulroney jumped like she'd been stung, her light swinging back to the body. "Holy shit. Holy. Fucking. Sh—"

"For Christ's sake Mulroney!" Collins snapped.

"But... *Jesus Christ* do you see her mouth? The teeth?"

"Yeah, I see it just fine, and so does the kid, so why don't you do your goddamn job and help me get these people out of here?"

"I told you it wasn't my mom," Birdy repeated when they started moving again. She quickly took the steps down to the next landing.

"Stay close, Birdy," the detective said. Tyreese had to edge his way down the stairs sideways, taking each step one at a time, and the detective didn't want anyone getting ahead of them. Not because he was concerned that he might be wrong about Tyreese, but because there might be more of whatever Elizabeth Finch had become. He hadn't said it aloud but he knew by the look of relief Tyreese had given him when he suggested they all leave that he was thinking the same thing too. And although the detective was having a hard time believing it, if Tyreese's account of the events on the stairwell were to be believed, their pistols would not be much help to them.

Detective Collins doubted that was the case. Over the course of his career he'd fired his weapon a total of three times in the line of duty, and each time he'd hit what he was aiming at. Twice the perp on the receiving end had never gotten back up.

Beyond the stairwell the wind had grown unrulier, rising in powerful gusts that rattled windows and shook the walls, the rain pummeled the sides of the building so hard it sounded to Collins like someone was outside throwing handfuls of gravel at it. The building creaked and groaned in the onslaught, driving home how unnaturally quiet it was in here.

At the bottom of the stairwell, Mulroney and Birdy waited while Collins and Tyreese caught up. Collins pushed open the door to the foyer, holding it for the rest to exit. The hinges shrieked as the door swung closed. All four froze, the sound like fingernails down a chalkboard.

"The car's parked right outside. Single file now," Collins whispered.

They were almost in the middle of the foyer when Mulroney, at the head of the line, let out a gasp of surprise. Her flashlight illuminated a shape that had been hidden by the darkness: an old woman standing silently in front of the double doors leading out to the street. She stared out through the glass, seemingly enthralled by the storm ripping through the night.

Collins guessed the woman must be in her late seventies, with thinning gray hair and loose folds of pale, wrinkled skin. Her spine was slightly crooked, stooped with age. She stood perfectly still, her back to the room, staring out through the glass into the night beyond. She wore a single pink slipper on her left foot and was dressed only in an ancient brown nightgown that had helped merge her with the shadows. This close, Collins could clearly make out the individual vertebrae of her spine against the thin material of the nightgown.

Mulroney glanced back at the detective. He nodded and the female officer took a step closer to the woman, her pistol half out of its holster.

"Ma'am? I'm a police officer, are you okay?"

The old woman's head tilted slightly at the sound of Mulroney's words but she showed no other sign of being aware of their presence.

Mulroney raised her voice, "Ma'am, can you step back from the door please." She moved in slightly closer to the woman.

"It's beautiful, isn't it?" The woman's voice froze the cop in her tracks. Collins felt an icy fist of fear squeeze his spine. He had expected a feeble voice relative to the woman's obviously advanced years. Instead what he heard was a strong, powerful tone, ringing with a sibilant edge that sounded as though the woman had a very slight lisp.

"Ma'am?" Mulroney took another step closer.

"The night, I never noticed before, just how *beautiful* it is. Now I see it as it truly is." The old woman sounded wistful, as though she was critiquing a wonderful piece of art that she had passed by many times before but whose beauty she only now recognized. The woman straightened suddenly, her crooked spine snapping back into place with six audible pops until she stood perfectly upright, shoulders pushed back. She gave a sinuous shake that started at her shoulders and migrated south to her feet, then the old woman let out a long sigh of contentment.

"That's *so* much better." She turned, slowly, her eyes blazing yellow, mouth open wide in a predatory smile that exposed the upper and lower fangs, black and glistening, protruding from her jaw. Her tongue, red and shot-through with thick black veins, caressed each tooth slowly, almost obscenely.

"What in God's good—" Mulroney's words were cut short as the old woman suddenly ran toward her, screeching like a banshee.

The cops' training overcame their shock, even as the woman launched herself into the air. Both drew their weapons and began firing almost simultaneously. Muzzle flashes turned the darkness into a flip-book movie of frozen moments that, while only lasting a matter of seconds, seemed to stretch to far more.

The old woman staggered backward under the hail of bullets, as round after round tore at her body, sending pieces of flesh flying through the air. The foyer suddenly filled with the sound of the storm beyond as the glass doors behind the old woman shattered into a million pieces.

Collins's mind registered all of this, even as he recognized that no blood flew from the impact of his bullets, despite using hollow-point rounds. Each hit knocked the woman backward, staggering her, until finally, the woman fell, collapsing to the floor even as the final round left Collins's weapon.

He ejected the empty magazine and slammed in a fresh one, then leveled the pistol at the old woman's prone body.

Mulroney edged closer to the old woman, her pistol aimed at center of mass.

*She has to be dead*, Collins thought, there was simply no way anyone... any *thing*... could have survived that fusillade.

195

"Let's go," Collins yelled, his ears ringing from the shootout. Birdy was cowering behind Tyreese, who had wrapped a big arm around her shoulder and placed his body between the kid and the crazy old woman.

"Birdy, you go fi—"

The dead woman sat up.

"You have *got* to be shitting me," Mulroney hissed.

Then the dead woman got to her feet.

"Get back to the apartment," Collins yelled at Tyreese as the woman stepped in front of the shattered exit, her bullet-riddled nightgown billowing in the wind roaring through the empty door frame.

Tyreese swept Birdy up in his arms and began to move as quickly as his prosthetic legs would allow back to the stairwell.

Collins turned his focus to the old woman just as Mulroney opened fire again, hitting the woman several times in the head and chest, dropping her to one knee. By the time Collins had made it to his partner's side, she had emptied the rest of her second magazine into the old woman, pushing her back.

"Let's move," Collins ordered, grabbing the cop's shoulder and swinging her around, pushing her in the direction of the stairwell. "Back up to the apartment." He could see the shock in Mulroney's eyes, the utter disbelief at what had just happened. "Move!" he yelled again as the old woman, who should be dead twice over by now, pushed herself to her feet again. The two cops sprinted to the stairwell and flung open the door. Tyreese and Birdy were halfway between the first and second floor landing.

"Keep going," Collins yelled, turning to look back through the shatterproof window in the door. Collins yelped in fear as the old woman's face suddenly appeared against the glass, spittle dribbling between her fangs. Collins ran, chasing after Mulroney, who was taking the stairs two at a time.

Collins's breath came in puffs; He was too damn old and out of shape for this shit even when the perps were human, let alone some godforsaken monster from hell.

Tyreese and Birdy had already made it to the second floor landing.

"Run!" Birdy screamed. "Run!"

Mulroney's upper torso appeared over the bars of the second floor landing guardrail above Collins, her pistol pointed at the door behind him.

*Don't look back*, Collins ordered himself. *Don't even think about it.* He ducked instinctively as the crack of Mulroney's 9mm pistol exploded through the confines of the stairwell.

"Come on, Boss. For fuck's sake, run."

Collins could not remember ever hearing terror in a cop's voice before, but he heard it now, could see it each time the swinging beam of his flashlight illuminated Mulroney's face as he pounded up the stairs to the landing where she covered him.

Mulroney's weapon fired again, and he heard the old woman screech behind him.

*Jesus! Oh, Jesus!*

Collins reached Mulroney, didn't even pause to catch his breath before starting up the next set of stairs toward where the kid and Tyreese waited. Glancing back down the way he had come he saw the old woman edging up the steps toward them. She was almost nonchalant about her approach, as though she thought she could sweep in any time she wanted. Half-way to the third floor landing, he pulled his own weapon and turned to cover Mulroney's retreat.

"Mulroney, get your ass up here," he yelled to her.

Mulroney turned and began to climb the stairs toward him. Her left foot was on the third step when the door to the second level opened and a yellow-eyed Hispanic man darted through the gap, grabbed Mulroney by the hair with both hands and dragged her back through the doorway. Mulroney didn't even have a chance to scream before she disappeared into the darkness and the door slammed shut.

"No!" Collins yelled. He dove toward the door but before he could reach it, the old woman was there in front of him, blocking his path.

Someone somewhere was screaming. It could have been

Mulroney, it could have been Birdy. Collins could not decide. Hell! For all he knew it could have been him. And that would be okay, because this was madness, utter madness.

The old woman edged up a step toward Collins. From above him, the detective heard Birdy's and Tyreese's voices screaming at him, urging him to turn around and run. He hesitated for a moment then fired two quick shots into the old woman's face, sending her spinning away into the corner. He reached a hand toward the handle of the door leading to the second floor... and stopped.

The detective glanced at the old woman. Even now she was struggling to her feet again. He looked at the door where his partner had disappeared as quickly as the prey of a trapdoor spider. Then Collins was backing his way up the stairs again. After three steps he turned and raced to join Tyreese and Birdy on the third floor landing.

If either of them had asked why he had not tried to rescue his partner, he would have told them it was because Birdy needed him more, that his partner was gone and that there was nothing he could have done to save her.

But that was a lie. The truth was that he was terrified.

# CHAPTER TWENTY-TWO

Detective Collins pushed Tyreese and Birdy through the apartment's doorway, then stumbled in after them, slamming the door shut behind him. He tried to slip the deadbolt across but his hands shook too much. Instead, he leaned his full weight against the door.

"Birdy," he gasped, panting from the exertion and adrenalin flooding his system, "can you... close... the... lock... please." He was surprised at how calm his voice sounded. It was odd because at that moment he wasn't even sure he was a part of this reality. Birdy jogged to him and slid the deadbolt into place. To Collins it felt as though he was somewhere else, watching the events unfold around him. A buffer of calmness surrounded his mind. It was shock more than likely, he realized, of course, helping his mind cope with what had just happened. He leaned over and placed his hands on his knees—*Jesus! They snatched Mulroney right off the stairs*—he took a deep breath and held it for a moment... then exhaled—*that could have been me... oh fuck. Fuck!*—took another breath and exhaled slowly.

After the fifth breath he felt his heart begin to slow, panic was gradually replaced with a throbbing ache in his knees and arms. Oddly enough though, the headache he'd had for the past couple of days had vanished. Tyreese was standing near him; Collins could see his mouth moving but he couldn't make out the words. "What?" Collins said, and then realized he could barely hear his own voice over the high-pitched ringing in his ears.

Tyreese stepped in closer to the detective, placed his hand on Collins's shoulder and said slowly and presumably loudly, "Are you hurt?"

It was going to take a while for the effects of the gunfire on Collins's unprotected ears to subside, but after a quick self-assessment, the detective gave Tyreese a thumbs up. "I'll live," he said, then, "We need to barricade the front door."

Tyreese agreed, nodding his head in the direction of the living room.

The detective followed Tyreese.

Birdy stood in the kitchen gulping a glass of water, watching the men. She seemed to be the calmest of all three of them, but her eyes were still wide and unblinking.

"Grab hold," said Tyreese, as he bent over and slipped his hands under the far end of the sofa. Collins did the same at his end, and together they lifted the sofa, manhandling it down the corridor. They placed it close to the door, then Tyreese tilted it up on its side and leaned it against the door.

"That should buy us some time," Tyreese said.

Both men headed back into the kitchen. Collins checked his pockets for his cell phone but could not find it. The last memory he had of it was when he had checked his messages in the car. He'd either left it there or lost it when he had fought his way back up here. "Do you have a land line?" he asked, moving his lower jaw left to right to try and clear the last of the discomfort in his ears.

Tyreese shook his head no. "But my cell phone's over by the coffee pot," he said.

Collins disconnected Tyreese's phone from the charger and dialed the number for the precinct front desk from memory. The phone rang and rang for almost two minutes. Nobody picked up. He mumbled an expletive, thought for a second, then dialed nine-one-one.

A woman's recorded voice answered, "All lines are currently engaged. Please stay on the line and we will—" The call abruptly disconnected. Collins tried the number again and this time all he got was a busy signal. That meant the phone systems were either malfunctioning or overwhelmed, but what about his unanswered call to the precinct? Sure, they had been shorthanded for the past few days. When you factored in the mother of all storms sitting over their heads, he mused, and a city that was in a general state of emergency, your resources were going to be stretched *pretty* thin... He let the thought trail off as a new, far more sinister idea took its place. *Maybe* those things in the hallway were just the tip of the iceberg. *Maybe* they had spread throughout the city, or even farther. The idea made him physically shiver. If that was what had happened, then they were on their own and in much deeper shit than he had imagined.

"What do we do now?" Birdy asked Collins.

That, as Collins's dad would have said, was the sixty-four-thousand-dollar question. "For now," he answered, "I think we stay put here, at least until we can find out exactly what's wrong with those... people."

"Those 'people' are *vampires*," said Tyreese, his tone of voice disconcertingly matter-of-fact. "I would have thought that was pretty goddamn obvious by now. How else do you explain the teeth, or their invulnerability to your bullets? *Shit*! Birdy killed her... she killed the creature on the stairwell with a *stake*? A freaking stake!"

The detective shook his head. "That's ridiculous. There has to be another explanation than... *vampires*, for Christ's sake."

"Like what?" asked Birdy.

"Like, maybe it's a disease or a bio weapon or something. I don't know. I just *know* it can't be vampires. It *can't* be vampires!" By the time he reached the last words he was almost shouting them.

"Maybe it's a virus. You know, like in the Walking Dead," said Birdy.

Now it was Tyreese's turn to look confused. "The walking what?"

"It's a TV show," said the detective. "About zombies." He thought he saw a flicker of a smile on Birdy's face at the fact that he knew the reference. "What? I watch TV." He smiled back. He liked the idea of having gone up in the kid's estimation.

"Yeah, well this ain't a TV show," said Tyreese.

"Don't forget the cops that were attacked in the apartments behind us," said Birdy.

"What? What cops?" Collins asked, shocked at what he had just heard.

Tyreese looked at Birdy, then back to the detective. "We thought you knew."

Collins shook his head and repeated, "What cops?"

"Earlier this evening some of your guys showed up a street over. Birdy, in one of her not-so-bright moments, went to take a look.

Birdy cut in, "There were cop cars and a SWAT van."

"Jesus Christ." Collins leaned against the wall for support while the information sank in. He turned to face Birdy. "Did you speak with any of the cops?"

Birdy shook her head. "There weren't any. Just their cars."

Collins looked taken aback. "No one? You're absolutely sure?"

Birdy nodded. "There was shooting... and screams. But when I got there, there was no one."

Rain thrummed against the windows. From somewhere distant, the dull rumble of thunder vibrated the glass in the living room window.

"So, what do we do now?" asked Birdy.

*The logical thing*, Collins thought, *would be to try and make another run for the car, but if the building's overrun with more of those... those...* things—his mind would not allow him to say the V word—*then there's no guarantee we would make it, so we'd have to—*

"Shit! Ah, shit!" Collins felt his heart sink.

"What?" Tyreese growled.

"The car keys. Mulroney drove us here. She had the car keys and she's..." he allowed the sentence to fade away. "I don't suppose either of you have a car we could use?" he asked.

Birdy shook her head solemnly.

"Not much use for one," said Tyreese.

"Great, just great," said Collins. "So, we stay here, until

morning at least. Hope those things don't notice us." He picked up Tyreese's cell phone and dialed the number for the station again but when he put the phone to his ear all he heard was dead air. There wasn't even a dial tone now. He hung up and tried again with the same result. Collins looked at his watch. It was just after eleven at night. He took his pistol from its holster, popped the magazine out and checked how many rounds he had left. He placed the weapon on the table, then fished out another two full magazines and a Taser. He laid them next to the pistol.

"So we stay here then," Collins said finally. "Wait it out, keep trying the phone until we reach someone that can help us. If we can't reach anyone, we wait until morning and then I'll go for help."

Tyreese shook his head. "Bad move."

"Why?"

"Because as far as we know, we're surrounded and outmanned. It's not going to take those things long to figure out where we are and come looking for us."

Collins stared blankly at Tyreese.

"They're smart," the big black man said. "You heard the old woman in the lobby. She was aware of us. She talked to us. Whatever they are, they're still able to think like us, and she was waiting down there to make sure we didn't get out of the building. Think about it. The old woman herded us back up here. She could have grabbed any of us if she *really* wanted to, instead they just took Mulroney. If they'd wanted to take all of us, they would have."

"That's ridiculous," said Collins.

"No," said Birdy. She stepped around from the kitchen. "The one on the stairwell, the one that used to be my mom, she tried to use it against me. Tried to get me to come down to her. And I would have gone, too, if it hadn't have been for Tyreese."

"You're saying they want to keep us here?"

Birdy nodded and Tyreese raised his eyebrows to confirm that that was exactly what they thought.

"That's just... just..." he was running out of adjectives to use in his defense. "Whatever! Leaving is out of the question. We stay here until dawn and if, and only if, I reestablish a line of communication with the emergency services, we'll talk about walking out of here. But until then, we wait. Am I understood?"

Birdy shrugged, pulled a chair out from under the kitchen table and sat down. She folded her arms and laid her head against them, but she didn't close her eyes. She watched the two men stare at each other.

"Not like I have much of a choice," Tyreese grumbled.

"Exactly. So, how about some food?" Collins said.

Tyreese looked at Birdy. She watched him with her big eyes, her face unreadable.

"Hungry?" he asked her.

Birdy nodded.

"I'll fix us some sandwiches," Tyreese said.

•••

"You ever heard of a slow earthquake?" said Tyreese, after the three survivors had eaten their sandwiches.

Collins shook his head, no. "Is that like the not-so-bright brother of a regular earthquake?" Collins joked.

Tyreese ignored the cop's poor attempt at humor.

"No, a slow earthquake is a quake that can go on for days or even months. Thing is, you don't even realize it's happening, but your world is breaking apart right under your feet, right under your nose. It's just as destructive as a regular quake, more so sometimes, but you don't know it's happening until it's just too late."

"So what's that got to do with this?"

Tyreese pondered the question for a moment or two, gathering his thoughts before speaking. "That's what I think's been happening; this slow, steady accumulation of destructive energy that's been building up for the last few days, maybe longer. It's gone unnoticed for most of that time, but at some point all hell is gonna break loose and the end result, well, it's gonna be devastating. The West Coast is not going to be safe with this storm hitting us. Emergency services are going to be stretched to breaking point, communication services are going to be intermittent, if they stay up at all, and the people are all going to be nicely contained in their homes. Easy pickings for those... those *vampires*."

"So it's sorta like the story about the frog slowly boiling in the saucepan of water; he just doesn't know how hot it really is until he's toast?" said Collins.

"Right. Everything's okay, everything is normal, just a *little* warm... until it isn't."

"Then we're dead," said Collins.

"Yes," Tyreese nodded his head in agreement. "Then everyone's dead."

•••

Birdy's eyes flickered open. She was curled up on the only chair in Tyreese's living room, her head laid against its padded armrest. She vaguely remembered Tyreese picking her up from the kitchen table where she had fallen asleep and carrying her here. A sound—she wasn't quite sure what had caused it—had snapped her from sleep.

Birdy listened. There was the quiet breathing of Detective Collins and Tyreese. Both men, exhausted, were asleep at the kitchen table; Detective Collins, head tilted back and snoring gently in his chair, Tyreese, his arms folded on the table, head resting on them.

Beyond the apartment walls, rain still drummed against the building, now such a continual background noise, Birdy barely registered it.

But neither of those sounds were responsible for having woken her. Birdy eased herself into an upright position and unfolded her legs from beneath her. She stood up, her calves cramping a little from being in one position for too long, then stretched—

*Tink!*

Birdy froze. There it was again; a sharp, but barely discernible noise that sounded like water dripping into a metal sink, except it had come from the other side of the living room, from the hallway leading up to the front door. She looked over at the kitchen sink to see if the faucet was leaking. It didn't look like it was. She cocked her head to one side, straining to listen for the sound again so she could identify exactly where it was coming from. A few minutes passed and Birdy began to think she had imagined it, but then...

*Tink!*

*Definitely from the hallway*, Birdy thought. She looked over at the two sleeping men, considered waking one of them, but then thought better of it, at least until she knew what was making the noise. She walked across the living room and leaned her head around the corner of the wall to the corridor; it was empty. The loveseat still leaned against the door. The door was still bolted and... something small and metallic glittered on the tiled floor of the entryway. She knelt down and picked it up; it was a small, short screw. There was a second and a third just a few feet away. She was quite sure they hadn't been there earlier, so where had they—

Birdy squeaked in surprise and jumped backward as something fell from the ceiling and clattered to a stop at her feet. It took her a second or so to recognize the white 12-inch by 12-inch piece of metal as the cover for a ceiling vent.

"Birdy?" Detective Collins's worried, still-sleepy voice reached her from the kitchen just as she looked up at the ceiling. Where the vent cover should have been there was now only the exposed opening of the ductwork.

She gasped as two golden orbs appeared in the black space. Something began to ooze out of the vent. First fingers reached down and gripped the ceiling on either side of the vent, then a grossly distorted head forced itself through the space.

Birdy heard Tyreese yelling her name as the two men scrambled to locate her in the tiny apartment, but she was frozen in place. A scream had lodged midway up her throat, unable to pass the sudden stricture created by the terror that squeezed her in its ever-tightening grip.

The *thing* in the air vent was almost halfway out now, using grossly elongated fingers to lever itself down. The squashed face, vaguely familiar to the terrified girl, began to fill out like a deflated football slowly pumped full of air. Then the shoulders and upper torso oozed from the ducting. Birdy saw a belly button, then hips... then the remainder of the creature popped free of the air vent and dropped to the floor, its legs swinging beneath it as it fell so it landed with almost perfect cat-like agility on both feet with an odd squelch like mud thrown against a wall. It waited for a few moments, yellow eyes rooting Birdy to the spot, as its body began to return to its normal humanoid shape.

Finally, she recognized the creature before her. It was Julio, sweet little Julio. The kid lived on the ground floor with his mom, just like Birdy. He was maybe eight, maybe nine, the kid was so skinny it was hard to tell. The few times they had talked he had told her his mom homeschooled him, but Birdy thought that maybe that wasn't true. Birdy didn't know how or why but she got the impression that his mom just didn't care enough about her child to send him to school. The kid always seemed so terribly sad, and Birdy had tried in her own childish way to befriend him.

Julio remained crouched in the corridor, his naked skin covered in a thin sheen of liquid that glistened like sweat, but was more of a goo. His body looked even more emaciated than she remembered, folds of skin hung limply from his body, and every bone within it looked broken, as though he had fallen from a great height instead of the eight or so feet from ceiling to floor.

"Julio?" she whispered.

The broken creature did not respond, instead he began to shiver as though he were frozen. Then his body began to rattle like glass marbles shaken in a mason jar.

"Jesus Christ on a fucking bike!" Collins exclaimed, as he and Tyreese rounded the corner into the corridor.

The sound of Collins's voice partially broke the spell that held Birdy, and her legs finally returned to her control. She began to back away but was still unable to tear her eyes away from Julio. Then, even as she stared wide-eyed at the boy, his bones began to snap back into place with audible pops. The goo that covered his skin began to seep back into his body, filling out muscles and tissue and sinew as it was absorbed.

Birdy felt Tyreese's hands clamp on each of her shoulders and pull her quickly backward until he had placed himself between the creature and her.

"How did *that* get in here?" the detective demanded. He was standing alongside Tyreese now, his voice a disbelieving hiss.

"Through the vent," Birdy said, her voice wavering, as she watched through the gap between the two men. "He... it... Julio came through the air conditioning vent."

Birdy saw Collins glance up at the vent. It was no more than a foot square. Birdy could almost hear the detective's brain stalling as he tried to figure out how the boy had managed to get through that impossible space.

The goo over Julio's body continued to soak into his skin, and his bones cracked and popped like freshly cut wood on a fire as his limbs mended. It was an insanity-inducing nightmare, yet not one of the three humans in the hall could tear their eyes away from the morbidly fascinating spectacle.

"Jesus! It stinks," said Collins, blocking his nose with the crook of his elbow. The corridor was filled with the stench of swamp mud, rottenness.

"Birdy, cover your ears," said Tyreese. He reached into the back of his pants waistband, pulled out the pistol she had brought to him and shot Julio once directly between the eyes.

Julio's head snapped backward, a hole the size of Birdy's fist blown momentarily through his skull, but a second later, the hole began to fill in.

"Where the fuck did you get that from?" Collins demanded, his eyes never leaving the injured boy.

Tyreese ignored the question and shot Julio again, this time in the chest where his heart should have been. The bullet blew a fist-sized hole in the boy's chest, but the boy was merely staggered by the impact.

Julio's mouth opened to reveal black teeth and a set of fangs...

he leapt straight at Tyreese.

•••

Tyreese spat an expletive, automatically throwing his hands up to protect himself as he stepped back. He backed hard into Birdy, sending her sprawling to the floor. Then he was yelling in pain as the vampire child landed on his chest and latched on like a crazed cat, its fingers digging deep into his shoulder and chest. Tyreese felt like he had been stabbed by hot knives, the pain so intense his own mouth refused to open and let out the scream that erupted from him. The boy's mouth opened inhumanly wide and it dipped its head down toward Tyreese's exposed throat, as Tyreese fought to bring his arms up and push the creature off him.

Collins dove forward, driving his forearm under the vampire's chin, forcing its head backward just as the jaws snapped shut with a sharp crack. He fastened his arm tighter around the thing's neck, securing it in a headlock.

"Got it?" Tyreese managed to blurt out between his clenched teeth.

"Yes... I think... Fuck! Do it," Collins yelled as the vampire struggled in his grip. It was wriggling so much he felt like he was wrestling with a shark.

Tyreese, his face contorted with pain, began to pry the talons from his flesh. The child vampire was unbelievably strong, but he was stronger. One after the other, the bloody talons came out from Tyreese's muscles and flesh until, finally, he had freed one of the vampire's hands. Tyreese gripped the boy's hand around the wrist. For some reason, he had expected the creature's flesh to be cold, freezing, but instead it felt uncannily hot, like he was holding his hand above a stove burner. He began to pry the other hand off. The pain was awful as the three-inch-long talons slid out from where they had embedded deep into his chest muscle. Finally, they slipped free and Tyreese seized the creature's other wrist in his meaty hands, Collins's chokehold ensuring it could not escape. The creature thrashed in the detective's grip while its jaws snapped at Tyreese, dark red mucous-like goo flying from its mouth as its teeth clacked together on empty air.

Tyreese could see sweat popping on Collin's forehead. The detective was having a hard time holding on to the boy. Tyreese felt blood trickling over his chest and left arm. His own strength was dwindling rapidly, too. They had to do something with this nightmare right *now*.

"On three..." Tyreese grunted, nodding toward the front door. "Then we make a run for the kitchen." He looked over his shoulder, Birdy was up on her feet, a graze above her left eye from where she had collided with the wall. "Get to the kitchen," Tyreese yelled at her. He didn't have time to see if she had complied, the creature's struggles only seemed to be growing stronger while he and Collins were getting weaker by the second.

"One. Two. *Three!*" He flung the vampire's arms away from him and stepped back out of reach. Collins, far more agile than Tyreese would ever have thought a man his size could be, rotated in place like an Olympic shot putter gearing up to throw, swinging the struggling vampire by its throat, then launched the thing that had once been a human child down the hall toward the front door.

Neither man stopped to check whether their maneuver had worked as they both scrambled to get to the kitchen, but a satisfying thud confirmed it had.

•••

Birdy was in the kitchen already, backed into a corner between the window and a cupboard. Collins thought she had his pistol in her hand but quickly recognized it was a Taser. He grabbed it from her and checked to make sure the safety was off, his breath was coming in shallow bursts, his heart thumped loudly in his ears and his vision was swimming like he was under water. He held the Taser out at arm's length, trying to focus his vision beyond his shaking hands.

Tyreese had grabbed a large Chef's knife from a block on the counter and he stood next to the detective, the knife held out in front of him.

There was no sound from the corridor.

"You okay?" Tyreese asked.

"Fine. I'm fine," said Collins, not sure if the words were to reassure Tyreese or himself. He was, of course, far from fine. His entire world had just been disassembled in front of him and reassembled into this... this *insanity*. There could be no doubt now that whatever was happening here could not be put down to some kind of virus or biological attack. This was something utterly outside the realm of humanity's doing. What he had just seen... it was impossible. Impossible!

Collins looked over at Tyreese. Blood stained the big black man's shirt at both shoulders and across his belly where the little bastard had sunk its talons into him. A horrible thought occurred to Collins, one he did not want to even consider: what if whatever was wrong with the kid was contagious? He'd seen enough TV shows to know that if you got bit by a zombie, you became one, right? Did the same apply to vampires?

"What do we do?" asked Tyreese, his voice low.

Collins heard nervousness in the man's voice for the first time since all of this shit had started coming down, and that did not make him feel any better. "We wait for it, right here," he said.

"Not much of a plan," Tyreese whispered back to him, with the slightest hint of humor.

"Best I could come up with under the circumstances." Collins's mind began going back over all the old B-movies he'd watched when he was a kid. Count Dracula, werewolves, zombies. They were all make-believe, but they had all also drawn from the same mythos, so maybe there was a common denominator that they could use to their advantage. Tyreese had said that Birdy had used the sharp end of his broken cane to stake her mother. It had undoubtedly killed Birdy's mom, and he had already proven that his pistol was as good as useless. He cast his eyes around the apartment looking for anything that they might be able to fashion into some kind of an effective weapon to use against the vampire—*There, I've said it*, his inner voice whispered, *vampire. I'm stuck in an apartment fighting a fucking vampire.*

The only wooden thing he could quickly lay hands on was the kitchen table and the four chairs that went with it. Everything else was either plastic or metal. They could use the legs of the chairs, but they would have to be broken apart first and then they would have to sharpen them before they would be of any use. He didn't think that the thing in the corridor was going to wait around for them to do that.

"Christ!" he whispered. *Listen to yourself, you're talking like this is real.* There would be time for analyzing the situation later, if there was a later. Right now, he needed to maintain full situational awareness because unless that little *bastard* had disappeared back up into the air vent, then it was still lurking back there, in the corridor.

As if it had read his mind—*And for all I know*, Collins thought, *it might just be able to*—a scuffling sound came from the corridor. To Collins it sounded like someone smacking the flat of their hand against the wall. Was it trying to lure them to it, because that sure as shit wasn't going to happen.

"No way! No goddamn way," Tyreese exclaimed, almost yelling.

Collins followed Tyreese's stare.

The vampire's head, gold eyes glinting in the apartment's meager light, had appeared around the corner of the room about halfway up the wall. The rest of the body followed as the vampire crawled across the wall near the ceiling like a giant white spider. Collins had no idea how it was doing it, but it was sticking to the wall. *Maybe it's using the same talons it used on Tyreese*, he thought, but there was no sign of any kind of damage to the wall. No, it was sticking to it somehow.

From behind him, Collins heard Birdy begin to cry. Long, deep sobs, interspersed with the girl's gulping attempts to pull in air.

*Jesus, hasn't she gone through enough already?* Collins felt an overwhelming surge of anger at the total injustice the universe had decided to hand down to the three of them, but in particular Birdy.

Julio scuttled across the living room wall, pulling himself hand over hand as if the wall were made of ice, then crossed into the kitchen.

Collins took a step forward and to the side, shielding Birdy, the Taser extended toward the creature that was now less than six feet away from where he stood.

"When I shoot it, grab Birdy," Collins said over his shoulder. "Grab her and make a run for it."

"No," said Tyreese, "we don't stand a chance out there."

"You don't stand a chance in here, either," Collins yelled, his eyes were filling with tears, not of fear but of pure, unadulterated anger. "Just grab her and—"

Julio jumped from the wall toward the Formica countertop.

Collins flinched, his finger squeezing the Taser's trigger, and it fired, sending two darts attached by leads across the space between him and the vampire in less than a second. The darts struck the vampire in the meat of its upper leg and just above its hip. There was a crackling sound as the Taser discharged 50,000 Volts into the vampire's body.

The effect was immediate, surprising, and devastating. The vampire crashed into the cupboards on the wall above the counter and fell hard to the floor, smoke rising from the two darts embedded in its body.

Collins stepped closer, afraid that the wires connecting the darts to the Taser might be torn free the thing was thrashing so much. The vampire screeched a high-pitched wail of pain, its hands and legs whipping wildly through the air, slamming against the cupboards, its head jerking up and down as it thrashed against the floor. One leg connected with the detective's right shin and he yelled out in revulsion at the creature's touch. His leg buckled, and he almost went down, but he felt Tyreese's hands on his arm, supporting him. Collins's hastily assembled plan had been that he would give Tyreese and Birdy a chance to get out of the apartment, buy them enough time that they could make a Hail Mary run into the storm, instead, it looked as though they had stumbled across a new way to destroy these creatures.

Both men stood side by side watching in fascinated horror as the vampire child continued to convulse and smoke. Eventually, the boy-vampire's screams subsided to a moan, its thrashing growing less and less violent with each beat of Collins's heart.

"Ah, Jesus," the detective said, as blood the color of shadows began to flow from the convulsing kid's nose and bubble up from its mouth, but still he refused to release the trigger of the Taser. *It's either him or us*; that was what it boiled down to. Within seconds, a pool of the blood had begun to spread across the floor moving out in an arc.

The kid's back arched one final time and then moved no more. It was as if the boy had suddenly been petrified; his body was rigid, his terrible jaws open wide in a silent scream of agony. One arm cocked above his head, the other frozen as it reached toward the two men.

Collins finally released the Taser's trigger. He kept his finger on the trigger guard, ready to activate the weapon again if the vampire looked like it was going to recover. But after a few minutes had passed in stunned silence, the boy's body had not moved.

"Is... is he dead?" Birdy's voice from beside Collins startled him back to reality.

"Yes, I think he is," Collins said.

"Good," Birdy said, with a vehemence that he should not have been surprised at but nevertheless was.

The apartment stank of blood and scorched flesh.

"Well that sure as hell wasn't in the movies," said Tyreese, quietly.

"No shit," said Collins, prodding the vampire's corpse with the tip of his boot.

•••

Ten minutes later, Birdy, Tyreese, and Detective Collins were still gathered around Julio's still-smoking body. The pool of black goo had stopped leaking from his wounds soon after the boy died. The blood had already begun to congeal and crust over. Here and there across the dead boy's body, thin, translucent pieces of skin, blackened around the edges like diseased leaves, had begun to flake away, peeling up from the epidermis.

"It almost looks like scales," said the detective, prying some of the skin loose with the tip of his pen.

"Now do you believe us?" Birdy asked Collins, gazing down at him with pleading eyes.

The detective did not look at her, he simply reached out his hand and placed it gently against the middle of her shoulder. "Yes, Birdy, I believe you."

The three of them had gathered around the corpse, at first to ensure that it would not simply get back up again, but after the first few minutes it became obvious that Julio was well and truly dead, and their concern had been replaced by a morbid curiosity.

"So, now we know two things that can kill them," Tyreese said. "You got any more charges for that thing?" He nodded at the Taser the detective still held in his right hand.

Collins shook his head. "I only ever carry one cartridge," he said, "but..." he paused as he popped what looked like a printer cartridge off the front of the weapon then held the Taser in front of his face. He pulled the trigger. A white lightning bolt of electricity crackled between two metal studs at the front. Collins smiled darkly. "I can still use it as a regular stun gun. Good for fifty or so uses. So even if it doesn't have as dramatic an effect as the darts, it'll give them a nasty surprise."

Tyreese nodded his approval. "We need to get out of here," he said flatly.

"I agree," said Collins, all resistance to the idea having evaporated. "So, how do we do it? And where do we go?"

Tyreese thought for a moment. "We've got to assume this outbreak or whatever you want to call it isn't localized to just this building or the area. It didn't just come out of nowhere, it's been a slow buildup, which means it's been spreading gradually, which also means it's probably spread much farther than we think. We need to get out of the city, head somewhere where there won't be as many people."

Collins walked across the living room to the window. He

pulled back the blinds and looked outside. The streets were awash with water. The city's storm drains were either blocked or unable to cope with the constant downpour from the storm. It didn't matter anyway; the result was the same, all the roads lay under almost a foot or more of water.

"Roads are completely flooded," Collins said. "No chance of us making it on foot. We need a vehicle."

"You're absolutely sure you don't have the keys to your car?" Tyreese asked again.

"Like I said earlier, Mulroney drove us here," Collins said, sounding irritated. "She had the keys."

Tyreese scowled and nodded.

Collins pulled out a chair from the kitchen table and sat down. "There has to be another way to find a vehicle. What about neighbors?"

"They keep themselves to themselves. I never bother them; they never bother me."

Birdy was hovering near the refrigerator. Now she joined Collins at the table, pulled out a chair and sat. "What about the cops?" she asked.

"What cops?" Collins questioned.

"The ones I told you about, the ones that were shooting. They left their cars open and those twirly lights on top were working." She made a swirling gesture above her head with the index finger of her right hand. "We could use one of them, couldn't we?"

Tyreese moved to the table and leaned against it. "Would the vehicles have keys in them?" he asked the detective who was now sitting upright in his chair. The paleness of the detective's face had been replaced with a bright red flush.

"Maybe. Depends on how fast they got hit. But they're not going to be of much use to us over there. We still have the same problem we had when we tried to leave earlier. Those things are going to be waiting for us."

"Yeah, but this time we have your Taser, we know that can kill them."

"Well, that remains to be seen. I'd say the best we should hope for is that I might be able to disable them long enough for us to make a run for it," said Collins.

Tyreese nodded. "And I can grab my stake from Birdy's... from the dead vampire in the stairwell."

The two men regarded each other across the table.

"It gives us a fighting chance," said Detective Collins, smiling grimly.

"That's all I ever needed," said Tyreese, returning the smile. "Next question is where do we go?"

"We have to assume that this whole area is infected, so we need to find someone in authority—military, police, fire—anyone that we can get this info to. 'Cause this outbreak needs to be contained fast."

"And we need photos," said Birdy. "Or they aren't going to believe us."

"Good idea," The detective said. "Use the cell phone."

Birdy got to her feet, took Tyreese's cell phone from the counter, walked over to Julio's body and began taking pictures.

With Birdy out of earshot, Tyreese leaned in closer to Collins and whispered, "But what if it's worse already, what if whatever this is has taken the city? What do we do then?"

"We need to plan to get away from the most densely populated areas." The detective considered the problem for a moment. "I've got a brother, we don't talk much, but he's reliable. Lives in a town about sixty miles west of Las Vegas called Waterrock. We can head there. There's enough empty desert between here and Las Vegas, the chances of this having spread that far should be slim to none."

"You hope," said Tyreese, grimly.

"Yeah, I hope."

"But that still leaves us with the problem of figuring out how we're going to get there," said Tyreese, leaning back into his chair.

"I have a plane," said Collins nonchalantly.

"You have a what?" Tyreese looked confused.

"An aircraft, a plane." Collins mimicked the action of a plane

217

taking off with the flat of his hand. "I always wanted to be a pilot, so when I got out of school I joined the Air Force. Didn't make the grade for fighter pilot school, eyes weren't up to it, but I still learned to fly light aircraft. I've got a plane. It'll fit the three of us."

Tyreese looked unconvinced. "Where is it?"

"Burbank. It's stored at a buddy's hangar at Bob Hope Airport."

"And you can fly us out of here in this weather?" said Tyreese.

Collins paused for a moment, considering the question, then nodded.

Tyreese allowed a smile to crease his lips. "That still leaves us with the problem of getting to the airport. We still need a vehicle."

There were a few more moments of silence between the two men, then Collins spoke. "I'm going to need you to stay here and watch over Birdy."

Tyreese's smile disappeared. "No, absolutely not. We all need to go together."

The detective shook his head adamantly. "It'd be stupid to risk us all."

"What would be stupid would be one person trying to make it down those stairs when we know what's waiting for us."

Collins drew in a deep breath. "You'll only slow me down."

"Bull. Shit. I didn't hear you complaining when I saved your ass out in the stairwell."

•••

Across the kitchen, Birdy pretended she could not hear the two men arguing in whispers between themselves. As she continued to listen she became aware of a fuse that had been burning inside her— a slow burning fuse that had run its course. It had reached the emotional explosive at the center of her. She was a human pipe bomb, packed tightly with shards of pain, jagged pieces of hurt and sadness, all encased in a shell of vengeance. It would be a slow but terrible explosion if she did not find some way to defuse it.

"I'll go," she said, her voice trembling.

218

The two men continued to argue, oblivious to the emotional chain reaction taking place just feet from them.

"I'll go," Birdy said again, this time loud enough that both men stopped and looked at her. She stood up from the table. "I'll go get a car."

"Don't be stupid," said Tyreese, "You can't go out there alone. You won't last five minutes on your own."

"I did just fine earlier," Birdy said, matter-of-factly.

Collins must have sensed some kind of a change in her because his eyes narrowed. "You don't even know how to drive a car," he said, then added with a quizzical tilt of his head, "Do you?"

Birdy shook her head, no she did not.

"Well then," the detective continued, "there's nothing more to be said. I'm going."

"No," Tyreese said firmly. "If you do this on your own you're going to put all of us in danger."

And with that, the two men were back to their argument, dismissing the girl as though she were not even there.

Neither man noticed Birdy as she slipped past them and headed to the living room. She pulled back the blinds, then opened the window. The rain was falling in sheets, she could actually see the waves of droplets in the air as the gusting wind caught the rain and blew it across the street.

Birdy raised a leg up onto the windowsill, then turned and grabbed the wooden frame for support as she ducked her head back into the living room. "Hey! I'm going," she called across the room.

Both men's heads turned simultaneously, both with almost identical looks of confusion, then shock.

"Jesus, kid! Get back inside," said Collins pushing his bulk up off the chair and heading toward Birdy. Tyreese was just a step behind him.

"Meet you downstairs," Birdy said as she pulled her hoodie over her head and climbed out onto the ledge.

By the time the two men had made it halfway across the living room, Birdy was already gone.

# CHAPTER TWENTY-THREE

Birdy shimmied out onto the two-inch ledge below the window. She reached for the drainpipe to her left and felt her fingers slip on its wet surface. If she had not had a tight grip of the window frame she would have fallen, that was for sure. She silently chided herself.

The storm lashed the side of the apartment so hard that rain bounced off the stucco and stung the skin of her face. The gutters were full to overflowing, mini-waterfalls cascading down to form a growing lake in the forecourt below.

She carefully let go of the window and pulled herself out onto the pipe. Her sneakers slipped once, twice, before she finally found some traction, the treads no match for the water-covered stucco. She was already halfway down to the next floor when she heard Collins's voice from above.

"Jesus Christ, girl. Get your sorry ass back up here right now," he yelled.

She stole a quick glance and saw the detective's face staring down at her. Tyreese's bulk was squeezed in next to him, an arm outstretched toward her. She ignored him and turned her attention back to her climb.

"Birdy... come back here right now." This time it was Tyreese urging her to return, but by the time she reached the second floor, the constant whoosh of the wind gusting past her and the thrum of rain drowned out the men's voices completely.

Thirty seconds later and Birdy's sneakers touched what should have been solid ground. Instead she felt cold water lap over the edge of her shoes and instantly chill her feet. The water was at least three inches deep this close to the apartment building. It looked like oil in the darkness, thick black oil.

Birdy released the drainpipe and crouched down in the shadows. The water quickly soaked into her jeans, turning them into cold clammy hands that lay heavily against her skin. A single streetlight near the security gate was still lit, but it flickered intermittently as if it felt it too should join its countless dead brethren. It gave off just enough light for Birdy to see across the forecourt to the road. Beyond that was the gully. At the other end of the gully, through driving rain so thick it seemed to hang in the air like a fog, she saw the flashing blue, red, and white lights of the cop cars.

*This is good*, she thought. Birdy knew enough about cars to know that if the lights were still working then the batteries must still be okay which meant that the car would start. *Right*?

*There's only one way to find out*, she thought. Birdy allowed herself two more seconds to make sure nothing waited in the semi-darkness for her, then took off toward the exit gate. There was no need to look back to check if Tyreese and the cop were still watching; she could feel their eyes following her.

Her feet kicked up big plumes of water that quickly soaked the front of her jeans as she ran. *God, it's cold.* She ignored the discomfort and angled for the gate. When she reached it she paused, her hands resting against the cold metal of the handle. She quickly checked the street, then pulled the gate open and stepped out onto the pavement.

A vicious gust of wind lashed at her, whipping up droplets of water from the lake that had once been a road. The wind forced itself through the leafless trees making their limbs creak and groan in protest, their branches rustle and whisper to each other. Another gust threw Birdy off balance for a second and she had to stop and lean into the wind or risk being blown flat. She held the hood of her jacket to her head. The material was sodden and felt heavy against her skull, her ears chilled as the wind tore past her.

When the wind finally moved on Birdy stepped out onto the road, except it was impossible to tell *where* the road actually was. Where it *had* been might just as well be a river. Neither the pavement nor the road were visible beneath the inches of rainwater gathered on its surface, a broad expanse that stretched from the apartments across from Birdy to where she stood.

She began working from memory, judging where the pavement should be in relation to the security gate she had just stepped through. Even so, it came as a surprise when her left foot finally stepped off the submerged curb and freezing water rose another six inches or so up her leg. "Ugh!" she spat, stepping fully into the water, shocked at the power she felt pushing against her as the water swept by. Moving across the road as quickly as she could, legs sloshing through the water, Birdy located the opposite sidewalk, then headed up a short way to the gully entrance.

At the farthest end of the gully, lights from the cop cars still danced their silent tango with the darkness. Birdy followed the same route she had taken earlier, sticking to the shadows, but this time she was accompanied by a new companion: fear. It burned in her mind, turning every shadow, every sound, into a vampire. She tried to manage her breathing but the farther along the gully she got, the more her anxiety grew.

Birdy stopped a few feet from the police car that was parked closest to the gully. She breathed in three deep lungfuls of air, while she tried to slow the frantic beating of her heart. Her body temperature was dropping quickly, her hands were already shaking with the cold and she had to fight the urge to throw her arms around herself as the cold bit into her with every snarling gust of wind.

*Keep moving, Birdy*, she heard Bryanna, her instructor, tell her. *Keep the blood pumping fast and your body will look after you.*

The door to the closest cop car was still open. Birdy ran at a crouch to it and slipped into the driver's seat. The leather gave off what sounded like the grossest fart she had ever heard as her wet clothes scooted across it and a little giggle escaped her lips despite the tension she still felt.

The interior of the cop car was a mess of computer screens, knobs and switches, none of which she knew how to use. A thick line of congealed blood was splashed across one computer screen in the center console. Birdy leaned to the right and quickly scanned the steering column until she found the ignition switch. She frowned, there was no key. There must be some kind of switch that allowed the emergency lights to run even if the engine was off. *What if all the cars are like this one?* she thought. *Then what do I do*? She pushed the thought from her mind, slid out of the driver's seat and crouched for a moment on the pavement as she assessed which of the other cars was closest.

She decided on the one about forty feet ahead of her. It was parked in the opposite direction to the cop car she was sheltering in, at a forty-five-degree angle to the curb, its hood pointing at the center of the road. That meant the driver's door was on the opposite side to this one, away from the sidewalk, facing a tall privet hedge emerging out of the shadows.

She took off running toward the car before she could change her mind. Her feet slipped halfway across the road, her shoes losing all traction. She tried to regain her balance but managed only to fall face first into the water covering the road. She was now thoroughly soaked through, and as she pushed herself back to her feet, spitting out dirty water, she saw she had badly skinned the palm of her left hand when she hit the concrete. She winced as she pulled a couple of pieces of gravel from the meat of her hand, the blood turning pink as the rain diluted it and washed it down her fingers. She sniffed back a couple of tears. *It hurt*. There would be time to deal with it once Tyreese and the detective were in the car with her, she told herself. *Focus*.

She was a little more careful now, walking rather than trying to run. When she got to the hood of the cop car she stopped and stared deep into the shadows that lay between it and the hedgerow that acted as a perimeter fence for the looming apartment building beyond. Stare as much as she liked, the flashing lights of the emergency vehicles were never going to allow her eyes time to acclimate. She had to move. *Now.*

Birdy jogged around the front of the police cruiser. The driver's door was closed. She grasped the cold door handle and pulled it open. The interior light came on. She didn't bother getting into the seat this time, instead she placed her hands flat on the seat and leaned in, keeping her feet outside the car.

The key was missing from this car too. "Fuck!" she said loudly, then unconsciously covered her mouth as she felt her face flush at the profanity. Her mother would have slapped her upside the head if she had heard her curse like that.

"Hey! Little girl. What are you doing?"

Birdy screamed and jumped at the sound of a man's voice. Her head collided with the car's roof and she tumbled into the driver's seat. Instinctively, she reached for the door and pulled it shut behind her. She flipped herself around and, all flailing legs and arms, pushed herself across the center console into the shotgun seat until her back was up against the cold metal of the passenger door. To Birdy, her breathing sounded like one of those old-timey steam trains, coming out in rapid, short chuffs. Her hands gripped the leather of the seat as she tried to find some way to make herself even smaller. Through the windshield she could just barely make out the shadowy outline of a figure, a little lighter than the darkness that surrounded it, but still too vague for her to identify exactly who it was.

The shape moved in closer and Birdy recognized the uniform of a mailman. She exhaled a lungful of air and felt her body relax a little. It was a *mailman*! He was standing just on the other side of the passenger door, his upper torso and face obscured by the roof of the car.

"You know, it's not safe for a kid like you to be out on the streets alone," the mailman said, his voice rumbling, so low it was almost a growl. She heard the sound of his hands pressing against the roof of the cruiser as he leaned his body against it. "Come on out of there, I'll take you somewhere safe."

Birdy couldn't identify what it was exactly, but this did not feel right at all. Why was this stranger just standing there in the dark? Why not come down into the meager light cast by the interior bulbs of the car? And why was he standing so his upper torso was obscured, almost as though he did not want to be seen?

"I... I... don't..." Birdy stumbled over her words, looking to buy herself a little time as she looked frantically around the interior of the police cruiser for something that she might be able to use as a weapon.

A hard rapping on the glass of the rear driver's-side window made Birdy jump. This time she screamed so loudly she thought she might just pee her pants. She levitated from the seat. An involuntary whimper escaped from between her lips as she saw a pair of yellow eyes staring at her through the window.

The eyes belonged to a young woman, maybe just a couple of years older than Birdy. She was crouched at the rear window, staring in at Birdy. The girl's lips were smeared with dried blood that stretched up to both her cheeks. The girl smiled at Birdy. Not a good smile—more like the smile of a fox that has a rabbit cornered in its burrow with no way out. The vampire's lips pulled back, exposing black fangs. She made a slow over-exaggerated snapping bite at the window, both sets of fangs cracking together like metallic jaws. Then she smiled, lasciviously.

"Come on out, come on out, come on out and play with us," the girl crooned in a childlike singsong voice. In a single blur of motion, she vaulted from beside the passenger window onto the hood of the car. She landed with a barely perceptible tremble of the vehicle as though she weighed little more than a feather.

The rain pummeled the girl, her close-cut afro glistened with collected droplets of water. Her clothes, torn in multiple places across her chest and arms hung in tatters, exposing the pallid skin beneath. The faint lines of what looked like half-healed welts ran down her chest, matching the tears in her shirt. On the girl's neck Birdy could see two puncture marks, puckered and angry looking.

Birdy glanced across the interior of the cruiser toward the

driver's side window. The mailman was peering in through the window. Birdy guessed he was in his early thirties, his shoulder-length blond hair matched the goatee outlining his lower jaw. He would have been cute when he was alive, Birdy thought, but not now. Not at all now. The two hot coals that were his eyes watched her through the glass with a coldness that was the opposite of the creature that sat on the hood of the vehicle. This one was cruel, Birdy decided. This one would hurt her, would want to make her suffer.

The mailman reached for the door handle.

Birdy exploded across the driver's seat and pushed the door lock just as she heard the vampire's fingers touch the handle. She flipped around and made sure the passenger door was locked too.

"Leave me alone!" she screamed, as loud as she could, her voice screechy and high with panic. Frantically she ran options through her mind: she was stuck in here with no way to start the cop car and no way to get past the two vampires that waited for her outside. She checked the steering column again but the ignition was still empty. She looked on the floor mat in case the keys had maybe fallen there, pulled down the visor, checked in the center console but found nothing. And there wasn't anything in the car she could use for a weapon, not even a flashlight.

She was trapped.

Birdy's head spun to the driver's side window at the sound of fingernails drumming against the glass. The blond vampire's face was pressed close to it, smiling a terrible smile. His fangs, barely hidden behind his lips, flashed at her when he spoke. "Come on out, little girl. We'll make it fast. Cross my heart and hope you die." He grinned at her hungrily but when Birdy did not comply, he slammed a fist against the window and yelled, "Open the fucking door!"

The female vampire moved off the hood. She stood outside the passenger door, her long fingernails tapping against the glass. Her jaw had distended three inches, the skin of her cheeks stretching almost to the point of breaking. Black drool dripped from the corner of her mouth as she slowly opened and closed her mouth, her tongue flicking in and out between her lips. The vampire drew her distended tongue slowly up the glass of the window, leaving a trail of dark saliva behind.

Birdy screamed as the driver's side window suddenly exploded, showering her with pieces of glass. Wind and rain engulfed the interior of the cop car, momentarily blinding her as she tried to clamber into the back seat, but a security screen separating the rear of the car from the front stopped her.

The blond vampire lunged through the shattered window, grabbing at Birdy as she tried to make herself as small as possible.

Birdy screamed again as she felt the mailman's hand close like a snare around her ankle. She twisted and saw his torso halfway through the broken window, his right hand locked around her ankle, jaw agape, eyes wild with furious anticipation.

In her peripheral vision, Birdy saw the female vampire disappear as she jumped onto the roof of the car then down behind the blond cop. The girl tried to force herself through the window too, blood lust driving her to claw at the other vampire in her desire to reach Birdy. The blond vampire turned slightly, opened his jaws wide then snapped them down hard on the female vampire's face, tearing away a chunk of flesh that he swallowed in two quick gulps like a hungry lizard. The girl screamed in pain, fluid—the same viscous shit Birdy had seen covering Julio in the apartment—spurted from the wound in her face. She flung her hands to the wound, screamed in outrage, and vanished below the door panel, mewling like a scolded child. Birdy could hear her cries of pain even above the roar of the storm.

Before the blond vampire's attention could return to her, Birdy pulled back her free leg and drove her foot hard into the creature's jaw. The vampire's head juddered at the impact, but besides that, all Birdy's kick did was draw the monster's full attention back to her. It reached another hand into the car, grabbed Birdy's other ankle and began pulling her out of the car through the window.

Birdy's scream of terror was cut short by a bleat of pain as her head cracked hard against the car's center console. Her hands blindly felt for anything that she could hold onto, but the rain had already soaked the interior of the car and her fingers slipped off every surface as the vampire dragged her inch by inch out of the vehicle.

Her hands closed around the edge of the car's window frame. She locked her fingers on it for a second and tried with all her rapidly dwindling strength to pull free of the monster's grip. But the vampire seemed indefatigable, and with a violent tug he wrenched her free of the door.

Birdy tried to scream again but pain and fear and panic had her now. A shrill whistling screech was all she managed, her cries caught by the wind and scattered into the night. Her head bumped hard against the door panel and she felt the skin of her left cheek split open, and the warm flow of blood across her face. Then she was completely outside, the rain hammering her body.

If Birdy had hit the ground on any other night than this, she would surely have suffered a concussion at best and at worst a fractured skull, or even death. Tonight the six inches or more of rainwater covering the pavement acted as enough of a cushion that only her breath was knocked from her lungs as she splashed down into the dirty water.

Birdy tried to breathe in but felt water flood her nose and mouth. The acid burn of bile flowed up Birdy's throat as she inhaled the dirty water into her lungs. She coughed, spat, gagged, then threw up over her chest, even as the vampire dragged her toward the waiting shadows of the nearby hedgerow. Through her rain-blurred vision she saw the other vampire, the girl, sitting cross-legged like a child in the water nearby, her hand still clenched to the now-almost-healed wound in her cheek. She stared at Birdy, her youthful face contorted into a strange mixture of desire, hunger, and anger. Whether the last was directed at her or her captor, Birdy did not know. Nor did she care, not anymore.

The girl vampire pushed herself to her feet, her eyes fixed on Birdy with a ravenous stare, drool dripping from her mouth as she edged forward.

*They're going to eat me*, Birdy realized. But first they were going to make her suffer.

Birdy closed her eyes.

She registered the sound first, a wet *thunk*, like a bag of flour hitting the ground then she opened her eyes just in time to see the young girl's head spinning through the night toward her. The decapitated head landed with a splash in the water near her, rolled a couple of times, then stopped against the lip of the sidewalk gutter, the lower jaw flopping uselessly back and forth as the water gushed down the road, buffeting the head like it was a soccer ball. The vampire's eyes continued to glow for a second longer, then dimmed and faded to nothing.

The blond vampire dropped Birdy's legs and began to turn at the sound of his comrade's headless body splashing onto the water-covered road. If he had been paying less attention to moving Birdy, he might have had time to deal with the shadowy figure as it rushed at him from the hedgerow. He might even have avoided the ax as it arced through the air, catching what little light there was on the edge of its blade before it sank into the top of his skull and split his head almost in two.

Birdy winced as bloody gore splattered across her face. The blond vampire's body toppled over and splashed to the ground next to her, the ax—she could see it was a bright red fire ax—still lodged in the dead vampire's skull.

Birdy's eyes followed the blurry silhouette of the vampire killer as it moved closer to her, gradually materializing into the form of a large black woman with the kindest face Birdy thought she'd ever seen. The woman knelt next to her and gently reached out a hand to touch Birdy's bleeding cheek.

The last thing Birdy registered before she lost consciousness was the woman's voice, "Genie's got you now, baby girl. And she ain't gonna let *nothing* happen to you."

# CHAPTER TWENTY-FOUR

Birdy drifted on the wind of the night.

At least, that's what it felt like to her; floating through the rain and the darkness. She felt sick, smelled vomit; hers probably, but she could not be certain. She tasted its acid burn in her mouth and down the back of her throat. And her head hurt. The further she rose toward full consciousness the more pain she became aware of, so she fought consciousness for a while, but its pull became too strong, inexorably dragging her back toward reality.

Birdy opened her eyes. She blinked away the raindrops that immediately ran into them. Her head swam almost as much as her vision but after a few seconds of disorientation it cleared enough that she was able to see the face of a woman... the woman with the ax, she realized as her memory returned. She was in the woman's arms, being carried... where? Panic swept through her, and she began to struggle weakly.

"Hey now, quit that," the woman whispered. "You trying to get us both killed?"

Birdy continued to try and free herself from the woman's grasp. "Put me down," she croaked.

"I said quit it, or by God I'll leave you right here for them monsters to get you, you hear me?"

Birdy stopped struggling.

"That's better. I ain't gonna hurt you. Look..." The woman nodded ahead of them. Birdy allowed her eyes to follow the direction of the woman's nod. Through the curtain of rain, its emergency lights flashing so brightly it felt like knives plunging into her skull, Birdy saw the big SWAT truck parked in front of the apartment entrance. She tilted her head in the opposite direction and saw the police cruiser she'd been trapped in about thirty feet behind them, the outlines of the two vampires' bodies sprawled next to it. The fire ax, she noted, was missing from the head of the blond vampire.

This woman—she had told Birdy her name just before she blacked out... It was... Jenny? No, *Genie*. That was what the woman had said her name was. *Genie*. Like the one in Aladdin that lived in a lamp.

She couldn't have been unconscious for too long. Birdy's mind struggled to comprehend what had just happened. This woman had saved her from the two vampires, rescued her from certain death. She remembered that much. If Genie hadn't come along she would have ended up just like her mom. Birdy shivered, not because of how cold the air was, but because the thought of becoming like *them* was soul freezing.

"Thank you," Birdy mumbled. Her lips felt dry, despite the constant rain.

Genie continued to whisper to the girl in her arms. "You ain't got to thank me for nothing. It's the Christian thing to do. You're pretty banged up, baby girl. But don't worry, Genie's got you. We gonna get you outta here, okay?"

"Put me down now, please," Birdy said; a request this time, not a demand.

Genie stopped and lowered the girl onto unsteady feet outside the door to the SWAT van.

"Got to be quick," Genie said. "There are more of those monsters 'round here. I can smell 'em." The woman's eyes darted left and right, constantly searching the shadows while the ax swung back and forth, pendulum-like in her left hand. Birdy realized Genie must have had it in her hand even while she had been carrying her.

"Get in," Genie said, and then waited for Birdy to climb into the SWAT van. It smelled of sweat and something else that Birdy could not place, something sweet and metallic. But at least it was dry. Her eyes automatically dropped to the steering column and she felt a small glimmer of victory when she saw the keys dangling from the ignition. Birdy slumped down into the passenger seat. Her vision swam for a second then cleared.

"If you'd been ten minutes later, I would've been gone already," said Genie, as she eased her substantial bulk up into the driver's seat. She slid the door closed behind her. "Time for you and me to get our butts out of this godforsaken city." She turned the ignition and the engine roared instantly to life.

"Tyreese...," Birdy managed to mumble, her world edging toward black again. "Have to get Tyreese..." The words sounded slurred to her, almost like she was drunk, and Birdy wondered absentmindedly whether maybe she had hit her head so hard she had a concussion. She shook her head gently, and instantly regretted it as a bolt of pain shot across her forehead and down the back of her neck. But her vision cleared a bit, enough that she could see the look of surprise on Genie's face.

"Tyreese? He your boyfriend?"

Birdy managed to screw her face into a position that conveyed how disgusting that idea was to her fifteen-year-old mind. "Friend. We have to get him and the cop."

"Cop?" The word came out of Genie's mouth like she'd tasted something sour. Then she let out a long sigh, "Okay, tell me where they are."

Birdy pointed in the direction of the apartment. "That way," she said.

# CHAPTER TWENTY-FIVE

Tyreese pushed himself to his feet, placed the palms of his hands flat against the windowpane and yelled, "Holy shit! She did it. She really did it."

Collins was sitting on one of the rickety chairs at the kitchen table, his elbows resting on the tabletop, his head in his hands. Tyreese had waited at the window the entire time after Birdy left.

"What?" Collins exclaimed, jumping to his feet. He joined a grinning Tyreese at the window and looked where he was pointing. The unmistakable twin beams of powerful headlights sliced through the narrow gully Birdy had taken.

"Open the window," said Collins, even as he reached and popped the latch himself. Cold air and rain blew in but it brought with it the unmistakable deep growl of a powerful engine.

"Christ! She really did it," said the cop, the look of disbelief on his face in complete contrast to the awe his voice carried.

Tyreese would have liked to have said that he had believed the tenacious kid was going to do it all along, but he knew that both he and the detective would have recognized it as a lie. Truth was, he had been sure Birdy was going to die horribly, she was just a kid, after all. He had just wanted to know if it happened. That was why he'd stayed here at the window this entire time. The kid had nobody left to watch over her. So, if not him, then who?

"Yes she did," said Tyreese. "She's done her part, you up for doing ours?"

A storm darker than the one raging outside passed momentarily over the detective's face at the thought of what was to come next. He breathed in deeply, held it, then released the breath in a long, slow exhalation. "Let's do this thing," he said, and began to move back toward the kitchen where he had left his Taser, pistol, and the flashlights.

The two men had fleetingly discussed how this would go down, neither really thinking that Birdy would come through. There was no way to get to the ground floor other than the still-not-functioning elevator, or one of the two stairwells. The detective had opted to try the second stairs, but Tyreese wanted the first, that was where the one weapon he knew he could use still waited, impaled in the chest of Birdy's dead mother.

"I want it back," he had told the cop. "I got nothing else."

Detective Collins had agreed, but only with the understanding that he would be on point, armed with the Taser. He had more than enough charge left in the weapon's battery, he hoped, to deal with the old woman, if she was still waiting for them. "You watch my back, and I'll take care of the rest."

Tyreese nodded.

They collected their equipment, checked that the flashlights still worked, then walked to the front door. Together they lowered the loveseat barricade and pushed it to the center of the corridor, but not so far that they could not grab it again if they needed to retreat back inside the apartment.

The detective put a finger to his lips. He leaned into the front door and placed his ear against it, listening for any sound that might give away whether some *thing* waited for them beyond it. After a minute, he turned back to Tyreese and mouthed, *Ready?*

Tyreese nodded in the affirmative.

The cop slowly pulled back the deadbolt, then unlatched the lock. Tyreese was pretty sure he saw Collins take another of those deep breaths, then the detective opened the door just a crack, his shoulder braced against it, ready to slam it shut again if anything tried to muscle its way into the apartment.

Tyreese stepped closer to Collins and placed his left hand on the older man's shoulder so he'd know he was there. The cop pulled the door open a tad wider, leaned his head and upper torso outside, then shined the beam of his flashlight into the darkness.

"Entire floor looks deserted," the cop whispered. He took a tentative step outside, playing the beam of the flashlight up and down the walls. He held the Taser at the ready as he checked every possible spot where a vampire could lie in ambush for them. Tyreese stepped out behind him and waited a few more seconds before he eased the door closed behind them. The click of the latch signaled they were on their own now. They were deep in bandit country and the only way either of them were going to live to talk about it was to keep moving.

To keep fighting.

The two men edged along the wall until they reached the first stairwell. The detective shined his flashlight through the safety glass onto the landing, then as much as he could, given the window's small size, he played the light up and down the stairwell. He reached for the door handle and pulled, cringing as the hinges complained loud enough to wake the dead. *Well, no need to worry about that,* Tyreese thought to himself, *because the bastards are already awake.*

The two men stepped quickly through the doorway. Collins pushed the door closed then leaned back against it as he moved the beam of the flashlight up and down the space of the stairwell again. There was no sign of anyone or anything.

From beyond the walls, the sound of the storm beating against the building reached their ears, but in the stairwell there was only the sound of the men's rapid breathing and the scuffing of their shoe leather against the concrete. Collins nodded toward the steps leading down. He went first, checking through the gaps of the metal handrail with each step he took.

Lizzie Finch's body still lay where it had fallen when Birdy had skewered her with the sharp end of Tyreese's cane. The body had begun to decompose, far quicker than a regular body would have, as though it was making up for lost time. The stink permeated the air.

Tyreese tried not to gag as he clasped both hands around the stake and pulled it free. It came away with a slurping noise that was quickly followed by a short hiss as gas escaped from the decomposing body. Black rivulets of fluid spilled out from the rupture in Lizzie's body and dribbled to the floor. Tyreese could not pull his eyes from the tip of the stake and the drops of black ichor that fell one-by-one from it, splashing across his boots as they hit the concrete floor.

"Come on," Collins whispered, taking Tyreese by the elbow and pulling him away from the body. "We have to keep going."

Tyreese carefully wiped the stake across the leg of his pants until none of the liquid remained.

"Tyreese? Come on." Collins was already halfway down the stairs to the next floor.

Tyreese hefted the stake in his left hand, it felt good to have something to defend himself with. He followed after the detective. His shoulder throbbed where the vampire had attacked him, and the stumps of his legs felt like someone had taken an industrial sander to them, but he did his best to ignore the pain and focus on staying alive. There would be time to heal when they were away from this place. Still, rivulets of sweat ran down his face even though the air within the stairwell was cold.

By the time the two men reached the ground floor, Collins was sure they had made it out scot-free. He leaned his shoulder against the door leading to the apartment building's foyer and looked through the window.

"What do you see?" Tyreese whispered, as he stepped off the stairs and joined the cop.

"Not a goddamn thing," Collins answered. He moved the beam of the flashlight around the foyer and then through the remains of the double doors and the pavement beyond them. A large pool of water had collected just inside the ruined doors, pushed in by the relentless wind. Pieces of the shattered glass twinkled and sparkled in the light as the beam passed over them.

"We'll wait here until we see Birdy's lights," he said. "Pointless leaving ourselves—"

Both men felt the breath freeze in their throats as from above them the sound of a door swinging open on unoiled hinges floated down the stairwell.

"Shit!" whispered Tyreese, his attention moving to the stairs, trying to see through the darkness that enveloped it.

"We move, now," said Collins, opening the door quickly, ignoring its creaking hinges. Collins stepped out into the foyer, Tyreese right behind him.

Flashlight beams crisscrossed like lightsabers as both men quickly played their lights across the room ahead of them. There was no sign of the vampire they had encountered earlier in the evening.

Through the ruined entrance of the building, the faint twinkling of oncoming headlights cut through the night moving painfully slowly up the street toward the apartments. Collins grinned at Tyreese, who allowed himself a smile in return as both men moved toward the entrance. They would meet Birdy outside of this place, the pounding rain and bone-rattling gusts of wind a welcome tradeoff to staying even a second longer in the apartment building.

"Quick as you can," said Collins, leading the way through the inch of water that had crept into the foyer. Tyreese had taken only a few steps after Collins when he sensed something was not right. This was just too easy. He stopped and slowly played his flashlight over the foyer.

"Collins!" Tyreese called out as he played the beam of his flashlight toward the stairwell back in the direction they had just come.

Collins stopped abruptly and turned to face Tyreese. "What the hell are you doing?" he hissed.

Tyreese looked over his shoulder at the cop. He said nothing but began to slowly back up, allowing his flashlight to illuminate the area around the stairwell.

"What in God's name...? Oh! *Shit!*" Tyreese heard Collins spit the words just as the detective's flashlight joined his, illuminating for a split second the four vampires waiting silently in the shadows, their bodies stuck to the walls around the stairwell exit like trapdoor spiders waiting for their unsuspecting prey. Another vampire clung to the ceiling, its eyes glowing fiercely. There were four women and a man, ranging in age from somewhere in their twenties all the way up to the old woman who had blocked their way out of this hellhole earlier. In unison, the vampires leaped from their roosts, arcing through the air toward the men, hissing and screeching in the repellent light of Tyreese's and Collins's flashlights.

"It's a trap!" Collins yelled. "Christ! They were just waiting for us." He started to turn back in the direction of the exit. "We've got to make a run—"

Collins's words stuck in his throat as the old woman they had encountered earlier made a beeline directly for him. Tyreese saw the detective bring the Taser up in a sweeping defensive ark, connecting with the exposed neck of the old woman. As it connected, Collins pulled the trigger.

The vampire convulsed as a continuous stream of high-voltage electricity ripped into her. She screeched and convulsed, smoke rising from where the Taser connected with her exposed skin. When the woman's eyes rolled back into her head, Collins pulled the Taser away and the woman crumpled to the floor. Collins took a step back from the smoking body, holding the Taser out in front of him like a knife.

A second vampire, this one a teenage girl no older than Birdy, hit the floor, opened her mouth wide to expose her fangs, then leapt to the right of the two men, disappearing into the shadows as the third and fourth vampire landed in front of the two humans. The smoldering body of their comrade lay between them. The two vampires hesitated, wary of whether the cop would be able to do the same to them.

Collins raised the Taser in front of him, waving it back and forth as though it was a sword. His gambit worked; both vampires backed up, dodging and feinting first right then left, hissing at him like scalded cats.

The fifth vampire, an obese man who must have weighed in excess of two-hundred-and-fifty pounds was not as reticent. Shirtless, his deathly-pale rolls of blood-splattered fat wobbling obscenely, he vaulted across the floor with impossible agility for a man of his bulk, barreling straight toward Tyreese. The creature's jaws hung wide, black flecks of spittle flying from between the glistening obsidian teeth, his arms thrust out ahead of him.

Tyreese set his feet wide, braced his body for the coming impact, and at the same time thrust the business end of his stake at the onrushing vampire, aiming for his heart. The vampire ran into the stake, impaling himself just below the left clavicle—missing the heart, Tyreese judged, by an inch or so. He felt the spear slide through the vampire's flesh and momentarily saw the tip appear out the creature's back. The man slid down the shaft of the stake, colliding with Tyreese. The full force of the vampire's impact knocked him backward, wrenching the weapon from his hands, sending Tyreese sprawling across the floor as his prosthetic legs failed him, buckling at the knees, as lightning bolts of pain lanced through his shoulder wound.

The impaled vampire screamed and thrashed, his legs and arms whirling. Thick black blood flew across the room splattering Tyreese, as he attempted to push himself away from the vampire toward Collins.

One of the two vampires Collins had been holding at bay now turned their attention toward Tyreese, hopping over the body of the old woman. Collins thrust the Taser at the creature... and missed, but the crackling blue bolt of electricity scared the thing enough that it backed up, giving Tyreese enough time to scramble on his hands and knees across the floor to the cop. Collins, his eyes never leaving the two creatures in front of him, held the Taser at arm's length, periodically pulling the trigger. The electrical bolt seemed to be frightening enough to the vampires that they did not want to risk attacking.

It would buy them some time.

Collins offered his free hand to Tyreese and pulled the man back to his feet. Tyreese staggered, wiping the spray of the obese man's blood from his face and eyes.

"Back up... slowly," Collins said through clenched teeth as he thrust the Taser at the two vampires again. The blue/white glow of the electrical arc cast flickering shadows across the creatures' faces, making them seem even more menacing, if that was even possible.

Tyreese looked across at the vampire he had stuck with his makeshift stake. The man's hands were clenched around the shaft of the cane and he was slowly working it free. Tyreese thought about rushing him, pulling it free and trying to finish the job but he knew that would be a mistake. The remaining vampires would be on him in a second. With a grunt of disdain that masked the lump of fear that had fixed itself in his throat, he abandoned any hope of retrieving his one weapon and instead began to edge his way toward the entryway.

Collins began to back up too. The two vampires he was holding at bay climbed over the body of their deceased comrade as they followed, but kept a respectful distance, encouraged to do so by the crackle of Collins's Taser. Each time Collins activated the Taser, the creatures stopped momentarily, snarling and spitting at the men.

"Hold on," said Tyreese as they reached the exit. The glass doorway had been shattered by Collins's and Officer Mulroney's gunfire earlier that evening, leaving behind shards of glass that jutted out of the frame like teeth. There was no way they would get through the opening without risking a severe laceration.

"Open the goddamn door," Collins ordered, his head facing the vampires but his eyes flicking to where Tyreese, his hands still slick with the blood of the fat vampire, fumbled with the door handle.

"I'm trying," Tyreese spat back, "just give me... Look out!"

The teenage girl leaped from the shadows where she had been hiding. Collins reacted just in time to keep her snapping jaws from slashing through his neck. Too late he realized it wasn't his *throat* she was going for; it was the Taser. He let out a scream of pain as the creature's mouth clamped down on his left wrist. Her teeth, like shards of glass, slicing through the material of his raincoat, jacket, and shirt with such force he thought he felt the bones in his wrist crack. The pain was unbearable but Collins refused to release the Taser. The girl's hands were fastened to his arm almost as tightly as her jaws. She began shaking her head violently from side to side like a rabid dog, tearing at his flesh, sending *his* blood flying through the air, all while pulling Collins back into the foyer and the waiting darkness. Collins screamed in agony, his fingers convulsing on the trigger of the Taser, discharging it uselessly into the air while he beat at the girl's head with his flashlight trying to dislodge her.

Seeing their chance, the two vampires Collins had been holding at bay bounded forward, then fell back again as Collins's convulsions continued to fire the Taser.

"Jesus! Fuck!" Collins screamed. "Help me, for Christ's sake, help me."

Tyreese staggered toward Collins, pulled back his arm and drove his meaty fist with sledgehammer-like power into the girl's face, collapsing her nose into a bloody mess. The creature's head flew back, dislodging her jaws from Collins's arm, but taking most of the layers of clothing with it, along with a chunk of the detective's forearm. Her left eye sailed from its socket with a wet slurping sound and spun almost comically by its optical cord a few times as she staggered backward, the detective's torn flesh dangling from her mouth.

The flashlight dropped from Collins's grip and went skittering across the floor as he clasped his uninjured hand to the wound on his wrist.

Tyreese threw a protective arm around the older man's shoulders, holding him up. "Move!" he yelled, trying to guide the cop back toward the exit.

The vampire girl, her eye still dangling from its socket, licked Collins's blood from her lips, then swallowed the piece of his forearm in two deliberate gulps. The two other vampires, emboldened by the scent of the detective's blood, advanced on the men like a pack of starving hyenas, closing in for what would now be an easy kill. And to their right, the fat man had freed himself from Tyreese's stake and was pushing himself to his feet, the black wound just above his heart oozing dark goo that trickled down his chest.

"Take it," Collins hissed, nodding at the Taser. He pulled his good hand from his bloodied forearm and tried to switch the Taser to it, but the weapon slipped through his blood-slick fingers and bounced to the floor.

"Shit!" Tyreese hissed, as the vampires surged forward again, the last-remaining threat now lying uselessly on the floor.

A deafening roar rattled the walls of the building as the room was suddenly and totally filled with a dazzling light and deafening roar. The vampires froze as they threw their hands over their eyes against the blinding white light filling the room.

Tyreese had a split second to glance over his shoulder and see the oncoming lights. He shoulder-barged Collins out of the way and the two men tumbled to the floor as the roar doubled in volume and the wall facing the street exploded into a million pieces. The vampires disappeared, replaced by the bulk of a huge tactical SWAT truck as it smashed through the entrance of the building, crushing the teenage vampire beneath its massive wheels in an explosion of black liquid, and sending the other once-human monsters cartwheeling into the back wall. The fat man was still standing, though. He cowered in the center of the room, his forearm slung across his face to protect himself from the vehicle's headlights.

The rapid crack of gunfire rose above the sound of the vehicle's engine as five shots rang out in quick succession, each bullet gouging out clods of flesh from the fat man's body, sending him spinning away. Tyreese fired a sixth and final shot that exploded half of the vampire's head. The fat man collapsed into a heap, thick black rivulets of blood flowing from the bullet wounds. But a second after the vampire hit the ground, Tyreese saw the creature's wounds were already beginning to heal.

The side door of the SWAT truck slid open and Birdy, her face bloodied and dirty, leaned out. "Run!" she yelled, her hand beckoning the two men toward her. "Run!"

Collins tried to stand, but his legs gave out and he collapsed back into the rubble that had been the building's foyer.

"Get up!" Tyreese demanded, but before Collins could even try to comply, Tyreese had slipped his hands beneath the cop's armpits and lifted him to his feet. Collins's legs seemed to have lost all their strength, and he wobbled precariously.

"Hold on to me," Tyreese said into Collins's ear, yelling to be heard over the rumble of the SWAT van's engine. The two men staggered and stumbled to the door of the truck. Tyreese all but threw Collins into the rear compartment next to Birdy then climbed inside himself, collapsing into a panting heap on the cold metal floor next to the cop.

From his position on the floor of the SWAT tuck, Tyreese saw the fat man sit upright, the damage from the fusillade of bullets he had fired at him now almost fully healed. *He sure as hell isn't going to win any beauty pageants*, Tyreese decided. The vampire's head was still a god-awful ugly mess, but even in the couple of seconds Tyreese had to view the vampire, he saw the broken skull and ribbons of flesh knitting back together again.

"It's a nightmare," Collins mumbled, from where he lay on the floor of the van. "I'm in a goddamn nightmare."

Birdy slid the door of the van closed. "Go!" she yelled and the van began to reverse out of the decimated foyer.

# CHAPTER TWENTY-SIX

"Pass me the first aid kit. There, behind the driver's seat."

Detective Phillip Collins heard the concern in Tyreese's voice despite the fact that he seemed to be talking from miles away. Right now, his world was a comfortable, reassuring blackness with only an occasional flash of orange to light the dark point in space he occupied, and remind him that he was *still* alive. He felt... disconnected from his body, detached from reality, as though the bare minimum of his personality still existed, compressed to the center of his brain; able to observe, but lacking the motivation to interact.

A ragged line of light flashed through his body. Pain—that was definitely pain. The light grew stronger, noise louder. Collins felt his mind begin to float upward, to some unseen surface, toward reality, as, nerve by nerve, his brain began to reconnect with his body.

His eyes opened.

He caught a brief glimpse of Tyreese kneeling over him, working on extracting a bandage from its protective wrapper. Birdy knelt on his left, her face painted with consternation. Collins's eyes moved, first left then right as his brain reestablished more connections. He was in the back of the SWAT van, Collins realized, and, judging by the tone of the engine and the rumble and rattle of the vehicle, they were moving.

"Who's driving?" Collins ground out; his tongue felt thick in his mouth, his lips dry as dead leaves.

"Quiet," said Tyreese, taking Collins's injured arm in his hands and winding the bandage he'd just unwrapped tightly around it.

Collins winced as pain shot up his arm.

"Who's driving this thing?" Collins demanded.

"I am." A voice, a woman's voice, drifted back to him over the roar of the engine.

"Who the hell is *that*?" Collins croaked.

"That's Genie," said Birdy. "She saved me, plus she knows how to drive."

Collins tried to sit up. He winced as the pain in his arm pulsed, once, twice.

Tyreese slipped an arm under the detective to support him, then eased him over to a metal bench running along the side of the truck.

"Thanks," said Collins, parking his ass on the cold metal seat. Tyreese remained standing, his hand holding on to a leather loop attached to the ceiling, swaying as the vehicle made its way through the stormy LA darkness.

"You okay?" Tyreese asked.

Collins nodded and gave a thumbs up. He watched Tyreese move to where Birdy sat on a bench on the opposite side of the truck. Only now that he was again in full control of his senses did he notice the kid was covered in dried blood and sported an inch-long gash on her cheek that was still oozing blood.

Tyreese set about cleaning the wound with some antiseptic wipes from the first aid kit.

"Don't think it needs stitches," he said after a second or two of inspection. "Show me your hand." Birdy extended her hand palm up, and Tyreese quickly cleaned up the grazed skin with another antibiotic wipe.

*She looks exhausted*, Collins thought, but the hint of a smile was there on her face.

"You did good, kid," Collins said as Tyreese checked the back of her head, carefully moving Birdy's hair aside to check her scalp.

The smile on Birdy's lips broadened and Collins saw a twinkle of satisfaction in the girl's eyes.

"I think you'll live," Tyreese announced finally.

Collins looked toward the front of the vehicle. All he could see was the back of the woman Birdy had called Genie, her short-cut afro and the profile of her face. He glanced down at his injured arm. A red stain had already begun to seep through the white bandage Tyreese had used to expertly dress his wound, but at least the fog filling his head was dissipating. That was both a good and a bad thing, because as his head cleared and his faculties returned to him, so did his appreciation for just how much he hurt.

"Does she know where she's going?" Collins asked, as he moved his good hand to support his damaged forearm.

"She says she does," said Tyreese.

"Is he going to turn into one of them?" Birdy asked abruptly, staring at Collins's wounded arm.

"No. I doubt it," said Tyreese, looking directly at Collins.

Truth was, Collins thought, none of them had any idea what would happen to him.

Genie's voice came from the front of the truck: "That's zombies. These things are vampires, got to suck you dry for you to become one of 'em."

"Here." Tyreese offered the cop a small bottle of water, twisting the top off for him.

Collins straightened up, gritting his teeth as pain shot through his injured arm to his elbow. He took the bottle and gulped down half of its contents. The water felt wonderful against his dry throat and parched lips. "What road is this?" he said.

"Victory," Tyreese called back, making his way toward the front of the van.

"We need to be on Sherman Way. My hangar's on the west side, away from the commercial airlines."

Tyreese tapped Genie on the shoulder.

"I heard him," she said. She slowed the truck, made a wide left, and began heading north.

•••

A couple of miles later, the truck's already sluggish movement slowed even more then ceased altogether with a squeak and hiss of brakes.

"Why've we stopped?" Collins asked, rising from the bench, cradling his injured arm. He had nodded off; lulled to sleep by the engine's growl, exhaustion, and the two pain killers Tyreese had handed him from the first aid kit. He walked to the front of the truck and stood between Genie and Tyreese. "What the...?" He squinted through the water-blurred windshield at a stretch of road blocked by an assortment of cars, vans, and trucks. Many of the vehicles' doors were open, as if the owners had simply walked away.

*Or run away. Or been dragged kicking and screaming from their cars.* Both these thoughts followed in quick succession through Collins's mind.

*But why had they left?* Collins scanned an array of switches and buttons on the truck's dashboard, found the one he wanted and flipped it. Instantly, the road ahead of the vehicle illuminated to almost daylight levels by the vehicle's multiple spotlights.

"Christ!" whispered Tyreese, leaning closer to the windshield.

Ahead, there *should* have been a bridge spanning one of the giant storm channels that crisscrossed the city. Hundreds of feet wide, the culvert was designed to move floodwater away from the city and out to the coast. But the bridge was gone, washed away by a raging torrent of water, nothing left of it now but ragged chunks of concrete and twisted metal. The rising flood had already slipped over the lip of the huge concrete culvert and was edging slowly but surely up the road, submerging the line of abandoned vehicles one-by-one.

"The storm's just too much for it," said Genie. The floodwater had already claimed several cars; their roofs were just visible. It was lapping at the tires of a Chevy just a couple of vehicles ahead of the SWAT truck.

Collins knew the LA storm drain system had been designed back in the nineteen-thirties as LA was still growing. He'd found himself wandering through some of them over the years as they were a prime dumping ground for killers to hide their victims. Those things were damn big, designed to carry millions of gallons of water an hour, but with the amount of rain that must be falling across the county right now... they just weren't capable of handling it.

"Guess that's why the cars all stopped," said Birdy, joining the adults at the front of the vehicle.

"And it's only going to get worse," said Collins. "Shit!" He thought for a moment, pulled up a mental map in his head. "We need to double back. Take Woodman north to Saticoy."

"But what if that's washed out too?" said Tyreese.

"Probability is that this is where the majority of the overspill pressure was focused, which is why the bridge failed. I doubt anything north of here is going to be affected."

Collins wished he felt as confident as he tried to sound. Truth was, every bridge south of Hansen Dam could be gone, for all he knew. And if that was true, well, then they were screwed, because there was no Plan B.

•••

They followed Woodman Street past stores and businesses, all shuttered or boarded up. Some had placed hastily stacked walls of sandbags around the entrances to their business, but that had done little to protect against the ferocity of the storm holding the city in its clutches. The brunt of the flood overflow now ran through the side streets, turning them into rivers.

"We should have stolen a boat, not a truck," said Genie, as the van pushed its way up the street. They were barely doing five miles an hour, the water reducing their traction to the point that it would be dangerous to go any faster.

Genie maneuvered the van around an abandoned Volkswagen in the middle of the road. Both its driver and front-passenger doors hung wide open, water gushing through the interior of the car.

Tyreese rose with a grunt of pain from the passenger seat and laboriously made his way to where Collins sat next to Birdy. There was a question that had been on his mind almost since the detective had suggested his plan to fly them out of the city: "Are you even going to be able to get off the ground in this weather?"

Collins considered the question, then shrugged. "Not like we have much of an option but to try," he said.

Tyreese did not like the answer, but he knew it was the truth. He'd rather take his chances flying than stay in this city a minute longer than was necessary.

"So how do you expect—"

Tyreese, Collins, and Birdy were all jerked from their seats as the SWAT van braked abruptly.

"God *damn* it," Collins hissed. His injured arm had collided with Birdy's shoulder. "What the hell are you—" The words froze in his mouth as the sound of the van's engine suddenly stopped. He was about to continue, but Genie was not listening. She was staring out her side window.

"Genie?" said Tyreese. "What's going on?"

Genie didn't answer. Instead she opened her door, letting in a gust of noisy, almost-freezing air and rain.

"Genie! Jesus! What's she doing?" Collins yelled as Genie slipped out of the truck.

Tyreese was up and moving immediately, scrambling to the front.

Genie stood just outside, one hand holding on to the door handle, staring out into the darkness that lay just beyond the pool of light of the van's headlights. She was soaked through already, but she didn't seem to notice or care.

"Genie?" Tyreese said, easing himself into the driver's seat and scooting over until he could lean in close to her. He kept his voice as low and calm as he could, "What's going on?"

For a few seconds Genie did not reply, then without turning her head, she said, "There's a child out here. I saw her when we made the turn."

"What? Where?" Tyreese struggled to try and see farther into the darkness.

"Hush!" Genie demanded, "I'm listening."

Birdy joined them, looking over Tyreese's shoulder. "What's going—" she fell silent when Tyreese put his finger to his lips.

The continual rattle of rain smashing against the floodwater was the only thing Tyreese could hear. He slid across the driver's seat and climbed down to the ground next to Genie, water almost up to his knees.

"There!" she whispered after a couple more seconds, "Hear that?"

"I can't hear a damn—" He stopped as his ears picked up the muffled sound of a child sobbing. He turned and stepped up onto the foot plate of the van, then leaned back into the cabin. "Hand me one of those," he said to Birdy, pointing over the back of the seat to a set of heavy-duty metal Pelican flashlights fixed to the wall next to her.

Birdy pulled a flashlight from its holder, reached over the back of the driver's seat and handed it to Tyreese.

Tyreese turned it on. The powerful beam cut through the rain and darkness. Tyreese played the light slowly left then right.

They had stopped next to a row of homes; small, single story affairs, their borders delineated by chain-link fences and the occasional privet hedge, their gardens and paths obscured below inches of water that lapped against the homes' front porches.

"Over there," Genie said, placing her hand on Tyreese's and guiding the beam to the front stoop of a home one house back in the direction they had come.

"I don't see anything."

"There!" Genie said, and pointed to a shape huddled on the porch.

It didn't look like a kid to Tyreese, more like some garden ornament that someone had moved out of the rain, but as he kept the light focused on the porch, he saw the top of the shape move upward and reveal the pale face of a child. Tyreese's mind finally made sense of what he was looking at: it was a kid in a raincoat, sitting on the front porch, knees brought up to their chest, her head (or his head, it was impossible for Tyreese to tell what sex the kid was from here) covered by the raincoat's hood.

There was no glow from the child's eyes. The kid was human. The first human they had seen since leaving the apartment building.

The child got to her feet, blinking nervously in the light from Tyreese's flashlight.

*Can't be more than seven, maybe eight*, Tyreese thought.

"What's going on?" Collins asked from behind Tyreese, his voice low. He felt Collins's hand on his shoulder as the man used him to lean outward to get a better look.

"There's a kid out there," said Tyreese.

"We can't leave her here," Genie said. She took a step toward the house where the kid still stood looking back at them.

"Hold on," said Tyreese, his voice carrying a firmness that stopped Genie mid-step. "Just wait for a second."

Genie turned back to face Tyreese. "I am *not* leaving her," she declared flatly.

"I'm not asking you to," said Tyreese. "We just need to think this through."

Collins exhaled a long sigh when he saw the child on the porch. "We can't hang around here all night. Is someone going to go get her... him, whatever the hell it is?"

Genie was off then, as though Collins's question had given her tacit approval to go grab the kid. She splashed through the water between the truck and the house in wide, almost comical strides.

"Genie, wait!" Tyreese called out after her. He didn't pause for Genie to stop before he too was splashing through the floodwater after her, leaving Collins and Birdy nervously watching from the driver's side door.

Tyreese caught Genie just as she reached the rusty metal gate separating the road from the path leading to the front porch. The kid stood on the wooden deck staring at them, wide-eyed.

"Wait! Would you wait just a goddamn second," Tyreese

snapped, grabbing the woman by the right shoulder to slow her. "Just slow down."

Genie flipped around to face Tyreese. "It's a *kid*," she snapped. "I'm not leaving her here."

"I'm not asking you to do anything except wait, just for a second. Okay?" Tyreese swung his flashlight back toward the porch. The kid was just standing there. He could make out the kid's face, pale and cold in the folds of the raincoat's hood; the child was terrified, he was sure.

"Hey kiddo," he called as calmly as he could, trying to keep the nervousness he felt at being so exposed out of his voice. "Your mom and dad there with you?"

The child, eyes wide, facial expression one of obvious fear, glanced first left then right, then shook her head, no.

"Is there an adult with you?"

Again a shake of the head, no.

"You all alone?" asked Genie.

Another shake of the head, no.

Genie looked at Tyreese, confused.

"Can you come down here to us, baby?" Genie asked.

A vehement shake of the head this time.

Genie started through the gate, but Tyreese held her back. "Let me," he said and gently pushed past her, following where he thought the path would be below the ebony sheen of the three or four inches of water that submerged the front garden.

The kid did not move. It was as though she was rooted to the spot, Tyreese thought as he carefully made his way the final few feet to the porch. He stopped, one foot perched on the first of two wooden steps leading up to the flat wooden deck of the porch.

"Hey, kiddo," he said, speaking gently, even as his eyes flicked left and right, "What's your name?"

The kid hesitated, then, "Stevie."

"Well, Stevie, I'm Tyreese, but you can call me Ty." He smiled. "That lady behind me," he continued, "her name is Genie."

It was impossible to see anything outside the cone of his

flashlight, the night was so damn dark, and that made Tyreese even more nervous. He beckoned to the boy again, smiling, "Come on, Stevie, we'll get you out of here. Someplace warm. You hungry?"

Stevie did not move, but this close, Tyreese could see the kid was shivering; whether it was from the cold or fear or both, he could not tell.

"Come on, kiddo, come here." He held his hands at arm's length and beckoned with his fingers.

"I can't," the boy bleated.

Tyreese took another step up toward the porch. "Why not?"

"'Cause they told me to stay here." Tears were running down Stevie's cheeks, snot trickled from his nose.

"Who's 'they' Stevie?" Tyreese asked, planting his feet firmly on the boards of the porch floor. The kid was just a few feet away now.

"Mommy and Daddy," the kid sobbed.

Tyreese was confused, "But I thought you said... Oh, shit!" Realization hit at about the same time he heard Birdy scream and Collins yell a warning.

Tyreese dove to his right, just as a shadow detached itself from the roof and swept down toward him, swinging down onto the porch. As Tyreese fell, his right leg cracked against a large concrete planter. He felt the prosthetic leg shift from its fastening, flopping uselessly in the leg of his pants, hanging there by its sleeve. He rolled out of reach of the vampire's grasping hands.

The vampire dropped to the deck, landing between the steps down to the path and where Tyreese now lay on the deck. If it had not been for her glowing yellow eyes, Tyreese would have thought the girl was still human. She looked to him to be maybe a couple of years older than Stevie. *Probably his sister*, he thought. She was dressed in a pretty, but blood-splattered dress that hung limply from her body, soaked through by the rain. The girl crouched, her arms spread wide like a linebacker trying to block any way past her. She snarled, a long guttural growl, then, lightning quick, lunged at Tyreese.

Tyreese sat up in time to throw a wild swipe at the vampire

with the heavy flashlight he held in his left hand. He missed, but the girl stepped back for a moment then dove at him again, coming in low at him, feinting to the right, then dodging to the left as she tried but failed to duck under Tyreese's clubbing swing.

The flashlight connected with the side of her skull with a satisfying *thunk* that sent her momentarily reeling sideways. She wasn't disoriented, Tyreese noted, as she almost instantly began to move back toward him.

Stevie started to scream, wailing like a tiny foghorn.

A movement from the shadows to Tyreese's left caught his attention. Something was coming up the wooden steps toward him. He swung the beam of the flashlight in that direction... illuminating Genie as she climbed the stairs. She threw her hands up to protect her eyes from the glare, then screamed as the vampire girl shifted her attention and darted at her, snarling.

Tyreese hadn't even noticed that Genie held her ax until she raised and swung it—almost reluctantly, Tyreese thought—at the girl's head. Genie's telegraphed intent allowed the girl to dodge the ax. She slipped beneath the swing and leapt back out of range.

Tyreese moved into a sitting position, his back leaning against the front wall of the house, a darkened window behind him. He pushed his back hard against the stuccoed wall of the house, then used his one good leg to slowly push himself upward, grunting with exertion as he used the wall for leverage, while simultaneously trying to point the beam of his flashlight at the girl. He heard the sound of shattering glass a millisecond after his mind registered the two arms thrusting on either side of his shoulders. They were big, masculine hands and they grabbed him firmly on each shoulder, pulling him backward through the shattered window.

"Jesus! Genie, help!" Tyreese yelled. He flung his arms wide looking for purchase as the vampire tried to pull him into the darkness of the house, only to have the flashlight slip from his cold, wet fingers and go spinning off into the darkness, landing with a splash somewhere below the deck.

Genie's face was a mask of confusion and fear. She didn't seem to be able to decide whether to help the kid or Tyreese as he struggled to pull himself free. With just the one functional leg it was almost impossible for Tyreese to get the leverage he needed to free himself, though. If he hadn't been so large, he would have been pulled into the pitch black interior already. If that happened, he knew he was toast for sure.

"Grab the boy," Tyreese yelled at Genie through gritted teeth as he continued to struggle with his attacker, trying to avoid the vampire's snapping jaws.

Genie did not move, frozen to the spot with indecision of who to help first.

Tyreese threw one shoulder forward then the other in quick succession, trying to shake loose the vampire's grip. He felt the fingers gripping his left shoulder slip away. It was enough to allow him to pivot around on his good leg and throw a pile-driver punch into the darkness of the room, right at where he estimated a face would be. His knuckles connected with something cool and oddly dry... and serrated teeth that sliced into his fingers. He felt the flesh give beneath the force of his punch. *Feels like punching that Memory Foam material they make mattresses from*, he thought.

Then he was free... and slipping back to the porch floor. Caught off balance, he waved his hands for anything to halt his fall, found nothing, and fell hard to the wooden deck. He looked up and saw Genie moving to grab the boy, but the girl — Stevie's sister, Tyreese was sure of it now — stood between the hysterical boy and Genie, like a hyena protecting a kill from a lion.

The girl bared her fangs, hissing a warning at the approaching woman.

Genie swung the ax. The girl dove out of the way, backing up. Genie took another step forward and swung again, forcing the girl farther into the opposite corner of the deck.

"There's gonna be more of these bastards," Tyreese called out as he began to pull himself across the deck toward Genie. "We need to grab the boy and go." He pushed himself to his knees. "Stevie, come here. Come on." He reached an arm out toward the kid, his fingertips brushing the child's coat, but the kid stepped back, his face a mask of fear as his eyes flicked back and forth between Tyreese, Genie, and his sister.

Genie's wild ax swings had managed to force the girl into the farthest corner of the deck.

"Grab him. Now!" Tyreese yelled.

Genie threw one more swing of the ax, dropped it to her side then turned toward the terrified boy.

"It's okay," she said, reaching for him. "I've got you."

The front door of the house flew open, crashing against the siding. A woman, her eyes yellow flame, darted from the darkness beyond the doorway, her bloody robe flapping as she flew toward Stevie.

"Mommy!" the boy squealed in fear as the vampire swept him up in her arms. Tyreese caught a last despairing look of Stevie's terrified face as the woman pulled him from his feet and dragged him screaming back into the house. A half-second later, the vampire-girl darted in after them, slamming the door shut behind her. A half-second after that, came the sound of locks being thrown into place

"*Noooo!*" Genie's cry was a drawn out note of despair. She began to move toward the door but Tyreese grabbed for her.

"Don't! It's what they want. It's a trap, goddamn it. A trap. Help me, for Christ's sake or we're both dead."

Genie hesitated, her body leaning first toward the front door the boy had been pulled through then back to Tyreese. For one horrible moment, Tyreese thought she was going to go for the boy and doom them both. Instead, Genie stepped toward him, grabbed him under his arms and heaved.

For a woman Tyreese estimated to be in her mid-fifties, Genie was *damn* strong. She hefted him to his good foot while she slipped a hand under his armpit and around his back for support.

"Get us out of here," Tyreese said. They moved toward the porch steps.

From behind them came the sound of something scuttling over the roof tiles.

"Run!" Collins yelled from the cab of the SWAT van. Tyreese saw him raise a carbine to his shoulder using his good hand, balancing the muzzle in the crook of the elbow of his injured arm. Two shots rang out so quickly Tyreese could barely separate them.

Something roared in anger.

Tyreese and Genie hobbled down the steps of the deck and into the waterlogged garden. Tyreese tried hard to resist the urge to turn around and check his six, focusing instead on moving forward.

Two more shots rang out. Tyreese flinched instinctively with each of them. Something big and heavy splashed into the water behind them. He heard the distinct sound of a second object splashing into the water. Tyreese twisted just for a second, just long enough to get a view of the house.

"Oh, shit!"

Two vampires, both male, their eyes glowing against the backdrop of night had begun to give chase. He could see where Collins's bullets had hit the one man in the chest, the wounds already healing, doing little more than slow the creature's pursuit of them.

Tyreese felt all hope drain from him. "Leave me," he told Genie. "Just leave me." There was no chance they could both make it; he was just slowing Genie down. If she left him, he could delay the vampire's pursuit long enough that she would at least have a chance to get to the van.

Genie said nothing, instead tightening her grip around Tyreese's shoulders. She kept moving forward, her eyes never leaving the SWAT van, Collins's silhouetted figure in the driver's doorway, the carbine still raised to his shoulder.

A succession of rapid, almost blinding, flashes lit up the night as Collins switched the carbine to full auto. The unmistakable *thud, thud, thud,* of full metal jacket rounds striking flesh was barely audible over the man-made thunder that now rocked the night. The vampires screamed; hurt, maybe. Stopped? Tyreese knew that the best he could hope for was that it would slow their pursuers down long enough that he and Genie could escape.

"Faster!" Collins yelled, then unleashed another fusillade.

Ahead of them, beyond the wan circle of light cast by the van's lights, Tyreese saw multiple pairs of yellow eyes in the darkness. He counted twenty or more just to his right, drawn from their hiding places by the cacophony of gunfire and the promise of blood.

"Christ! Move, move, move," Tyreese yelled at Genie.

"I'm going faster than I have in twenty damn years," Genie hissed back at him, "*and* I'm carrying your ugly ass."

"Yes, ma'am," Tyreese offered back.

They reached the side of the SWAT van just as a vampire landed with a reverberating thud on the van's flat metal roof. The middle-aged man stared down at the two humans, his jaws dripping black saliva, his face full of malice and hunger. Then its head exploded with three gouts of black liquid as several rounds from Collins's weapon ripped through it. The vampire spun around and fell head first, splashing into the water at Genie's feet. Even with three holes in its head, the vampire still reached a limp hand toward the two humans, clawing at them. What was left of its lower jaw opened and closed, snapping on nothing but air.

"Get your asses in here," Collins screamed. He tossed the still smoking carbine onto the passenger seat, then reached down with his good hand and grabbed Tyreese under his left armpit while Birdy used both of her hands to grab him around his right arm. Together they heaved Tyreese inside as Genie pushed his bulk through the door. They dragged him unceremoniously into the back of the truck, collapsing into a tangled heap on the floor. Genie climbed into the driver's seat, slamming the door shut behind her. She turned the ignition keys. The engine fired up and Genie slammed the truck into gear, accelerating far faster than she should, sending the back end of the truck fishtailing first left then right.

Something thudded against the front of the van, followed almost instantly by a bucking of the floor as the wheels rode over what could only have been a body, then the wheels found a semblance of traction and they were moving away.

Nobody said a thing for the longest while.

Finally, as his breathlessness began to fade, Tyreese found his voice; "The airport," he said, "get us to the airport and get us the hell out of here."

"It was a trap. A goddamn trap," Collins said, between panting breaths.

"What?"

"They used the kid to lure us. I mean, we know they keep their intelligence after they... change... but Jesus! I think they become more devious."

"It's like they're demons," said Genie. It was a statement not a question.

Tyreese's instinct was to poo-poo Genie's observation, but the truth was he thought she might just be right. These things were utter evil. They had used the kid to lure them to the house; a level of deviousness and inhumanity usually best left to al-Qaeda or ISIL.

Collins caught Tyreese's eyes; there was no sign of any disagreement in them.

# TUESDAY

# CHAPTER TWENTY-SEVEN
CHAPTER TWENTY-SEVEN

"What time is it?" Collins asked. He had dozed briefly, not long enough to get any meaningful rest, but enough that he woke momentarily confused and unsure of where he was.

Tyreese glanced at the truck's dashboard clock. "It's a little after four in the morning."

They were making painfully slow progress. Genie was keeping their speed at about five miles an hour, not just because of the waterlogged roads, but also to avoid the numerous abandoned vehicles that littered the streets and the debris that had been dislodged by the floodwater. That flotsam and jetsam drifted by on an almost continual basis; mainly small branches and the odd errant trashcan, but occasionally a fallen tree would tumble by and Genie would have to carefully maneuver the van to avoid it.

And then there were the bodies.

They had seen five dead bodies float past them in the last twenty minutes, twisting slowly in the swell of the rushing water.

"At least they're dead," Genie had muttered. The three others said nothing.

*Still a couple of hours or so until dawn*, Collins thought, watching the road over Genie's shoulder. A couple more hours until he would finally have an answer to a question that he was sure had been on all their minds, but no one had voiced yet. He leaned back against the bench, "Given their aversion to the flashlights, do you think the movies and stories are right about vampires being unable to move around in daylight?" he asked. He had to speak loudly to ensure everyone would hear him over the noise of the engine and the constant shush of water beneath the tires.

"Makes sense," said Tyreese after a few moments consideration on the question. "The fables and old wives' tales usually have some kind of truth at their root. And they sure as hell don't seem to like the flashlights."

"Or the headlights," Birdy chimed in.

"Well, come daybreak, I guess we'll find out," Collins said.

"I sure as shit hope we're not going to still be here to find out," Tyreese returned.

"Hey!" said Genie, "sorry to interrupt you boys' chit-chat, but I think we're here."

Collins got up and carefully made his way to the front of the truck. Genie was right. Off to the right he could see the razor-wire topped chain link fence that ran around the perimeter of the airport.

"It's a few hundred feet farther," he said.

Gradually, the dim outline of buildings emerged from the darkness beyond the security fence.

"Pull into the parking lot over there," Collins instructed Genie. He pointed off to the right toward a large modern-looking multi-story building made from huge panes of glass and aluminum, flanked on either side by two more-conventional looking office buildings.

Tyreese guessed there was probably a parking lot in front of the building, but the only way it was distinguishable as such was by the cars lined up in neat rows; the rising floodwater totally obscured the concrete lot.

Genie swung the truck off the road and into the submerged parking lot. As they moved toward the glass building, the shadowy forms of several huge aircraft hangars revealed themselves in the SWAT van's headlights.

"That's the place," said Collins. He pointed at the hangars.

"How do we get in?" Genie asked.

"Follow the road—" Collins paused as he oriented himself in the darkness. "—over there." He pointed toward the front of the hangars.

"Looks expensive," said Tyreese, shooting a look at Collins. The inference was obvious; *how could he afford somewhere like this on a detective's salary?*

"I did a favor for the owner of the company that runs a charter service out of here. He lets me keep my plane in their hangar," Collins explained.

They drove slowly around the front of the buildings, all four of them crowded at the front of the van, staring through the windshield.

"There, it's the second one." Collins gestured to a door between a set of metal roll-ups. Genie brought the van to a stop next to the building and reached for the door handle.

"Wait a second," said Collins. He shifted the SWAT van's exterior spotlight slowly across the front of the hangars, then out over the ground in front of them, past the eight-foot high chain-link fence that separated the buildings from Saticoy Street beyond. The only movement was the constant dance of rain on the surface of the flooded roads.

"Where are all the lights?" Birdy asked.

Collins thought about what the girl had said for a moment. He reached across the dashboard and switched off the van's floodlight, leaned across Genie and extinguished the headlights, too. Outside the vehicle was now nothing but a perfect darkness that stretched off in all directions, unbroken by any of the lights that could be expected within a modern city.

"Not even a candle," said Genie, her voice suddenly a whisper.

*There should be something,* Collins reasoned. Some hint or glimmer of human activity; headlights, the flicker of a flashlight behind a curtain, even the house lights of people lucky enough or smart enough to have a generator. But there wasn't even a distant glint. The airport, which Collins *knew* had backup generators that could last for days was equally shrouded in darkness.

Collins felt a chill run up his back. *Dead. Everyone is dead.* The entire population of LA had been consumed by the sweeping darkness that had crept into the city from god-knew-where. "Jesus!" His stomach twisted as the realization that he had greatly underestimated the extent of what was happening here floated up to the surface of his understanding like a dead and bloated body. *Hell,* he thought, *who was to say it wasn't happening across the entire western seaboard?*

"Come on," Collins said after a couple more seconds, looking directly at Tyreese. "We need to get the hell out of here as fast as possible."

•••

"Back it up... another foot or so... that's it." Tyreese's voice echoed through the interior of the SWAT van. He hung out the side of the van, directing Genie while she reversed the truck until its side door was parallel with a door that Collins said he thought would get them into the aircraft hangar.

"Woah! That's perfect," said Tyreese, holding up a hand.

Genie put the vehicle in park and reached for the ignition.

"Best you leave it running," said Collins. "Just in case we need to make a quick getaway." He was the one who had suggested they reverse the van parallel to the door to the hangar. That way they could open the van's side door while the vehicle provided cover for them.

"I don't have the keys to the building," Collins had explained to the others. They had been on his key ring with his car keys. And his car keys had been with Mulroney when she'd been snatched off the stairwell back at the apartment complex. "So, we're going to have to improvise."

They had spent the last five minutes prepping, pulling weapons and the heavy-duty police-issue Pelican flashlights from the storage racks in the SWAT van. They hadn't found any more Tasers, and the firearms would do little more than temporarily slow down any vampires they might encounter, but Collins was willing to take any advantage right now. He now carried the Heckler and Koch assault rifle he had used earlier, slung over his shoulder. Tyreese had a Benelli M4 shotgun, loaded with double-ought buckshot and a box-full of extra shells stuffed into his jacket pockets.

Genie refused the second shotgun Collins had offered her. "I'll stick with this old bitch," she said, patting the cold metal head of her ax.

"Can I get a gun?" Birdy piped up.

Collins raised his eyebrows, shook his head and handed her a Pelican flashlight instead. The detective smiled grimly at Tyreese. "Would you do the honors?"

Tyreese nodded, picked up the pry-bar he'd found in a toolbox in the rear of the SWAT van and hefted it in his hands. They had hoped for a portable battering ram but the SWAT team must have taken that with them on their ill-fated assault of the apartment building.

Tyreese stepped out through the truck's side door into the narrow recessed doorway that Collins assured him led into the hangar. Water fell in a torrent from the roof of the hangar, creating an icy waterfall that soaked Tyreese in a second, hammering against his head and shoulders as he negotiated himself into the narrow space between the truck and the hangar door. He slid the pry-bar into the space between the door and the frame just below the lock, then pushed it into the gap as hard as he could. Collins and Birdy watched intently from inside the van. Genie remained in the driver's seat, in case they needed to make a quick getaway.

"I can't... quite... get enough... leverage," Tyreese grunted as he leaned his weight against the pry bar. The sharp flat edge of the bar would not stay in place, the rain making it slide across the slick surface of the door.

"God*damn* it!" Tyreese spat as the bar slipped again and the knuckles of his right hand rapped painfully against the sharp wooden edge of the door's surround.

Collins continued to stare at Tyreese's back. "Just take your time," the cop said.

"What I *need* is a hammer," Tyreese said, "something that I can use to force the bar into the crack of the door."

"How about this?" asked Birdy, offering the Pelican flashlight to Collins.

Collins took the flashlight from Birdy, hefted it in his good hand. "Might just work," he said. "Here..." He passed the flashlight to Tyreese.

"Back up. Give me some room to swing," Tyreese said, taking the flashlight. He flipped it over so he held it by the lens, pushed the sharp end of the pry bar into the crack of the door, drew back the flashlight and brought the battery-heavy shaft down hard against the curved end of the bar with a resounding clang.

"Yes!" Birdy shouted as the pry bar bit deep into the gap between the door and the frame. She clapped excitedly, then stopped, embarrassed at how uncool she must look.

Tyreese drew his arm back again, and slammed the flashlight down even harder. The tip of the pry bar dug in another half-inch.

"Okay!" Tyreese exclaimed, a smile of accomplishment cracking his rocky face. "One more time should—"

"Oh, sweet Mother Mary!" Genie swore from the driver's seat.

"What is it?" Collins asked. He leaned his head inside the van far enough to see Genie.

Genie pointed through the windshield into the darkness.

"What?" Collins asked again. He ducked back inside and moved toward the front of the van, then stopped. "Oh... shit!"

Beyond the chain link fence that separated the road from the airport, a hundred or more pairs of eyes stared at the van, moving points of yellow light in the darkness.

"What's going on?" Tyreese called from the doorway.

Collins made his way back to him. "We've got company. Vampires. A lot of the bastards."

"Shit!" Tyreese leaned hard against the pry bar, forcing it in deeper, then gave it one last thump with the Pelican, enough to push the bar's tip almost all the way through to the other side of the door. He switched position so his back was to the door, pushed hard against the bar, leveraging his weight until, finally, with a loud crack of splintering wood, the door popped open.

Tyreese, caught momentarily off balance, tipped forward, dropping the pry bar as he caught himself. The bar disappeared into the water with a splash but it had done its job. Floodwater began to pour into the interior of the hangar, forcing the door open and briefly staggering Tyreese with its force.

"Genie, let's go," Collins yelled from the van's door.

"Move it. Move it," Tyreese said. He offered his hand first to Birdy then Collins, helping them down and ushering them into the hangar's interior. Genie was a few seconds behind them and, once she was safely inside, Tyreese turned to follow them.

•••

If Tyreese had taken a second longer he probably would not have seen the shape split from the shadows and jump onto the front of the SWAT van. It barely touched the hood before launching itself into the foot-wide gap between the hangar and the van.

"Jesus!" Tyreese yelled, ducking his head to the right to avoid the taloned hand of a woman in her mid-twenties, clad only in a pair of red panties and what had once been a white bra. She snarled like a rabid dog as she tried to force herself deeper into the narrow gap between the wall and the SWAT van, scraping skin from her naked back.

Tyreese lurched backward, thought he was going to fall, but Genie's hands against his shoulders steadied him enough that he could turn and stumble into the room.

"We've got to get out of here, now!" Tyreese yelled at Collins.

The cop was trying to push the exterior door closed with his shoulder but the force of the water gushing through the opening made that next to impossible. He backed off, moved his flashlight onto the face of the young woman trying to squeeze through the gap, and allowed the beam to linger for a second. The woman hissed and screamed even louder, but she did not try to get away. If anything, she seemed even more determined to get to them. The light seemed to cause discomfort, but there was no physical effect that Collins could see.

"Collins?" Tyreese called, breaking the cop's momentary fascination with the vampire.

"Coming," said Collins. He moved the light quickly around the room's interior. He'd always used the back entrance to get into the hangar, so he wasn't familiar with this part of the building at all.

They were in a waiting area. A reception desk, filing cabinets, and a big brown sofa with a magazine-scattered coffee table in front of it were all that was in the room. Another door on the opposite side of the room had a plastic sign fixed to it that said HANGAR — NO ENTRY UNLESS ACCOMPANIED BY STAFF MEMBER.

"Maybe we can move a filing cabinet to block the door," Birdy suggested.

"Not enough time," said Tyreese. He splashed his way through the rapidly rising water to the second door, turned the handle and pushed. "Goddamn it!" This door was locked too.

"Where's the pry bar?" Collins demanded.

Tyreese shook his head. "I dropped it outside."

"*Shit!*" Collins cursed. "Jesus! Shit. Shit."

"Step back," said Tyreese. Tyreese took three steps back into the room, turned his shoulder toward the door, then with a mighty roar, he charged.

Birdy winced as Tyreese smashed full force into the wooden door.

There was a loud crack as bits of wood flew from the doorframe and the door opened partially, canted two-inches at the top, the lock still holding, but only barely.

"Here, let me," said Birdy. Before anyone could object, she stepped forward and stomped her foot against the door just to the right of the handle.

It flew open.

Tyreese gave her an appreciative nod. "Quick, everyone in," he said, glancing back at the vampire who was still pushing her way through the gap. And she was succeeding, he noticed. Her head was already visible halfway up the doorway, her eyes fixed on them as she somehow managed to maneuver one of her arms over her head and grab the wooden surround. A second hand appeared and she began to pull herself slowly, but inexorably into the room. The sound of more bodies scrambling over the exterior of the SWAT van reached the four humans.

"Did you lock the van's doors?" Collins asked Genie.

"I... I... don't think—"

Before Genie could finish, the unmistakable sound of the SWAT van's rear door flying open confirmed that she had not.

There was a moment of silence as each of the four survivors looked at each other, then: "Run!" Tyreese yelled. He pushed Collins through the doorway, then waited for Genie and Birdy to follow before he stepped through too. He pushed the door closed but it wouldn't shut properly, the top hinge having shifted at least two inches from the force of his hit and Birdy's kick. He ran his flashlight around the area they stood in. They were inside the main area of the hangar. When he shined the beam toward the front of the hangar he saw the big doors were wide open. *Well at least we don't need to worry about how we're going to get out of here, but if the vamps figure out they're open, we'll be overrun in seconds*, he thought.

"This way," said Collins, oriented now that he had seen the hangar doors. He moved off at a jog, the beam of his flashlight bobbing left and right as he moved toward the back of the building. Tyreese took Genie by the elbow and guided her after Collins. Birdy ran on ahead.

There were several aircraft in the hangar; huge private jets, bright and shiny, and a couple of double-prop planes, each worth millions of dollars, Tyreese suspected as he, Genie, and Birdy wound their way quickly between them. They ducked beneath the underbelly of a massive private jet, following behind Collins as closely as possible. Tyreese knew there were crooked cops in the LAPD, but he was confident that even the rotten ones didn't make enough in bribes to own one of these beasts. So how could a cop like Collins afford one, he wondered.

He got his answer when they caught up with Collins next to what could only be described as a 'well worn' airplane that looked like it had seen its heyday back when Reagan was still dreaming of being president. The single-prop plane's paint was flaking in patches, its windshield cracked in a couple of places. There was a small puddle of what might be oil beneath the engine.

"You want us to fly in *this*?" Birdy asked incredulously.

Collins stopped what he was doing and looked at her. "Hey, I'll have you know this is an '86 Cessna 172. It's a classic. Sure, she needs a little work, but she's no hangar queen. She'll get us where we need to go."

Tyreese had to smile despite their situation, the old man actually sounded offended.

"She ain't pretty but she's the best chance we got," said Genie. She reached up and opened one of the plane's doors. "So what are we—" Her words were cut short, turning instead into a shrill screech of surprise as a vampire plummeted from the darkness above them, landing in the center of the four humans.

The vampire's name was Bill. Tyreese knew this because it was stitched into the blood-splattered blue shirt he wore, and in the split-second before the vampire lunged at him, Tyreese's eyes had been drawn to his name tag.

Tyreese stepped backward, hitting the support strut of the Cessna's wing as Bill lunged at him, grabbing him by the shoulders. The vampire opened his jaws wide and snapped for Tyreese's throat just as Tyreese brought his arm up hard, forcing his forearm under the vampire's chin, pushing his head back. Bill's jaws snapped shut an inch or less from Tyreese's throat. The vampire had his hands-on Tyreese's chest, pinning him against the plane's strut. Bill was almost as big as Tyreese, and strong enough to hold him in place despite Tyreese's desperate attempts to push him away.

•••

271

Collins brought up his rifle, aiming for the vampire's head, but hesitated to fire; the creature was too close to Tyreese and the plane to be able to risk firing without hitting them. Instead, Collins stepped in close to the struggling man and the monster, and swung the stock of his rifle with as much force as he could muster against the vampire's skull. Instead of the hard thud Collins was braced for, the impact felt more like he was hitting something soft, yielding beneath the club. The vampire's head seemed to almost mold around the stock of the rifle, but it had the desired effect. The creature released Tyreese, who pushed the vampire away from the plane.

Collins flipped the gun around and opened up on full-auto with his weapon, unloading a hail of bullets into the creature. The vampire went spinning away, but almost immediately began to stand right back up again. Bill was halfway to his feet, his left arm dangling by sinews where Collins had raked his body with bullets when Genie jumped from the Cessna. She brought her ax around in a sweeping curve, like a boxer throwing an uppercut, and let loose a mighty yell.

Genie's ax blade caught the vampire under his chin and sent his severed head flying into the shadows. The headless body slumped to its knees, black goo spurting from the stump, then collapsed to the floor.

Tyreese, Collins, and Genie stood splattered in the dead vampire's gore, their hearts pounding with adrenaline, panting from the exertion.

Genie looked at both men then quickly glanced around her.

"Birdy?" she said, "Where's Birdy?"

It was only then that the two men realized the girl had vanished.

# CHAPTER TWENTY-EIGHT

The preceding sixty seconds were little more than a blur for Birdy. She'd screamed when the vampire dropped from the ceiling, watched it lunge at Tyreese, seen the cop try to shoot it, and had taken several involuntary steps away from it. But she had not even registered the second shape crawling across the hangar floor like some obscene reptile until it was too late. None of the adults had seen it either, and before she could even think to shout a warning, the vampire had sprung silently at her, sweeping her from her feet. She felt a hand clamp down hard across her mouth, silencing the scream that had risen to her throat as the vampire carried her off into the shadows.

Flashes of light flickered in the darkness syncopated with the *thud, thud, thud* of the cop's machine gun covering any sound the vampire that clutched her so tightly to its chest might have made. And with each brief flash that illuminated the darkness, Birdy saw the vampire's face; it was an old man, probably in his eighties, her mind, sharpened by terror, decided. His face was drawn and wrinkled, his thin arms exposed beneath a nicotine-stained white wife-beater shirt. He had that same stale smell of muddy-decay she had smelled on Julio, back in Tyreese's apartment. The vampire's spindly arms were almost as thin as Birdy's yet they were like iron clamps around her, she could feel the faint pulse of warmth from them against her own

273

skin. And when the old man looked down at her, it was with a desire and hunger that almost stopped her heart.

Birdy tried to struggle free, but the vampire's grip on her chest was like nothing she had ever felt before, she could barely breathe. Her muffled screams only faintly reached her own ears.

The gunfire stopped. She thought she heard Genie calling her name, but her mind reeled as the vampire sprinted through the darkness. Shapes, hidden within the darkness, flashed by. Her head grazed something sharp that cut into her scalp, and she felt blood begin to flow. Hot tears of pain welled in her eyes.

Then as suddenly as she had been snatched away from her friends, Birdy found herself thrown violently to the ground. She skidded across the floor hitting something hard and unyielding with a metallic thrum. Birdy pushed herself upright, as good as blind in the darkness of the hangar, her hands flailing around her as she tried to find something, anything, that she could use as a weapon. She felt cold corrugated metal against the flesh of both her hands. She backed up a few inches and felt the same cold metal behind her; she was in a corner of the hangar.

From somewhere in the darkness ahead, Birdy heard Tyreese calling her name, his voice echoing off the walls. Then Collins's and Genie's voices joined in too. She tried to scream for help but her throat was *so* tight, and *so* very dry that nothing came out. She let out a tiny gasp of fear as a pair of yellow eyes appeared just inches from her face. She tried to push herself even deeper into the corner, her wet feet slipping on the slick surface of the floor.

A second pair of eyes appeared to her right, then a third, and a fourth.

Birdy was sure her heart had stopped. She tried to scream again but managed only a weak whimper. Fingers touched her right ankle. She pulled her legs up to her chest, but a pair of hands grabbed her foot and yanked her so violently that her head hit the floor, snapping her jaw shut, her teeth sinking into her tongue, filling the darkness with sparkles of light that floated and pulsed across her vision. Birdy tasted blood in her mouth, felt it trickle down her throat as the pain in her tongue finally registered in her concussed brain. She moaned with pain and kicked blindly at her assailant, but the hands that had grabbed her were like steel traps. Inescapable.

*Pain*, like she had been stuck by a fistful of needles exploded in Birdy's right arm; something horribly sharp had pierced her flesh just above her left wrist. A second burst of agony seared her left leg as she felt another set of fangs sinking into the meat of her calf. Her right arm was wrenched so hard above her head the sudden pain hid the bite of the third vampire as its teeth sank into her other wrist.

When she felt bony fingers grab and twist her hair, yanking her head to the right, felt teeth bite deep into the flesh of her neck, Birdy finally managed to scream.

•••

Tyreese heard Birdy's scream echo off the walls of the aircraft hangar. In Afghanistan he'd heard the screams of dying men, of terrified women and children; this was worse.

"Dear God," Genie said.

Tyreese hissed an expletive and took off in the direction he thought Birdy's terrified scream had come from. Collins hesitated for a second. If he went after Tyreese and the kid, they were all being put at risk, and he sure as hell couldn't leave Genie here by herself. Genie apparently had other plans; she was up and running after Tyreese.

"Well, shit!" Collins said, then took off after the beam of Tyreese's flashlight as it bounced off the hidden surfaces of walls, and glass, and the glistening bodies of aircraft. He ducked under a plane's fuselage... and almost collided with his two companions.

"What the hell are—" Collins forgot the rest of the sentence when he saw what the beams of Tyreese's and Genie's flashlights were illuminating. Three vampires were caught in the pool of light like butterflies pinned to a board. *Really goddamned ugly fucking butterflies*, Collins thought. The feet of another of the bastards was just disappearing into the shadows as Collins's eyes moved to the still form lying spread-eagled on the floor nearby.

"Oh... no," he managed to whisper.

Birdy lay on her back, her left leg straight out, her right leg akimbo, both arms were stretched above her head. Her head was tilted to one side, her hair pulled upward to expose her throat. There was not much blood, not really, just the multiple puncture marks, puckered an angry red, against the pale skin on Birdy's wrists and throat, a trickle of blood flowing from each bite. *She looks like she's doing a pirouette*, Collins thought. He had left his weapon in the back of the Cessna. He looked across at Tyreese; he had not brought his weapon either.

But Genie had her ax.

As if she had read Collins's mind, she raised the ax to her shoulder and rushed at the vampires, a scream of rage roaring from her mouth. She was a Berserker, with nothing but death and fury on her mind.

She swung the ax at the first of the blinded vampires. It connected with the old man's head just above his left ear, dug deep, and separated the creature's lower jaw from the rest of the head. The vampire collapsed backward to the floor. Genie placed her foot on the side of the man's head and pulled the ax free, raised it again and swung at the second vampire, a skinny woman. The ax hit the vampire on the meat of her upper back as she turned to flee into the darkness.

*The ax should have stuck*, Collins thought as he watched the fight play out as if in slow motion. Instead, Genie's ax sliced through the vampire's meat and bone as momentum drove it through the strangely transmuted flesh. It *did* stick when it hit the woman's hip bone. Genie gave a deep growl like the vengeful mother bear she now resembled, and kicked the screaming creature, tearing the ax free, ripping the blade the rest of the way through the vampire. The woman's entire left side, along with the arm, tore away from the rest of the woman's body and lay twitching next to Birdy's feet. The vampire screamed and thrashed, spraying liquid and pieces of flesh though the air.

Genie raised the ax again and brought it down with a grunt of satisfaction, splitting the vampire's skull diagonally from the crown of her head to her left shoulder, instantly silencing the screams. The final vampire, confused and disoriented by the light, scrambled away into the darkness, disappearing faster than either Tyreese or Collins could follow with their flashlights.

"Birdy!" Genie whispered. She rushed to the girl's side, slipped her arms beneath her back and raised her gently upright. Birdy's head lolled like a broken doll's onto her chest, her arms hung limp at her side.

"Birdy!" Genie yelled. "Birdy?"

The girl did not move.

"Put her down," Tyreese ordered, almost pulling Birdy's body from the woman's hands. He laid her gently back down onto the floor, dropped his head to her chest and listened.

Collins stood at Birdy's head. He swung the beam of his flashlight back and forth across the hangar floor, cutting through the darkness, forcing any remaining vampires to stay deep in the darkness.

"Is she alive?" Genie asked, her voice filled with fear, almost to the point of breathlessness. "Is she?"

"Shut up," Tyreese commanded, he pushed his ear closer against Birdy's chest.

Apart from the hammer of the rain on the metal roof, and the scuffing of Collins's shoes as he shifted from one foot to the other, all was quiet inside the hangar. Tyreese's hand found its way to Birdy's arm and pressed two fingers to her wrist just above a set of puncture wounds.

"She's alive!" he finally declared.

Collins wasn't sure who exhaled louder, Genie or him.

"Come on, let's get her into the plane," Collins said. He helped Tyreese to his feet, then along with Genie, lifted the girl into Tyreese's waiting arms.

Collins led the way back to the Cessna, sweeping his flashlight across their path.

"Genie, get in," ordered Tyreese. Genie threw her ax to the floor of the plane and climbed into the rear bench seat.

"Hand her to me," she said, when she was seated.

Slowly, ever-so-slowly, Tyreese slid Birdy onto the seat next to Genie, lowering the child's head into the woman's lap.

"We have to get her to a hospital," Tyreese demanded.

"Yes, but not here," Collins said. He ran around the front of the plane, his flashlight slashing the darkness, and climbed into the pilot's seat.

"She's going to die if we don't get her medical attention fast," Tyreese insisted. He stood on the copilot's side of the plane, one hand on either side of the doorway leaning into the cabin, making it clear that he had no intention of getting in until he had a satisfactory answer.

"We have to head to Nevada," Collins said as he pulled a lightweight earphone and microphone set from the dashboard, plugged it in then placed it over his ears. "Now will you get in the goddamn plane?"

"Not until you tell me we're taking her to the nearest hospital," Tyreese demanded. "If we don't she's going to—"

Collins cut him off. "How? How are we supposed to do that?" he yelled.

"It's not up for discussion," Tyreese yelled back. "We get her to a hospital. *Now!*"

"Again, how the fuck do you propose we do that? Are you gonna drive her? And which hospital are you going to take her to? Hmmm? How many lights did *you* see on our way here? I'll tell you how many I saw; none! Not one! Know why? 'Cause every last goddamn man, woman, and child is dead... or one of those... those goddamn vampires. And you can probably count every doctor and nurse between here and Santa Barbara among them. And even if the hospitals haven't been overrun yet, how long do you think it's going to be before they are?"

"You can fly us there," Tyreese insisted.

"And land *where*?" Collins implored. "How many hospitals do you know with a convenient airstrip? And this storm is all along the West Coast. Who's to say it's going to be any better in Oregon? Or Washington? Hell! For all we know, this could have come up from Mexico. No, the only hope for her and us, is if I get us to Nevada."

Collins paused. "Now, are you gonna get in the goddamn plane or are we leaving without you?"

Tyreese hesitated for a moment, then heaved himself into the cockpit and closed the door behind him. "What are you doing?" he hissed as he strapped himself into the shotgun seat. Collins was flipping switches and checking gauges on the plane's console.

"Pre-flight check. Making sure everything's flight ready."

From across the darkened hangar, the sound of movement within the room they had just left could be plainly heard.

"We don't have time for this," Tyreese insisted. His voice sounded like escaping gas.

•••

"Listen," Collins shot back, "It's going to be hard enough getting us off the ground in this goddamned weather. I don't want any surprises if... *once...* we're in the air. So you better just let me get this done." Before Tyreese could argue any further, Collins flung his door open and was jogging around the exterior of the aircraft, running his flashlight over the plane's wings, tires, engine, checking whatever it was that pilots needed to check before takeoff.

"Christ!" Tyreese turned sideways and opened his door. He pressed one foot against the bottom of the door to keep it from swinging closed, then turned his attention back to the hangar. His rifle lay in his lap but now he brought it up to his shoulder, holding the flashlight under the barrel as he swept back the darkness with its beam. "Hurry up, for Christ's sake," he whisper-shouted at Collins.

The detective ignored him, ducking under the fuselage as he moved back toward the front of the plane.

From the direction they had just come, Tyreese heard the sound of something moving, or rather *things*, plural. Footfalls, shuffling sounds that he could not identify, which made them all the more terrifying because there were almost certainly no other living humans in here besides the four survivors. *Three survivors huddled together in a deathtrap of an aircraft while they waited for the fourth to finish checking they wouldn't explode the second he put the key in the goddamn ignition or however the fuck you started this thing.*

"Okay, let's motor," said Collins, climbing back into the pilot's seat.

"That wrist gonna give you any problems?" Tyreese asked, nodding at the cop's bandaged forearm.

"You know how to fly?" Collins asked Tyreese.

Tyreese shook his head.

"Then it's not like we have any choice is it. Now close the goddamn door."

Tyreese pulled his feet inside and closed the door, fastening it shut, while Collins checked the plane's fuel valve, quickly tested the brakes, primed the engine, set the throttle to idle, then turned the ignition key. The engine fired up instantly, the propeller twirling into a blur of motion in seconds.

"See," said Collins, turning to face Tyreese, his voice raised loud enough to be heard over the thrum of the propeller, "I told you there was nothing to worry about."

The vampires appeared as if from nowhere, but Tyreese's mind, hyper-vigilant from adrenalin, instantly figured out that they must be dropping from the ceiling, having climbed up the corrugated metal and then used the girders that crisscrossed the roof-space to move silently and quickly to where the humans sat, like canned meat inside the Cessna. He yelled a warning, instinctively trying to bring the rifle to bear on the nearest vampire. Genie yelled something that was probably an expletive but her voice was so run through with fear that her words were indecipherable.

Collins gunned the engine and released the brake.

The Cessna began to move forward even as the first vampire flung itself at Tyreese. It smacked against the window, its jaws wide, teeth scoring the glass, thick black saliva running from its mouth, yellow eyes burning with an evil hunger. In the darkness over the creature's shoulders, Tyreese saw more eyes than he could count moving through the darkness, climbing over aircraft like spiders, along walls, and across the roof beams. He couldn't shoot the thing hanging onto the side of the plane, it would shatter both the window and the eardrums of those sitting beside him. Instead, Tyreese unlocked the door and threw it open with all the force he could muster, stopping abruptly when it was halfway open. The sudden jolt caused the vampire, a skinny white teen boy with blond hair cropped all the way down to his skull, to lose his grip and drop away out of sight. Tyreese closed the door and locked it again, turning his face forward in time to see six more vampires drop to the ground ahead of them, forming a cordon and blocking the exit from the hangar.

"Oh no," said Genie from the back seat.

"Fuck 'em!" Collins yelled. He gunned the throttle. There was an audible increase in the whine of the plane's engine as its revs surged. Collins aimed the nose of the Cessna directly at the vampires. They tried to move out of the way, leaping into the air, but they were too slow. The propeller turning at thousands of revolutions a minute tore into their bodies, turning them into tiny pieces of flesh that splattered across the windshield and sent body parts flying away as though a grenade had been detonated inside them. Another tried to leap out of the way, but the left wing caught it with enough force that it almost snapped the woman's body in two. She fell to the ground in a bloody pool.

And then they were outside, the rain hammering against the plane's body.

"They're following us," said Genie.

"How many?" Collins asked.

"All of them," Genie blurted back, unaware of how unhelpful she was inadvertently being.

Tyreese looked over his shoulder and sucked in a gulp of air. "She's right," he said to Collins, then matter-of-factly added: "Go faster. Go much faster."

The hangar was quickly fading back into the darkness, but bobbing and weaving like fireflies in the night were the gold eyes of vampires; hundreds of them streaming out of the deeper shadows of the hangar's doorway. Tyreese looked to his left; there were more coming after them from across the airfield, more than he could easily count. So many the otherworldly glow of their eyes had become a golden wave that undulated within the darkness; a beautiful yet terrifying sight.

Tyreese forced himself to look straight ahead into the darkness. A darkness lit only by the intermittent flash of the aircraft's running lights.

"Faster," he repeated. "You have to go faster."

Collins held on to the steering yolk with one hand, grabbed a microphone with the other and keyed it. "Burbank Ground and Tower, this is Cessna November-six-one-four-Juliet-Sierra at parking ramp, have information Tango, request permission to taxi to runway fifteen for immediate departure to the north, over."

There was no reply.

"For Christ's sake, we don't have time for this," Tyreese said.

Collins did not take his eyes off what little of the runway he could see ahead of him. "I don't have a damn choice," he said. "If there's another plane out here with us, there's no way I'll see them in time to stop. If the tower's still operational, it'll be the only way to avoid a collision."

He repeated the radio call. Again there was only silence.

"Well... shit!" Collins said, exhaling the words.

"They're getting closer," said Genie. Her voice was just above a whisper, as though if she spoke any louder it might draw the creatures to them faster.

Tyreese glanced out the side window. A wave of vampires was moving across the airfield toward them, less than twenty feet away.

"They're almost on us. You have to—" Tyreese's voice was drowned out by a sudden increase in engine noise as Collins throttled up. The plane began to pick up speed.

Visibility was down to maybe thirty feet thanks to the swirling rain, and as the Cessna accelerated, just how insignificant that distance was became all the more obvious. They would stand no chance, none at all, Tyreese realized, if there was any kind of obstruction ahead of them. For all any of them knew, there could be a 747 parked on the runway ahead, or a refueling truck. Truth was, anything in their way would spell doom for them; there would be no chance of avoiding it. Tyreese reached out both hands and grabbed the dash, his knuckles white against his dark skin.

"Oh God, Oh God!" Genie repeated, as a sudden gust of wind caught the plane, buffeting them hard, pushing the Cessna to the right toward the edge of the runway.

"Come on, baby. Come on," Collins urged as he fought to guide the aircraft back toward the center of the runway. He grimaced and pulled his injured hand from the yoke, flexed his fingers a couple of times, then grabbed the controls again as another gust of wind swept under the left wing, pushing it up. Collins fought the plane's controls, leveling the wings. "Almost there, baby. One more time. Come on," he whispered, as if his words might persuade the plane to do his bidding. "Hold on, here we go," he called out as he eased back on the yoke.

"Oh!" said Genie, as the plane momentarily left the ground. She clutched Birdy's limp body to her bosom like the kid was a doll, then let out a louder exclamation as the wheels touched down again with a bump. They left the runway for a second time... and continued to ascend into the oily black sky.

"Yes!" said Tyreese, "Yes!" He thumped the console lightly with his clenched fist. "Good job!" he said, turning to smile at Collins.

Collins nodded. The plane was already a good hundred feet or so in the air. "See," he said, his eyes finally leaving the windshield to look at Tyreese, "I told you she'd make it."

"Never doubted it for a moment," Tyreese said, trying to keep the sarcasm from his voice.

A sudden downdraft of air hit the plane like a giant fist.

"Jeezus!" Collins exclaimed as he fought the aircraft's controls.

Tyreese grabbed onto the seat, his eyes wide as the plane dropped then surged back up again.

"We've got to get out of this goddamn storm as fast as possible," Collins said, through gritted teeth.

"Can't we just fly above it?" Tyreese asked.

Collins shook his head. "Not a chance. Storm's way too big and the plane's ceiling is way too small. Our best bet is to just head toward Vegas and hope we hold together long enough to get to quieter air."

Collins banked the Cessna until it was heading north, raised the nose so they were in a gradual climb to higher altitude and throttled up the engine.

•••

"How's Birdy holding up?" Collins asked. His eyes were focused beyond the *swish-swish* of the windshield wipers to the storm still plucking at the airplane.

"Not good," said Genie, her voice was quiet, barely audible above the constant thrum of the Cessna's engine. "Can you go any faster?"

"I'm going as fast as I can," Collins replied. Truth was, he was going faster than he had expected; the storm was giving them a swift kick in the pants thanks to an extra fifteen-knot tailwind. "She has to hang on. We're going to make it," he insisted.

The next forty-five minutes went by in almost complete silence as the plane headed northeast. With each passing minute the storm's ferocity diminished until the rain had all but ceased its constant hammering against the windshield and all that remained was thick cloud.

"How long until we land?" Genie asked.

"I'd estimate another fifteen minutes or so," said Collins. "When we get a little closer, I'll contact the—" Collins was interrupted by an electronic buzz and a red flashing light on the Cessna's control panel. "Ah, shit!" Collins spat.

"What? What?" said Tyreese, sitting up straight. His mind had drifted off for... how long? Minutes? Seconds? He had no real idea.

"We've got a major problem," Collins said. He leaned forward and tapped at a dial on the control panel. "Shit!" he hissed again.

"What the hell is wrong?"

"The fuel gauge. They were supposed to have... I assumed they had... they were supposed to replace the damn thing. It's faulty. I told them to change it out. Shit!"

Tyreese looked at Collins in disbelief. "So?"

Collins sighed, a deep unhappy exhalation, "So... we don't have enough fuel to get us to Waterrock."

"That's just great. Jesus!" Tyreese pounded a fist against the console.

"No need to panic, not yet anyway. I think we have enough to get to Vegas. It's not as far."

Tyreese felt the plane gently bank as Collins adjusted the Cessna's heading. "It's twenty miles or so. We should have just enough to get us—"

Collins's words stuck in his throat as the Cessna's engine sputtered twice, coughed, then died. The propeller at the front of the plane went from a blur of motion to a slow rotation.

"What? What just happened?" Genie asked.

Tyreese looked across at Collins. The detective was grim-faced, his jaw set as his hands moved quickly through what Tyreese figured must be the engine restart procedure. Nothing happened. Collins tried it one more time with the same result.

"We're going to have to put her down," Collins said.

"Where?" Tyreese and Genie said in unison.

Collins nodded at his feet. "Down," he said, and immediately put the plane into a gradual descent.

"But, there's nothing down there," said Genie.

"Not that we can see, but we're still in cloud. I've got to get us beneath this cloud bank before I'll have any idea where we *actually* are."

"But... but," Genie kept repeating. Birdy still lay across the leather seat; her head in Genie's lap. Genie's hand gently slid back and forth over the girl's forehead.

"Listen," Collins hissed, "Other pilots might tell you that we're 'gliding' right now. Me, being the eternal realist that I am, I like to tell it as it is: we're essentially falling out of the sky, so I'd appreciate it if you'd let me keep one-hundred percent of my attention on flying this goddamn brick."

•••

Tyreese sat back in his chair. The plane was frighteningly silent now that the engine was off. There was only the sound of air rushing over the wings and past the cockpit, and the quick inhale-exhale of the occupants' breaths. *We might just as well be sinking to the bottom of a pitch black ocean*, Tyreese thought as the plane dropped down through the impenetrable darkness surrounding them. And they could hit bottom before they even knew it was there.

"Sweet Jesus!" Genie said, suddenly. "There, over there." She pointed over to the right of the plane. Both Collins and Tyreese turned their heads to where she indicated.

"Ho-lee shit!" Collins exclaimed.

Tyreese just smiled. Ahead of them and perpendicular to their approach was the outline of a freeway. The road was dark, but the lights of vehicles moving along it glowed in the darkness like a shower of shooting stars. North of the road, like the Emerald City at the end of the yellow-brick road, was the unmistakable electronic glow of a city.

"Las Vegas," Collins said. "Never thought I'd be so happy to see her."

"Will we make it?" Tyreese asked, leaning forward to get a better view, as Collins gradually brought the plane around. They were flying directly over the freeway and the plane's nose was pointing straight at the distant lights of Vegas.

"Not a goddamn chance," said Collins.

"What?" Tyreese exclaimed.

"We don't stand a chance of making it to Vegas but I can put her down on the freeway... if we're lucky." He flipped a switch on the control panel, turning on a pair of landing lights that illuminated the thin veil of misty rain like tiny diamonds.

The plane continued to drop as Collins fought against the crosswinds buffeting them from both sides. The rain had all but disappeared this far from LA, replaced by a light drizzle. As they dropped silently through the air, the freeway resolved into greater detail: two three-lane highways, the headlights of cars and trucks cutting through the misty rain that still fell.

They were still a good hundred feet or so above the ground, Tyreese estimated, but he could already hear car horns honking. The headlights of oncoming vehicles in the southbound lanes flashed warnings to the drivers directly beneath the Cessna. Their lights dazzled Tyreese, but Collins seemed unfazed by them, his eyes focused directly ahead as he coerced the plane toward the center lane of the north-bound freeway looking for a space in the traffic to put them down.

"Over there," said Genie, pointing off to the right. "There's another road."

Tyreese looked in the direction Genie was pointing. She was right, there was another two lane road that ran along the side of the freeway, nowhere near as wide as the main freeway. It must be some kind of emergency access road, Tyreese guessed, but other than the headlights of a couple of cars that had drawn Genie's attention, it looked to be completely free of vehicles.

"Hold on," Collins said. He banked the Cessna toward the access road, then lined the plane up with the road and began to purposely descend. "Brace yourselves," he said, when there was less than twenty feet between the plane's tires and the blacktop.

The sudden downdraft of desert air hit the left wing of the Cessna like a giant fist. The Cessna's nose dipped, and the plane went into a steep dive.

Genie screamed in surprise and fear as the plane plummeted toward the ground.

With no visual references to help him orient himself and with just a second before impact, Collins fought the controls to level the plane out, but it was too late. The Cessna clipped some unseen object in the gloom, sheering away the right wing. The plane began to corkscrew, then tumble before its nose hit the ground, sending shards of the propeller flying through the air like shrapnel. The remains of the aircraft cartwheeled once, then smashed into the ground before sliding another fifty feet and coming to rest in the frontage road's southbound lane facing east, smoke and flame billowing from the engine.

# CHAPTER TWENTY-NINE

Tyreese wasn't sure if he had lost consciousness or not; one moment he was watching the road approach from below, the next he was staring at the console through a red haze and his head hurt like a *mother*. It took a few more seconds for him to realize there was smoke all around. It wafted past him like a ghost. Within the smoke an orange light jumped and danced.

*Fire!* The flames flickered in front of him. He could feel the heat against his face. The flames were giving off a thick black, choking smoke that stung his eyes and clung to his throat and nostrils with each breath he took. And there was something else, something within the smoke that his watering eyes could not quite focus on.

His head *really* hurt.

*Where the hell am I?* He tried to think back to the last thing he could remember, but it was like trying to grab a piece of paper blown by the wind; his thoughts just would not stay still long enough for his mind to grasp them.

"Tyreese, please, you have to help us." The voice—it was a woman's voice—came from behind him. It sounded familiar but when he tried to put a face to it there was just a blur of color.

"What happened?" he asked. The words were hard to form, his lips were *so* dry.

The woman was crying, he could hear her sobbing behind him. He tried to turn to look and see who the voice belonged to but for some reason he could not move his upper body, so he turned his head in the direction instead.

There was someone next to him. He could not make out the face because of the smoke, but there was a vague but unmistakable outline of a person. Tyreese felt a cool breeze waft across his face, and a light splash of water carried on it cleared the smoke away for a second... just long enough for him to see that he was strapped into a seat, and he was looking into the blank eyes of a dead man.

That the man was dead, was obvious; a long ugly piece of metal protruded from his right side, just below the armpit. The metal bar had entered the man's body on his left side and penetrated all the way though the upper torso, pushing the dead man's right arm up so that it looked as though he was waving at Tyreese. The bloody end of the metal bar was just inches away from Tyreese's head. Luck was probably all that had saved him from ending up just like him. The real question was who was the dead guy? Tyreese felt he should know who he was, but his thoughts still refused to be herded into focus.

*Collins*! The name came to him like a thunderclap. The dead man's name was Collins. "Detective Phil Collins... like the rock star," Tyreese said. And as if he had uttered the magic words to unlock the mental prison holding his memory hostage, it all came flooding back to him.

"Collins!" he whispered, unable to keep the painful emotion he felt from his voice as he looked at the glassy-eyed, ghostly-white face of the dead detective. Blood ran from the corner of Collins's mouth. It had pooled on his thigh before dripping down onto the seat.

Blood.

Vampires!

"Oh, Jesus!" Tyreese was suddenly and completely alert as everything came rushing back to him. "Genie! Can you hear me? Are you okay?" He tried to turn again but felt the same pressure against his chest stopping his upper body from moving. He looked down. His safety harness was still doing its job. He popped it open and turned to look into the back of the wrecked cockpit, careful to avoid the metal spike that had ended the detective's life.

The crash had ripped the tail section of the Cessna away completely, exposing the rear of the cabin to the elements. It had also pushed the bench Genie sat on about a foot or so closer to the front of the plane on her side, trapping the woman against the back of Tyreese's seat.

"Are you hurt?" Tyreese asked Genie.

She took a second to answer. "No, I... I don't think so."

Tyreese had to give the woman credit. She had just survived a plane crash, something that would have left most people shocked and mentally broken, but she was handling it with little more than a lip tremor. Tyreese repositioned himself, pulling his feet from the crumpled dashboard of the plane. If he'd had toes, they would surely have been broken, maybe even severed. He maneuvered himself until he was kneeling on his seat, looking back into the rear of the cabin. A cool gust of wind blew in through the exposed hole where the tail had once been, driving rain in with it, fanning the flames of the fire and pushing the black smoke momentarily clear.

"Is Birdy okay?" he asked.

"I... I can't tell," Genie said. "I can't move."

Tyreese repositioned himself so he could look down into the gap between the seats. Birdy still lay with her head in Genie's lap. Her body looked unscathed by the crash but he couldn't actually see her head, trapped between Genie's lap and the seat back. He reached a hand down and took the child's left arm, trying to ignore how terribly pale she looked or the two scabbed-over puncture marks on her wrist. He felt for a pulse. It was there, but just barely.

"I'm going to get you two out of here," Tyreese said to Genie. "Can you push Birdy toward the opposite end of the seat?"

"I can't get my safety belt off," she said. The bench seat Birdy and Genie sat on had been pushed far enough forward that Genie could not reach the restraint release on her left side.

Tyreese pushed an arm into the gap between the two seats, felt around for a few seconds until he found the safety belt's release just below Birdy's collar bone. He pushed his arm all the way down to his shoulder, gently lifted Birdy's body with his fingers, and fumbled for the release button with his thumb. He heard the metal belt fastener pop free.

"What's wrong with the cop?" Genie said suddenly, a puzzled look on her bloodied face.

"He didn't make it," Tyreese said, matter-of-factly.

Genie paused for a moment, considering her next words. "He was a good man; you know... for a cop." She turned her attention back to Birdy. "I can't move her," she said after a few seconds. "Can't get any leverage."

"Can you wriggle free?" Tyreese asked.

Genie tried. Her torso moved up a bit, but that was it. "I think my leg is hurt. Can't put much weight on it."

"Okay, here's what we're going to do," said Tyreese. He pushed both of his hands under the woman's armpits. "I'm going to help you. You ready?"

Genie nodded. "As I'll ever be."

"Okay, on three... three." Tyreese pushed his hands up into Genie's armpits with all his remaining strength. Genie grimaced with pain and exertion, but after a few seconds, she was able to get first one hand then the other free. She placed them on the front and back seat and applied her own strength to push herself the remaining way until, finally, she was free, sitting precariously on the ridge formed where the rear seat and the back of Tyreese's seat met. The right leg of Genie's pants was torn just below the knee about six inches. It was stained with blood. Genie winced as she probed through the slashed material to the wound beneath. Her fingers came away bloodied.

"Can you walk?" Tyreese asked.

Genie nodded. "Maybe... yes... I think so." She was sucking down big gulps of air.

The fire at the front of the crashed plane, where the engine used to be, was growing hotter, Tyreese could feel it singeing the small hairs on the back of his neck.

"We need to get out of here," Tyreese said. "Can you open the door?"

Genie reached over from her perch atop the crushed seats and tried the door handle; the door opened a couple of inches but would not budge any farther than that.

*The hinges had probably been crushed during the crash,* Tyreese thought. He reached across Genie and gave the door a good hard push, but it refused to move. "Shit," he mumbled, then turned and looked at Collins's body. He leaned across the man, and unlatched the lock to the pilot's-side door, then pushed; it was stiff but with the application of a little force, he was able to push it open. He took a deep breath then pulled himself as carefully as he could over the dead man's lap, snagging his jacket on the jagged piece of metal protruding from Collins's body, tearing out the pocket.

Tyreese grimaced as he stepped out of the wrecked plane; what should have been clean air stank of burning rubber and oil and the memory of aviation fuel.

How in God's name had they survived that crash? He looked over the crushed wreckage of the unrecognizable aircraft; the wings were gone, torn off somewhere in the rut of broken earth and fractured blacktop they left behind when they hit the ground. It was a miracle any of them were alive at all, and he would happily take the cards he had been dealt. As it was, only Collins had been dealt a bad hand; he could see now that it was the strut that supported the plane's left wing that had been thrust through his cabin door by the impact, impaling Collins. Tyreese was sure the man died instantly, never knowing what had quite literally hit him. Tyreese was surprised at how badly he felt for the detective; he had been a good man, shouldn't have had to die that way. But there were worse ways to die, much worse ways. If dying to a vampire could even be described as death. Not if you come back from it.

The freeway was about two-hundred feet from where they had crashed. Tyreese saw several cars had pulled over, the silhouettes of drivers caught in the headlights. They were waving to him and yelling, asking if he was okay. He raised a hand and beckoned them to come help but they were stuck behind the wire fence that separated the freeway from the access road they had crashed on.

"Give me your hand," Tyreese said, turning his attention back to Genie. He reached a hand into the rear cabin for her. His head was throbbing badly now. His eyes watered from the smoke blowing through the demolished cabin from the small but fierce fire that burned in the plane's engine. If there had been any fuel left in the tank when they hit... well, he didn't think any one of them would have made it out alive. His vision swam for a moment and Tyreese grabbed for the fuselage to keep himself from falling. He coughed loudly as his lungs filled with the thick black smoke.

"You okay?" Genie asked, taking his still-outstretched hand.

"Fine," Tyreese croaked. He pulled Genie toward him. She slid across the top of the seats, then not very elegantly climbed over the dead detective.

"Lean on me," Tyreese said as the woman stepped down to the ground.

"I don't need no more help," Genie said as she propped herself against the plane's fuselage. "Get the girl out of there."

Tyreese leaned back into the cockpit, supporting himself with his right arm against the exterior fuselage—his head spun as he inhaled another deep breath of the noxious fumes burning off the engine. He reached down with his left hand, searched blindly for a few seconds and finally found Birdy's legs. His hands were so big he could wrap one of them around both the girl's ankles. He pulled... and almost fainted.

His world had suddenly turned into little more than a kaleidoscope of colors reeling around his head. His blood pounded in his ears.

"You okay, son?" Genie asked.

Tyreese felt Genie's hand against his shoulder. "Yeah, yeah. I'm fine." He fixed his grip on Birdy's ankles and pulled again. Birdy slid closer. He moved his hand up her leg until he found the waistband of her jeans, and pulled her all the way to him. Leaning over the back of the seat—his head swimming crazily, Tyreese slipped a hand under

Birdy's back and gently lifted the girl free. There was an opaque haze around the peripheral of his sight; the haze was gradually contracting, toward the center of his vision.

"Here, let me take her," Genie said. She was standing just behind Tyreese with both arms extended.

Tyreese didn't argue. His head was pounding. His vision barely there. He swayed from side to side as he placed Birdy's limp body into Genie's arms. He felt *so* tired, all he wanted to do right now was lay down and close his eyes.

*Concussion*, Tyreese thought as he followed Genie toward a sandy embankment just off the side of the road. He tried to help Genie as she lowered Birdy to the ground, but all strength seemed to have left his body. He tumbled to his butt; the world was swaying in and out of focus now. He turned and vomited onto the sand then collapsed onto his back. Tyreese looked to the east through the smoke and flames of the destroyed Cessna; a glow had begun to push away the darkness of the night painting the eastern horizon with red and orange.

Sunrise.

The last thing Tyreese registered before he tumbled into the deep well of unconsciousness that opened up around him was the wail of emergency vehicles approaching in the distance.

# CHAPTER THIRTY

"*Wake up.*"

Tyreese heard his wife's voice calling to him, but he didn't want to wake up, not yet. Emma must be somewhere else in the apartment because her voice sounded different; muffled, distant. His head ached horribly, and all he wanted to do right now was stay here in the darkness that enveloped him, a little longer; at least long enough for the throbbing pain that started above his right eye and ran down into his jaw to go away. The pain in his head made him want to stay very, very still. It hurt even when he breathed.

"Mr. Douglass? Wake up." The voice sounded much closer this time, and much clearer. And it did not belong to his wife.

Tyreese opened his eyes. He wasn't in the apartment. He wasn't... well, he had no idea where he was. A woman in her mid-forties with tired eyes leaned over him, her face about eight inches away from his. She was close enough that he could smell mint on her breath when she spoke, "Ah! There you are. Welcome back." The woman stood upright and smiled at Tyreese.

He looked around, his head moving slowly, a disorienting fog clung to both his sight and his brain. He was in a hospital room, that much he could tell from the machines that sat on either side of his bed, beeping quietly. His eyes smarted as he tried to focus on a window in the wall opposite the bed he lay on, but the light, *daylight*, was just too bright. He closed his eyes again.

"Who..." he croaked, his throat dry and voice raspy. "Who are you? Where am—" Tyreese was shocked into silence by a lightning bolt of pain that exploded from left to right across his forehead. Blackness closed in on him again, momentarily...

Only it must have been longer than a moment, because when Tyreese opened his eyes again, the woman was gone. He glanced over at the window; it was dark out there now.

His mind was a maelstrom of competing memories and images, all jumbled together within his brain by the constant throbbing ache in his head. He remembered everything up to the plane crash, but it was as though he were looking at it from a distance, as though the events had been related to him by someone else. It all seemed so impossible now, here in the sterile normality of this hospital room.

Tyreese put a hand up to his head, and felt some kind of bandage or gauze stretched across his forehead. Everything after the plane crash was just a blur. He remembered bits and pieces of it, but it was all a jigsaw of confusion. *I've obviously suffered some kind of head injury*, he thought, touching the bandage on his head again. That would account for his screwed-up recollection.

The door squeaked open and the woman he had seen earlier walked in. She was dressed in a white jacket and had a stethoscope hanging around her neck. "Hello again, Mr. Douglass, I'm Dr. Wu," she said as she walked across to his bed. "How are we feeling?" She took his left arm and checked his pulse.

"Where am I?" Tyreese asked in a croaky whisper.

The doctor took the stethoscope from around her neck, placed the eartips in her ears then put the diaphragm against Tyreese's chest.

"Sounds good," Wu said, after listening for a few seconds. She replaced the stethoscope around her neck. "You're at Sunrise Hospital, in Las Vegas. Can you tell me what you remember?"

Tyreese thought for a second, trying to get his memories into some semblance of order. "We came in from Los Angeles... Ran out of fuel and had to put the plane down... But we crashed. *Shit!* The people I was with, where are they?"

Doctor Wu gave a contrite smile and ignored the question. "Anything else you remember, after that?"

"Collins, the cop, he was the pilot. He didn't make it. But Genie and Birdy, I got them out." He paused for a second as the vague memory of him helping Genie get Birdy out of the crashed Cessna came back to him. "Are they okay?" he asked. "Birdy and Genie."

The doctor sat on the edge of the bed. "Are you related to them?" she asked, her voice low.

Tyreese almost said no, instead he said, "I'm the girl's uncle. Genie's a... family friend."

The doctor gathered her thoughts for a second. "And why were you all in the plane in such bad weather? I mean the storm they're having out there in California is pretty serious. The power's out in lots of places, emergency services aren't getting in or out, and I've heard that the National Guard is being mobilized. Must have been pretty bad?"

"Doc," Tyreese interrupted, "how are my friends doing?"

Doctor Wu inhaled slowly. "Ms. Prescod, Genie, is doing well. She has some minor injuries, but she'll recover. We expect her to be well enough to be released in the next day or so, but she's refused to answer any of our questions."

"And Birdy?"

Doctor Wu cocked her head quizzically.

"Annabelle," Tyreese said, "she prefers to be called Birdy. The girl who was with us on the plane."

Doctor Wu took an even deeper breath. "I'm very sorry to tell you that Annabelle... Birdy, died as a result of her injuries."

*Jesus! Oh, no,* Tyreese thought. Collins had been so damn sure that she was going to make it. He had been too, even after the crash.

The doctor smiled sympathetically at him. "If there's anyone you would like me to contact, or—"

It was the blood loss from those goddamned vampires, Tyreese was sure of it. They had drained her until there was almost no life left in the kid. He felt hot tears roll down his cheeks. His emotion was quickly smothered by a terrible, terrible thought.

"Was she dead when the paramedics got to us?" Tyreese interrupted.

"I'm not really sure how that is—"

Tyreese's hand flashed out and grabbed the doctor's left wrist.

"*Was she dead when the paramedics got to us?*" He enunciated each word individually and slowly, as if talking to an imbecile.

Doctor Wu looked startled, her expression of sympathy slipping. She tried to pull her hand free of Tyreese's grip but he was far too strong.

"Mr. Douglass this is just not—"

"*Was she dead when the paramedics found us?*" Tyreese repeated, almost yelling the words this time, spittle flying from his lips.

Doctor Wu gave a little yelp, like a surprised puppy. "Yes," she blurted. "Yes, she was already dead when the emergency crew reached the crash site. She had bled out at some point; she was completely exsanguinated."

"What?"

"She had no blood left in her body. It was all gone."

Tyreese felt his mind swirling.

"Where did you put her body? Is it here, in the mortuary?"

"Yes," Wu said, "but Mr. Douglass—"

"Jesus!" he whispered. "God help us. God help us all," Tyreese said, then added, "How do I get to the mortuary?"

"Please," Doctor Wu said, "My wrist. You're hurting me."

Tyreese released Wu's wrist. The doctor looked puzzled, then outright concerned as Tyreese pulled the drip from his arm, flung back the bedsheets, and swung his legs out of the bed. Only his legs were not there, they had been removed at some point while he was unconscious. His eyes searched the room for his missing prosthetics. They had been placed neatly next to his bedside table. He reached over and grabbed them, then quickly fitted them to each leg stump.

"Mr. Douglass, I have to insist you return to your bed," Doctor Wu said. She placed a hand on his elbow as he climbed unsteadily to his feet. "Please, Mr. Douglass, you're in no condition to be moving around."

Tyreese shrugged her hand away. When he looked down at himself he saw he was wearing one of those standard issue hospital gowns; the ones that leave you bare-ass-naked. "Where are my clothes?" he demanded.

"They were incinerated," Doctor Wu said. "We had to cut them off you when you were brought in."

Tyreese scowled at her. Then took a step toward the door... and staggered, as his head did loops around the room. He felt the doctor's hands against him, holding him up.

"You see? I told you. You're not well enough to be on your feet, you need to get back in bed."

Tyreese allowed her to support him just long enough for his vision to clear then he pushed his way past her, pulled open the door of his room and stepped out into a brightly lit corridor; the faint sour smell of disinfectant stung his nostrils. He checked the corridor, looking for anything that might tell him where the mortuary was. Ahead of him, a young nurse with a shock of auburn hair watched him from behind the desk of a nurse's station. He shambled toward her, Doctor Wu following behind.

"Which way is the morgue?" he demanded of the nurse.

"Mr. Douglass, you *have* to return to your bed." Doctor Wu's voice came from over his shoulder but he ignored her.

"I... I..." the nurse stuttered, her gaze moving between Tyreese and the doctor.

Tyreese slammed a fist down hard on the top of the desk. The nurse jumped in her seat. "Which way!"

"That way," the nurse spluttered, pointing off to her right. "Down the stairs. It's in the basement."

Tyreese moved off in the direction the nurse had pointed, then stopped and walked back to the desk.

"That," he said, pointing behind the nurse, "give it to me."

"What?" the nurse said, looking to where Tyreese was pointing.

"The planter, give it to me." Tyreese beckoned with his right hand at a large brown plant pot that contained some kind of half-wilted shrub. "Give it to me."

The nurse looked at Doctor Wu, a confused expression on her face. "No," she said, "I'm sorry I can't let you—"

Tyreese sighed and walked around the counter to the planter. Whatever species the plant was, it was large enough that it needed an equally tall wooden pole to support its growth. The plant was secured to the pole by three pieces of green plastic tape which Tyreese quickly snapped before pulling the pole free of the pot. He wiped dirt off the bottom of the pole and nodded grimly when he saw the pointed end used to drive it into the dirt. *This would have to do.*

Doctor Wu buzzed alongside Tyreese as he made his way back around the counter, "Mr. Douglass, please, for your own good, I have to insist that you return to your room." She was starting to sound exasperated now, and more than a little nervous. When she saw him heft the three-foot long stake, she took a step back from him.

"You've got nothing to worry about, not from me, at least," Tyreese said to her when he saw Doctor Wu reach for a phone sitting on the nurse's station countertop. He turned and headed toward the door the nurse had pointed to.

Behind him, Tyreese heard the doctor talking on the phone: "Security, I need you at station four, right now!"

•••

Tyreese headed unsteadily down the flight of steps until he reached the basement. Ahead of him was another short corridor with a single door. There was no sign to indicate that it was the mortuary, just the letters B1 stenciled above the door. There was a push-button security lock next to the door handle.

Tyreese gave the handle a couple of tries anyway but the door wouldn't budge even a little. He cursed under his breath and took a step back to look around, but there was no other way in. There wasn't even a window in the door to see inside the room.

*Which means that if there's anyone in there, they can't see out,* Tyreese reasoned.

He rapped his knuckles hard against the door three times.

It took about thirty seconds, but eventually a man—probably a morgue attendant, Tyreese guessed—in his late forties with an annoyed look on his face, opened the door wide. He blinked a couple of times when he saw Tyreese standing there dressed in his hospital gown, and holding a plant stake, then said, "I think you're—"

Tyreese reached out and grabbed the attendant by the scruff of his shirt and jerked him out into the corridor. He hit the wall and stumbled to the floor.

"What the hell are you doing?" he yelled.

Tyreese ignored him, slipped through the slowly closing gap and pushed the door closed behind him.

Ahead of him, two large doors were still swinging shut. Tyreese eased his way between them and found himself in a large room. The attendant who had opened the door must have been the only employee down here, because the place was empty. In the center of the room were two large glistening steel tables, on the right was a mortuary rack; three rows of stainless steel doors, four bays in each row. The constant thrum of a refrigerator motor whirred quietly somewhere within the storage unit. Off to his right was an elevator door that Tyreese assumed was used to transport bodies down here.

He was in the right place then.

Across the other side of the room was a door, propped open by a gray plastic doorstop that Tyreese assumed had been left open to get some fresh air into the room, or maybe the morgue attendant had just been out there for a quick smoke on his break. Tyreese leaned his head around the open door to make sure he really was alone. A single orange sodium light illuminated the area just enough that he could make out a concrete loading dock where funeral home employees came to discreetly pick up bodies. There was no sign of anyone else, so he ducked back inside.

From back down the corridor he could hear the thump, thump, thump of the attendant banging against the door. He was yelling something but Tyreese couldn't make it out.

Tyreese placed the wooden plant stake against the side of one of the cadaver tables then walked over to the mortuary rack. He started with the top-left bay; a wave of cold air rolled over him when he opened the door, but the space within was empty. The next two bays were empty too, but when he opened the fourth door, inside was the body of an old man in his eighties; cold and stiff and withered. Tyreese quickly closed the door and moved to the next bay; another body, this time of a middle-aged woman. He continued opening doors until he reached the next-to-last bay; that was where he found Birdy.

Birdy's skin was almost as white as the sheet her naked body was wrapped in. Her eyes were closed, her face peaceful, a slight sheen of frost, already beginning to melt, covered her hair.

Tyreese stifled a moan of sadness as he looked at Birdy's still, bloodless face. He had failed her, he knew that, and he felt the icy-hot spike of guilt at his failure thrust deep into his own heart. As deep as he knew he was going to have to drive the stake into Birdy. That was the only way he could make up for what had—*would*—happen to her if he left the unnatural process he was sure she was undergoing run its terrible, terrible course.

Tyreese drew in a long, deep breath, steadying his nerves while attempting to calm his emotions, but succeeding only enough to slow the trickle of tears that ran down his cheeks. He wiped them away with the back of his hand then reached down and rolled the metal tray Birdy's body lay on completely out of the mortuary rack. He leaned over her, slid both of his hands under her cold form and lifted Birdy off the rack.

*She's so light,* Tyreese thought as he carried Birdy's almost weightless body to the metal examination table. He laid her down gently, and brushed away an errant frost-stiff lock of hair that had fallen across her closed lids. *She looks so peaceful,* he thought, *so perfect.* And it was in that moment that he knew that he was right to be afraid for her, afraid *of* her, because the cut to Birdy's cheek, the one she had gotten when she was trying to get to the SWAT van, was gone. Vanished, healed as though it had never been there, leaving behind flawlessly smooth skin.

He had to work fast.

Tyreese pulled back the cloth Birdy was wrapped in enough to expose her budding left breast, reached down and picked up the wooden garden stake he had taken from the nurse's station.

"God, forgive me," Tyreese whispered and raised the stake in both hands until his arms were above his head.

"Stop right where you are and drop the weapon."

Tyreese spun around. He hadn't heard the door open, certainly had not heard Doctor Wu and the security guard enter the mortuary. The guard had a large caliber pistol aimed directly at Tyreese.

"Drop the weapon," the security guard repeated. "I won't ask again." The guard must have been ex-police or maybe military or maybe he had gotten some half-decent training, Tyreese thought, because his shooting stance was perfect. The guard's eyes were focused on Tyreese, his pistol aimed directly at his torso; center of mass, just like he'd been trained to do.

"You don't understand what you're dealing with," Tyreese said, his voice surprisingly calm to his ears. "I can't take the chance that she'll turn... into one of *them*."

No way was anyone going to listen to him, Tyreese knew that. There was zero chance they would believe his story. At best, if he laid down his weapon and surrendered he was looking at hours of interrogation in some cop station, and, if by some stroke of good luck, he found someone who *did* believe his story (a story, that quite frankly he himself still found hard to believe), by that time it would be too late and Birdy would have been unleashed on Las Vegas. And he could not allow that to happen.

Tyreese turned his back on the guard. "*I don't have a choice,*" he said flatly. He raised his hands above his head again and brought the stake down with all the force he could muster. He felt the hammer-blow slam into his left shoulder a split-second before he heard the gunshot.

There was no pain, not immediately, anyway. Tyreese staggered. He half-turned and looked back toward the security guard and the doctor; Wu's eyes were wide open, her mouth forming an 'o' of surprise and shock. The guard was yelling something at him, the man's lips moved but Tyreese could not hear what he was saying. His world had gone completely and terribly silent.

Tyreese felt the beat of his heart reverberating inside his chest; the frantic *bump, bump, bump* echoed against his eardrums. His left arm hung uselessly at his side. A thick stream of blood ran down past his elbow to his wrist and over his fingers, and a bright red pool had already formed next to his naked feet. His eyes moved to Birdy; a crimson spray covered her face, droplets of his blood had splashed across her lips.

Tyreese raised the stake again in a feeble last ditch attempt to finish what he had started.

The second bullet hit Tyreese hard in the back. He let out a deep grunt as the force of the bullet spun him 180 degrees. He stumbled backward, grabbing for the edge of the cadaver table. His fingers found no purchase on the slick stainless steel. The stake clattered to the tiled floor as Tyreese slowly sank to a sitting position, his back against the cold steel of the table.

A thick ribbon of blood flowed across the tiles, following the slight decline toward the open mouth of a small drain. *His* blood, he realized as he looked down at his chest and the bright red bloom that had seeped into the cloth around a jagged hole in his hospital gown.

*Through-and-through wound,* Tyreese thought. *The rent-a-cop isn't as bright as I gave him credit for, the idiot's using full metal jacket rounds.* He heard his breath rasping with each intake and exhalation of air he made, small bubbles appeared in the blood around the exit hole. *Nicked a lung,* he thought. *Fuck!* He tried to speak, but his jaw just wouldn't cooperate. He managed to raise his head to look at the security guard; he still had the pistol pointed at him, his face was almost as ashen as Dr. Wu's.

"Get on the ground!" the guard screamed. He sounded close to snapping. And for a second, Tyreese thought he was going to be shot again. Truth was, he would welcome it; he was tired now. So goddamned tired. And the pain of the two bullet wounds was beginning to pulse through him, like sharp lightning bolts.

Dr. Wu stepped in front of the guard, her eyes fixed on Tyreese as she started to move toward him, her instinct to protect and heal her patient overwhelming the desire to run away.

She was halfway across the room to Tyreese when Birdy sat up.

"Jesus Christ!" The guard screamed in surprise. His gun moved to Birdy, then back to Tyreese.

Doctor Wu yelped too, danced away from Birdy, then stopped in her tracks and stared at the supposedly 'dead' kid, her mouth agape. "Oh my God," she whispered and rushed toward Birdy.

Tyreese tried to speak. He wanted to tell the guard to shoot Birdy, but all that came out of his mouth was an incomprehensible mumble.

"Get some help...," Doctor Wu yelled at the security guard. "...Now!" she ordered when the guard didn't move.

"What about him?" the guard said, nodding toward Tyreese.

Doctor Wu turned for a second and looked at Tyreese. "He's not going anywhere," Wu said, "Now get—" Wu's words turned into a yell of surprise as Birdy's hand flew to the doctor's head, her fingers grabbed a handful of the woman's hair and tugged the doctor's head toward her. The doctor's astonishment almost instantly turned into a scream of pain as Birdy bit deep into the soft flesh of the woman's throat.

The guard advanced across the floor toward Doctor Wu and Birdy, his gun lowered, mouth open as though he had forgotten what he wanted to say, and stopped. He took a step backward and raised the gun at Birdy, then dropped it again as he realized he could not fire without hitting the doctor.

"Let go of her," he managed eventually. "Drop her right now."

Tyreese did not know whether Wu somehow managed to free herself or if Birdy simply was done with her, but the doctor suddenly staggered back from the cadaver table, one hand clasped to her throat as blood gushed from between her fingers. The doctor spun in a slow pirouette and briefly met Tyreese's eyes with her own; they were wide with terror and confusion, and, Tyreese thought, a terrible understanding that he had been right. She staggered toward him, her right arm stretched out in front of her, a trail of blood spurting in a red arc through the air behind her.

The security guard opened fire. Four rounds in quick succession. Two hit Birdy in the chest, spinning her around. The other two shots missed, ricocheting around the room.

Birdy's eyes snapped to the guard, a crimson spray flying from her blood-soaked mouth. She snarled viciously, like some gutter dog, then jumped from the cadaver table straight up. She hit the ceiling, her hands sticking to it as if she were a giant naked fly, and snarled at the guard. The two exit wounds in her back were both almost healed.

The guard gibbered a string of nonsensical words that could have been a prayer, staggering backward in disbelief. His legs tangled and he went down hard, sprawling across the tiles, the pistol in his hand all but forgotten. He scrambled upright and began a panicked sprint toward the exit, arms flailing.

Birdy scuttled across the ceiling, launched herself through the air, and landed on the guard's back. The man screamed in terror as the momentum of the collision toppled both he and Birdy through the two doors separating the mortuary from the exit into the rest of the hospital.

Tyreese heard two final gunshots, followed by a scream that seemed to last forever before finally fading to nothing.

Tyreese's vision had begun to blur, the room growing dimmer then brightening again as shapes swam into then out of focus. The pain was beginning to burrow through his muscles, eating its way to his brain. It hurt every time he breathed in; each breath sounding raspier than the last.

Doctor Wu lay on her side facing Tyreese, one hand behind her head, the other stretched out in front of her. She did not move. She did not even blink as blood continued to seep from her, forming a pool in front of her head that slowly expanded across the floor.

Tyreese's world faded out again. When his vision returned Birdy was sitting cross-legged in front of him, staring intently, like a child inspecting a particularly fascinating bug, her wounds all healed.

"Hello... Birdy," Tyreese wheezed. He supposed that he should have felt a sense of fear or panic, but all he actually felt was indifference. He was a dead man either way, that was an undisputable fact, and he was okay with that. He was tired of fighting, tired of all of it.

"Birdy," he whispered. "I'm sorry." He reached out a hand toward the child's face.

Birdy snatched his arm from the air before his fingers could reach her, drew it close to her mouth as her lower jaw distended, and bit down into his flesh.

Birdy began to drink deeply.

As the last reserves of blood left Tyreese's veins, warmth was replaced by cold, stillness, and light was replaced with welcome darkness.

And now I see with eye serene
The very pulse of the machine;
A Being breathing thoughtful breath,
A Traveller between life and death;

***She Was a Phantom of Delight***
*~ William Wordsworth ~*

# EPILOGUE

A narrow stream of rainwater gurgled across the floor of the storm drain. Above the curve of the drain's ceiling, through layer-upon-layer of desert dirt topped by a crust of asphalt, the dull rumble of passing Las Vegas traffic accompanied the constant *thud-thud-thud* of music as it echoed through the tunnel, reverberating off the concrete walls; the heartbeat of Las Vegas.

For most of the last forty-eight hours, Birdy had hidden within this tunnel system snaking beneath the city; hundreds of miles of drains and interconnected flood channels spread out across Las Vegas like arteries. Perhaps it would have mattered to her if she were still a human child that the drains were surprisingly clean thanks to the rain that had recently swept through them. But Birdy was no longer human, and the only thing that mattered to her now was that the permanently dark concrete tunnels offered her shelter from the destructive rays of the sun.

There was food down here, too. Wretched humans living their lives within the confinement of the tunnels; social outcasts, the mentally ill, the lost. Easy prey for Birdy. Over the past two days she had gorged herself on the pathetic creatures she stalked, the perpetual darkness allowing her to never have to sleep, never have to nest. The constant commotion of the city above drowning out the cries of terror and pain of her victims.

She was strong now, powerful beyond anything she had ever imagined when she was alive. Although it would be impossible to describe Birdy as being even close to human any longer, at her core she was still a child, with a child's delight and fascination for her new existence. Her past life was little but a memory, a fading remnant that fluttered within her brain like decayed clothing, her previous personality all but consumed by the constant gnawing hunger woven through the very core of this new being she had become; it was a beautiful driving force that she could barely restrain. But Birdy sensed she needed to be patient. There was another to watch over now, her progeny; one that would soon join her in her strange new world.

Birdy looked down at the body concealed within a bundle of old and faded blankets that had once been a tunnel dweller's bed, cocooned and hidden while the time of change took its course. If any human accidentally stumbled across her nest they would think they had found a dead body, but Birdy saw with stranger eyes the changes taking place beneath the skin of what had once been a man. The powers altering his organs and bones and muscle into something new were ancient and dreadful, they pulsed and throbbed within him, radiating an invisible light, imperceptible to all but vampire eyes.

A slow pulse began to beat at the center of Birdy's brain, the interval between each beat shortening with each passing minute.

Soon, darkness would return.

As if the body lying next to Birdy had sensed her thoughts, the tangle of bedding shifted slightly. She moved closer, loosened some of the sheets enough to see the body and two freshly grown limbs beneath, the darker skin still mottled with spots of new pink flesh.

Birdy sat back on her haunches and waited as the drumbeat within her mind grew faster and faster until it was almost a hum, building to a crescendo as some supernatural ability sensed the day was finally done.

Several hundred feet away at the mouth of the tunnel, the dying light of day lost its battle and succumbed to the darkening world, and with its arrival, the beat within Birdy's head was silenced.

Tyreese opened his eyes.

~ Fin ~

# Acknowledgments

My thanks go out to my editor Karen Boehle-Johnson for her incredible work on helping me pull this book together. I am in your debt. And to Kelly Graffis — the best beta reader a writer could ask for. Also to Lance MacCarty for his patience and hard work designing The Darkening's cover. I'd also like to thank my wife for always being willing to listen to my thoughts and questions, and always being ready to give me her input.

And last, but not least, I want to thank you, dear reader, for choosing to spend your precious time in my imaginary worlds.

## About the Author

A native of Cardiff, Wales, Paul Antony Jones now resides near Las Vegas, Nevada, with his wife. He has worked as a newspaper reporter and commercial copywriter, but his passion is penning fiction. A self-described science geek, he's a voracious reader of scientific periodicals, as well as a fan of things mysterious, unknown, and on the fringe. Paul is the author of six books, including the bestselling Extinction Point series and Toward Yesterday.

You can learn more about Paul and his upcoming releases via his blog at www.DisturbedUniverse.com or his Facebook page www.facebook.com/AuthorPaulAntonyJones/

15926701R00181

Printed in Poland
by Amazon Fulfillment
Poland Sp. z o.o., Wrocław